THE ORACLE YEAR

DISCARD

ALSO BY CHARLES SOULE

Letter 44

Curse Words

Strange Attractors

Death of Wolverine

Daredevil

THE *ORACLE* YEAR

A NOVEL

CHARLES SOULE

HARPER ⬤ PERENNIAL

NEW YORK • LONDON • TORONTO • SYDNEY • NEW DELHI • AUCKLAND

HarperCollins books may be purchased for educational, business, or
sales promotional use. For information, please email the Special Markets
Department at SPsales@harpercollins.com.

FIRST EDITION

Designed by Jamie Lynn Kerner

Library of Congress Cataloging-in-Publication Data has been applied
for.

ISBN 978-0-06-268663-3

18 19 20 21 22   LSC   10 9 8 7 6 5 4 3 2 1

For three women:

Mary

Amy

Rosemary

THE ORACLE YEAR

PART I

FALL

CHAPTER 1

*A*nything can happen, Will Dando thought. *In the next five sec-onds, in the next five years. Anything at all.*

He tipped his beer up, finishing the last few swallows. He set about the task of getting the bartender's attention, which looked like it could be an ordeal. The bar hadn't been crowded when he'd arrived three or so hours earlier, but it had filled up once the game started—Jets/Raiders.

The Jets were down by three with not much time left on the clock. Will wasn't ordinarily much for sports. He wasn't sure he'd ever watched a football game all the way through.

This one was different, though. It was important.

It was important because its outcome was one of a hundred and eight things Will knew that hadn't happened yet.

The bar was just a dive near his apartment, without much to rec-ommend it other than the base level offered by every bar in the world: drink there and you weren't (technically) drinking alone. Will had picked the second-best seat in the house—a stool as far away from the door as possible. Unseasonably frigid November gusted in every time anyone came in or out, sweeping along the bar, stirring the little puddles of spilled beer and wadded napkins.

The first-best seat in the house, the stool farthest from the door and the wind, was directly to Will's left. It was occupied by a truly lovely girl with chestnut-colored, slightly curly hair. She seemed to be a friend of the bartender. She certainly got her refills more quickly than Will did, and a good two out of three seemed to be left off the tab. But there were any number of reasons for that, really. The hair alone.

Will had caught her name—Victoria—and he was considering saying hello to her. He had been considering it, in fact, for most of the past three hours.

His phone buzzed. He looked down—*Jorge* on the ID, which meant a gig, a good one. Probably a party at some cool venue downtown, for solid money. Even the worst Jorge job was generally a pretty good time, and on occasion they were spectacular. He had hired Will for lingerie fashion shows, postconcert after-parties packed with industry people, no-joke studio session work, even a few opening band tours. Any future Will might have as a working bassist in New York City was tied more or less directly to Jorge Cabrera.

Will tapped the front of his phone, declining the call, just as the bartender finally worked his way down to his end of the bar.

"One more?" he asked, gesturing to Will's empty beer bottle.

"Yeah," Will said. "Same again."

On an impulse, Will turned to his left and smiled at Victoria.

"Get you a drink?"

Out of the corner of his eye, Will saw the bartender pause slightly as he reached into the cooler. Maybe they were more than just friends, then. But so what?

Victoria turned her head to look at Will.

"Oh, thanks," she said, just friendly enough, no more, "but I know the bartender. I drink for free."

"Sure, right," Will said, "but . . . just thinking out loud . . . paid for's better than free, right?"

Victoria tilted her head slightly.

"That's okay, thanks."

She made a point of looking back at the television, about as emphatic a shoot-down as she could give short of changing seats. The bartender returned, skidding a cardboard coaster out in front of Will and slapping a fresh beer down, maybe a bit harder than necessary.

The Raiders scored a touchdown and made the extra point, extending their lead to ten. Groans rolled up from most of the crowd in the bar, including Victoria.

On the bar in front of Will was a black, spiral-bound notebook, the cover creased like an old leather wallet. Spilt coffee had stained the pages along the bottom edge a fungusy brown. Will ran a thumb down one corner, flicking through the pages. He stared at the back of the bar, at the multiple distorted reflections of himself in the bottles lined up on the long shelf. He gripped the notebook, bending it along the creases.

He thought about what he knew, and what he could do with what he knew.

Shots from inside the deli. The Lucky Corner. Two quick, then a pause, then three more, one after another. Then a long break. A held breath. Decisions were being made inside. More shots. A lot of noise. A splash against the front window of the deli, from inside. Dark at the center, tinged red at the edges where it wasn't as thick and the sunlight could shine through it.

Will toyed with the label on his half-finished beer and considered the beers he'd already had. He thought about good decisions, and bad decisions, and how hard it could be to tell them apart.

Will turned back to Victoria.

"Jets fan?" he said.

"Yeah," she said, still watching the television.

"You want to know who's going to win this game?" Will said.

"I think I already know," she said.

"You might be surprised," Will said. "The Jets will win by four."

Victoria snorted, which still somehow managed to come out cute.

"Two touchdowns, with two minutes on the clock? Come on. Maybe I should have Sam cut you off."

"Wait and see," Will said.

"And how are you so sure? You the Oracle?"

Will hesitated.

"That's right," he said.

Victoria finally looked away from the television.

"Uh-huh," she said. "You know how many times I've heard that line in the last few months? But you're using it wrong. You're supposed to predict that we'll wake up together tomorrow morning."

Will grinned.

"I don't know about that. But the Jets will win this game."

"By four," Victoria said.

"That's right."

"If that happens, then I'm all yours. You can take me home and do whatever you want with me."

Will's eyes widened.

"Huh."

"Don't hold your breath," Victoria said.

On the second down in the Jets' next possession, one of the New York receivers caught a thirty-yard pass and ran it all the way to the end zone. The bar erupted.

Will glanced at Victoria. She was staring at him.

"See what I'm saying?" Will said.

"Yeah," Victoria said. "But they've got a long way to go, and not much time to get there."

"Mm-hmm," Will said.

The Jets kicked their extra point, and the Raiders took possession again.

A dark splash, red at the edges where it wasn't as thick.

Will stood, grabbing the notebook and tucking it under his arm.

"Where are you going?" Victoria asked.

"I'll be back in a sec, don't worry. We've got a bet, remember?"

"I very much do."

Will walked quickly to the back of the bar. He slipped into the men's room and locked the door. He put his hands on either side of the sink's cold porcelain and looked into the mottled mirror.

A cloudy, utterly ordinary reflection stared back: late twenties, scruffy, underemployed. But of course, the cover wasn't the book. He hadn't been ordinary for a while now.

Another cheer from the bar. Will couldn't see the TV, but he knew what had happened. The Jets had forced a fumble and ran it in for another touchdown. The bar was going nuts, and a gorgeous girl was starting to think that maybe she actually had met the Oracle that night. He could have her, and every other woman in the place. He could have the entire bar, if he wanted it. It would only cost him about ten words per person.

Will closed his eyes. He rolled the notebook into a cylinder and squeezed it with both hands, his knuckles turning white.

Good decisions, and bad decisions.

"Goddammit," he said.

Will realized he'd left his coat draped over his barstool. Stupid.

He slipped out of the men's room, risking one glance back into the bar. The beautiful Victoria was staring at the television, clapping as the Jets prepared to kick the extra point. They'd make it. Up by four.

The bar had a back exit near the kitchen. Will stepped outside, feeling the air spike his lungs as soon as he took a breath. He walked out into the night, not looking back.

CHAPTER 2

eigh Shore stared down at her salad. She'd allowed herself some excesses. Croutons, cheese, sliced-up bits of fried chicken, the good dressing (which they should just call pudding and be done with it). Almost fifteen bucks' worth of moral support via the build-your-own bar. She'd managed maybe two bites.

Leigh pushed her fork into her salad and wiped her hands on a paper napkin. She crumpled it and dropped it on her tray. Reflexively, she grabbed her phone and swiped it open. A Reddit thread popped up on her screen, with a single post pinned to the top.

At the top of the page, two short sentences:

TOMORROW IS TODAY.
THESE ARE THE THINGS THAT WILL HAPPEN.

Below that, a list: twenty brief descriptions of events, none longer than a few sentences. Each was accompanied by a date, spread over a period of about six months. This list was all over the web—every news aggregator site maintained its own copy, each with its attendant thread of thousands of comments beneath it—but the Reddit post was the place it had first appeared, via a link to an anonymously posted pastebin.

The Site. Everyone knew what you meant when you said it.

Leigh scrolled to the bottom of the list. Nothing had changed in the five minutes since she last performed exactly this same maneuver. She looked up from her phone. Around the café, roughly eight out of ten people were on their phones. She saw the Site on at least two of those screens, just in her eye line right at that moment.

Leigh clicked away and pulled up her e-mail. Nothing—or at least not the e-mail she was waiting for.

She hesitated, frowning, then pulled up another document on her screen—an article, her article—about three thousand words, nicely supplemented with images, links . . . everything the discerning readers of Urbanity.com expected in their content.

The article was about the Site. Leigh could have chosen anything. But the Site was . . . fascinating. Ever since its appearance, it felt like the only thing that really mattered. The only puzzle worth solving.

She'd been in line at a Starbucks when her phone had buzzed with a text—a link, sent to her by her friend Kimmy Tong. Clicking through, not understanding why Kimmy thought this was worth her time. Giving her order, then googling around a little bit while she waited for her latte, realizing what the Site was actually claiming to be, and just . . . staring at it. Reading it, over and over again. Not hearing her name when the barista called it, until he all but shouted it right in her face with the bitchiest possible inflection.

The Site emerged into the public consciousness so quickly it was like a UFO appearing over Washington. From one day to the next—one hour, it seemed, as she remembered it—it became the only thing anyone could talk about.

Twenty events, all accompanied by dates. The first two had already happened by the time the Site went viral, but the rest all were slated to occur in the future. Since then four more of those dates had passed, and on each, the event on the Site occurred, exactly as it described. Or more accurately, predicted—by an unknown person, presence, supercomputer, or alien that had become known as the Oracle, in the same way that the Site had become the Site.

Leigh continued scanning the text of her article, doing one last check for sense and typos. She had chosen to write about the Oracle precisely because the subject had already been so exhaustively covered. A strategic thing. If she could bring some new angles, new interpretations, then it was almost more impressive than writing about something less familiar.

She thought she might have pulled it off—she'd tried to get into the Oracle's head in a way that most articles didn't seem to attempt, ignoring any discussion of the effect of the Site's prophecies on the world and focusing more on how they might affect the prophet. That was the idea, at least. She'd read the piece too many times to be sure what it was actually about anymore—but her intentions were good.

Leigh's current beat at Urbanity.com was "city culture"—shorthand for list-based clickbait about New York's clubs and shows and celebrity squabbles and the best bagels in Brooklyn. Urbanity did produce some actual reportage—not much, but a little, in some of the other sections—and her Oracle article was something like an audition to get over to that side of things.

Leigh flipped back to her e-mail account—still nothing. She frowned, frustrated, then tapped her phone a few times and her article went live, now freely available to every one of the site's millions of readers. The die was cast.

She stood up and emptied her tray into the trash bin, reflexively twinging a bit at the waste. She walked the two blocks back to the office, her stomach churning.

Urbanity had a few floors of a nondescript building at Fiftieth and Third. Just a cubicle farm with conference rooms along the sides on six, and the executive offices up on eleven.

Leigh sat down at her desk, glancing at the small mirror hanging on one wall of her cube. Her relationship with her reflection was evolving in a frustrating way as she neared thirty. Every look was accompanied by a little held breath. She didn't know what she expected to see—maybe some echo of her mother's face—streaks of white in her hair or lines fanning out into the dark skin around her eyes.

Why did you do that? she asked herself.

She had a job in New York City, writing for a living, actually using her journalism degree. More or less. She could pay her bills with a minimum of month-to-month shuffling and humbling calls home. Fully half her friends couldn't come close to any of that.

So why did you just do that? she repeated to herself.

A head appeared over Leigh's cubicle wall—Eddie, one of the company's photographers. Approaching middle age, not fighting it all that hard, and very good at what he did. Eddie had taken some of the photos for her article about the Site and helped her lay it out.

He was smiling.

"Just saw your article went live, Leigh. Good for you. I told you it was solid. Did they say anything about moving you over to News, or was this a onetime thing? Either way, they almost never take work from people on other desks, long as I've been here. You should be proud you got the green light."

Leigh looked back at him, saying nothing. Eddie's eyes narrowed a little.

"You didn't," he said.

The fundamental truth to Leigh Shore was this—something she'd realized years back but could not seem to change, no matter the opportunities, long-term relationships, and overall happiness it denied her—nothing was less interesting to her than something she already had. And nothing was more interesting to her than something someone told her she could not have.

"I was tired of waiting, Eddie. I e-mailed them the article over a week ago—and they didn't even respond. You know what I'm capable of, right? You just said so. I needed to show them something.

I've been asking for a change of assignment for coming up on two years, and they just keep sending me out to bullshit club openings or whatever. When the verticals come back on this article, it'll speak for itself. Sure, maybe it's a little bit of a gamble, but—"

Eddie exhaled loudly, more of a grunt than a sigh.

"You know this site is owned by a multinational entertainment conglomerate, right? You can't just . . . post things. It's not your Tumblr. People get sued over this sort of thing, Leigh, and they most definitely get fired."

Eddie turned away.

"I'm going to go check your goddamn article and pray you didn't credit me on it."

Leigh opened her mouth, about to say she'd pull the post off Urbanity's site. But what would that do, really? It was already out there.

The first prediction to happen while people were paying attention was a claim that fourteen babies would be born at Northside General Hospital in Houston on October 8, six male, eight female. Exactly correct, even though the last infant was born at two minutes to midnight, and the mother was a woman who showed up at the hospital about half an hour earlier. She wasn't even from the area—she was driving through with her husband.

Not easy to stage, but naysayers on blogs and message boards came up with all sorts of ways it could have been done. The most popular was that the CIA ran the Site and had induced labor in a number of women at a secret facility near the hospital, lining them up like brood mares to make sure everything worked out as planned, sending out the lucky lady to the hospital a little bit before midnight.

Never mind that the CIA worked exclusively outside the United States, and inducing labor was far from a precision maneuver subject to split-second timing, and why would any woman agree to something like that, and and and.

The next prediction was dated about two weeks after the births:

PACIFIC AIRLINES FLIGHT 256 LOSES CABIN PRES-
SURE ON ITS DESCENT FOR LANDING IN KUALA
LUMPUR. ALTHOUGH THE PLANE LANDS SAFELY,
SEVENTEEN PEOPLE ARE INJURED. THERE ARE NO
DEATHS.

Again, the Site was dead-on. A bird hit a window weakened from lack of maintenance, and it cracked just enough to cause a blowout. Exactly seventeen people were hurt, no more, no less. And even that could have been faked, people claimed, but the world was much less willing to take the conspiracy theorists seriously on that one, because that event had been caught on film.

A crew of enterprising Indonesians brought a camera out to the airport and filmed Flight 256 as it came in for a landing. The clip was online within hours, and it very clearly showed the flock of birds entering the frame. Most turned at the last minute. A few didn't. When you started asking people to believe that the CIA had developed the ability to remotely control birds, and had somehow rigged the plane so that only seventeen people would get hurt, it became easier to just believe that the Site was real.

Someone out there could predict the future. The Oracle.

Most religious groups either denounced the Site or pointedly ignored it. A few embraced it. Politicians and pundits incorporated the Site into their rhetoric without a blip. Invitations to the most exclusive events, offers of sexual favors, payments, employment were extended to the Oracle, all of which were, as far as anyone knew, ignored.

Fads appeared based on the content of the predictions—chocolate milk was the drink of choice for children and adults alike due to:

APRIL 24-MRS. LUISA ALVAREZ OF EL PASO, TEXAS,
PURCHASES A QUART OF CHOCOLATE MILK, SOME-
THING SHE HAS NOT HAD IN TWENTY YEARS, TO SEE

IF SHE STILL ENJOYS THE TASTE AS MUCH AS SHE
DID WHEN SHE WAS A CHILD.

Bartenders across the country had learned to mix Brownouts: chocolate milk, amaretto, and vodka.

And if the Oracle wouldn't make him- or herself known, the public satisfied itself with the people named in the predictions. Luisa Alvarez had been snapped up as a spokesperson for Hershey's. She seemed to enjoy the spotlight immensely, until some sort of fanatic tried to assassinate her at a press event. The would-be killer's motive: to prevent the Oracle's prediction from coming true. To "save the world" from the pernicious influence of a false prophet.

Luisa had been placed under heavy security after that, her public appearances drastically curtailed. Hershey's didn't want anything to interfere with her ability to buy that milk when the big day came.

The word from Anonymous and its various allied hackery organizations was that the Site had been set up using simple, existing anonymization tools that all but guaranteed that no one but the Oracle would know who the Oracle was, or be able to issue new predictions. Their current verdict: whoever set things up for the Oracle was extremely conversant with the ins and outs of modern data security. Beyond that, they didn't have much to say.

The world's markets endured a series of roller-coaster climbs and reversals. The outcome of the next presidential election was suddenly thrown into doubt when Daniel Green, the incumbent, fumbled his first few opportunities to comment on what the Site's emergence meant to the country.

There were no answers—not yet, really, just the hope that at some point, all this would make sense. Clearly, a plan was at work, but what, how, where, when . . . and most importantly, why . . . no one knew. Not yet.

Leigh settled back into her chair as she read the last few lines of her article. It was better than she remembered. Not perfect, but at least as good as most of what Urbanity published on what passed for their news desk. Eddie needed to relax.

A ping—an e-mail hitting her work account. Leigh pulled it up

From: jreimer@urbanity.com.

Upstairs, please.

—Reimer

Leigh stared at her monitor for ten seconds or so. Her hand reached out slowly and clicked her mouse, minimizing the e-mail app and revealing a previously hidden browser window behind it. Showing the Site. Of course it was.

Reflexively, Leigh's hand moved. She hit refresh, even though she cringed a little bit inside as she did it. The Site never changed.

But it had.

At the bottom of the page, after the last prediction, six new words had appeared:

THIS IS NOT ALL I KNOW.

Below that, an e-mail address.

CHAPTER 3

"PLEASE TELL ME WHEN MY DAD WILL COME BACK."

"GOD WILL PUNISH YOU, DEMON. REVEREND BRAN-SON SAYS—"

"COMBIEN D'ANNÉES JUSQU'À CE QUE LA FRANCE GAGNE LA COUPE DU MONDE?"

Will replaced the sheet of paper on the stack piled against the wall of his apartment, one of three, each about four feet high, totaling thousands of pages. Every sheet was densely covered with small-font text, both sides. Questions, mostly—for the Oracle. Since the e-mail address had gone live on the Site, millions of messages had come through, which could be broken down into variations on three questions:

Will I get what I want?

How can I get what I want?

Why can't I get what I want?

The first hundred thousand or so had been printed and now sat piled between some of Will's instrument cases—basses and guitars standing upright, guarding the questions like sentries.

"Stop reading them, Will," came a voice from behind him.

"I know. It's not easy," Will said.

Will flipped open one of the cases and pulled out a well-worn Fender P-bass. He slung it over his neck and turned to face the rest of the room. Not much to see—a trash-picked coffee table, top like a Spirograph, all interlocked drink rings and long, swirling scratches, standing between some hand-me-down living room furniture. The rest of the apartment was crammed with gear. Instruments, music stands, neatly looped cables, effects pedals, a small set of digital production equipment—more storage unit than living space.

Sitting in the apartment's sole armchair was Hamza Sheikh. Smiling eyes, tightly cropped hair, extremely white teeth.

"None of those questions matter anymore," Hamza said. "We got what we needed from them. They're just noise."

"I bet they matter to the people who asked," Will said.

"Can you answer any of them?"

"Not really."

"Then you don't have to feel guilty. Those questions were always unanswerable. Don't beat yourself up just because people want to know things."

"This isn't a logic thing," Will said. "It's . . . I just feel bad about it. Giving people hope for something I know we won't ever deliver."

Hamza looked back down at the laptop he had open on the coffee table, next to sloppy piles of paper, binders he'd assembled full of research on the people they were about to speak to, spreadsheets.

"Get your head on straight," Hamza said, typing a few updated figures into one of the tables on his screen. "This is the most important day of either of our lives. If we pull this off, you can help anyone you want. Be my guest, brother."

Will began to play a bassline on the instrument slung around his neck—a four-note repeating pattern.

"I know that one," Hamza said, not looking up from the keys. "What's it called?"

"The O'Jays," Will said. "'For the Love of Money.'"

"Yeah, that's right," Hamza said. "My favorite song. Get over here. It's almost time."

Will walked over to the couch and sat down, unslinging the bass and leaning it up against the cushions. He shifted one of the piles of paper on the coffee table, revealing his own laptop—almost as banged up as the table itself—and the Oracle notebook.

Will flipped open the screen of his computer, then took the notebook and held it up, showing it to Hamza like a tent revival preacher presenting a Bible to his flock.

"Before we do this," Will said. "Let's talk it through. One last time."

He lowered the notebook, twisting the cover in his hands.

"You really think this . . . this is it?" he continued. "The reason I was sent these predictions? Just . . . money?"

Hamza took his hands off the keyboard and sighed heavily.

"Okay, Will. One last time."

He looked up, directly at Will.

"We have an opportunity here like nothing I have ever seen in my life. Big enough that I quit my job to help you—a job at an investment bank that, in a bad year, netted me a quarter mil with bonus. Big enough that I've been lying to my wife about why I did that. I'll put aside the fact we have been each other's best friend for over ten years, and that I'd expect there would be more trust happening here."

"Hamza, come on, it's not—" Will began. Hamza held up a hand, and Will stopped midsentence.

"I will also not mention that you need this so much more than I do. I will not say any of that because, as your good friend, it would be rude. However—"

Hamza reached for the notebook, and Will yanked it back. A pause, as they both processed that particular reflex. Hamza slowly lowered his hand, staring at Will.

"Look," he said, his voice quiet. "You got the predictions. You trusted me enough to tell me about them. We talked for a long time deciding what to do. This is what we came up with, and it will change both our lives forever. Forever.

"You didn't get instructions. You didn't get rules. If you find a twenty-dollar bill on the sidewalk, did it come to you for a reason? Are you obligated to do one thing or another with that twenty? Fuck no. It's yours. Do whatever you want with it."

"You always go financial," Will said.

"That is not a bad thing. In fact, it is a good th—" Hamza stopped, shaking his head. He slapped down the cover of his laptop, setting the coffee table a-wobble again.

"You know what?" he said, standing up. "Forget it. Let's take the Site down. Let's just . . . agh."

Will watched Hamza pace back and forth. He didn't have much room to work—his path bounced between the entrance to the phone booth kitchen and the bathroom door, about four steps each way.

"You get cold feet now, when, in, oh—"

Hamza pulled out his phone and checked the time, then held it out so Will could see it.

"—seven minutes, everything we've been working for will be right in our hands?"

Hamza shoved his phone back in his pocket.

"You're a guy with, forgive me, no future, and then you are lit-erally given the future, but the possibilities in that just seem to ter-rify you," Hamza said. "I mean . . . it's overwhelming, sure, but does that mean you should just sit on all this? Ignore it? Pretend you don't know the things you know? I mean . . . what the fuck, man?"

Will watched his friend pace.

"You're just as nervous as I am, aren't you?" he said.

Hamza stopped, then collapsed back into the chair, rubbing his face with one hand.

"Pff," he said.

"You weren't at the Lucky Corner," Will said. "It happened before I told you I was the Oracle. You don't know how wrong this shit can go. I do. Once you put this information out into the world . . . once you unleash it . . . you just have to sit there, and watch what happens, knowing you did it. Everything that happens next is your fault."

Hamza sighed.

"I know, brother. Look. We can still turn this ship around, if we do it now. In about twenty minutes, that won't be an option anymore. The predictions came to you, not me. I won't push it. If you want to stop, we'll stop. Don't even worry about it. I can get another job. And you . . ."

Hamza gestured out at Will's shabby, overstuffed apartment.

"You'll still have all this."

Will put his hand flat on the notebook, feeling the cardboard cover under his hand. It didn't feel warm. It didn't feel alive—but of course it was, in its way.

He sat there, thinking, for what seemed like a long time. He tried to think it through, the same way he'd tried to think it through a thousand times before, finding, as always, that it was just too big.

Will let his mind go blank. He opened his mouth, curious to see what he would say.

"Yes. Let's do it," he said. "Tell me who I'll be talking to again."

"Right," Hamza said, flipping his laptop open. "It's a hedge fund. Starrer, Wern, Bigby and Greenborough. They manage assets valued in the neighborhood of thirty-five billion dollars, investing in a wide variety of concerns, from pharmaceuticals to agriculture to nanotech.

"What that means, Will, is that while we don't know what SWBG will be asking you about, we do know that it will concern one general area."

"Money," Will said.

"Yes. And they'll be tough. Expect them to try to bully you. That's how they do business. But remember there's nothing they can actually do to you.

"They will absolutely threaten to sue you at some point, but whatever. They have no idea who or where you are. They'll be talking to the Oracle. They've never heard of Will Dando, and they never will."

Hamza frowned.

"Assuming, that is, that the Florida Ladies didn't screw up the security on this whole chat program thing they set up for us."

"They didn't," Will answered. "The Ladies know what they're doing. And besides, with what these hedge fund guys paid to talk to me, the last thing they'll want to do is try to hack us somehow and scare me off."

"Right, right," Hamza said, holding up a hand to concede the point.

Will flipped his laptop open. The chat program was already up and running. Nothing fancy, just untraceable communication, text only, running on a Tor browser through some sort of anonymized Deep Web channel.

"Okay, all set, but they have a few minutes yet," he said. "Can you check on the money? Make sure they didn't back out?"

Hamza typed rapidly on his own machine, then grinned. He spun the laptop so Will could see the screen, displaying an account summary from a bank in the Cayman Islands.

ACCOUNT # 52IJ8549UIP000-LF8
ESCROWED BALANCE: US$10,000,000.00

"Still there," Will said. "Jesus."

"Still there," Hamza said. "The bank will release it from escrow to us in about three minutes."

"Unless something gets screwed up."

"Nothing will get screwed up. Once it's out of escrow, it's ours, no matter what happens."

Will smiled.

"Easy," he said.

Hamza nodded.

Will's computer chimed, and his grin faded.

"Shit, that's them," he said.

"Okay, okay," Hamza said, "you're ready?"

Will looked at his screen. He cracked his knuckles and set his hands on the keys.

"Ready," he said.

Words appeared on his screen:

SWBG: Is this the Oracle?

Oracle: It is.

SWBG: We will require proof before we authorize release of funds from escrow.

Oracle: No. You will release funds now, or we will leave. You have thirty seconds.

He looked at Hamza. "Gave them the ultimatum," he said. "Thirty seconds. Let me know."

Hamza stared at his screen, chewing on the edge of his thumb. Seconds ticked by.

Will reached out his finger toward the keys, hesitated, then pulled them back. If this didn't work . . . he couldn't imagine getting up the nerve to try again, no matter what Hamza might say.

"They paid," Hamza said. "Transfer complete."

Will's entire body seemed to thrum, like a well-struck chord. His share was five million dollars, no matter what happened next.

"Okay," he said, putting his hands on the keyboard, "time to earn it."

The bank spoke first:

> **SWBG:** You have received ten million dollars from us. If our ten-minute timer has begun to run, please be assured that we will pursue legal action as a consequence of your lack of response.

"These guys are assholes," Will said.

"What are they doing?"

Hamza started to get up to see. Will waved him back to his chair.

"Threatened to sue me. Assholes. I'll call out the questions as they ask them."

Hamza cracked his knuckles and poised his fingers over his own keyboard.

"You are speaking to the Oracle. The interview begins now," Will typed.

Hamza hit a timer on his screen, and ten minutes began counting down. Almost immediately, the first question appeared.

> **SWBG:** Will the Medicare reforms described in H.R. 2258 be approved by Congress and the president?

Will laughed.

> **Oracle:** No idea.

SWBG: When and how will the following individuals die: James Starrer, Joseph Wern, Eduard Bigby, and Ira Green-borough?

"Hmm," Will said. "Creepy."

"What?" Hamza asked.

"They want to know when they're going to die."

"Yeah. Do you know?"

Will hesitated, feeling Hamza staring at him and willing himself not to glance at the notebook.

"No," he said.

SWBG: On what date and time will the Dow Jones In-dustrial Average exceed twenty thousand points?

Oracle: I do not know.

Will typed, and then he typed it again, and again, after each new question appeared on his screen, wishing he'd just copied it to the clipboard.

"God, they have to be pissed," he called to Hamza. "Ten million bucks for a whole lotta nada. Are you getting anything from the questions they're asking?"

"Tons," Hamza answered. He was furiously typing notes to himself, flipping through his papers. "They're tipping their hand left and right, telling me where they plan to invest. I can use that Medicare question alone to turn our ten mil into a hundred, at least."

"Explain it to me later," Will said. "I almost feel bad for th—"

He stopped, looking at the screen.

SWBG: Do you have any information on the Florida citrus crop for this year's growing season?

"Whoa, wait, I can answer this one. They got lucky," Will said. "What do they have, like a minute or two left?"

"Forty-five seconds, actually," Hamza said.

"Okay. I'll type fast," Will said.

Like every time Will recalled a prediction, it was perfectly clear, every word, as if the notebook was open in front of him. He began to type.

Oracle: Unusual weather patterns will cause a very late freeze that will sweep across much of the southeastern United States. This freeze will have a serious effect on the Florida crops. The freeze will occur on—

"Stop!" Hamza said.

Will looked up.

"That's it?"

"Ten minutes on the dot."

"Huh," Will said, taking his hands from the keyboard and looking at Hamza. "I could only answer one of their questions, and even that one I didn't finish. Sort of a shame."

Hamza grinned at him.

"No, my friend, not a shame! These guys knew the deal. We made no promises, and anyway, they make like ten million bucks a day. Who cares? Besides, if they want more time, they can just buy it. Another ten million buys another ten minutes."

"Ha," Will said. "Not likely. Would you, after that?"

"Who knows? These people don't think the way we do."

"Aren't you one of them?" Will said. "Great and powerful banker type?"

"Not anymore. I quit, remember? Now I'm just an independent businessman. Part of the backbone of this great nation."

SWBG: We wish to purchase another ten minutes. The

funds are being transferred to your account now. Please complete your response to the question concerning the Florida citrus crop.

Will stared at his screen. He reached out and typed.

Oracle: The freeze will occur on May 23. Below-average temperatures will continue for approximately one week. The Florida crop will be 40% off normal numbers.

SWBG: Is this all the information you can provide on this event?

Oracle: Yes.

Will waited. For the first time since the chat began, there wasn't an instant follow-up question. He glanced over at Hamza, who was giving him an odd look.

"One of your predictions was specifically about the weather this May in Florida and how it will affect the number of oranges in the supermarket?" Hamza said.

Will nodded.

"And not only did these guys happen to ask a question that would require that specific piece of knowledge to answer, but they asked it at exactly the moment that would require them to buy another chunk of time with us?"

Will shrugged.

"I've been asking myself questions like that since I had the dream, Hamza. I'm sort of beyond surprise at this point."

More words on the screen.

"Okay—here we go!" Will shouted. "Your turn, Ham."

"Ready," Hamza said, very focused, staring at his computer.

SWBG: Is it possible for this information not to be released to any other parties?

Oracle: Yes.

SWBG: Under what terms?

Hamza lunged for one of the binders on the coffee table. His knee knocked the edge, and the table finally collapsed, spilling spreadsheets, printouts, and laptops in a wide arc across Will's floor.

"Fuck," Hamza said, very deliberately.

Will ignored him and typed.

Oracle: Make an offer. The timer on the remainder of your audience period will be halted during these negotiations.

SWBG: What assurances do we have that once we purchase the exclusive rights to this information, it will not be sold to others?

Will had prepared for this one—it seemed likely that this question might come up.

Oracle: My word. And the assurance that if you don't make a deal with us, I will definitely sell this information again, if another buyer appears.

Will lifted his hands from the keys, then had another idea.

Oracle: Or I could post it on the Site. You've bought the right to know about the Florida freeze, not to own it. If you want exclusivity, tell us what you'll pay for it.

A lengthy pause from the other side of the screen. Will imagined frantic calculations being made in a masters-of-the-universe conference room, high above some city, stuffed with expensively suited old men he was visualizing as something like human buzzards. Behind him, he could hear Hamza shuffling rapidly through the papers on the floor, cursing to himself.

SWBG: We will pay you an additional ten million dollars for the exclusive rights to this information.

"Ten million," Will called over to Hamza. "Is that a good offer?"

"Fuck no," Hamza said, sitting on the floor, holding up double fists of spreadsheets. "I'm not finished yet, but I can tell you these guys are heavily invested in California agriculture. What do you think they grow out there?"

"Oranges?"

"Oranges, grapefruit, tangelos, you name it. And if Florida is off this year, that means California is way up. So their portfolio companies make lots of money there. Also," Hamza said, brandishing another piece of paper, "there are rumblings that this fund is looking at investing in Florida farms too. If there's a frost, a lot of farms will be hurting, looking to sell out. So they get a big foothold in the Florida market for cheap."

"Okay," Will said, "break that down."

"Breaking that down, it means SWBG will probably make around a billion off knowing about that Florida freeze ahead of time,"

Hamza said. "So they'll have to pay a hell of a lot more than ten million for it."

Hamza grabbed a pencil and started scribbling on the nearest sheets of paper, mumbling to himself. He dragged his laptop across the floor, and Will watched him pull up statistics on agriculture markets, historical impact of unseasonal weather, and all sorts of random esoteric financial data. It was alchemical.

"Almost there?"

"Time, Will, time. This is hard as hell. I want to get it right. If we underbid, we could be losing millions of dollars."

Will's heart was pounding. It had taken about twenty minutes for him to become the kind of person who gives out cars as birthday presents.

"Four hundred fifty," Hamza said. He threw his pencil on the table. "Four five oh. That's my best bet. I'll tell you, there aren't many people who could have modeled that out for you in a couple of minutes. My brain's about to slide out my nose."

Will couldn't speak for a moment. He put his hands over the keyboard. They were shaking.

"Is that our opening offer?" he managed.

"No, that's it. That's what they have to pay if they want the info. That leaves them a healthy profit, an incredibly healthy profit. I even shaved some off to account for their reluctance in light of . . . well, the fact that this is all so fucking bizarre."

Will shook his head.

"How can you be sure? What if we just piss them off?"

"We won't. They have the same information I do, and they can create the same projections. If you know how to do it, it's not guessing at all. It's fact.

"Of course," he added, "they probably had to put about thirty people on it to get the same answer."

Will's forced his hands to steady against the keyboard.

Oracle: $450 million. There will be no further negotiations. This is the final and only price I will accept.

Again, a pause, longer, like a stunned silence.

SWBG: That is a considerable amount. It will take us some time to amass those funds.

"Holy shit," Will said. "They went for it."

"Of course they did," Hamza answered. "And now they know we know what the hell we're doing."

"They say they need time to get that much cash. How much do I give them?"

Hamza thought for a few seconds.

"Seventy-two hours. They can liquidate some assets if they have to, but their last fund prospectus said they had almost that much in investment accounts ready to go. They'll need some approvals and things, though. It's probably a valid request."

Oracle: Funds must be received within 72 hours.

SWBG: Agreed. To the same account?

Oracle: Yes. Should we complete the remainder of your interview period?

SWBG: Yes, but one last thing. If you have defrauded us, please know that we will use every resource at our command to destroy you and get our money back.

Will frowned, glaring through his laptop's screen. His hands were suddenly very steady indeed.

Oracle: Destroy me? Ten words on the Site. That's all I'd need. For you, or for anyone in the entire world. Think about that, assholes.

Will finished the interview. He thought the fund seemed a bit muted after that last exchange—understandable. He didn't know the answers to any of their remaining questions, which was well and good. The pressure of another hit might have killed him.

He closed the chat program and looked at Hamza, who was back in the armchair, staring at their bank account balance on his computer. He seemed stunned, or even maybe a little bit stoned.

Will leaned back on the couch and closed his eyes.

Just oranges, he thought. *Fruit, for God's sake. How much harm could it possibly do?*

CHAPTER 4

Reverend Hosiah Branson blinked the sweat out of his eyes and focused on the young woman in front of him. She smiled up at him, her eyes glazed in rapture. She wasn't beautiful, but she was earnest, and devoted, and that made up for any plainness in her features.

Branson could feel the surge coming over him. He threw his head back, closing his eyes. A stream of ecstatic noise poured out of his slack mouth, his tongue moving with its own will. He stiffened and reached out. He placed both hands on the woman's face. Her eyelids fluttered closed against his palms in spidery little spasms.

One last gasp, and he pushed the girl's face away from him, his ululations ceasing at the same moment. He brought his arms around in a wide circle to clasp his hands in front of him. He opened his eyes.

His deacons had caught the girl as she fell. She lay cradled in their arms like a newborn, her spindly, pale limbs draped bonelessly this way and that. Branson reached out to her, his face clothed in a broad, reassuring smile.

The girl grasped his hand. Her grip was faint, and he could feel her trembling. Hosiah pulled her to her feet.

"Go now, and walk in God's light," he said, his voice amplified a hundred times by the microphone on his lapel.

The girl's face collapsed into a mess of overwhelmed tears and red-faced huffing. Spotlights nestled in the ceiling high above flared into life, painting out a path for the girl to walk back into the audience. One of the Sisters appeared and took the girl's arm, gently escorting her away.

Branson was tired. It was good work, but draining. She would be the last for today.

He turned to face his audience: thousands upon thousands of people, arrayed in loose rows on the cathedral floor below him. Unceasing motion filled his view—people swaying, dancing, clapping their hands, all overcome with the glorious truth of the Lord.

The sound of the crowd, somehow perfectly supported by the singing of the choir in their loft off to the left of the altar, rose to fill his cathedral, his beautiful stained-glass palace.

Branson lifted his hands above his head, and the choir held a long chord and abruptly ceased singing. The crowd quieted quickly, ready for what they knew was coming: the day's final sermon.

"The Oracle," he said, speaking softly, his voice picked up and amplified throughout the cathedral by his lapel mic.

A few shouts from the crowd—condemnations—but mostly hushed, expectant silence.

"The Oracle is a poison," Hosiah continued. "That monstrous thing, peddling lies to this world through the Site. I am so, so sad—to my very soul—to see that some few small-minded, faithless individuals have been suckered by its con game."

He paused, took a handkerchief from his breast pocket, mopped his brow. A deep breath, then a launch into the next phase . . . the red-faced, forceful blast of brimstone his audience expected.

"Exodus 20, verse 5. Thou shalt not worship false idols, for God will not *tolerate* any affection for other gods!

"Do you hear that? God will take his vengeance on those who worship pretenders. He is a *jealous* god! And rightly so, because he is the one true God, and woe . . . I say *woe* . . . to those who would challenge him!

"Exodus 20, verse 6. But if you worship the Lord, and obey him, he will grant you love, and care, and great prosperity for all your days!

"The Oracle is a tool of the devil—he may well *be* the devil, active in our daily lives in a seductive, novel fashion. The Site . . . giving us lies packaged as if they are great gifts. Is it any wonder that so many foolish people have bought into the devil's game in these godless times?

"But in spite of all this, I am hopeful, my friends. I have hope, for I know that you, my soldiers of Christ . . . you are well equipped to do battle with that sly trickster. You already have the only weapon you will ever need."

Hosiah reached behind him and held out his hand, palm up. An attendant slapped a leather-bound book into his hand, making a meaty, satisfying sound. Hosiah held the book up to the crowd, stage lights glinting off the golden words etched into its cover.

"Right here! The Word of the Lord himself! The Holy Bible!"

A resounding cheer rose up from the crowd, amens and hallelujahs and such. Hosiah noted his ushers circulating through the aisles with the collection plates.

"Denounce the Site. Denounce the Oracle, wherever and however you can. Know that I am with you in this fight, as are all our brothers and sisters around the world. God bless you all, and I will see you soon!"

Hosiah nodded to one of his deacons, a large man named Henry, and he and the rest of the men quickly positioned themselves behind him in a wedge with him as the point at the center. Television cameras on either side of the stage repositioned themselves, catching the scene from multiple angles.

Hosiah raised his arms heavenward. He knew the deacons behind him had done the same. They wore bright blue suitcoats and red trousers, like a platoon of French Zouaves. His own little army, and him in a blinding white suit, brighter than anything the spotlights were putting out, standing out in front like a general, the focal point of the stage's pageantry.

The lights cut out, and Hosiah slipped through a door set just behind and to the left of the stage, followed by his deacons. He entered a long, softly lit hallway. The carpet was a thick cream, and the walls were painted in exactly the same shade. As soon as the door closed behind him—the deacons stayed outside to make sure it stayed that way—the noise of the crowd vanished. The hall was thoroughly soundproofed. After the chaos of the stage, stepping into the hallway was like sliding into a bath of warm milk.

Branson walked down the hallway, through another door, and entered his office. He dropped heavily into the seat behind his desk, a sigh escaping his lips. He rubbed the bridge of his nose, pushing his glasses up toward his forehead. Letting them fall back into place, he ran that same hand across his hairless scalp. He grimaced, feeling a wash of sweat against his palm.

Hosiah checked his watch—just a cheap model, the sort of thing you could buy at a drugstore. It wouldn't do to have the television cameras picking up anything too fancy. He reached across the top of his desk—an unadorned white expanse, like an ice floe—extending one finger toward a button set flush with the desktop. He rested his index finger on the button, but hesitated before pressing it.

Come on, Hosiah. Pull off the damn Band-Aid, he thought.

He pressed the button. It moved downward with a slight, whispery click, and almost before it had returned to its original position, a knock sounded from the wall opposite his desk.

"Come," Hosiah called.

A previously invisible seam opened in the wall and expanded into a door. A young, extremely slim man entered—Brother Jonas Block, Branson's executive assistant. His pinched, frowning face sat above a black suit and tie, with a crisp white shirt beneath. Undertaker chic.

"How can I help, Reverend?"

Brother Jonas' complexion was never robust, but at this moment he looked positively cadaverous, like a man made of white candle wax. His eyes darted to either side—he wasn't able to meet Branson's gaze. Not a promising sign.

"It happened, I assume?" he asked.

"Yes, sir," he said. Jonas' mouth twitched, and his eyes rolled toward Branson briefly before skittering away. "The Site's prediction about the woman in Boulder winning the lottery. Confirmed true, just a few minutes ago. But that's not—"

Branson slammed his right hand down on the surface of his desk. He'd spent almost twenty thousand dollars to make this office as acoustically neutral as a space could be—even so, his palm hitting the desk was a gunshot, cracking out into the room.

He spun his chair to face away from Jonas, cradling his wrist in one hand. He looked around his office, decorated in muted tones, except for a few tasteful splashes of color here and there. A blue lamp, a couch upholstered in celadon silk. A large painting on the wall directly behind his desk.

A sanctuary.

Branson's hand was already starting to hurt. He looked up at the painting on the wall, his eyes narrowed.

It was a work by a Filipino artist, depicting in thickly applied oils a procession of penitents being carried through the streets of Manila on Easter Sunday. Each year, certain individuals opted to demonstrate the depth of their faith by allowing themselves to be crucified. The truly devout put nails through their wrists and thorns on their heads.

"Sir . . ." Jonas said, his voice tentative. "That's not all."

"What else?" Branson said, his voice tired.

"You know that new predictions occasionally appear on the Site—a few at a time?"

"Yes, of course."

"A new set of predictions was released just after the Colorado lottery prediction came true. Just three, but one of them . . ."

Jonas trailed off.

Hosiah spun around in his chair. He slapped another control on his desk, and without a sound, a screen rose up, followed by a keyboard sliding out from just below it. Branson sat down and tapped a few keys, pulling up the CNN home page.

He stared at the screen. A long moment passed.

"Sir, one of them . . ." Jonas began.

He swallowed, producing a froglike sound fully audible in the silent office, then finished.

". . . it's about you."

And so it was. Shorter than most of the predictions, just a single innocuous sentence:

AUGUST 23: REVEREND HOSIAH BRANSON WILL PUT PEPPER ON HIS STEAK.

"I'm so sorry, Reverend," Jonas said.

Just over ten words, and yet they changed everything.

Everything.

CHAPTER 5

The waiter—an elderly, aproned man—gingerly placed a large white platter down on the middle of the table. The platter contained a single enormous steak, a porterhouse, resting in a near-to-boiling, savory-smelling lake of juices.

"Very, very hot," the waiter said in a slightly German-accented voice, making eye contact with both Will and Hamza. "You touch, you'll be sorry."

"Understood," Hamza said. "I've been here before."

The waiter produced a set of carving tools and went to work on the steak, slicing it into bite-size chunks and serving out portions, dragging the meat through the sizzling puddle of melted butter on the platter before depositing it on each of their plates. A little bit of creamed spinach, some mashed potatoes, topping up of wineglasses, and he withdrew, with one last finger wag toward the platter.

Will picked up his fork and speared a piece of steak. He stared at it.

"I get it," Hamza said. "Savor the moment. From now on, your life will be forever divided between the time before you've had that bite and after. There is no place in this world like Peter Luger's. This is the best steak in the world, since 1887, right out here in Williamsburg. Make it count."

"That's not why I'm waiting," Will said. "I'm just . . . it's hard to process all this. This is a ninety-dollar piece of meat. This meal will cost like three hundred bucks. That's a month's grocery budget for me. It all seems . . ."

Will put his fork back down on his plate. Hamza watched it go, frowning.

"No, don't let it get cold, man."

"You said you've been here before, Hamza. I haven't. I never, in a million years, thought I ever would go to a place like this."

"We can afford it, Will. You could buy every meal served here for a month and not even notice."

"That's not the point. All my instincts are off. I don't know what to do. I've spent a good part of almost every day of my life since I moved to New York worrying about where my next gig would come from. If I'd get hired enough to make rent, and pay bills, and eat."

"You don't have to think about that anymore."

"I know. But I don't know what I'm supposed to think about. I wanted all this money because you're supposed to want money. And now . . . it's hard to believe any of this will last. It's too big. I keep waiting for something to happen to balance it out, to fuck it up."

Hamza pointed to Will's fork.

"Pick that up, and eat it. Then, I'll tell you how to deal with this."

Will glanced down at his fork, then popped the bite into his mouth. The steak was tender, and savory, and buttery, and without a doubt one of the best things he'd ever eaten in his life.

"Well," he said.

"Right," Hamza said. "Now, you keep working away at your plate, and just listen to me. Back at Corman Brothers, I regularly saw completely talentless assholes, managing director level and above, take home five million bucks as their annual bonus. These were miserable people, who had gained their positions because they were, in general, willing to be more evil than the people around them on the way up."

Hamza leaned forward.

"They didn't deserve five million dollars. But they got it anyway, and nothing ever happened to them. There was no karmic justice. They lived their lives, they were total shits to everyone around them, and next year, another five million bucks."

He leaned back and speared his own chunk of steak, popping it into his mouth, almost angry. He chewed, swallowed, then pointed his fork across the table.

"You're in shock, Will. It makes sense. Change can be tough, and what's happened to you . . . to us . . . it's seismic, as far as life events go. You'll get used to it—but the biggest step you can take in that direction is to stop looking for some meaning in the predictions. You're stuck on this whole destiny thing, but there is no such thing as destiny. What happens, happens.

"My dad used to say it all the time. He was always frustrated by the way people in the States have this assumption, this moral certainty that there's some bigger plan. It sure as hell wasn't that way for him and my mom back in Pakistan. For them, life was chaos. None of us are meant for anything, and none of us are meant for nothing. Life is chaos, but it's also opportunity, risk, and how you manage them. If you're smart, you get this . . ."

He gestured at the table, laden with expensive delights.

"If you're not, you don't. There's nothing else to it."

Will swirled his fork through his creamed spinach, considering. Hamza took a sip of wine, not taking his eyes off his friend across the table.

"The numbers, though," Will said.

"Numbers?"

"Twenty-three, twelve, four. The last prediction, if that's what it is."

"Come on, man," Hamza said, a little edge creeping into his voice. "You don't have any evidence that those numbers mean *anything*. You've gotta work with what you know, not with what you feel."

"Uh-huh. But if there's no higher purpose to all this, then I'm just some asshole musician who got really lucky. If the predictions don't mean anything, then neither do I."

"Fuck that," Hamza said. "If you're rich, you matter. That's the world we live in. And we are both very rich, no matter what happens. Don't . . . don't self-sabotage."

"Is that what I'm doing?" Will said.

"I don't know," Hamza said. "I hope not. I did notice that you put three new predictions up on the Site, though."

Will looked up.

"Yeah. Innocuous stuff."

"But the third one . . . about Hosiah Branson," Hamza said.

"Yeah," Will said. "You've heard the things he says about me. And I had a prediction about him—seemed too perfect not to use."

Will ate another bite of steak, chewing very deliberately. Defensively.

"Branson doesn't say things about you, Will," Hamza said. "He says them about the Oracle. We don't want to let things get personal. Ever. We just sold a prediction for half a billion dollars. I'm not sure it makes sense to just give them away anymore. The Site's served its purpose. It's not Facebook. We don't have to keep updating it."

Will frowned. Hamza's worst quality was his tendency to explain.

"I know I'm just a stupid bass player, Hamza, but give me a little credit, all right? I think I can tell when a prediction's worth something," he said. "And besides, how much money do we actually need? When are we going to stop?"

"When we have enough that it literally does not matter how we got it. Even if we eventually get exposed as the people behind the Site, we'll have enough so that we're totally bulletproof."

"How much is that?"

"More than we have right now. I'm making plans, though," Hamza said. "It's keeping me busy. Money means work. Shell corporations, multiple accounts, the whole bit. It's one thing to have a few billion in offshore accounts, but making it accessible at your local ATM is complicated. The couple hundred thousand I got you might be it, at least for a little while."

Will considered this.

"Did you talk to the Florida Ladies?" he said. "They might be able to help. That's what we pay them for, right?"

Hamza frowned.

"I'm not going to involve them any more than we already have. I'm sure they're wonderful, and worth every penny of the excessive fees they charge us, but if it's all the same to you, I'd rather they didn't know our bank account numbers. I'm on it, Will. I'm taking care of it."

An uncomfortable pause.

"Anyway," Will said.

"Anyway," Hamza agreed. "It's not all bad. I paid off the credit cards I've been running up since I quit the bank, and my student loans. Miko's, too. Not that sexy, but, goddamn, it felt good."

Will finished his glass of wine. He stared fixedly at the bottom of the glass.

"How did you explain the money? Is she still asking questions?"

"No, Will. She's just accepting that Providence has blessed her brilliant husband with millions of dollars. Of course she's asking questions."

"What are you telling her?"

"I'm telling her that you and I are getting a lot of VC money in, which is more or less true. She doesn't believe it, but we've got sort of an unspoken pact. She loves me, right? And she knows I love her. If I don't want to tell her what I'm doing, then she trusts me enough to know that there's a good reason, and that I'll tell her the truth when I can.

"But," he added, "that won't last forever. And I don't want it to. It's this growing thing between us."

Will looked at his friend.

"I get it, Hamza. But the more people that know . . ." He lowered his voice. "I'm the Oracle, right? I take the hit if people find out who I am. I know you'll have to tell Miko eventually, but we're almost out. We'll sell a few more predictions, get bulletproof, like you said, and then the Oracle disappears. Then you can tell her. Yeah?"

Hamza hesitated briefly, then nodded. He refilled Will's wineglass and topped off his own. He raised it in a toast.

"Enough with the recriminations and all that bullshit. This is a celebration, man. To the weirdest business idea anyone's ever had, and to the fact that we actually made it work," he said. "And to one hell of a business partner."

"Absolutely. On all counts," Will said, and clinked glasses with Hamza.

They ate in silence for a while, working through the steak. It had cooled a little, but that made it no less effective.

"Hey," Hamza said, his tone casual, verging on forced. "The next time you want to change something on the Site, maybe talk it over with me first? The one thing that could sink us is someone finding out who you are before we're ready. You put up those new predictions the way the Florida Ladies told us, right?"

"Yeah," Will said. "But I thought you didn't like the Ladies?"

"I know why we need them. I just wish our operation was a little more self-contained, that's all. Anyway, I'm sure it's fine. If it weren't, we'd probably be sitting in some FBI holding cell right now."

"The FBI?" Will said, lifting his wineglass. "Come on. We're not criminals."

CHAPTER 6

Jim Franklin, current holder of a hard-won and cherished position as the nation's top cop—director of the Federal Bureau of Investigation—was thinking about crime. He was thinking about committing one.

"Gentlemen. Here we are again," said Anthony Leuchten, current White House chief of staff, and the person against whom said crime was being considered.

Franklin stared at the thick, unhealthy-looking pouch of fat distending Leuchten's neck. He couldn't believe the other man managed to put on a tie every day—his shirts had to be specially tailored. He looked like a bullfrog. A bullfrog with pink skin, snowy white hair, and round glasses that made his eyes look watery and weak.

He wanted to reach deep into Leuchten's neck pouch and strangle the man, to push his thumbs deep into the fat until he could be absolutely certain he would never have to hear the chief of staff's condescending, sanctimonious voice ever again.

Franklin looked away, trying to shake the impulse. Another man stood nearby on the snow-covered South Lawn of the White House—a short, extremely slim, odd-looking person in the uniform of a three-star general of the U.S. Army. This was Lieutenant General Linus Halvorsson, the head of the National Security Agency.

Franklin didn't know him well, despite the frequent collaboration between their organizations. The NSA had earned itself a reputation as a home for marginally socialized math geniuses and code breakers, or Peeping Toms who got their jollies from reading the country's mail. From the few times Franklin had dealt with Halvorsson directly, the man fit the bill on both counts.

Leuchten was holding a broken-off length of tree branch about two feet long. He tapped it against the fleshy palm of his free hand, then threw it as far as he could across the lawn.

A fluffy black-and-white Siberian husky at his heels took off after it. The men watched the dog run.

"It's really too hot here for her in the summers, but the president was stuck. Abandoning the family pet back in Minnesota would've hurt him more in the polls than any three diplomatic incidents. People do love their dogs," Leuchten said.

"I suppose so," Franklin answered. Linus Halvorsson remained silent.

The husky returned, proudly bearing the stick in her jaws. Leuchten knelt to retrieve it, ruffling the dog's shaggy fur.

"That's a good job, Anouk. Good dog."

Leuchten looked at the two men, his gaze cold.

"One of you would have called me by now if you had a name," he said, "so I know you haven't found the Oracle yet. You've had a month. What's the goddamn problem?"

Franklin spoke.

"Tony, listen, we've been sending you the progress reports, you know . . ."

Leuchten held up a finger. Franklin's jaw clenched.

"The reports are dogshit, Jim. Hell, Anouk manages that much twice a day."

Franklin's hands actually twitched, clenching spasmodically in his pockets.

"Time is short, gentlemen," Leuchten continued. "It's an election year, and the man behind both of your appointments is up for his second term. As I happen to be responsible for making sure he wins that second term, I am stunned that you aren't doing more to make me happy.

"The wars for freedom our country is currently fighting, the economic issues facing the middle class, gun control, the health-care mess we inherited, immigration reform, blue and red state tension . . . none of it is unexpected, and none of it presents an insurmountable problem."

Leuchten's mouth tightened.

"But somehow I could not predict the appearance of a man who, to all indications, can foresee the future. Despite all the other issues facing this country, the American people care about the *Oracle*. The president's illustrious opponent, that shitbag, has already referenced the Site in three separate speeches. His position is simple—he draws attention to the fact that we can't locate or explain the Oracle, which makes the president, your boss, look weak.

"I'm sure you see the difficulty. Beyond the fact that we cannot actually locate or explain the Oracle, we can't issue a position, either. We can't act until we know whether the Oracle is just some Vegas trickster, or that the Site is some elaborate effort by a foreign power to destabilize us, or God knows what. And this is hurting us, badly. This . . . *fortune-teller* might actually keep President Green from a second term."

This speech had caused Leuchten's face to flush the shade of cotton candy. He paused, letting himself relax, and addressed the two men.

"And so now I would like you two to give me some good news."

Halvorsson and Franklin looked at each other. The NSA head shrugged and spoke first.

"We've intercepted communications that suggest that the Oracle has met with high-level representatives from several large, multinational corporations, as well as a few wealthy private individuals."

"I see. Who?"

"Barry Sternfeld, for one. We're ninety percent certain about him. Ngombe Mutumbo is another, although he's less sure."

"Sternfeld? He contributed millions to the president's first campaign. He's a friend of this administration. You say he met with . . . the Oracle's taking meetings? Why the fuck don't we know his name? Why can't we set a goddamn meeting?"

Halvorsson cleared his throat.

"It's done clandestinely, sir. It all takes place over the Internet, deep down, using custom-coded, onetime-use tools specifically designed to make monitoring all but impossible. Nothing's recorded. We're good, but we aren't miracle workers. If we knew about a meet ahead of time, we might be able to do something, but we're finding out about all this after the fact. With time, perhaps . . ."

Leuchten interrupted, his face darkening.

"More dogshit, Halvorsson. I'm getting extraordinarily sick of the smell. Call Sternfeld! Ask him how he managed to get in contact with the Oracle. It's not brain surgery, man."

Franklin interrupted.

"Say, Tony, here's an idea. Give us a few minutes to tell you what's going on before you jump in with your little suggestions. Don't assume we're idiots."

Leuchten's expression cleared. He turned to face Franklin, a small smile crossing his lips.

"I'll assume you're idiots until you prove otherwise, Director. And as for my suggestions, you may not enjoy hearing them, but I can assure you that the president does. For instance, I might suggest to him that the FBI could use a change in leadership. Shake things up a bit. In with the new blood, out with the old. From my lips to the man's ear. Just something to think about."

Leuchten peered at Franklin over the top of his glasses, his blue eyes cold.

"But please, continue. Tell me what's going on."

Franklin looked to Halvorsson for support, but the man had chosen to stare at a nearby tree.

Franklin took a deep, frustrated breath of wintry air and held it in his lungs. On the exhale, he looked back at Leuchten.

"Fine," he said. "Here's how it is. My people have heard about the Oracle meetings Director Halvorsson describes, but we can't get any details. Either the Oracle's clients are too frightened to talk, or he gave them something so valuable that our threats don't outweigh it. I'm sure Linus has encountered the same difficulties."

He glanced at Halvorsson. The man nodded, slowly, once, but didn't say a word. Now Franklin wanted to hit *him*, too. This meeting needed to wrap up quickly, or he'd end up in court on assault charges.

He had hoped that Halvorsson's NSA drones had figured out something spectacular, but it didn't seem like that was the case. With every moment, it was becoming increasingly clear that Franklin would have to do something he really, truly did not want to do.

"We think the Oracle is selling predictions," Franklin continued.

"Ahh," Leuchten said. "I was worried this would happen. It's what I would do if I had access to the future. What's he selling? Specifically, I mean."

Franklin gritted his teeth.

"Once again, we aren't sure. As Director Halvorsson mentioned, the meetings take place over entirely secure networks, and our sources aren't the people in on the discussions with the Oracle. We get everything secondhand—men's room gossip; executive assistants overhearing bits of conversation, that sort of thing. We can't get near anyone who has actually received the information. They paid a lot of money for it, and they don't feel like sharing."

Anouk bounded up to the men, spraying powdery snow with each step, and frolicked around the chief of staff's legs. Leuchten reached down and yanked on a choke chain attached to the dog's neck. She yelped and fell sideways, looking up with a wounded expression.

"Dammit, get this animal inside," Leuchten said. He turned and motioned to one of the Secret Service men standing a few paces away. The man spoke quietly into his lapel mike, then came to lead Anouk away. Leuchten planted his hands on his hips.

"I refuse to accept this," he said. "This person is creating a power base, allying himself with some of the most powerful men and corporations in the world. Why? Do you have a single useful piece of information for me? Anything?"

"There is one thing," Halvorsson said.

Franklin looked at him, surprised.

"We have been able to cross-reference certain large payments made by the individuals and organizations we know have been in contact with the Oracle. The payments have all been to the same bank in the Cayman Islands, although each to a different numbered account."

Leuchten pursed his lips.

"How much?"

"The payments vary, but never less than ten million dollars," Halvorsson continued. "The largest are on the order of hundreds of millions. They total just over two billion."

"Fine. What is he spending it on?" Leuchten snapped. "You can buy one hell of a lot of AK-47s with a couple billion dollars. You could set up terrorist training camps all over the Middle East. It'd get you pretty far down the road to building a nuclear bomb. *What is he spending it on?*"

Franklin and Halvorsson stared at him. Silence stretched over several seconds. Leuchten crossed his arms and turned away.

"All right, that's it, then," he said. "I've got other work to do. Find the Oracle. Get it done, gentlemen, or leave me your suggestions for who should replace you."

Halvorsson inclined his head and turned to walk back across the South Lawn. Franklin hesitated.

"Tony, if I could have just another few minutes," he said.

Leuchten looked up, surprised. Halvorsson was already a few steps away; his gait hitched—he clearly didn't want to leave anymore if the conversation wasn't quite finished—but it was too late to smoothly turn around in any way that would maintain his dignity.

"You can have two, Jim," the chief of staff replied.

"Let's walk," Franklin said, gesturing toward the end of the South Lawn, even farther away from the retreating Halvorsson. They walked back out, through the trail Anouk had broken, taking a circular path through the snow.

"What's this about?" Leuchten asked.

Franklin took a deep breath, fervently wishing that he were speaking to the president instead of this access-hoarding toad.

Leuchten was staring at him with undisguised, greedy curiosity.

"There might be another way to find the Oracle," Franklin said slowly.

Leuchten raised an eyebrow.

"Oh? And yet we can't discuss it in front of Director Halvorsson?"

Franklin nodded.

"It's an unusual approach, Tony, and it's my opinion that you'll want as few people as possible to know we had this discussion."

"I see. Are you certain we should have it, then?"

"Yes," Franklin said flatly. "The truth is, I don't think we'll find this guy for you any time soon. He's smart about the way he's using technology. The Oracle's whole system has been designed to not really give us anything to hack. We aren't the NSA, but my tech people are damn good, and they tell me we just don't have the technology to crack the Site's security in a reasonable period of time. Could take years, maybe. We're working on it, but at this point we don't even know where the e-mail address goes.

"Now, my crew might get him through pure investigation, but the Oracle would need to make a mistake for us to find him, and it's all different now that he's got money. Sometimes that helps—money leaves a trail. But it also lets you hire people who can help you hide your tracks. Either way, detective work takes time. You've made it clear that we don't have that time, and I am inclined to agree."

Leuchten exhaled, a long plume of breath steaming out in the winter air.

"Explain why I'm still standing here listening to you, Jim. I mean, if I wanted to freeze my balls off, I'd fuck your wife."

Franklin smiled at Anthony Leuchten. It was a very thin smile.

"I'm getting to it, Tony," Franklin said, then paused, forcing himself back to calm. "I know someone who could find the Oracle. Maybe."

Leuchten frowned.

"Alone?"

"Not exactly. There are usually teams of specialists involved."

Franklin hesitated. He considered, thinking about the rat's nest his next few words would kick open, deciding whether the Oracle was worth it.

He considered . . . and then he told Leuchten about the Coach.

CHAPTER 7

Reverend Hosiah Branson sat in his living room, staring moodily at a television displaying footage of his own home.

Jonas Block stood at the entrance to the room, directed there a few moments earlier via a curt sentence or two from Maria Branson. The reverend's wife normally affected the personality of a cheerful talking animal in a Disney cartoon, but this evening she seemed grayed out, drained. The stresses affecting the Ministry since the Oracle's prediction three days earlier had clearly made their way home.

Jonas cleared his throat. Branson turned his head, and his expression flipped over completely, surging from morose frustration into a confident, welcoming grin.

Branson stood and walked over to Jonas, clasping his hand and shaking it in welcome. He wore jeans and a T-shirt, his hair was unkempt, and his face was covered with a rough layer of stubble, but his smile . . . it was like the neon cross atop the Ministry headquarters, lit every day at sundown and visible for miles.

"Thank you for coming, Brother Jonas," the reverend said.

"Of course, sir. I'm just glad you called. We were all very worried. But you should know, we've been getting calls from . . . well, everyone. About the Oracle's prediction. We haven't been sure what to do."

Branson gestured at the television, which now featured a reporter breathlessly speculating as to why the reverend's personal secretary might have been summoned to his home this evening.

"I'm aware of the media's surge of interest," Branson said. "It's abundantly clear every time I look out my front window."

Jonas nodded.

"Have you been praying on this?" he asked. "Asking for a solution?"

Branson reached for a remote control and clicked off the television.

"In a sense," he said.

He walked across the living room, passing a large, heavy, wooden door, out of place against the Crate & Barrel chic that characterized the rest of the room, and the vibe of mild, inoffensive comfort that suffused the house in general. It looked like a teleporter accident had partially fused the reverend's living room with an old English country estate. The door seemed purposely designed to generate inquiry as to what was behind it.

Branson arrived at a side table holding a number of bottles, with glasses and other various drink-making paraphernalia arrayed next to them. He took a decanter filled with an amber liquid and poured two generous portions. He handed one over, then raised his own in a silent toast and took a sip. He raised an eyebrow at the younger man, holding it until Jonas lifted the glass to his own lips.

"Delicious, isn't it?" Branson said. "This is the Byass Apostoles. I don't think there's a better Palo Cortado to be found."

Jonas nodded politely.

"It's very good, Reverend. I'm not much of a drinker, but this is very tasty."

He watched Branson, waiting for him to explain why he'd been summoned, but nothing seemed to be forthcoming. The reverend lifted his half-empty glass, swirling it in the air, his expression turning pensive—but only for a moment, until the broad smile returned, right on the edge of unsettling.

Jonas found himself getting annoyed.

It was as if the man had no idea what was happening outside his home. In his church. His people left leaderless while he boozed it up in his living room. The congregation was asking questions. They thought the reverend was *frightened*.

"Sir, I realize that the Oracle naming you on the Site must have come as a shock, but please, we need to know what to do. We need a plan."

"Oh, I have one, Jonas. After all, it's been three days. Time for me to rise again, eh?"

Branson turned toward the heavy wooden door, considering. He took another long sip of his sherry, then looked back at Jonas.

"Do you think I'm a good man?" he asked.

To this question, Jonas knew, there could only be one response.

"Yes," he said.

"Good," Branson said. "I'm glad. I do too. The Branson Ministry brought in over a hundred and thirty million dollars last year, and a lot of that went right back out. The clean water initiative in Africa. The schools. The drug outreach work. I'm not one of those huckster preachers taking his flock for every penny and spending it on Ferraris and plastic surgery."

He glanced at the wooden door again for a moment, then back to Jonas.

"To put it another way, would you agree that this Ministry is valuable, and it would be a great loss to the world if it were to disappear?"

"Well, of course, Reverend. I'm not sure anyone could say otherwise."

"I agree with you," Branson said. "Therefore, we've established that I'm a good man, and that everything I've built is important."

He rubbed the side of his face, causing a distinct, weary scratching noise as his palm was abraded by his stubble. He stared into the middle distance for a long moment.

"I've got a secret," he said.

Branson pointed at the wooden door.

"It's in there."

Jonas took an involuntary step backward. He set his mostly untouched glass of sherry down on the coffee table.

"Reverend, I think maybe I should go."

Branson walked toward the wooden door, pulling a heavy iron key from his pocket.

"Don't be foolish, Jonas," he said.

He unlocked the door and opened it, revealing dimness beyond. He stepped inside, vanishing into the gloom.

"Come in here," the reverend's voice floated back. "And bring your sherry. It's expensive."

Shaking his head, Jonas picked up his glass and followed Branson into the next room.

It was a study of some kind—a dim, windowless chamber with its illumination generated by a single, small lamp on a table in the middle of the room. The pool of light was too small to see much—a few glints of metal from the walls.

Branson closed the door, sealing the room with a smooth click as the latch engaged, then flipped up a bank of switches to the right of the entrance.

A series of spotlights set into recesses along the walls came to life. Below each light sat a niche containing a small, ornate object of metal and glass. The walls were crimson, and the few pieces of furniture were carved from dark wood, with leather upholstery. The aesthetic could not have been more opposite to the calculated, milk-bath neutrality of Branson's office back at headquarters, or even the bland ordinariness of the rest of his home. It was lush, almost sensual.

Branson tapped another switch. A gas fireplace leapt to life, sending warm, dancing reflections off the metal objects in the alcoves arranged around the room.

He walked to a niche containing a glass cylinder about a foot high, chased with silver, standing on four little golden feet. Inside, an unrecognizable yellow-brown lump. He picked it up and turned, showing it to Jonas.

"Do you know what this is?" he asked.

Jonas looked, his face puzzled.

"I'm not sure, Reverend."

"A reliquary. These are the mortal remains of Saint Gratus of Aosta. He died in AD 470. I believe it's a vertebrae. Or so they told me when I bought it."

Jonas glanced around the room, taking in the many other alcoves, each with its own little chest and container of glass and metal, holding a lump of flesh and bone nearly indistinguishable from the one Branson was holding.

"Are all the rest of these . . ." Jonas gestured helplessly around the room. "Reverend, these are Catholic saints. I don't understand."

Branson smiled thinly.

"Don't worry, Jonas. I'm not a closet Papist. I'm still a good, old-fashioned American Protestant."

"But then why do you . . ." Jonas began.

Branson stepped closer to the fire, which, to Jonas, seemed like a bizarre choice. The room was much too warm.

"Saintly relics are tourist attractions," Branson said. "For thousands of years, churches all over the world have used relics to pull in the faithful, and next to every single one is a donation box."

Branson stared at the bone inside the reliquary.

"Is this actually a piece of old Gratus' spine? Or did some church just need its roof fixed, and so they went down to the boneyard out back and dug themselves up a miracle?"

He looked at Jonas, his face calm.

"My secret. It's simple enough," he said. "I don't believe in God."

Jonas frowned.

"Your faith has lapsed?" he asked. "It happens, Reverend, or so I've heard—if you want my help, we can pray together. I'll do everything I can, and I'm honored that—"

"No," Branson interrupted. "I've never believed in God. I don't particularly see the point."

Jonas remained silent.

"Well, that's not exactly true. I believe in spirituality, and goodness. But the stuff in the Bible? The specifics? No. God's not real. At least, not the version we sell to our congregation. That's all pablum. An ad campaign."

He held up the reliquary again.

"Belief is a commodity. It can be packaged, bought and sold. It's true of saint's bones, and it's true of my ministry."

Jonas could feel his eye starting to twitch.

"You know our congregation doesn't believe either, right?" Branson said.

"That's not true," Jonas said, heat leaking into his voice.

"Sure it is. If those folks really believed God was up there judging them, they'd be better people. But you see how they are. They lie, they cheat. They're brazen about it."

Branson drained his sherry glass and looked at it ruefully.

"Should've brought the bottle," he said.

He set the glass down on a nearby table.

"A long time ago, I spent a while thinking about the good a person might do in their lifetime. The things they might really do to help their fellow man. Like a math problem. How much good could one ordinary person accomplish with their life? I figured it was quite a bit, if they really wanted to go that way.

"But then, I looked at what people actually do, and I realized . . .

it's not a lot, is it? Not very much at all. Folks look out for their own, and maybe they don't actively hurt anyone else if they can help it . . . but reaching out a hand to those in need? Forget it. Most people have a hard-enough time just getting through the day."

He smiled at Jonas.

"I didn't like that math. I found it frustrating. So I decided to do better. I decided to do this."

He gave the reliquary another rattle.

"Now, I don't want to sugarcoat things. I take money—buckets of it—from many, many people. But I'm not a thief. I give good value. Our congregation . . . our customers . . . want to feel good about themselves, and better than other people, and they're willing to pay top dollar.

"That is what our ministry is for. That's what every ministry is for. That's all they really want from us. Look me in the eye and deny it."

Jonas wanted very much to look up, deny the reverend, defy him, but his eyes remained fixed on the reliquary, watching the flames dance across it.

"My flock gives me their energy, their power, their money, and they're happy to do it. If I was selfish about how I used it, that would be one thing. I'd be a devil. But that's not what I do, is it? I gather up all those little scrapings of goodwill and put them together, into *me*. And then I create change in the world. I bring light.

"And now," Branson went on, "I have the ear of captains of industry and titans of entertainment, because I have an *army*. My flock. I call something the devil's work, and they despise that thing. I call another thing blessed by God, and my people buy it, or vote for it, or go see it. That is my power, and it lets me walk with powerful men. You know President Green calls me once a month, Jonas? Just to chat.

"All that power, and I've tried to do nothing but good with it. How many people could say the same, if they were in my position?"

Jonas realized that he had just listened to a man spend ten minutes justifying the fact that he lied for a living.

"I don't believe in God," Branson said, "but I believe in belief, and its power to do good in this world. I've devoted my life to that principle. But now . . ."

He lifted Gratus of Aosta's reliquary again and smiled at it.

"Who gives a shit?" he said.

Branson threw the reliquary into the fire. It smashed, and an odd, mushroomlike odor immediately wafted up.

He stepped to another alcove and removed a second reliquary, brandishing it at Jonas. The reverend's face was turning red—the room had become stifling, and the overpowering odor of burning human remains didn't help.

"Anthony of Padua, Jonas. Asses. The patron saint of donkeys, for God's sake!"

A crash, as Anthony joined Gratus in the flames. Jonas shied back from the heat. The Oracle's prediction had clearly broken the reverend's mind. He wanted to run, wondering in a panic if he should try to warn Maria, get her out of the house. He considered what might happen if he actually had to fight Hosiah Branson—he couldn't even picture it.

Branson stepped to the next alcove and picked up a small crystal chest—into the fire it went. The scents wafting out of the flames had taken on a new quality—notes of nutmeg, mixed with a sharp, chemical odor.

A vision popped into Jonas' head, very clear—the reverend's wife opening the study door some hours from now, and finding both her husband and his assistant dead on the rug before the fireplace, poisoned from the fumes generated by some ancient preservative.

Jonas stepped forward and put a hand on Branson's arm.

"Please stop, Reverend. What are . . . what are you doing?"

Hosiah swiveled his eyes toward Jonas. Sweat was pouring down his forehead, beading in his eyebrows. He wiped it away with his sleeve.

"That prediction was a direct attack, Jonas! He's trying to destroy my credibility—make me a joke. And not just me, either. Hindus, Muslims . . . we'll all get it. We can't compete. The Oracle hasn't come out and said he's the voice of God yet, but it's only a matter of time, and then . . . a prophet whose predictions actually come true? We're done. Faith is fickle, I'm sorry to say. The Oracle's doing what we do, just . . . better, and people are paying attention. Shifting their loyalties. The Site's only been up for three months and our donations are down by . . ."

"Fourteen percent," Jonas answered, without hesitation.

"Fourteen percent," Branson echoed, nodding his head. "We have to stop him. I won't let my life's work be ruined by some charlatan."

"Charlatan?" Jonas said. "I mean . . . the predictions he's making . . ."

"Yes, a charlatan. A fraud," Branson said. "I can admit to some doubt, early on. That prediction about me . . . pepper on my steak . . . I couldn't get my head around it. Not at first. That's why I had to take this time—these days away—just to think it through. But now . . . I know what to do.

"We'll take him down, Jonas. You and me, and some of my powerful friends. It'll work. I know it. After all, we've got God on our side."

Branson smiled again—that neon-bright grin.

"Do you really think it'll be that easy, Reverend?" Jonas said. "I mean, the Oracle does seem to be able to predict things before they happen. We don't know what else he's capable of. What powers he might have."

"No. We'll be fine," Branson said.

"But . . . how do you know?"

"The Oracle isn't a god. He's got no magic. He's just a man. Without a doubt. Do you know how I know that?"

"How, sir?"

"Because he fucked up."

Branson eased himself down onto one of the couches, the leather creaking under him.

"He got rattled," Branson said. "He sent that prediction at me like a sniper's bullet, like some kind of attack, but it'll bite him in the ass, I promise you that."

He sipped Jonas' sherry, savoring it, taking his time.

"I didn't see it at first. I'll admit, I was probably a little rattled myself. The Site is so pervasive . . . even I sometimes forget that it's all a lie. But I tell you this—there is nothing supernatural about the Oracle.

"The fool said I'll supposedly put pepper on my steak on such and such a date. Well, I have a choice, don't I? I have free will. When the time comes, Jonas . . . it's simple. I just won't do it."

"But I don't see how . . ."

"Because," Branson said. "I'll have that steak live, in the ministry's cathedral, on television, with the signal going out all over the world. And I'll lift that pepper shaker, and then I'll look at it, and I'll smile, and I'll set it right back down, unshook.

"Everyone on the planet will see that the Oracle can be wrong. And between now and then, we'll use every resource this organization has at its disposal, every connection I have, every favor I'm owed, to find him. We will name him, and we will take away his power, and that . . . will be that."

He raised his sherry glass and drained it.

"The Oracle gave us the weapon we'll use to defeat him. He fucked up. That's how I know he's just a man."

Branson shifted his gaze toward the fireplace, the flames fueled by blackened, smoking, shattered saints.

"God doesn't make mistakes."

CHAPTER 8

At his kitchen table, surrounded by stacks of thick-bound books and scattered web page printouts, Hamza examined the table of contents of *The Swiss National Bank Law: A Treatise*. He flipped to the section on international currency exchange regulations.

Even the introductory paragraph was a rat's nest—a set of sentences so convoluted that they had to be combed for meaning like a weaver preparing wool.

Hamza sighed and began to take notes.

Fifteen minutes later, as he was attempting to understand the reasons Switzerland preferred to keep its American dollar reserves in money market accounts, he heard a phone ring. Without taking his eyes from the page he was reading, he reached across the table for his phone.

And then he realized it wasn't his cell phone that was ringing. The sound was coming from the bedroom, where Miko was grading papers. Also where he had set up the extremely secure (and extremely expensive) satellite line he was using to maintain contact with a very select group of people.

Hamza's eyes shot up from the book, and he half rose out of his chair.

He started to move toward the bedroom, already knowing he'd be too late. The phone cut off in midring, and he heard Miko's voice say, "Hello?"

Hamza stopped at the bedroom door. The look on Miko's face as she listened told him everything he needed to know about the person on the other end of the line.

"Just a moment," she said, "I'll get him for you."

Her voice held the forced-calm tone she tended to use when she was struggling mightily to hold it together. He'd seen her use it when she was talking to her class, at moments where the fourth graders were on the edge of erupting into full-blown chaos.

She carefully placed the heel of her hand over the phone's mouthpiece and turned to her husband.

"Hamza," she said.

Still the same tone—which made him the fourth grader in the scenario.

"Meeks, listen . . ." Hamza answered. She held up a hand. He closed his mouth.

"The man on the other end of this telephone just asked to speak to His Majesty Hamza Abu al Khayr Sheikh, King of the Coral Republic."

Hamza stared at her for a moment.

"Right, hon, uh, that's for me. I'll just take it in the other room."

He held out his hand for the phone. Miko didn't move.

"I know it's for you, Hamza. He said his name was General Muatha Kofu."

They stood, staring at each other. Hamza's mouth had gone dry.

"Miko, I really have to take that call."

"I'm sure you do. But there's only one way you're getting this phone. You swear right now that when you finish, you tell me what the hell is going on. You tell me what the Coral Republic is, you tell me how you got to be its king, and most importantly, you tell me what you're doing with Will Dando. I have been incredibly patient with you, but this is it. No more."

She hovered a finger from her free hand over the phone's disconnect button.

"No!" Hamza said, half leaping for the phone.

Miko stepped away, giving him a disdainful look.

"Okay, Miko," Hamza said. "Okay."

"Swear it!"

"Dammit, Miko. I swear."

She handed the cell phone over.

"General!" Hamza said in a cheery voice. "I apologize for the delay. I trust it did not inconvenience you."

He left the bedroom. Miko followed him. He sat down at the kitchen table, facing a corner. Miko moved a chair and sat down directly in front of him, so close that their knees touched, an intent look on her face.

Hamza frowned, but kept his voice light.

"That's excellent news, General. I will wire the second half of the payment to you as soon as the United Nations publishes notice of your recognition of the Coral Republic in their register. I appreciate your speedy attention to my request."

Miko's look changed to blank incomprehension. Hamza listened to the voice on the other end of the line. He hesitated, glanced up at Miko, then continued.

"Yes, that's the amount we agreed on. Fifteen million U.S. dollars."

Miko's mouth dropped open. Hamza gave her a pleading look and held a finger to his lips, begging her to stay quiet.

"Certainly, General. The UN recognition won't take long. Our countries will be competing against each other in the Olympics before you know it. And let me say that I am pleased, very pleased, both for myself and on behalf of my subjects that we have an ally such as yourself in Africa."

He listened again.

"Yes, we'll speak soon. Good-bye."

He hit the cutoff button. Miko stared at him, her mouth still not fully closed. Hamza gave her a weak smile.

"All right, let's get through this—honestly, I think it will be a relief. Let me show you something."

Hamza rummaged through one of the piles of paper on the kitchen table and extracted a manila folder. He opened it and removed a glossy photograph, which he handed to his wife.

Miko looked at the photo, an aerial view of an island. It felt small, the palm trees just off the beach providing a sense of scale. A white sand beach took up most of one coast, and the rest alternated between black volcanic-looking rocks and lush green vegetation, with no evidence of human habitation.

"What . . . ?"

"That's the Coral Republic, Miko. That's what I was talking about with the general just now."

Miko laid the photograph on the table.

"The general called you a king."

"Yes. Will's the prime minister." He paused. "Uh, let me point out that makes you the queen."

Miko settled her head in her hands. She stared at the photographs on the table. Behind her, the refrigerator motor clicked on with a slight whir.

"Hamza, sweetheart," she said, "what the fuck are you talking about?"

Hamza leaned back in his chair, thinking. After a moment, he looked at his wife.

"Okay. Let me start by saying that we're rich. Richer than we ever would have been if I'd stayed at Corman. We never have to think about money again."

Miko blinked.

"That's not a bad way to start," she said.

"True," Hamza answered. "Any chance you'd just be willing to leave it there?"

Miko gave him a flat stare.

"Zero chance. How did we get this rich, and how is Will involved? Didn't you have to pay his electric bill for him once last year?"

Hamza's mouth twisted into a quick smile.

"Huh. I'd forgotten about that. But listen, Meeks, Will paid us back for that a million times over. Literally."

"*How*, Hamza?"

Hamza looked away, running a hand through his hair. Miko's eyes never left his face.

"Ahh, shit," Hamza said, finally. "It's the Site, Miko. Will and I are working on the Site."

Miko slowly raised her eyebrows.

"What are you talking about? The Site? The future Site?"

"Yes. Will's the Oracle, and I'm helping him."

Miko's eyes narrowed. Hamza waited. He knew what she was doing—waiting for him to decide he'd milked enough humor out of the joke and laugh, or smile, something. Miko frowned. She stood up from the table and walked to the refrigerator, where she clinked a few chunks of ice into a glass from the dispenser and filled it with water.

"You want one?" she asked.

"No, that's all right . . . actually, yeah, that would be good."

She poured Hamza a second glass and placed it in front of him on the kitchen table. Her mouth twisted.

"I'll be right back," she said.

"What?" Hamza said. "Don't you want to hear the rest?"

Miko didn't answer. She left the room. Hamza watched her go, momentarily left with nothing to say.

He heard the sound of the printer in their tiny home office spitting out a few pages. A moment later Miko reappeared, holding two sheets of paper. She sat down at the kitchen table and laid the papers flat, side by side. Hamza read them upside down, seeing the all-too familiar text of the Site.

She studied the predictions, taking her time. Hamza remained silent, letting her read. Finally, Miko looked up and met his gaze.

"The Site. My God. I was just grading my kids' essays in the bedroom before that call. The topic was free choice—I just asked them to write about something affecting the world today. Almost every single one of them wrote about the Oracle, Hamza."

Miko tapped the printouts with her index finger.

"Where did Will get these?" she said. "Where did the predictions come from?"

Hamza shrugged.

"I don't know. Neither does he. According to Will, he woke up at about five A.M. one day, just launched out of a dream. You know what that's like—no break between sleep and reality. You're awake, but it doesn't really feel like it.

"The dream was just a voice, he said, reciting a series of events, each with a date. A hundred and eight separate things, all set to happen over the next three years or so."

"One hundred and eight? Why that particular number?"

"No idea. That's just how many there were."

Miko processed for a moment. She gave a little involuntary shiver and looked up at Hamza, half angry, half embarrassed.

"Hamza, I just realized—I sent a question to the Site, when you set up that e-mail address so people could write in."

"You did? What did you ask?"

"None of your business. It was personal. That's the point. I thought I was asking the Oracle, and it turns out I was just asking *Will.*"

"Well, I never saw it, and Will never mentioned it, if he did. We've gotten millions of e-mails, Miko, and we've only made it through maybe a hundred thousand. Most of them won't ever be read."

"Why did you ask for questions from people in the first place?"

Hamza took a sip of water.

"The idea was to give corporations and wealthy people a way to contact us without being obvious that we were offering to sell predictions about the future."

"But you must have had so many people writing to you for answers, for hope. Did you ever respond to any of them?"

Hamza suddenly felt extremely small.

"Why did you lie to me?" Miko said, her eyes flaring. "You could have told me. You've been lying to me for months. That day you came home after quitting, and you wouldn't give me a real reason why. That bullshit about a biotech startup you were shepherding along, and all that VC money . . ."

"I wanted to tell you, Miko, but Will has a huge bug up his ass about staying anonymous, and he was afraid that the more people who knew who he is, what he knows, the greater the chance it'd get out somehow."

"I'm your wife! Not some . . . random! You didn't think you could trust me?"

Hamza reached out and touched Miko's hand.

"Listen, I can trust you with *anything,* I know that. That's the point. That's why you're my wife. But this secret wasn't mine to share."

Miko let her hand stay where it was, Hamza noticed with some relief.

"So why are you telling me now?" Miko asked. "Did Will change his mind?"

"No. I'm telling you because you're my wife and I can trust you with anything."

The corner of Miko's mouth twitched upward.

"You're goddamn right. What else?"

"There's not really that much more. We did some work to figure out the rules, you know, whether the stuff he saw had to come true, or if it can be changed."

"Can it?"

"Not as far as we can tell. Everything so far has happened just like he dreamed it, even when we try to get in the way of a prediction, or push it in another direction. It just . . . doesn't work."

"Creepy."

"It's actually a great thing from a sales perspective—means we can have confidence in our product . . . but yeah. Not everything Will knows is good, and he's getting wrapped up in the causality of the whole thing. He's wrong—none of these things are his fault—but I sympathize. It's not easy for him."

Hamza paused and looked across the kitchen for a moment.

"He's probably the most famous person in the world, but not really in a good way. You know how people feel about him. Half are terrified of what a guy out there who sees the future means, and the other half are terrified *and* they want to kill him."

"Not everyone."

Hamza rolled his eyes.

"Oh, sure," he said. "Crazies who think he's the second coming, maybe, or UFO freaks."

Miko shook her head.

"No, that's not true. My students are fascinated with him. He confirms their suspicions—they're still young enough to think there's magic in the world, and the Oracle plays right into that. And I've had lots of conversations with people who think it's hopeful that the Oracle's around. It means there's a plan. Life isn't just random."

She wrapped her hands around her glass of water.

"I hope so, anyway," she added.

"Why's that?" Hamza asked.

Miko looked up and met his eyes.

"Because I'm pregnant," she said.

Hamza sat, stunned.

"Okay," Miko said. "Now tell me why we need an island."

CHAPTER 9

"Christ, look at this," Eddie said.

Union Square was filled by a mass of people—a demonstration of some kind, maybe a protest. Signs poked out of the crowd here and there, too far away for Leigh to read.

"Don't turn, Eddie," Leigh said. "I want to see what's happening."

"If I don't get off Broadway, we'll get stuck in that clusterfuck," Eddie said, pointing to the snarl of traffic ahead of them, cars inching along through the overflow of pedestrians from the square. "We're already going to be late, and if we don't turn, we're going to be so late that the guy you're supposed to interview will be long gone by the time we get there."

"I'll take responsibility," Leigh said. "Just get closer."

Eddie shrugged and left the queue of cars preparing to turn off Broadway. The van inched closer to Union Square, and Leigh realized that most of the signs had at least one word in common—Oracle

"I know what this is," she said. "The Oracle demonstration."

"That's today?"

"Sure as hell looks like it," Leigh answered. "I want to get in there. This is huge. I had no idea it would be this big."

"Oh, Leigh, no. You can't."

"This is more important. We can get past the barricade with our press pass."

Eddie's hands remained frozen at ten and two on the steering wheel.

"I'm sure New York 1 has it covered," he said.

"Just do it, Eddie!"

Leigh tossed her notes for the interview with some celebrity chef she had been scheduled to meet—oh, fifteen minutes ago—on the van's dash. She turned and snagged her purse from the back and plopped it on her lap, rummaging through it for a notebook and a pen. Tools secured, she shoved the bag to the floor and started composing a cold open, jotting down questions for prospective interviewees in the margins.

She felt frigid air as Eddie rolled down the window to flash his press credentials at the police officers manning the barricade, and was dimly aware of the van's slow progress as it nosed its way through the crowd to find a spot to park.

"All right," Eddie said, turning off the van's engine. "Let's do this and go. You'd better stick up for me if Reimer gets a hair up his ass about it."

"He won't fire us for missing some dumb interview," Leigh said, checking her makeup in the mirror on the sunshade. "It was filler, just in case some other piece ran a little short on the edit."

"He won't fire you because you missed the interview. He'll fire you because he already thinks he should have fired you because of the stunt you pulled with that Site story you ran. I don't know why you insist on giving him ammunition by doing shit like this."

Leigh looked at him, annoyed.

"If that's how you feel, then why did you stop?"

Eddie grinned at her and opened the driver's-side door.

"Because I want to see what's happening too. And if Reimer does get pissed, I know it'll all land on you. I'm too talented to replace."

Leigh snorted.

They got out of the van, Eddie sliding open the passenger-side door to pull out his camera, battery packs, and assorted additional gear. Leigh checked her own equipment—her wireless microphone and its connection to the signal pack clipped to her belt in the back, under her coat. Satisfied that everything was working properly, she buttoned up her long coat and adjusted her scarf, pulled on her gloves, and snagged her notebook from the front seat of the van.

Eddie was still getting ready, so Leigh looked out into the crowd, trying to get a sense of what was happening, trying to remember what she'd read about the demonstration.

At the far end of Union Square, a strident, amplified voice rang out over the crowd. She couldn't make out the words, but every so often everyone would react—boos and cheers in equal number.

The signs waving above the crowd were finally visible—a schizophrenic assortment of pro- and anti-Oracle views. SAVE US FROM OURSELVES, ORACLE! ORACLE = HOPE.

THE ORACLE LIES FOR THE DEVIL! was a popular one, printed in vibrant red ink, with horns and a spiked tail added to the *O* in Oracle.

Mounted police were stationed at the edges of the park, and more officers patrolled through the crowd in groups of two or three, watching carefully for . . . what? From what Leigh could remember, the rally was part of a mass call to the Oracle to reveal himself, one of a number of similar assemblies happening at the same time in cities across the world. But she hadn't ever thought it would be this big—ten thousand people had crammed into the park, if not more.

"You know Reimer won't run this, either, no matter what we get," Eddie said, hoisting the camera to his shoulder. "You aren't on the news beat. He couldn't have been clearer about that. It's a principle thing for him."

"I know that," Leigh snapped. "This isn't about Johannes

Reimer, and it's not about Urbanity dot fucking com, for God's sake. We're reporters. This is news. We should document it."

Eddie pointed at live broadcast antennas poking out into the air above the crowd at various points around the square.

"You don't think those guys have things squared away? I don't like the vibe in here."

Leigh looked away from the crowd. She gave Eddie the sweetest smile she could muster.

"Just ten minutes, Eddie, for me. One or two interviews, and we can go. Maybe we'll find something amazing, and even if it never runs, we can leak it to the net, put it on our résumés and get out of this shitty gig."

"Your shitty gig is my fifteen-year career, kid. I'm perfectly happy."

God help me if I ever get that happy, Leigh thought.

She put her hand on his arm. She looked into his eyes, giving him an intentionally oversincere smile.

"Please," she said.

Eddie looked back at her for a moment, then rolled his eyes.

"Fine, ten minutes," Eddie said. "Pulitzers all around, I'm sure."

Leigh circled the outskirts of the crowd, Eddie following, looking for someone to put on camera. The demonstrators were a mixed bunch—age, gender, apparent walks of life . . . all over the map. The only consistency was a seriousness of expression. This wasn't a fun day out in the park, not for any of them.

Two men, hands in their pockets, shoulders hunched against the cold, stood on the sidewalk on the north end of the park near the entrance to the W hotel. They were watching the demonstration, just staring, fascinated. Neither held a picket sign. Leigh pointed them out to Eddie.

"How about those two?" she said.

"Whatever," Eddie said.

Leigh approached the two men. One was Caucasian, the other looked South Asian, maybe Indian, and both appeared to be in their mid- to late twenties.

"Excuse me, my name's Leigh Shore, from Urbanity.com," Leigh said. "I was wondering if either of you would like to do a short interview about what's happening here today."

"No, thank you," the Indian man said. "We're just browsing."

"How about you?" Leigh asked the other man.

He hesitated before responding.

"All right," he said.

"Hey," the Indian guy said to his friend.

"It's fine," the second man said.

"Great!" Leigh said. "What's your name?"

Another brief pause, then, "John Bianco."

"All right, John, would you mind letting your friend here hold your bag? It's got a logo on it, and rather than blurring that in post it'd be easier just to keep it out of the shot."

John Bianco removed his shoulder bag and handed it to his friend. Said friend appeared to be having some sort of quiet, mostly internal seizure.

"Fantastic. Now, if you could just stand here." She pulled John by his sleeve, positioning him so the demonstration was at his back. "And when you answer my questions, talk to me, not the camera. Okay?"

"No problem," John answered.

"Eddie, you good?" Leigh said.

Eddie nodded.

"All right, set. Go ahead," Leigh said.

"Taping in five, four, three," Eddie said, counting down on his fingers at the same time, indicating the last two numbers silently, pointing at Leigh as he hit zero.

"I'm Leigh Shore," Leigh began, "and I'm here in Union Square, at the site of New York City's Oracle demonstration. These events have been staged today in major cities across the globe, with the intent being to coax the mysterious prophet into revealing his identity. I'm talking to John Bianco to get his thoughts on what's happening here today." Turning to face him, she continued, "John, have you been here all day?"

"Since this started, yes."

"And you live in New York?"

"That's right."

"What brought you down here today?"

"Same thing as most of these people, I suppose. I wanted to see what will happen."

"Do you think these rallies will bring the Oracle out of hiding?"

"I doubt it," John said.

"Really?" Leigh said. "You seem very certain. Why not?"

"I just think that if he's keeping himself out of the public eye, he probably has a good reason. I mean, you think he isn't already aware that the world wants to know who he is? What, he's going to come out of hiding just because all these people say please?"

Leigh nodded, smiling. She liked this guy. He had a point of view.

"A lot of people here today think that the Oracle has a responsibility to share his gifts with the world more directly than he already has," she said. "To make himself available, to help humanity navigate away from any disasters that might be looming on the horizon. What's your take on that?"

"I think it's his business. I think we don't have the whole picture about what's going on with this guy, so when people assign him motives or responsibilities, it's just sort of silly and frustrating."

"Frustrating? That's an interesting choice of words. Why are you frustrated by how people feel about the Oracle?"

"I just think people need to get over it, I guess. Let the guy be."

"But yet, here you are."

John Bianco gave a short, quick laugh.

"Yeah, I guess I am."

Behind them, from somewhere deep in the middle of the crowd, shouts rose up, loud enough to drown out the speakers at the south end of the park. Leigh and John Bianco turned to see what was going on, but it was hard to make out anything from where they were standing.

Eddie grabbed her arm.

"Come on. We're leaving," he said.

"Why?" Leigh said. "What's happening?"

He nodded at the mounted police at the edge of the crowd. They were all on their radios, and some were beginning to push inward, letting their horses clear a path.

"They can see better than we can, and I'm sure they have spotters on the rooftops. Something's going on in there, and we don't want to get stuck in the middle of it."

The noise from whatever was happening in the center of the crowd was growing louder, and now a few screams could be heard. The mobile uplink antenna for the van closest to the disturbance was swaying in increasing arcs, presumably as the van hidden by the crowd was pushed back and forth. As Leigh watched, it toppled slowly into the crowd like a felled tree.

Leigh glanced at John Bianco and his friend. They were transfixed, staring at the burgeoning chaos. The Indian man turned and grabbed Bianco's shoulder, trying to pull him away.

"Oh . . . oh no," she heard John Bianco say, quietly.

He took a step toward the crowd, and the Indian man put his other hand on Bianco's arm, forcibly rotating him away from the center of the park.

"There's nothing you can do," he said. "We have to get out of here, Will, right now!"

"But it's happening again!"

Leigh had a moment to wonder what that could mean, until a fresh round of screams reached her ears. Her head whipped around, back toward the center of the square, where she could see clouds of white smoke billowing up in the midst of the demonstrators.

"Eddie," she said. "We need to get in there. We need to see what's going on. Document it."

A bottle smashed onto the pavement two feet away, exploding into a hundred tiny blades.

"Fuck that. That white smoke is tear gas," Eddie said in her ear, taking her by the arm. "The crowd will stampede, any second. Leigh, we have to—"

A second bottle crashed directly into the camera Eddie was holding in his free hand. He dropped it, cursing, and the camera fell to the ground with a crunch. Eddie held up his hand, staring at it in disbelief. Blood streamed freely from deep gashes in his palm and wrist.

Leigh bent to retrieve the camera, snatching it up from the ground, and then a sound from behind them, like the roar of a fire stoked with new fuel. They turned to look, and saw hundreds of red-faced, terrified people surging toward them out of the white gas clouds covering the south end of the park.

They ran.

THE ORACLE IN THE DESERT

On the horizon, shapes appeared, round dark lumps shimmering in the heat haze. The village. Arnaud Teulere slowed his Jeep, thinking hard.

Teulere could admit that the chances of the Oracle living in a hut in the northeastern deserts of Niger were . . . remote, to be charitable. But he had been in Africa for a long time, and he had seen stranger things. Besides, there was more hope in his breast than he'd had in years, and perhaps that was worth a nine-hour drive into the wastes. Even a single prediction of the future could be sold for enough to get him back on his feet, to return to France and start over. What else did he have to spend his time on? Contemplating failure? That had grown tiresome a decade ago, when his uranium mines stopped producing.

The Jeep was now close enough to the village for details to be discerned. It was small, six or seven huts surrounding a well sunk deep into the earth. Teulere stopped his vehicle and stepped down into the desert. He made a display of pulling his pistol from his belt and checking the loads. Only two bullets, but the villagers wouldn't know that. He didn't want to start things on an aggressive note, but he was very far from safety here, and if these people turned out to be hostile, he wanted them to know that he wouldn't be easily taken.

Teulere holstered his revolver and plodded through the dust toward the village. A group of men walked out to meet him as he approached. Four of them, in long, light-colored robes, with leather-skinned faces framed by turbans and scarves. Behind them, the rest of the villagers stood and watched, curious. Teulere noted a number of young men—children, really, boys—squatting in the shade of the huts, staring at him with reddened eyes, keeping their balance by leaning on AK-47s planted stock-first against the ground.

The eldest member of the advance party stopped a few feet away and held up a hand. He spoke. Teulere struggled to understand—it was some kind of Hausa, but thickly accented.

He responded in that language, with a basic greeting. Whether the elder comprehended or not, the old man seemed to know why he was there. He curtly gestured for Teulere to follow him, then turned and walked directly to the largest hut in the village.

The boys unfolded themselves, standing and slinging their rifles over their shoulders, holding them loosely. The child soldiers closed in around Teulere, silent, red-eyed. The only open direction was along the path the elder had taken.

Teulere kept his hands far from his pistol and stepped forward.

The large hut had a hanging cloth for a door. The elder pulled it aside, grinned, showing a set of mottled, wooden teeth, and pointed into the dark depths of the hut.

"Who is there?" Teulere asked the old man in Hausa. No response.

Teulere sighed and ducked into the hut. His eyes took a moment to adjust to the gloom. The little round building was cool, almost pleasant after the heat outside.

"Hello, Monsieur," a voice said in French, from the far side of the hut. Teulere shaded his eyes, peering into the darkness, trying to see who had spoken. He took a step forward.

"Who is it?" he said. "I have come to see the Oracle. Are you he?"

A man was seated on a rug at one end of the hut, surrounded by platters of food, rifles, delicate items of stonework, and other gifts. He looked just like the other villagers—perhaps his clothes were a bit finer, but otherwise he was just a man, about thirty years old.

"Why have you come here?" the man said.

"Talk in the city has it that the Oracle lives here, and that he is willing to sell visions of the future. If this is true, then let us make a deal. I have brought items to trade."

The man began to laugh and continued for a long ten seconds. Teulere waited, growing more certain every second that he had wasted his day and several canisters of gasoline he could barely afford.

"My name is Idriss Yusuf. And yes, I am the Oracle," the man said, his chuckles tapering off. "I was able to predict the day a small plane would crash near here. It was full of supplies stolen from a United Nations outpost in Burkina Faso. My village has been eating well ever since. And now, people come to me with their questions

about what tomorrow will bring, and I do my best to answer them."

"So it is true," Teulere said, feeling a little awed. "But how?"

"How?" the man said. "It is very simple. I am the only man within a hundred kilometers who can read French."

He laughed again.

Teulere's mind filled with confusion.

"I don't understand."

The Oracle reached to the ground next to him and opened a cloth satchel. He pulled out a newspaper and held it up. Teulere took a step forward. It was a copy of Le Republicain, dated some months earlier. Prominently featured on the front page was a story about the Oracle, which reprinted the predictions from the Site. One of them—one of the first, date-wise—referred to a plane crashing in the Niger desert.

Teulere understood. The crash had occurred before the Site had truly erupted into the world's consciousness. Back then, no one would voyage into the trackless wastes of the Niger dust lands on the off chance some American website could predict the future. Now, of course, it was different. The location of each of the Site's predictions had become spots of great interest as their occurrence dates drew near, attracting Oracle tourists from across the world and extensive media coverage.

This man had seen an opportunity and taken it. That was all. A gamble that had paid off.

"So you see, then," the man continued. "People come from far away to ask my advice and give me the wealth of their villages. It has made me and my tribe rich. You are the first white man to come see me. Ask me your question, give me your gifts, and I will reward you with what you seek."

"Fuck you," Teulere spat. "You are a fraud. I will give you nothing."

The faux Oracle shook his head sadly.

"That is unfortunate, my friend. I have plans, you see. In this dead land, people are desperate for a future. Any future. Why should I not be the one to give it to them?"

His eyes narrowed.

"Better than your kind, who only take."

The man lifted his head and rattled off a loud string of Hausa, too fast for Teulere to follow. Still, he didn't need to hear it clearly to understand. He cursed and reached for his pistol, spinning around.

The first shot caught him high in the chest. He had just enough time to see two of the child soldiers at the entrance to the hut, holding their rifles high, before the second entered through his cheek and exited through the back of his skull.

PART II

WINTER

CHAPTER 10

Thirty miles west of Duluth, Minnesota, a navy-blue-and-white Sikorsky H-92 helicopter holding the designation Marine Two touched down on the front lawn of a large Victorian home, throwing up huge clouds of billowing, pristine snow, sparkling in the cold sunshine.

The house stood alone on an estate of a hundred acres of rolling midwestern hillsides and woods, and a large section of the lawn had been cleared of the three feet of snow on the ground in anticipation of the aircraft's arrival. Two hundred yards to one side from Marine Two sat a sleek black executive copter fitted with wide skids to allow it to land on the snow, tiny in comparison to the huge Sikorsky, like a shiny, dark-skinned beetle.

Several other helicopters were dotted along the lawn and the long, curving drive leading from the house to the nearest road, over a mile away. These were matte black, with discreetly mounted weapons pods, and had disgorged contingents of Secret Service agents and U.S. Marines in winter gear, who now stood at strategic points on all sides of the house, looking both inward and outward.

A lone figure sat on a glider on the home's wide front porch, sipping from a thermos and swinging slowly forward, back, forward. He was bundled against the cold—puffy coat, earflapped hat, thick scarf.

Inside Marine Two, Anthony Leuchten peered out the window at the figure sitting on his porch. He was smaller than expected, the name "Coach" having conjured up images of burly midwesterners with red cheeks and girthy waistlines. But this man seemed short, almost delicate.

"That's him, huh?" he said. "The Coach."

"Yeah," Jim Franklin answered. "More or less."

Leuchten frowned. The details for this meet had only been finalized earlier that day—a matter of hours, really—set to occur at his family home in rural Minnesota, completely snowed in, accessible only by air. And somehow, the man had arrived first, and was already sitting on his porch drinking coffee when the advance security teams arrived.

Leuchten found that extremely irritating.

He turned back to the FBI director, sitting across from him in a beautiful, pale leather seat with the presidential seal incised into its headrest.

"You aren't wasting my time here, are you?" Leuchten said. "Because this would be a really bad time to have my time wasted."

Franklin gave him a very dark look, black as pitch.

Leuchten knew the FBI director hated him. He was used to it. A lot of people hated Anthony Leuchten.

People hated him because he won. Mustering energy to care that people were frustrated when he beat them seemed like a tremendous waste of time—which was something he did care about, very much. There was a vision to be realized, after all, and only so much time in this life to get there.

He locked eyes with Franklin, keeping his face blank, and then he winked. A flicker of confusion rippled across the other man's face, which Leuchten enjoyed immensely.

He leaned forward and rapped on the helicopter door. A marine standing just outside opened it, letting the warm cabin air out and the

freezing Minnesota winter in. Leuchten made his way out of the aircraft and along the shoveled-out path to his own front porch, where
the Coach sat waiting, still swinging, watching him.

As he drew closer, the Coach's face—smiling—came close
enough for him to make out. And then Leuchten stopped cold, because the Coach was not a small, delicate man after all. The Coach
was a woman.

Leuchten forced himself to take another step, watching as the
woman on the porch got to her feet. He thought back to the conversations he'd had with Franklin about the Coach, and not once could
he remember the FBI director mentioning that his mysterious fix-it
man was in fact a mysterious fix-it woman. Franklin hadn't corrected
Leuchten, either, not in all the times he'd referred to the she as a he.

Leuchten resolved to ask the man why he had done such a rude,
suspicious thing—right before he fired his insubordinate, ineffec-
tive ass.

All this ran through Leuchten's head as he approached the porch,
his polished loafers slipping on the snowy path. As he neared the
steps, the briefest shadow of displeasure crossed the Coach's face, but
it was wiped away instantly, replaced by an even larger grin.

"Mr. Leuchten, sir," she exclaimed, stepping forward with hand
outstretched as Leuchten reached the porch, "it is an honor and a
privilege to meet you."

Leuchten reached out his ungloved hand to meet the Coach's
mittened one.

"Goodness, look at me," the Coach said, quickly tugging the mit-
ten off her hand. "No manners at all. I'm just excited, sir, that's all."

She grasped his hand and shook it warmly, a firm, dry grip.

Leuchten considered the Coach, deciding that she reminded him
of Bea Arthur. High-cheekboned face surmounted and defined by
a thin, aquiline nose like half an isosceles triangle. Sharp, clear blue
eyes behind rimless spectacles, with that smile powering the whole

thing. Overall, it gave the impression that under her puffy winter coat, she was wearing a T-shirt that said WORLD'S BEST GRANDMA.

Even with a career spent around good politicians and all their native charisma, and being able to exude no small amount of charm himself—when necessary—Leuchten felt himself warming to the Coach's aw-shucks demeanor. He pulled back, forcing himself to remain aloof. He knew frustratingly little about this woman beyond Franklin's stories of her superhuman ability to solve problems no one else could—and he'd been skeptical when he'd thought the Coach was a man. Now that he knew she was a woman . . . it all just seemed ludicrous. Some sort of ridiculous game.

"Believe me," Leuchten said, "after the things Jim Franklin's told me about you, the pleasure is all mine. Coach, is it?"

The woman ended the handshake.

"That's right, sir. Just Coach does just fine. Been called that so long, seems like that's the only name I've ever had. Describes my professional capacity pretty well, besides."

Leuchten held up a hand, gesturing toward the front door of his house.

"Let's get inside. No reason to stand out here on the porch in the cold."

The Coach nodded.

"Sounds just about all right to me, Mr. Chief of Staff," she said.

"Call me Tony, please."

Leuchten opened the door and held it for the Coach, who entered the house and stood in the foyer, looking around at the decor. Leuchten glanced back. Jim Franklin stood in the snow just off the porch, clearly unsure whether he was invited in.

Leuchten let him wonder for a moment longer.

"Come on, Jim," he said graciously. "Let's not keep your, ah, friend waiting."

Franklin nodded tightly and climbed the porch steps.

Leuchten took off his coat and hung it on a stand by the door. He glanced out through a window at the snowy landscape, deserted in every direction except for the various government vehicles and the Coach's helicopter.

Four or five Secret Service agents waited impassively inside the living room, arms folded. Leuchten and Franklin watched as the Coach sat on the stairs leading up to the second floor and tugged off her boots.

"Sorry about melting on your floor here, Tony. Get me some paper towels and I'll wipe it right up."

"That's all right, Coach," Leuchten said, marveling at the surreality of the entire encounter. "Someone will take care of it. Come into the dining room. Can I get you a drink?"

"Why the hell not?" the woman said. "Scotch, one ice cube. Nice to have something warming on a cold day."

The trio entered the dining room and sat at the long mahogany table. Leuchten took the seat at the head, with a huge picture window behind him, knowing that glare from the snow outside against his back would leave his face shrouded in shadows. Franklin sat to Leuchten's left, and the Coach slipped into a chair about midway down the table on the other side, stopping first to hang her coat over the back of the chair. A Secret Service agent entered with a tray of drinks.

"Now, Tony, I've got a question for you," the Coach said, after whisky was sipped and pleasantries had been exchanged.

"Sure, Coach," Leuchten said, smiling broadly.

"Where the fuck's the president?" the Coach said, her genial tone not varying in the slightest.

Leuchten choked on his mouthful of scotch, spluttering. He composed himself quickly, storing away for future reference the satisfied,

I-told-you-so look on Franklin's moony, blue-collar face. He set his drink down on a coaster. The woman waited, unhurried, patient. Leuchten forced a smile back to his lips.

"I don't know if Jim Franklin gave you the idea that President Green would be meeting you today, Coach, but obviously there was some miscommunication. The president's a busy man. That said, he's very interested to hear what you might be able to do for us."

Leuchten paused. The Coach stared at him, unblinking.

"Is there a problem?" Leuchten said.

The Coach ignored him. She turned to Franklin.

"Jim, you told this guy about me, right? Didn't sugarcoat it any?"

Leuchten watched, incredulous, as Franklin answered as if he weren't even in the room.

"I did, Coach, but the chief of staff tends to have his own ideas about the best way to do things."

The Coach made a hard-to-define noise that nonetheless very clearly communicated her disapproval. She looked out the window, apparently deep in thought.

"Excuse me?" Leuchten said. "I have full authority from the president here. If you have any questions, Coach, you can ask me. Actually . . ."

He stood up from his chair and folded his arms.

". . . no. I've had about enough of this. There is no such thing as a mystical black-ops fix-it person. If there were, I'd know about it. Franklin told me you found a terrorist cell the FBI couldn't, stopped their boat with a dirty bomb aboard about a hundred yards from the Statue of Liberty. Told me you figured out who actually blew up the *Columbia*. Told me all manner of other horseshit. I don't know your game—either of you . . ."

He glanced at Franklin, who was watching him, his face almost . . . amused?

". . . but I'm not playing. Coach, whatever your name is, I'd like you to stand up, leave my house, get in your little helicopter out there and fly away, right now, or I'll hand you over to the marines."

The Coach didn't move. They stared at each other, unblinking.

"Well," the small woman said. "You do seem to know quite a bit about me. You did your homework. That's good."

She reached down, below the level of the table. Leuchten flinched back, involuntarily, even though he knew that the Secret Service had gone over the woman with a fine-toothed comb, and there was no way she'd have been able to sneak in a weapon—they had even checked out her thermos. But still.

The Coach came up from under the table with a paperback book, a very familiar book indeed.

Leuchten's eyes widened, not understanding.

The Coach dropped the book onto the table, where it landed with a dull whap.

"Your autobiography, Tony," she said. "Read it on the flight up. I liked it. Funny thing, though . . ."

She reached out a finger and rotated the book slowly on the table, bringing its cover around to face him. She looked up at Leuchten and smiled thinly.

". . . you left out Annie Bridger."

All the blood seemed to drop out of Leuchten's head. The room receded, and a hollow ringing noise echoed in his ears. He fell backward, hitting the seat of his chair—a five-thousand-dollar handmade piece of Baker furniture—hard enough to strain the wood. Somewhere, deep in the distance, he heard it crack.

"How do you know . . . that name . . . ?" he managed, hile in the back of his throat.

The Coach didn't answer. She didn't have to.

Just as suddenly, the woman reverted back to genial grandmother mode. She lifted her glass and tipped it in Leuchten's direction.

"No better way to understand a man than to see how he talks

about himself, in his own words. How he tells his own story. What he puts in, and what he leaves out. Now, from this . . ."

She skated the manicured index finger of her free hand—nails painted bright blue, he noticed—across the cover of Leuchten's autobiography.

". . . it's pretty clear to see that you feel you've been tapped to use the skills God's seen fit to give you to guide the world into a better future. You can see things other people can't—consequences, opportunities. Would you say that's true?"

Leuchten didn't answer. He hadn't put any of that in the book—but that didn't mean the woman was wrong.

"I'd even go so far as to say that the way you handled that situation with Ms. Bridger was the point where you realized that you didn't have to let events carry you along. You could make the world into what you wanted it to be. You could take control."

The Coach set her glass down on the paperback, right over the smiling portrait of Leuchten that graced its cover.

"You know, my original sales pitch was going to be to President Green, but I've learned to roll with the punches in my career. Honestly, it might even be better that it's you, Tony."

She settled back in her chair, eyes sparkling.

"You believe you're a man of destiny, Mr. Leuchten. Literally. You think you're the one steering the world, keeping it safe from disorder. The lone torchbearer bringing the American dream into the twenty-first century. The puppet master. And so, you must hate that things are getting so out of control. Those poor people killed in the Oracle riots, the Site, all those billionaires buying predictions they won't share with you and yours."

Leuchten shot a glance at Franklin, mentally adding treason to the list of reasons he was planning to have a new FBI director come Monday morning.

Franklin just shrugged and looked back at the Coach, who was still talking.

"In fact, all this Oracle business . . . it's such a stick in your eye that it's almost hard to think that wily old prophet isn't doing it to you on purpose, like a big fuck-you aimed right at your face."

The Coach looked down at her hand. She languidly extended a single middle finger, examined it, then retracted it back down into her fist, just as slowly.

"After all, Tony, you're the one who's supposed to be able to predict the future, right? That's how you win elections for people. You see what's coming down the pipe and pivot in whatever direction you need to."

Leuchten searched his mind for any way he could regain control of the conversation. The woman was just some nobody. If she were somebody, he'd have heard of her. He thought of all the people he'd beaten over the years—Supreme Court justices, senators, journalists, canny rat bastards of all description—and pulled himself together.

"The Oracle?" Leuchten asked. "Why did you bring him up?"

The Coach folded her hands around her glass. Her lips thinned into a smile.

"Oh, please. The Oracle's the biggest game in town. Who he is, what he is, why he's doing what he's doing. Everyone wants to know, and everyone has an opinion. Except"—she pointed at Leuchten—"for your guy. Almost nothing at all from the president of the United States. That tells me that either the Oracle is one of yours, or you have no idea who he is and you don't want to risk alienating him by taking a position one way or another."

Ouch, Leuchten thought, keeping his face neutral.

"But I don't think he's yours," the Coach continued, "because if he was, you'd have some story out there, something you'd prepared ahead of time. The silence says that you don't know who this guy is any more than anyone else. And Jim here"—she nodded at Franklin—"wouldn't have gotten in touch with me, considering what that would mean for him, unless you guys had a problem, a big problem. One the U. S. of A. couldn't solve.

"Put it all together, and it's clear as day—you can't find this guy, and you want me to take a crack at it."

Leuchten took a long sip of his drink, buying time. The good scotch was doing its work. He was beginning to feel a bit like himself again.

He looked at the Coach, meeting the woman's eyes. She stared back, unfazed.

"Let's say you're right, and we want the Oracle," he said. "Director Franklin seems to think that you can find him for us. Tell me your plan."

"Plan? I don't have a plan. I mean, you haven't hired me yet. Why should I do the work before I have the job? That would be crazy," the Coach said.

Leuchten frowned.

"Fair enough," Leuchten said. "What I need to hear, though, is what makes you so damn effective. Give me your sales pitch. Tell me why you think you can do better than the entire U.S. government. So far, I haven't seen anything particularly impressive."

The Coach shrugged. "I bet that's what Annie Bridger said," she responded.

Leuchten leaned back in his chair, his mouth pressed into a tight line.

The Coach grinned.

"Where will you be, Tony, if your boy loses that election? He'd be just another guy. And you . . . well, you'd just be out there. Unprotected. Guy like you, lots of enemies, am I right?"

The woman lifted her drink and took a swallow. She very deliberately replaced the glass, not back on the book, and not on the coaster she'd been given, but about three inches to the right, on the polished surface of Leuchten's twelve-thousand-dollar Baker table.

"I am so damned effective, sir, because I know people. I remember people. I have one hell of a Rolodex up here."

The Coach tapped her temple.

"Comes in handy. Must be about a million people up in my skull—all different kinds. Bakers, butchers, cleaners, cooks, and carpenters. Someone comes to me with a problem, I sit back and think on it, and before I know it, names start popping out of my brain like bread out of a toaster. But knowing the right people for the job is only the first part of what I do. Once I have my team set up, I start to live up to my name. After all, a team without a coach is just a bunch of people playing with each other."

The Coach gave Leuchten a serene look.

"You know," she began, "outside all this Coach business I'm as ordinary as you like. I've got a nice old husband, some great grandkids, and a garden that I dearly love. I'm about eighty-five percent retired, too. There's not much to do in life, good or bad, that I haven't done.

"This Oracle thing, though," she added, "this has my back up. He seems *interesting,* in a world that, from where I'm sitting, isn't interesting enough. If you hadn't called me on it, I might have tried to figure out who this fellow is myself. Nothing like a good mystery, right?"

Leuchten digested that.

"So, here's my offer," the Coach said. "I find the Oracle for you. You get control over the future again, one way or the other. I get to meet him—which is almost pay enough. This guy's a mover *and* a shaker, tell you what."

"Just like that?" Leuchten said.

"Just like that," the Coach answered.

"I'll need more. I need details. I can't take this back to the president."

The Coach stood up, pulled out the seat directly next to Leuchten's at the head of the table, and sat back down. She leaned in. Behind her mildly stylish glasses, the woman's eyes were very blue and very clear.

"Very respectfully, Mr. Chief of Staff, I don't think you do need details. If you hire a plumber, do you get down there on your hands and knees and watch him mess around with the pipes for three or four hours? Nope. You wait until he tells you the john's unclogged. You don't want to hear about all the shit he has to wade through to solve your problem.

"If we have a deal, then you'll get the Oracle delivered to you, in person. He'll be alive and well, and I'll throw in whatever other information I discover about what he's up to along the way. That's it. Done."

The Coach waited for Leuchten to respond, keeping her face close. She smelled like scotch and peppermint and damp wool.

"So what this means, ultimately," Leuchten said, not pulling back, "is that we have to turn you loose, with absolutely no control or authority over the actions you will take in the name of President Green, and in the name of the United States of America."

The Coach inclined her head.

"And the price?" Leuchten asked, his voice clipped. "You said meeting the Oracle would *almost* be enough compensation. What else do you want?"

The Coach leaned back, a smile appearing on her face.

"Well, it's not about money. I've made so much over the years, I don't need a dime. Hell, I even cover my own expenses.

"Here's how it'll work. Someday, I might want your boss for one of my teams. Now, there's no guarantee I'll ever need President Green at all. I'm almost retired, like I said. But if I do call, then he'll come, and he'll do what I ask. I've got a few ex-presidents on my roster, but a sitting one is a whole other thing. He's got a year and change left in this term, and I'll make sure he gets a second one, so that's over five years he could be available to help me out."

"You're insane," Leuchten said. "The president cannot hold superseding allegiances. And thank you for the offer, but getting Daniel Green a second term is my job. I think I can handle it."

The Coach laughed a little.

"Maybe. But I'll do it better. You broker this deal, you can just sit back and relax for another four years, Tony. Trust me."

Leuchten considered this. Senator Aaron Wilson, the president's esteemed opponent, was proving to be a wily competitor—he was young, vital, with a clean background that included combat service in Desert Storm, and he was damnably quick with a sound bite. If that wasn't enough, Leuchten was running Green's campaign in the face of an amazing chain of unrelated events that had somehow locked together to tank the U.S. economy—uncertainty over the Oracle, of course, but also unrest in South America, a couple of hedge fund failures that had shaken Wall Street, spiking gas prices, and on it went. If it weren't impossible, he'd almost say it had been planned. Whatever the real cause, though, everyone blamed the president for their 401(k)s shrinking, even if there wasn't a goddamn thing he could have done about any of it.

"I'm sorry, Coach," Leuchten said, pulling his head back to the moment, "but you have to understand that the president can't be compromised in the way you're proposing."

"Well, he wouldn't be *compromised*, sir," the woman answered. "Oh, no, it's not as bad as all that. For one thing, it would only be just the one time. I ask him to do one thing for me, could be anything from having me over for dinner to making a phone call—who knows? Once he helps out, he's done, and he never hears from me again. Nothing to get upset about.

"Here. Let me show you."

The Coach raised a hand in the air and called out across the room.

"Hey, Fred. You want to come in here for a second?"

A beat, and then one of the Secret Service agents entered the room, his face set in the same emotionless mask that they all held while they were on duty. Leuchten didn't know his name—but apparently the Coach did, and apparently it was Fred.

"Nice to see you," the Coach said. "Have a really quick question for you. Being on one of my teams . . . would you say it's a good thing?"

"Yes, ma'am," Fred replied, without hesitation. "Absolutely."

"And that whole favor payout back-end deal? No issues with that?"

"None. I'd do it again in a heartbeat, and whatever you need, I'm ready."

Fred's face didn't change.

He just admitted to high treason . . . without blinking, Leuchten thought, almost in despair. *Jesus. And we had no idea. With all our screening . . . and he's next to the president every single day. No fucking idea!*

"Thank you, Fred, I appreciate the recommendation, and consider that favor repaid. Now, chances are you'll need a new gig after this—why don't you fly on home with me and we'll set something up for you."

Fred nodded his head.

"That's very kind of you, ma'am. I'll wait outside, if you don't need anything else?"

The Coach waved her hand toward the home's front door.

"Sounds good. Bundle up, though. Cold out there."

Leuchten and Franklin watched as Fred reached inside his coat and removed his badge and gun. He laid them on the dining room table, turned, and left without a word, closing the front door behind him.

They turned to look at the Coach, who was staring out the window, still smiling. She never seemed to stop smiling. She reached out, picked up her glass of scotch, and took a long sip, placing it right back in the ring of condensation on the tabletop when she was done.

"Franklin," Leuchten said. "A word, please."

He stood up and walked to the front door, snagging his coat as he went. Franklin stood, but turned toward the Coach before following Leuchten.

"Thank you," Leuchten heard him say.

"Of course, Jim," the Coach replied. "Anything for an old friend."

Leuchten left the house, shrugging on his coat. He looked out at the Coach's helicopter, where Fred the ex–Secret Service agent could be seen through the cockpit's front windows, waiting patiently. Franklin appeared, closing the door behind him.

"I'll need your resignation on the president's desk in the morning, Jim," Leuchten said.

Franklin's gaze went very cold.

"And why is that?" he asked.

"You were obviously a member of one of the Coach's teams at some point in the past. That's how you know who she is and what she can do. The president can't have people in his administration with conflicting loyalties. You're out. Honestly, I have no idea why you told me about her in the first place. You had to know this would come out."

Franklin's eyes didn't move.

"I told you, Anthony, because I am trying to protect my country," he said. "People are dying. I think those Oracle riots are just the start. Something enormous is happening, and we need to understand it. Get ahead of it. The Coach seems like our best shot to do that."

Franklin took a step closer to him.

"This might be hard for you to understand," he said, "but I don't do this job for myself. I do it for the people I can help by doing it."

You sanctimonious prick, Leuchten thought. *Like I don't help anyone? I'm trying to save the goddamned world!*

"Not anymore," he said.

"Excuse me?" Franklin replied.

"Not anymore. You don't do this job at all, in fact. Not once we're back in DC."

Franklin smiled, just a little.

"I don't think it'll go that way," he said.

"Oh? And why is that?"

"Because I run the best investigative agency in the world, Leuchten. And the first thing I'm going to do when I get back is look up Annie Bridger. Unless you'd rather I put a team on it? I could absolutely do that. You're the boss."

Franklin put his hand on the door handle.

"I'll wait inside while you call the president to go over the Coach's offer," he said. "It's cold as hell out here."

He pushed open the door.

"Don't worry about the Coach, Tony. She always gets it done, and she looks after her own."

Leuchten watched Franklin slip back inside, wondering how the hell he could have been outmaneuvered so utterly and completely. He felt dazed.

The White House chief of staff pulled a secure phone from his pocket and dialed.

"Mr. President," Leuchten said.

A light snow had begun to fall, filling in the tracks created by the vehicles and the security staff. The scene was extremely peaceful. The conversation lasted for perhaps ten minutes. Once it was done, Leuchten stood and watched the snow for a moment, then turned and went back inside.

CHAPTER 11

W ill lifted the slip of paper and looked at the computer screen, cross-checking the sequence of numbers and letters written on it—thirty-two characters long—against what he'd typed. It looked right.

Will extended his index finger over the enter key. One tap and that was it. No more Oracle.

He looked to either side. Most of the other terminals were occupied, mainly by European tourists checking e-mail and posting to various social networks. He'd spent a fair amount of time in places like this since the Oracle's debut. The Florida Ladies called it a low-tech solution to a high-tech problem: hiding in plain sight by using public Internet access points—cyber cafés, coffee shops, libraries, parks. The sheer number of users online through the same IP address at once helped to disguise his own use, especially when combined with the anonymizing tools he used to access the Site. Most of the time when he used a terminal at an Internet café, his preferred apps—Tor, IRC, et cetera—were already installed on the machines. Clearly he wasn't the only person using these machines for nefarious operations.

No one was looking at him. The end of the Oracle, and they had no idea. Too busy trying to score cheap Broadway tickets and Skyping back home.

The sequence of numbers and letters was a burn code; it would activate a series of programs the Florida Ladies had set up to erase the few bits of data out there that allowed the Site to run—the original pastebin with the predictions, and the e-mail address and its end point in New Jersey. They had designed the system so there wouldn't be very much to connect the Oracle to Will Dando. Once he hit enter, there would be nothing at all.

Will's hand hovered over the keyboard. He stared at the screen.

His finger moved two inches up to the delete key. He watched as the burn code vanished, character by character, from right to left. He closed the window, deleted the tools he'd downloaded at the beginning of his session, and stood up, grabbing his coat from over the back of his chair.

Coward, he thought.

Will paid—cash—and left the Internet café, stepping out onto the sidewalk on the northern end of Times Square.

He zipped up his coat and walked east, no particular destination in mind.

More than two hundred people had died in the Oracle riots, all over the world. Twelve had died at the Lucky Corner.

He could hear Hamza's voice in his head, telling him that those things were not his fault. How people chose to use information the Oracle put out into the world was not his responsibility. He hadn't killed anyone. He hadn't hurt anyone.

All that was true. But it didn't change the fact that if he hadn't put up the Site, then those people would still be alive. Hamza didn't get it, or chose to pretend he didn't, and that was why Will hadn't spoken to him since Union Square.

He continued east, weaving through the scrum of Times Square tourists without thinking about it, walking with that sidewalk auto-pilot longtime New Yorkers developed.

Will had gone to the Internet café with the idea—the hope—that if he shut down the Site and the Oracle went silent, maybe the world would just move the fuck on. The whole thing would just be one of those blips people barely remembered five years down the road, like the Chilean miners or the winner of the last World Cup.

No one else would get hurt. No one else would die.

And then the moment came, and all he'd needed to do was hit that enter key, and he hadn't, and so the Site was still up.

Why? Money?

He considered, trying to come up with a single purchasable thing—anything at all—that he didn't already have enough money to buy.

Hamza had finally figured out a way for them to access the Oracle funds safely from inside the United States. It involved Caribbean shell corporations, an ersatz Panamanian hedge fund that had hired them both as its sole, insanely highly paid employees while relying on automatic algorithmic trading to operate, and a thousand other things that ultimately meant they were hiding in plain sight.

It wasn't too far from the methods the Florida Ladies used to handle their data security, even if Hamza would never admit it. The Oracle network of businesses paid every fee, every tax bill, on time and in full. Everyone got their cut, everyone was happy, so there was never a reason to look into things too closely.

Hamza was convinced that once they'd been in operation for a few years, it wouldn't matter where the money originally came from, because they'd have a history of legitimate business activity to hide behind. They didn't need to hide the money. They just needed to hide the fact that it was the Oracle's money.

The main thing, as far as Will was concerned, was that he could go to any ATM and see a seven-figure bank balance. He had a few thousand dollars in his wallet right at that moment. The only other time he'd had that much at one time was at the end of a tour a few years back, when the promoter had paid the band in cash for the whole run all at once.

So, no. Not money.

Will looked up, realizing where his feet had brought him—Forty-Eighth Street, between Sixth and Seventh Avenues. What was once known as Music Row.

During Will's first several years in New York, he'd been on this block nearly constantly, at least once a week. Until fairly recently, it had been the home of a number of guitar shops—Sam Ash, Rudy's, several others—each with its own staff of frustrated working musicians trying to take advantage of tiny employee discounts to keep themselves stocked with gear while suffering through the indignity of selling instruments and effects pedals and amps and strings to the city's many, many amateurs.

Will had worked at one of these shops when he'd first moved to New York. That was back when he'd still assumed the break was coming. Maybe one of the bands he was playing with would get signed, or one of the tracks he'd cowritten would blow up, or he'd find his way into the really high echelon studio work with stars who could afford to pay their bands salaries whether they were recording or not, plus benefits.

Players with all that and more were everywhere in New York. You ran into them all the time, at open mics or at the stores or just in the bars where musicians hung out. There was no real reason Will couldn't be one of them.

After all, Will had been far and away the best bassist—the best musician, really—in his high school. College, too. He could sing, and more importantly, he could write. His was a special talent. Musical fame and fortune were his destiny. It was just a matter of time.

And then that time had gone by, and Will had come to realize something very important. There was good, and then there was New York good. Will Dando was Chicago good. Austin good, definitely. L.A. good, probably.

But New York good? No.

It turned out that Will Dando, at least from a musical perspective, was not particularly special.

And then he woke up from a dream with a hundred and eight bits of the future in his head. Not what he would have expected, not what he would have chosen.

But pretty fucking special.

Will walked out of Music Row into the broad concrete plazas laid out beneath the skyscrapers on the western side of Sixth Avenue. An electronic news ticker ran around the façade of a building a block south, displaying an endless, ten-foot-tall stream of headlines.

His cell rang. Will checked the ID—his mother. He sent it to voice mail and slipped it back into his pocket.

She called a lot, and so she got his voice mail a lot, as did Hamza, Jorge Cabrera, and anyone else who tried to get in touch with him these days. Will couldn't remember the last time he'd actually spoken to his mother, or his father, or his sister. He texted, sent the occasional e-mail—they knew he was alive, and vice versa, but he didn't want to speak to them. He didn't know what he'd say.

Will felt like he was on the edge of a long, fast, bone-breaking tumble—into booze, maybe, or women, or just ugliness. He knew what was going to happen, and he was coming to understand that *no one* should know what's going to happen.

And yet the Site was still up.

More than two hundred people in the Oracle riots. Twelve at the Lucky Corner.

Will had spent almost every waking minute since sprinting out of Union Square with Hamza trying to decide what the hell he was going to do. He'd considered going public. Had considered going to the cops, or the *New York Times*. He'd thought about sending money to the families of everyone who had died at the Lucky Corner, and in the riots. But it was hard to see how he could do those things without putting Hamza at risk, and that wasn't fair.

The safest, best idea he'd come up with was just to pull down the Site, but when the moment came, he couldn't bring himself to do it, and he knew exactly why, if he could just be honest about it with himself.

He *liked* being the Oracle.

Beyond that, there had to be something more to this than just two guys making a fuckload of money. He still had so many predictions left that he hadn't used. There had to be a reason for all of it, something he was supposed to do.

But the next step wasn't clear. He was paralyzed. He was a prophet with absolutely no idea what came next, and maybe a few more people would die because he was too dumb to figure it out.

A kebab cart caught Will's eye, steam billowing out from its grill into the frigid air, and he realized he was hungry. Eating had been sort of hit or miss, recently. It happened when he reminded himself that he needed to do it, not on any sort of regular schedule.

Will walked up to the cart and asked for a chicken pita; the cart's proprietor, a swarthy man in a thick, grease-stained coat and a plaid hunter's cap pulled tight over his head, earflaps and all, tossed some raw chicken on the grill to sizzle.

The cart owner looked up at the news ticker, still running in the distance, and squinted.

"Heh," he said. "Look at that."

Will followed his gaze, and read:

REVEREND HOSIAH BRANSON ANNOUNCES PUB-
LIC CHALLENGE TO ORACLE PREDICTION: "NO ONE
TELLS ME HOW TO EAT MY DINNER!"

Will thought that over, then shrugged. Branson could say whatever he wanted. The prediction would still come true. They all came true.

"What do you think about all that?" Will asked, gesturing at the ticker.

"What do I think, sir?" the vendor said. "I think it's just more BS. Everything BS. This Oracle, so powerful, he can see the future, and he just gives us predictions about lottery tickets or chocolate milk? Why never anything useful? Why never anything that helps?"

He pointed at Will with his tongs.

"Everyone I know—everyone; me, too—writes the Oracle with questions about important things. Things that, if I knew, would maybe change my life. *Everyone* does this. But how many get answers? I ask you. How many people you know get an answer from this Oracle?"

"None," Will said.

"None!" the vendor said, snapping his tongs together with a loud metallic clack.

He turned angrily back to his grill and pulled the spiced chicken together onto a spatula, which he dumped onto a waiting pita. He added a little tahini sauce, some lettuce, tomatoes, and onion, then wrapped it up in a sheaf of wax paper and aluminum foil.

"Everyone thought maybe this time something would be true, that it would matter, that things could change. But you know . . ."

He pointed at the news ticker with Will's pita. The scroll now read:

NIGER CAPITAL CITY NIAMEY BESIEGED BY SOJO GABA FORCES.

". . . just because the Oracle says things that are *true,* it does not mean that they *matter.* The world is as ugly as ever. I just don't understand why he bothers at all. What is the point?"

Will stood there for a moment, staring at the man holding out the foil-wrapped sandwich toward him.

"Hello?" the vendor said, one eyebrow raised. "Hello?"

Will reached for his wallet. He looked, extracted a bill, and handed it to the man, taking his pita sandwich at the same time. The vendor looked down, frowning.

"Hey, you crazy. I can't break this. Give me something smaller," he said and held the hundred-dollar bill back out toward Will.

Will turned and walked away, heading back the way he'd come, back toward the Internet café. He took a bite of the sandwich, ignoring the sound of the vendor calling after him.

That's good, he thought. *That's really good.*

CHAPTER 12

You feel like this is the right way to go?" the president asked.

"I do, Daniel," replied Hosiah Branson, relishing, as always, calling the man by his first name. It just never got old.

"Read me the bit about Niger again," Branson said.

A pause, and then the president's voice over the phone, low and rich—say what you would about Daniel Green's talent for governance, but he was a hell of a public speaker.

"Our commitment to freedom cannot stop at our shores. The human rights abuses perpetrated by Sojo Gaba and its leader, Idriss Yusuf, must end. He is taking the children of Niger and turning them into his army—forcing them to murder their countrymen in an effort to take control. Niger is one of the poorest lands on the planet. It has suffered under oppressive regimes for generations, and its people have been unable to develop on pace with other nations in the region, despite their abundant natural resources and vibrant culture. Even more, the lack of a stable government has made it difficult for them to police their own state, allowing for the growth of aggressive terrorist organizations such as Sojo Gaba. Niger may seem far away, but events there can absolutely affect the safety and security of the American people. Evil seeds may flower from its hidden training—"

"Root," Branson said.

"What was that?" Green said.

"Seeds take root. They don't flower. It's a better metaphor, in any case. Roots burrow in—they need to be rooted out. Flowers . . . who's afraid of a flower?"

"Mm," the president said.

A beat, which Branson presumed was due to the president correcting his speech.

"All right," Green said, after a moment. "I think that's got it. Not that it will help all that much. That bastard Yusuf's telling people he's the Oracle, and people down there believe him. He's already got an army together, and half his soldiers are just kids. Even if we do send troops to Niger, the idea of big, bad U.S. soldiers gunning down nine-year-olds is . . . well, shit. I might as well hand the election to Wilson."

"Daniel, come on," Branson said, his tone forceful. "You know this is a long game. Election day is still quite a ways off."

"I realize that, Hosiah," the president replied. "And I can see about a hundred ways things can get worse. Not so many ways they can get better. We've got troops on the ground in Afghanistan and Syria, and now we're seriously talking about going into a third country. The Dow's fallen over a hundred points every day this month, and most of the other economic indicators aren't much better. China can't get its house in order, and we're tied so closely to them that anything bad that hits their markets ripples out and nails ours within a day.

"Honestly," he went on, "I don't know why the hell anyone even wants this job."

"You could always resign," Branson said. "No law says you have to run for a second term."

"Uh-huh," Green said. "I'd miss the free plane, though."

The president cleared his throat, which Branson knew was a signal that the conversation was wrapping up.

"Thank you, Hosiah," Green said. "I appreciate you taking the time—you know how important your perspective is to me."

"Of course, Daniel. I am at your disposal, any time you need me. But if there isn't anything else, I have a—"

"There is one thing, actually," the president said. "The Oracle."

Branson's grip on his phone tightened.

"Yes?" he said. "What about him?"

"I've seen you, Hosiah. You're on every talk show that will have you, writing editorials . . . you're going full-on scorched earth as far as the Oracle goes. Pretty much calling him the Antichrist."

"I'm just following my gut on this one, Daniel. I truly believe everything I'm saying. People think of the Oracle like a . . . party trick. Or maybe some sort of savior. As I see it, not enough people understand that he's dangerous. I've been blessed with a pulpit, and I feel obligated to use it."

"I get that, Hosiah. But I need you to back off."

Branson's face went hot.

The president had never—not once in all the years he'd been the man's spiritual adviser, since almost a decade before he got anywhere near the White House—attempted to exert any sort of influence over Branson's Ministry. He'd never asked for a favor, never asked Branson to campaign for him, even in those states where a few words during a sermon could have made a real difference. It was one of the reasons their relationship stayed strong, he'd always felt. Neither one of them asked for anything from the other beyond friendship and advice.

Until now. The goddamned Oracle, thrusting himself into Branson's affairs again.

"Back off?" he said. "What do you mean?"

"You just need to tone it down. The thing is, we still don't know much about the Oracle, but if he can really do what it seems like he can do—"

"He can't," Branson said, his voice flat and certain.

The president paused, then continued.

"I'd prefer if you didn't interrupt me again," he said, his tone gone cold. "I understand that you have a point of view, Reverend. But everyone knows you and I are close, and if the Oracle does turn out to be . . . what he seems . . . then I want him as an ally. Period. We've got our own plans in place to make contact with him—Tony Leuchten is handling that situation, and I don't want anything to interfere with what he's doing."

Green's voice changed, softening.

"We've been friends for a long time, Hosiah. Nothing would hurt me more than having to cut ties. That is the last thing I want to do."

Cut . . . ties? Branson thought.

He thought about the ripples that would spin out from the president no longer being willing to take the calls of Reverend Hosiah Branson. Green would be first, but word would spread, first to the politicians, then to the businessmen, then to everyone else. He'd be done. Done.

And the Oracle would have won. No. It couldn't be allowed.

"Daniel, I'll do what you say—I'll back down—but I've already authorized a small ad campaign that will be putting out some . . . ah . . . strong rhetoric about the Oracle. We've already paid for it, and we can't get the money back. I'll do my best to distance the Ministry from the ads, though."

Silence from the other end of the line. Branson swallowed once, then continued.

"And I'm going ahead with the live broadcast when that bastard's prediction about me is supposed to come true. That's my life, Daniel. My life. The Oracle might as well have called me out for a showdown at high noon. I will eat every bite of that steak, without a damn bit of pepper anywhere near it, and the whole world will watch me do it."

Still nothing from the other end of the phone. Five seconds passed. Ten. And then, finally, the president spoke.

"I'm sorry, Hosiah, I didn't catch that. An aide was just talking to me . . . I need to go," he said.

The line went dead. Branson slowly lowered the phone from his ear. He set it on the counter in front of him and looked at his reflection in the large, three-paned mirror set onto the wall.

"You can come back in," he called out.

Three people entered the dressing room—his stylist, his makeup girl, and Brother Jonas, in his dark suit and tie, frowning down at his phone like it was a pet gerbil that had just taken a crap in his hand.

The makeup artist took a small gauze pad from a makeup dish sitting on the counter in front of Branson and started dabbing powder on his forehead without a word. She'd been about halfway through the task when the president called and he'd ordered his staff out of the room.

"Jonas," Branson said, "I've decided to go ahead with the ad campaign we talked about. Go ahead and send the initial payment to the agency, and tell them to get started immediately."

The ads were a full-court press—Internet, radio, print, even a few carefully chosen TV spots, all designed to raise doubts about the Oracle's origins, intentions, and abilities. The ad agency had focused on a single key concept during their presentation—they wanted to encourage the congregation to become "Detectives for Christ," investigating their friends and neighbors for signs that the Oracle might be among them.

The other man hadn't moved. He was still frowning down at his phone.

"Jonas," Branson said. "Did you hear what I just said?"

"Yes, Reverend," he said, his voice hollow. "You need to look at this."

He thrust out his phone.

The screen was displaying the Site; familiar lines of black text, with the twenty-some predictions Branson had read so many times they were almost as familiar to him as scripture. Below those should have been the Oracle's e-mail address, with the tantalizing "This is not all I know" line, but that had been moved farther down the page. Now, below the old predictions, new sentences had appeared—twenty-three of them, numbered in sequence just like the first set of predictions. The format looked identical—a date in the future, and then a few words describing an event set to happen on that date. But the new predictions were not entirely like the old.

Each was written in red text, the color standing out starkly against the plain white background. Blood on a snowfield.

Branson devoured the twenty-three new predictions, reading them once quickly to see if his own name was anywhere in them, then a second time for content, and a third time, much more slowly, delving for meaning.

"Out," he said. "Everyone but Jonas."

The stylist and the makeup artist both set down their tools and left without a word.

"It might not be as bad as it seems," Jonas said, sounding a bit desperate. "We can increase funding to our outreach programs. Our Ministries help people all over the world. We just need to explain that . . ."

"Enough, Jonas," Branson broke in. "Either he has to go, or we will. It's that simple."

"Does this change things for the meeting in Dubai?" Jonas said.

Branson thought for a moment.

"Yes," he said. "Move it up. As soon as we can get everyone there."

He stood up, handing the phone back to Jonas. He removed the paper collar from around his neck and straightened his bright blue tie underneath. He studied his reflection in the mirror.

Strong, he thought. *You look strong. No one would ever know you just got kicked in the balls.*

Branson strode out of the dressing room and headed to the stage, hearing the swelling music, the shouted exhortations of the laypeople who warmed up the congregation for him, the cheers of the assembled crowd. He walked faster, wanting to get out there, to feed off the energy of his people, recharge his batteries with a little of that old-time Jesus love.

He walked through the wings to the edge of the stage and took the microphone and encouraging smile offered to him by an attractive young intern. He stepped out in front of the crowd, listening to the roar as they caught sight of him. A joyful noise, and that was a fact.

Branson's view of the audience was blotted out by the spotlights shining on him—he only had a clear view of the first several rows.

And in those rows, at least every third person was staring down at their hands, enraptured. In those hands, glowing rectangles of white light, about the size of a deck of cards, with red lines running across them.

CHAPTER 13

A bright, impossible-to-ignore, rectangular light, a few rows down and to the right.

Hamza let out a loud, theatrical sigh, pure exasperation. Miko put her hand on his leg.

"Don't say anything," she whispered. "You get mad every time and it never does any good. They just get angry right back, and then you sit here pissed for the rest of the movie."

Hamza leaned over and spoke softly into her ear.

"It's just so goddamn rude," he said. "Ten ads before the movie telling people to shut off their phones, and that guy decides the rules are for other people."

"Just relax," Miko said. "He'll turn it off in a second."

The man using his phone turned to the woman next to him and spoke to her, showing her the screen. A moment later, she had her phone out as well.

"Come on," Hamza said, no longer whispering. "Shut it off."

The couple ignored them. Another phone lit up, then another. The infection spread rapidly, until all around them, on every side, screenlight invaded the darkness, and for Hamza, realization finally dawned.

He reached into his pocket and pulled out his own phone, pulling up a browser.

"What are you doing?" Miko said. "Two wrongs don't make a—"

Hamza showed her his screen—the Site.

"Has it changed?" he said. "I can't look."

Miko took the phone and swiped her thumb upward along the screen, scrolling through the predictions. The text turned red, and Miko frowned. She read the new lines, then silently handed the phone to Hamza. He scanned the text, then clicked off the phone and sat, staring at the movie screen.

He took a deep breath, held it, let it out. Then another.

"Come on," Hamza said, grabbing his coat and stepping through the row toward the aisle.

All around him, lit phone screens bobbed in the dark theater, people speaking to each other—excited, at full volume, the film forgotten.

Hamza walked into the lobby. Almost everyone in sight had their phone out. He walked past the concession stand, toward a quiet corner next to an external window. Everything outside looked gray—from the buildings to the city-tainted piles of slush to the people trudging through them. He leaned forward, closing his eyes, touching his forehead to the window, feeling the cold leaching through the glass.

A hand on his arm. Hamza opened his eyes and saw Miko, her head tilted slightly, her mouth turned down.

"You didn't know he was going to put new predictions on the Site?" she asked.

"No," Hamza said. "We haven't talked—really talked—in a little while. Just some housekeeping stuff, about the money. He took the riots really hard. It seemed like he just wanted some distance from all of this."

Miko's face twisted, her mouth turning up and one eye scrunching a bit—her version of a shrug.

"Apparently he's over it," she said. "Okay. Take a step back. Tell me what this means."

"What it means? I'll show you what it means."

He held up his phone, pointing at one of the red lines of text.

"This could be worth a hundred million," he said. He moved his finger down slightly. "This one, maybe a billion. These predictions are literally the most valuable things in the world, and he's just . . . giving them away!"

"Relax," Miko said, putting her hand on Hamza's forearm, pulling his hand down. "If they're that important, why did he do it? He must have had a reason."

"I have no idea, Miko!" Hamza said, his voice rising. "I don't even know where he is. I call him all the time, text, whatever—he won't get back to me."

Miko frowned. She plucked the phone from Hamza's hand and stared at the screen.

"You know," she said. "These new predictions. They're different from the first set."

"I know," Hamza said, his voice flat. "The first group was supposed to be worthless, or as near as we could get. The lottery ticket in Colorado, the chocolate milk thing, that crappy actor in Uruguay. They wouldn't even make the news, if they hadn't been on the Site. Why give it away for free, you know?"

"Right. But that's not what I mean," Miko said. "I don't think Will was thinking about money here."

She read from the screen.

"A bridge is going to collapse in Milwaukee. A car factory will catch fire in Pusan. A ship's going to run aground near Rotterdam."

She looked up at him.

"Hamza, these are warnings. These are all awful things—people could die. But none of the new predictions talk about that. Will doesn't say how many people will die. Because maybe now no one will."

Hamza took his phone back and read through the list again.

"The predictions can't be changed. None of these things can be stopped."

"They don't have to be," Miko said. "If people know what's coming, they can, you know, just get out of the way."

"Okay, even if that's what this is—and I'll grant that could be a good thing, even a great thing—Will promised me he wouldn't put up more predictions without talking to me first. He's not *alone* in this, Miko."

Miko raised an eyebrow.

"He thinks he is, Hamza, or he would have talked to you first."

Hamza glanced down, at the slight curve that had only recently become visible above Miko's waist.

"This is about the riots," Miko said. "And every other bad thing that's happened because the Oracle showed up. He feels guilty, or responsible."

"He's not," Hamza said. "That's ridiculous. I've gone over it with him a hundred times. What other people do isn't his—"

Miko put her hand over his mouth, gently.

"He's obviously not convinced," she said. "I know you're frustrated, sweetheart. You're a control freak. This is your worst nightmare. But the Site, the Oracle . . . they aren't yours. They belong to Will. They always did, even though he brought you into it. The weight of it . . . the weight of what he knows—we can't even imagine. If this is how he wants to deal with it, well, it's his call. And are you really saying he shouldn't try to save lives? Honestly, I can't believe you guys didn't post these in the first place."

Hamza looked at his wife's face, her good, earnest expression, a few wisps of dark hair spilling down over her cheek. He breathed in the scent of her skin from her hand covering his mouth.

People try to break into the Site constantly, he thought. *Every day. The Florida Ladies send us reports. And this isn't teenagers in their basements. Japan, Israel, corporations—they're relentless. The Ladies tell us we can't be hacked, and that there's nothing to find even if someone broke through the security . . . but yeah. Sure.*

Every time Will does something outside the plan, he gives those hackers more data to crunch—more ways to get a foothold. I don't know what's going to sink us—maybe the Ladies are right, and nothing can or will—but why is he taking chances with it?

If it gets out that Will's the Oracle . . . then . . . everyone would sue him. And then they'd sue me, the minute they figured out I'm involved, and how much money we made from all this. And then maybe some D.A. somewhere would try to prosecute us for breaking some law or other. Every penny we have would be gone, just from trying to stay ahead of it.

Assuming some fanatic doesn't just shoot all three of us in the head. Or . . . all four of us.

Hamza reached up and gently removed his wife's hand from his face. He kissed Miko's palm, and smiled at her.

"I just don't like it when Will goes off the reservation," he said. "You're right about the weight of all this. He's too deep in his own head. He doesn't think about the consequences of what he does."

"I don't know," Miko said. "He just posted predictions that will save hundreds, maybe thousands of lives. I think he's only thinking about consequences."

Hamza nodded.

"Yeah. But there's you, and the kid. The stakes are high, you know?"

Miko did her face-twisting shrug maneuver again.

"Of course. That makes sense. Hey, here's a question: Have you told Will that?"

Hamza rubbed his hand down the side of his face, then shook his head.

"No. It would be an awkward conversation, because in order to get him to really understand why I get so worried about this stuff, I might have to tell him that I brought you into all this."

Miko raised an eyebrow.

"So each of you is just building up lists of things you're not talking to each other about. Seems like a sound strategy."

Hamza looked at Miko for a little while. He lifted his cell, thumbed it on, and dialed.

"You're right," he said. "Let's just hope the asshole picks up this time."

CHAPTER 14

Will tapped his phone, sending Hamza to voice mail.

He lifted his head to let the sunlight wash over his face, enjoying the complete lack of winter. The air held a pungent, thick smell. Sea salt for sure, and something else. Life. Will took a few deep breaths and leaned back against the side of his rental car.

The Gulf of Mexico wasn't crystal clear, but compared to any of the waters around New York City, it was like something out of a surfing movie. Will had pulled over when he was about halfway along the causeway from Fort Myers to the outlying islands off the Florida coast. The mile-long series of bridges dipped down periodically to tiny islands, just sandy scraps of land, really, and Will had chosen one when the view became too overwhelming not to stop. He had no idea how people could live in a place like this, with jobs, obligations. He'd just stare out at the ocean all day long.

As if to prove his point, a school of dolphins curled up through the surface a few hundred yards offshore, and Will gave silent thanks that he hadn't seen that while he'd been driving—chances are he'd have gone right through a guardrail and into the Gulf.

He stretched, folding to touch his toes, then knelt on the sand and bent at the waist, touching his forehead to the ground and reaching as far as he could with his hands. He felt his spine elongate and sighed with pleasure, the exhalation making a little crater in the sand. The move was a holdover from a yoga flirtation. He wished he had kept up with it—yoga hadn't stayed in his life much longer than the girl he had taken it up for.

Will stood up. Better. His muscles still felt tight, and there was an ache between his shoulder blades, but there was only so much a minute or two of stretching could do. He'd been sitting in a car for five hours as he cruised through central Florida, across the state from Orlando. Direct flights to Fort Myers did exist, but he'd wanted the drive.

Will walked back to his car, leaned in, and reached across to the passenger seat, fishing around inside his shoulder bag. He came back out of the car holding the creased black notebook that had rarely been more than a few feet from him since the Oracle dream.

Some of the small islands along the causeway were equipped with public picnic tables and barbecues—this was one. A few small, ash-filled grills set on dark, corroded metal poles sat nestled in the sand not far away. Will walked to the nearest one, pulling a Zippo lighter from his pocket.

Will placed the notebook on the grate. He centered it, looking at it for a moment, watching as the breeze from the sea rifled through the pages, as if it were just as interested as the rest of the world in what was inside.

The Zippo produced a slight rasping noise, a spark, and ultimately, a little bit of fire. Will held out the lighter to the notebook and lit it at each corner, holding the flame steady until the paper caught.

It burned well, the flames flickering about six inches above the cover of the notebook, black smoke curling lazily up into the air. In just a few minutes, the predictions were reduced to a blackened strip of spiral wire and a layered pile of ash in the bottom of the grill. Will found a stick nearby and poked through the remains, looking for anything readable. Dark flakes drifted up and were caught on the breeze, floating toward the sea. Nothing. Not a single word left—except in his head, where the predictions blazed as strongly as ever.

Will inhaled deeply—smoke and sea. He realized that it was the first free, easy, lung-filling breath he'd had since the Oracle dream.

He returned to his car, pulled back onto the causeway, and continued west along the bridge toward its end point, a place called Sanibel Island. He paid a surprisingly pricey toll—he supposed maintaining bridges across the ocean didn't come cheap—and rolled on to real land.

Sanibel was a tourist preserve. A few signs of year-round inhabitants popped up from time to time as Will drove along the road through the island—a school, what looked like a little suburban neighborhood—but they were the exceptions. Most of the real estate was covered by low-rise hotels, seafood restaurants, and tennis courts, with the balance covered by overdesigned strip malls filled with interchangeable tchotchke shops selling T-shirts and seashell-based art.

And on top of all that: Christmas decorations. Palm trees wrapped with blinking lights, the big plateglass windows at the grocery store still painted with evergreens and snowflakes.

How many lives did I save? he thought. *I'll probably never know. Not an exact number. But it's a lot.*

He'd already seen a few articles online talking through this exact question—How many people would avoid death or injury because the Oracle put warnings up of future disasters on the Site? He shook his head, a smile coming to his face.

Thousands? Maybe. Probably.

The GPS on Will's phone ordered him to turn right—he saw a sign with an arrow pointing in that direction marked CAPTIVA—his ultimate destination, still several miles down the road.

His mistake, he was beginning to realize, had been waiting for the predictions to tell him what they meant. They were never going to do that. They meant what he decided they meant. Superman didn't wait to be told what to do with his powers. He just used them.

Will caught his eyes in the rearview mirror. Yes. Superman. And that was just fine.

The tone of the road under the car's tires changed briefly as it crossed another bridge, much shorter than the causeway from the mainland, leading to a second island—Captiva. The way narrowed. To Will's left, across an expanse of white beach, was the sea, shining blue and bright. On the other side of the road was a mangrove swamp, lush and impenetrable.

He thought about his plan, and about the predictions he hadn't released yet in one way or another. Between the ones he'd used at the start to understand the rules—the Lucky Corner prediction and other, less tragic events—the original set released to the Site, those he and Hamza had sold and now the warnings, most had been used. He still had some left, just a set of oddities he hadn't been able to figure out how to use, but none would find their way into the world—not unless he was sure they could help somehow.

The dates on all of them would pass eventually. After that, he wouldn't know anything more than anyone else. He'd be done. The Oracle wouldn't—couldn't—exist.

The road turned away from the beach and cut inland, running beneath a canopy of palm leaves that blocked out much of the sunlight, turning the road into a green cave.

Will scanned the mailboxes beside the driveways poking out from the jungle on either side of the road. Each had a cutesy name painted on it—things like SEABREEZES or MARLIN'S REST.

About two miles into the island, Will finally found the address he was looking for. The mailbox for this house read JUST BEACHY.

A gravel driveway wound a little way back into the trees, leading to a pleasantly sized house, white with light blue trim, set up about twenty feet off the ground on a wooden stilt framework. A white Lexus—almost all the cars down here were white—sat in a carport built into the space beneath the house.

Will parked, got out, and walked up the stairs to the front door of the house. He rang the bell. Through the cut glass panels on either side of the door, he could see a shape moving, resolving into a figure walking toward him.

He stepped back. He wiped his palms on the front of his jeans. He was sweating—he wished he had dressed for the weather a little better, but had somehow stupidly not expected Florida to be so warm. Not at Christmas.

"John, John, John, John," he muttered to himself.

The door opened.

A woman stood there. She was probably north of fifty, but she had either the resolve or the cash to take care of herself, because she just looked like an aged echo of a young woman—certainly older, but not old. Her hair was short and mostly white, but her face looked younger than the color, a Steve Martin sort of look. It was styled in a sort of upswung do that Will associated with suburban moms. Actually, that was her look: well-off mom.

"John Bianco," the woman said.

"Hi, Cathy," Will said. "How are you?"

"Surprised to see you," Cathy answered. "It was my understanding that we had a deal. Safer for everyone if we kept all contact online only."

"You'll be happy I came down."

Cathy smiled.

"Well, of course, John. I already am."

Cathy stepped aside and ushered him into her home.

The entrance hall opened into a spacious living room with enormous floor-to-ceiling windows that looked out on a spectacular view

of the beach and the Gulf of Mexico beyond. Ceiling fans set at least twenty feet off the floor spun lazily. The decor relied heavily on wicker. It was all very tasteful and expensive-looking.

Cathy pointed at a couch set in the middle of the room, and Will sat.

"Something to drink?"

Will shook his head. He'd had drinks with Cathy Jenkins before, and he wanted to keep a clear head. He could get drunk later, back at the hotel, if he felt like it—which he absolutely would. He had celebrating to do.

"Well, I'm going to have something," Cathy said. "It's past noon, right?"

Will watched as Cathy walked over to a little bar built into one side of the room. She took a large tumbler from a row of glasses on top of the bar. Ice, three cubes' worth, out of the mini fridge. The rest was vodka.

Will stared. The woman took a container of cranberry juice and held it up.

"For color," she said and splashed no more than a teaspoon's worth into her glass.

A quick stir with a long, thin spoon, and she took a sip.

"Ah, yes, that's just the thing," she said, looking at Will. "You sure you don't want anything?"

"That's all right, thanks," he answered.

Cathy walked across the room and sat in an armchair. She crossed her legs gracefully, adjusting her cream-colored linen pants. She took a coaster from a basket on the coffee table in front of the couch and set her drink on it.

Then, with everything properly arranged, she looked up at Will and raised a perfectly tweezed eyebrow.

"So?" she said.

"Is Becky coming?"

"She'll be here shortly. She called just before you arrived. Traffic on the causeway in from Fort Myers."

"Let's wait for her, then. I'm sure she'll want to hear this."

Cathy sipped her drink.

The Florida Ladies. Two women he'd "met" online, down in the Dark Web, after being pointed in their direction by a keyboardist friend who had done significant spelunking down there in search of exotic pharmaceuticals.

It wasn't difficult—you downloaded a piece of software, a web browser that both anonymized your own travels through the Internet and allowed you to connect to sites hidden from mainstream search engines. Tor was one, I2P was another, and new ones popped up all the time, promising better access to the net's hidden corners and better security once you got there.

The site addresses weren't standard URLs—they were just a hash of letters and numbers, almost like a code. If you didn't know exactly where you needed to go, you'd never get there. Will's keyboardist friend had given him a few links, to the boards where "security consultants" supposedly hung out—criminals, really. The sort of people who would dig into Amazon and Expedia and other huge e-commerce sites, harvesting them for credit card numbers they could resell in lots of a thousand each. Or they would search for security vulnerabilities in government and corporate sites, hoping to sell what they knew to the highest bidder, often the target itself. Or they would make themselves available for special projects—targeted assaults on sites or networks their clients wanted taken out of action.

Will had tried to strike up conversations with these people, but it hadn't been easy. Most seemed to be based in Eastern Europe, and he had to deal with a significant language barrier compounded by a nonexistent trust factor.

Eventually, though, he'd found an operation run by an individual using the handle GrandDame, who spoke (typed) excellent English and seemed willing to meet him halfway.

Negotiations had ensued, with Will in the role of John Bianco, one of several supposed employees working under the Oracle, a mysterious man who could see the future. Even saying that much had almost ended things right there—GrandDame's skepticism had almost palpably radiated from the computer screen, like standing in front of an oven with the door open—but getting the Ladies to believe in the Oracle had worked the same way it originally had with Hamza. Will gave them a prediction due to happen in the next few days and simply let it come true.

Disbelief, mental trauma, denial, eventual acceptance, and then much wheeling and dealing, until finally an arrangement—Cathy and her partner, Becky Shubman, the other Florida Lady, would devise a set of protocols that would allow the Oracle to accomplish four specific objectives. They were: release predictions to the world; add new predictions from time to time; receive e-mails; and make it all vanish without a trace at some point down the road, all with complete, impenetrable security that wouldn't require day-to-day maintenance or upkeep by the Florida Ladies, the Oracle, or anyone else.

Three weeks later, they'd presented their results. The system they'd devised didn't rely on hiding a server in some sort of data vault behind multiple layers of heavy-bit encryption, or setting up the Site in a privacy-friendly jurisdiction somewhere in the world, or any of the other standard methods of protecting information. All those could be hacked with enough time and effort—no good.

Instead, they had sent Will to an Internet café and told him to download a Tor browser. Through that, he had opened a onetime-use dummy account on a freemail service, which he had used to open a corresponding dummy Twitter account. That was used to post the first set of predictions to a pastebin-esque clone the Ladies had coded themselves—like an anonymous bulletin board that could be seen by anyone with an Internet connection, but only updated if you had the encryption key.

The key for this particular bin changed every ten seconds and could only be retrieved through the use of an algorithm built upon a key phrase Will had chosen himself—he'd picked the first line of the second verse of Hendrix's "Little Wing." Those sixteen words were used as the building block for the encryption key, which was about a hundred characters long and morphed and changed constantly, now so far removed from the original code phrase that it couldn't be reverse engineered.

Ultimately, it had all worked as promised. The Oracle's name remained the best-kept secret in the world.

In exchange for accomplishing all this, the Ladies were paid large sums of money, but more importantly, the Oracle had promised to give them a prediction once all was said and done, a prediction that would save both their lives.

Will still felt bad about that last bit. There was no prediction. He didn't know anything specific about the Florida Ladies' futures. He simply needed to offer them something that would inspire complete loyalty from them, something that could come from no one else. Other people could bribe them with billions to give up the Site, but only the Oracle could give them the future.

When everything was over, once he knew he wouldn't need them again, Will was planning to tell the Florida Ladies to avoid Albuquerque on such and such a date, without elaboration. They would stay out of New Mexico, they would stay alive, and the Oracle would maintain his perfect record.

The front door opened. Becky Shubman shouldered her way in, accompanied by a blast of hot, humid air. She shoved the door closed and marched across the living room to stand directly in front of Will. Becky always walked like she was moving against a gale-force wind.

"Johnny B!" she said, sticking out her hand. "You keeping the city safe for me up there?"

Will took Becky's hand and was immediately hauled up out of his chair into a bear hug. Becky released him after a few seconds, then plopped herself down on the couch next to Cathy, eyeing the half-consumed cocktail in her hand.

"I see you didn't waste any time this morning."

"Would you like a drink?" Cathy asked.

"Sure, make me a smoothie," Becky said.

Cathy stood, taking her vodka with her, and vanished into the kitchen.

"How long are you staying, Johnny?" Becky asked.

"Probably just the one night. I have to get back."

"That's too bad. I've got a daughter you'd absolutely adore."

"So you've mentioned," Will said. "Many times."

Becky snorted. The sound of a blender could be heard coming from the direction of the kitchen.

She crossed her legs at the ankles and settled deeper into the couch cushions.

"Gotta say," she said, "I liked that last set of predictions your boy put up on the Site. Those warnings. They'll help a lot of people. Save some lives, I'm sure. Made me proud to be part of the organization."

"Me too," Will said. "Me too."

Will didn't know much about the Florida Ladies' origin story. They'd apparently bonded when both their husbands died within a few months of each other. They met at a volunteer group at a Fort Myers museum and somehow, not much later they were partners in a freelance computer security business. What Becky actually did in that arrangement was unclear to Will—Cathy was clearly the technical genius. She'd been one of the only female engineers at the Xerox PARC lab in the '80s, working to set up the backbone of the world's networking infrastructure—much of which had formed the foundation of the current Internet. Becky, on the other hand, was your classic Long Island widow. She'd been a wife and mother for the majority of her adult life and had moved to Florida once her kids graduated from college.

Cathy returned from the kitchen holding a pink concoction in a tall glass. She handed it to Becky and sat down next to her. Will looked from one woman to the other. Becky Shubman looked like a white Shirley Hemphill, and Cathy Jenkins always reminded him of Jackie O.

The women didn't match. They were like a beat-up old Chevy pickup next to a vintage Ferrari. But somehow, they worked. Cathy wouldn't make a single decision, no matter how small, unless she'd run it by the inimitable Mrs. Shubman.

"All right, John," Cathy said. "Here we are. Why are *you* here?"

Will reached into his pocket and pulled out two cards, each printed with a long string of numbers. He reached across the coffee table and handed one to each Lady. They looked them over, then back up to Will, both mildly confused.

"What are these?" Becky asked.

"Numbered accounts, at South Cayman National Bank. You each have one set up in your name. Five million dollars apiece."

In unison, the women's heads snapped back up to look at Will, their eyes wide.

"What the hell for?" Becky said. "You're already paying us."

Will nodded.

"The Oracle reads the security reports you send up. We know the sort of people who are trying to get access to the Site. Governments, big corporations. And they haven't gotten in. We're still safe. You're both doing an incredible job, and you've earned this. Merry Christmas."

"I'm Jewish. But I'll take it," Becky said, staring at the card in her hand.

Cathy stood up, laying her card on the coffee table. She walked to the bar and started mixing another drink.

"Olive or twist, John?" she asked.

Will sighed.

"Twist," he said.

A moment later, she returned holding a vodka martini, filled to the brim, with a bright yellow curl of lemon peel moving lazily in its depths as Cathy walked. She handed it to Will.

"And so," she said, holding up her glass.

They clinked glasses, and Will tasted his drink. It was ice-cold, smooth, and incredibly strong. The first taste went down well enough, and it wasn't as if martinis tended to get *less* enjoyable.

"I'm not complaining, Johnny, but was that the only reason you came down here? I mean, you could have told us over the phone."

Will took another sip. Delicious.

"How many times in your life do you get to give someone five million bucks?" he said. "That's an in-person sort of job. I wanted to see your faces."

He set his glass down on the coffee table.

"But there is something else. This whole thing, the Oracle, the Site"—Will took a breath, feeling lighter even just for saying the words—"it's almost done. I wanted to discuss the logistics in person. Will we have any trouble shutting the Site down when we need to?"

Becky and Cathy exchanged a glance.

"No," Cathy said. "It's simple. You can pull it off-line any time you want, and you've got the codes to run the deletion program I wrote for you. Once that runs, the e-mail system stops cold, and that's the only hard point of contact. Even if that somehow got tracked down, there's still no way to trace it back to you, unless you somehow happened to be physically there when the bad guys found it."

"Not likely," Will said. "The Oracle doesn't need it anymore. So no trail? Nothing at all?"

"None, just like you asked for. No way to trace it back to your people, assuming the Oracle's been following the rules. Everything anonymous, random access points, all that?"

"Absolutely," Will said.

"So, John," Becky said, "unlike Cathy during her college days, looks like you're impenetrable."

Becky grinned and looked over at her partner, who shrugged and lifted her glass to her lips.

"Yeah, well," Cathy said.

Becky turned back to Will, her smile fading a bit.

"Can I ask why you're planning to shut things down? Is the Oracle going to . . . is something going to happen?"

Will looked at the Florida Ladies. They'd both tensed when Becky asked her question. Everything the Oracle had done for them, and they were still frightened of him.

"Nothing's going to happen," he said. "It's just time to end it."

"And when it's done, we get the prediction? The one the Oracle promised to give us?"

"Absolutely. The moment the Site's off-line, it's all yours."

The Ladies relaxed, evidently reassured. Will lifted his martini, draining the glass. He stood up.

"Just one, Johnny? Come on. Stay awhile," Becky said.

"Thanks, but I need to get back. Early flight tomorrow. I'll just walk along the beach, clear my head before I head back to Fort Myers."

Will stood and left the house, after a quick hug from Becky Shubman and an escort to the door plus a quick nod from Cathy.

He stood on the path leading from the house to his car and took a deep breath, smelling—almost tasting—the dense, saturated scent of sea salt and green things. Of *life*.

CHAPTER 15

We are at war, my friends," Hosiah Branson said, "but we are fortunate. Our armies are billions strong."

He reached into the breast pocket of his suitcoat, pulled out a clean white handkerchief, and mopped his forehead. He was sweating like a hog.

Branson sat in a leather chair at the head of the long, polished mahogany conference table that took up most of the boardroom. He had expected some tension to erupt in connection with the seating arrangements, but the holy men had taken their place-card-marked chairs with a minimum of discussion. That was good—he had put the Pakistani Sunni cleric as far from both the Hindu priest and the Iranian Shiite as he could, who themselves needed to be at opposite ends of the table, with the placement of Rabbi Laufer yet another complicating factor. But perhaps he had overthought the issue. For this one day, at least, differences seemed to have been put aside.

Translators and assistants stood behind each chair, ready to provide whatever services their masters might require. Several televisions on wheeled stands sat at the opposite end of the table. On their screens, heads and shoulders of an additional few religious leaders who had been unable or unwilling to make the journey to Dubai watched through a videoconference link.

The holy men looked expectantly at Branson, waiting for him to continue.

Hosiah took a moment to relish his accomplishment at gathering these men together, then cleared his throat and spoke.

"My friends, thank you for coming today. This is a historic moment, with leaders from so many of the world's great faiths gathered in one room. Such an event has not happened within my lifetime—unless, of course, I simply wasn't invited."

The translators finished. A smattering of laughter, but the majority of the room's faces remained locked in expressions ranging from blank to outright hostile.

Hosiah swallowed, ignored the sweat running down his back, and continued.

"I am honored that so many of you responded to my call, and I believe it speaks to the gravity of the issue that we currently face. Between us, we are the stewards of faith for, as I said, billions. And when threats to that faith appear, it is our duty to battle on behalf of our people, savagely and with no thought of retreat.

"A battle looms, and I am sure the enemy's name is familiar to all of you. The Oracle."

The room began to shift uncomfortably before the translations came through. *Oracle* was a word everyone knew.

"In my faith, we often refer to our constituencies as our flocks, in the sense that we are their shepherds, guiding them through a dangerous, ugly world.

"I love my flock, and I would do anything to protect it . . . but it has dwindled of late, my friends. The Oracle is a wolf in among the sheep, culling them away from the truths we provide."

Branson spoke carefully. There was a sensitivity to be maintained. Despite his emphasis on their unity of purpose, the truth was that this was closer to a gathering of heads of rival corporations than anything else. He had no illusions that, absent the Oracle, these men would give him the time of day. Their livelihoods and power bases were under siege, that was all. Combining resources might deliver a solution, but certainly not any sort of lasting accord.

But that wasn't the sort of thing you wanted to come right out and say.

"I would like to begin by saying that my position, from the very start, is that the Oracle is to be approached as an enemy of *all* our faiths. I do not know how he receives his information, but I am of the belief that it comes from either scientific origins, somehow, or that he is a fraud, creating the events he predicts after the fact. No true prophet would act as he has."

"What do you propose?" the Sunni cleric said bluntly in heavily accented English, waving his translator back. "We know that the Oracle is a problem, otherwise we would not be here. What solution do you offer?"

Branson smiled through his irritation at the interruption.

"Of course," he said. "Let us move on to the meat and potatoes, as we say in America. No pork, though, I promise."

Silence—although several seats away, the Right Reverend Michael Beckwith, a prelate of the Episcopal Church and the representative at this particular meeting of Anglicans worldwide, some 165 million worshippers, smiled down into his coffee. Branson felt momentarily heartened—at least *someone* in the room had a sense of humor.

"I suggest two courses of action, gentlemen. First, I believe that we should speak out more publicly against the Oracle. To our congregations, to the press. We should make it clear that there is no common ground between our faiths and this . . . this magician. Some of you have already taken action along these lines, but I humbly recommend a unified party line, if you will."

"What good will this do?" This time it was one of the Hindu priests—Bhatt was his name.

"Why, it will make people think about what the Oracle is, where he comes from. It will raise the seed of doubt in their minds. If the world's religious leaders all say the same thing—that the Oracle is evil, not to be trusted—it may not stop whatever his plan may be, but I believe it will . . ."

"But we do not know if he is evil," Karmapa Chamdo said quietly.

Heads turned to look at the man who had spoken—the eighteenth Black Hat Lama, chief of the third-largest sect of Buddhism, with authority to act on behalf of the Dalai Lama himself. He wore maroon-and-saffron robes that appeared infinitely more suited to the creeping desert heat than the suit and tie Branson was wearing.

"The Oracle is outside our present experience," Chamdo continued, "but do our belief systems almost all, to a one, include the concept of prophets? How can we condemn a man who appears in our midst exhibiting the very divine abilities we describe in our sacred texts?"

"He first offered his predictions on websites connected to the United States, in English," the Sunni cleric said. "He is not our Prophet."

"And they say he is asking for money, selling his predictions," Bhatt said, as if this settled the matter. "We have all heard this. What use would a divine being have for money?"

"The same use our own churches do, perhaps," persisted Chamdo. "If we can ask our worshippers to donate to support us, why is he forbidden to do so? And I would point out, the Oracle has never claimed a divine origin.

"He is here, with us, in the material world," the Buddhist continued. "He is part of the natural order of things, part of the great wheel on which we all turn. Surely it would be best to find a way to adapt to his presence, rather than fight it?"

The sentiment in the room was rapidly turning against the Lama, Hosiah was pleased to note. Subtle cues from the other holy men communicated a very strong collective attitude of *Whose side are you on?*

Karmapa Chamdo seemed to notice this and stopped speaking. He nodded at Hosiah, his face suffused with what was apparently his only expression—extreme calm.

"His Holiness makes excellent points," Branson said, "but I submit that many of our worshippers are not prepared for the subtle philosophical distinctions we might debate here today. Clothing the Oracle in the guise of evil when we speak of him to our congregations is a simple concept that they will easily be able to understand. However, you all may do as you like, of course."

Heads nodded around the table. Not all, but most.

"You mentioned a second component to your plan, Reverend?" Beckwith said.

"Yes, thank you, Bishop. This may perhaps be more palatable to Karmapa Chamdo. I believe that a large part of the reason the Oracle is so fascinating to the world is that his nature remains a mystery. If we could discover his identity, show to the world that he is just a man, that his predictions have a secular explanation, why, our problems would be over.

"This brings me back to my original point. Our congregations, taken together, constitute the largest army in the world—*billions* of people, in every country across the globe.

"We will become generals. We will tell our forces that the Oracle is an *enemy of God,* and we will set them to *hunt* him. I have already set this in motion within my own flock."

"Your Detectives for Christ," Rabbi Laufer said, his tone amused. "Like something from a film."

"Yes, I know," Branson said, forcing an easy smile to appear on his face. "Unsophisticated, of course . . . but it can work. You can all present the idea to your own people however seems best, but it is important that we combine our efforts. I can only do so much alone.

Most of my influence is focused within the United States. That's why I wanted to bring all of you into this."

"Is that why?" the rabbi said. "Or is it perhaps that you are worried about a certain prediction from the Oracle about a certain steak, and you wish to discredit him before he makes a fool of you on the live television broadcast you have announced?"

Branson turned to Laufer, no longer pretending at a smile.

"I'm in the thick of all this. I won't pretend I'm not. But you're a fool if you think he'll stop with me. The Oracle reached out and stabbed at me, a spear thrust at my heart. It's a message to me, yes"—here he gestured around the table, taking in all of the assembled holy men at once—"but also to all of you.

"He wants to take me down so that none of you will challenge him. He's as bad as any dictator, oppressive government, or pogrom that has tried to destroy men of God in all the long centuries we have been doing our work."

He pointed at Rabbi Laufer.

"What if he releases a prediction that the Jews will attempt to take over the world financial system?"

A head tilt toward the Sunni and the Shiite.

"Or another large-scale attack by Muslims inside the United States?"

Frowns around the table.

"None of you have been on the receiving end of the Oracle's abilities. I have, and I will tell you, none of us has ever faced anything like this. With ten words, he could make any of our faiths the enemy of the entire world."

Branson shifted in his chair.

"Humanity needs us. They need our direct aid, and our good counsel, and our example. Our faiths are the mortar of the world. We must act.

"The Oracle must have a neighbor, a brother, a friend. One of those people is among our faithful, or is known to them. We will *find* the Oracle. And once the man is uncovered, we will expose him as exactly that—simply a man."

"What will be done once we have him?" asked the Iranian.

"What we must," Branson answered.

"And if he is not a fraud? What if he is, indeed, a messenger from God? What then?" Karmapa Chamdo broke in.

Hosiah folded his hands and looked at the man.

"In that case, my friend, I suspect we're probably screwed."

CHAPTER 16

Will watched as the concierge handled yet another set of hotel guests with the skill and charm she brought to every single encounter. He didn't know how she did it, but every time, the same bright smile, the same warmth. Will had worked in service jobs a time or two, and he knew how quickly customers transformed from people into annoying problems to be solved. But this concierge . . . masterful. A-game every time. Will had seen her every day for the past few weeks, and he was always impressed. She was just fun to watch.

It also didn't hurt that she was arguably the most beautiful woman Will had ever seen.

Don't stare, he told himself. *She's just trying to do her job, probably deals with creeps all day long. Don't be a creep.*

Will was sitting on a couch in the lobby of the Hotel Carrasco—a palatial, high-ceilinged confection of marble pillars, crystal chandeliers and mosaic floors, the highest-end hotel available in Montevideo. It was packed, guests milling around, pulling rolling luggage behind them, heading out into the bright sun of the Southern Hemisphere summer.

A cocktail sat on the table in front of him—something with a lot of mint and lime—and next to that, a low stack of bound reports, about fifteen, of varying thickness, which had cost him a hundred and fifty thousand dollars.

It didn't even seem like that much money anymore.

Will reached out and flipped through the stack—presentation binders with clear plastic covers, perhaps ten in all. Each had a spiffy, thesislike title, and many had logos from high-end consulting firms. *Twenty-Three Twelve Four: A Numerological Analysis. The Astrological Significance of the Numbers Twenty-Three, Twelve, and Four.* The cover page on the binder from MIT's math department was just the numbers, alone in big black type, in a vertical row:

23
12
4

He pulled the top binder off the stack—the astrological analysis. He flipped through it. This guy had gone the extra mile, running through possibilities related not just to the Zodiac, but palmistry and phrenology as well.

More money than Will had earned in the last three years, to find out that geniuses of all descriptions thought the numbers were probably a date—April 23, 2012, 4 P.M. on December 23, maybe December 4, 2023.

Which was, of course, what Will figured too. It seemed possible that the . . . transmission, or whatever the dream with the predictions had been, was cut off midstream, and the numbers were just the start of the next one coming through.

All the expensive geniuses started their reports there. Beyond that, though, almost no consistency.

A poli-sci professor at Harvard pointed out that India has thirty-five states, and they break down geographically into groups of twelve, twenty-three, and four, depending on how you decide to draw your borders.

The numerologist had exhaustively detailed every mathematical combination of the numbers, from the most mundane—their sum—to the esoteric. To wit: twenty-three times twelve divided by four is sixty-nine. She put that in a section all by itself, called "Combinations of Interest."

Will kind of liked the numerologist.

Then there was the report from the cryptographer, a man in Idaho. His specialty was finding hidden messages in famous books— the Bible, the Constitution, things like that. He'd gone through every book of the King James Bible with at least twenty-three chapters and twelve verses in the twenty-third chapter—nineteen books. Taking the first letter of the fourth word of each verse resulted in a set nineteen letters long. Gibberish, but the man had been able to reorder them into something that made sense.

A message, if you decided you wanted to see it that way: "God quit the sad task," with two letters left over. W and D.

The cryptographer hadn't known what those last two letters meant—Will Dando had commissioned the reports using his John Bianco alias.

And it didn't mean anything—it couldn't. The King James Bible was first printed in 1611. Will had looked it up. The whole thing was tinfoil hat conspiracy theory nonsense.

But it also wasn't great.

Will set down the report in his hand and lifted his cell—a new, razor-thin model he'd bought upon his arrival in Uruguay. He wondered how many texts and voice mails were sitting on his old phone, waiting for him to come into range of a U.S.-based cell tower, probably ninety-nine percent of which were from Hamza.

Will thumbed it on, checking the time. It was getting late, almost eleven in the morning. Now or never.

He lifted his lime/mint/rum concoction, draining it—fortification.

Will gathered the reports together and shoved them in a shoulder bag. He stood and walked over to the concierge desk. The woman smiled as he approached, the same smile he'd seen her give to a hundred other guests. Will sat in one of the two chairs opposite her, setting his bag on his lap.

"Buenos días, Señor," she said. "I am Iris. How may I help?"

Her English was perfectly imperfect. Her name sounded like water hitting the basin of a fountain.

"Good morning," Will answered. "I was wondering if you could tell me about the performance of *The Tempest* this evening?"

"Ah," she said, "an Oracle tourist, then."

"I . . . suppose," Will answered. "Is that bad?"

"Not at all," the concierge replied. "The city is full of people like you, from all over the world."

She gestured out at the packed lobby.

"I have never seen the Hotel Carrasco so full, in fact," she continued. "A wonderful thing. Keeps us busy."

Iris pulled out a city map from a drawer in her desk and unfolded it. She took a pen and marked the location of the hotel with an *X*, then drew a line northeast along the beachfront—across the street from the hotel—to a large green area.

"The government has set up screens in many locations around the city, for people to watch the play live. It's a bit of a festival—we need no excuse in Montevideo to celebrate, as you will see."

She tapped the green area on the map.

"Here is the Parque Roosevelt. It is the closest public screen to the hotel, just a short walk along the beach. I think you will enjoy it—a very lovely spot, and there will be many vendors with food, beer, everything you might want."

Will looked at the map, then back up at the concierge.

"Where is the actual show happening, though? Which theater?"

The concierge tilted her head at Will—she hadn't stopped smiling, but he caught a little sense of *How much of my time do you think you're entitled to this morning? Did you not notice when I mentioned how busy the hotel happens to be?* from her posture.

Iris tapped another spot on the map, a good way to the hotel's west, in the center of an area labeled "Ciudad Vieja."

"Here. The Teatro Solís. A beautiful place, very old—but there are no tickets. They have been gone for months, from the moment the prediction about the standing ovation for José Pittaluga appeared on the Oracle Site."

"None at all?" Will asked. "Isn't that what you . . . can't you guys get tickets to anything?"

He felt incredibly awkward. He knew there was a way these things were done—Hamza would know, probably—but Will wasn't sure he'd ever even stayed in a hotel with a concierge before, much less one that looked like Buckingham Palace.

Fortunately, Iris seemed to be willing to meet him halfway.

"Ordinarily, yes, of course," she said, "but tickets to the forty-third performance of Pittaluga's *Tempest* are not like restaurant reservations. There may be a few seats available here or there, but the cheapest I have heard is two hundred and seventy-five thousand Uruguayan pesos. Over ten thousand U.S. dollars."

"That's fine," Will said.

Iris froze briefly, just for a fraction of a second. Will understood. When she'd first seen him, she'd put Will in a box. His clothes, maybe his demeanor . . . they suggested he was a certain type of person, at a certain level. He might be staying at the Carrasco, but it was a stretch. Or maybe he wasn't paying with his own money—he was an assistant to a real guest, perhaps. Something like that.

But now, with just a few words, Will had put himself in another box, and Iris had to adjust. Recalibrate her expectations.

"Señor," she said, speaking deliberately, "I would of course be happy to assist, but before you spend such a significant amount, let me tell you something about José Pittaluga. No one is expecting a masterpiece this evening.

"He has been part of our theater for many years. He is short, and he is round, and his roles are rarely of the significance of a Prospero. He has been a bit player, as you say. A comedic actor. A clown.

"The producers of *The Tempest* hired him for the role because the Oracle named him on the Site. He was not even auditioning for the part. They simply saw an opportunity and took it."

She looked down at the spot on the map where she had circled the Teatro Solís.

"My understanding is that they have done very well—every show sold out. But the reviews have been . . . unkind."

Will nodded.

"I know. People want a piece of the Oracle, however they can get it. I'd still like to go. I just want to be there. To see it. It's history, you know?"

Iris smiled.

"I do indeed. If I had the funds, I might also be tempted."

She inclined her head, almost apologetically.

"And speaking of such things, did you wish to give me a credit card, or—"

Will reached into his bag and pulled out a thick stack of Uruguayan currency—one- and two-thousand peso notes.

"No," he said, "cash will be fine."

The concierge looked at the money in silence. Will could feel himself moving into yet another box. Iris would never forget that this had happened, and while the chances she would actually figure out he was the Oracle had to be almost nil (in Will's opinion), he was still advertising that he was an extremely wealthy man, far from home, who carried a ton of cash.

Hamza would hate this. If he knew about it. Which he didn't. And wouldn't.

Will looked at Iris, who still hadn't taken her eyes from the stack of bills. He smiled.

"Actually," he said, "if you're free tonight, why don't you see if you can get two seats?"

CHAPTER 17

athy Jenkins sprawled in a deck chair on her back patio, her tablet on her lap, both hands curled around a steaming mug, looking out at the waves. A flock of pelicans had gathered just past the edge of the beach. She watched them swooping down to snatch breakfast from the surface of the sea.

Not very pretty birds, she thought. *Flying coat hangers.*

It was still fun to watch them fish. They'd dive-bomb the water, smacking into the surface with all the grace of a basketball, and come up a moment later to bob along the waves with fish hanging from their beaks, looking very self-satisfied.

Cathy turned on her tablet and pulled up the home page for the *Tampa Bay Times,* skimming the headlines. President Green's lead in the election polls had eroded to the point where it was an even race. She'd have thought Green had a lock on a second term, but Aaron Wilson had somehow stolen away a lot of his support.

She scrolled the rest of the page. At first, she was surprised not to see anything Site related. This would be the first day her employer hadn't made the front page in weeks. And then, an item down toward the bottom—an interview with José Pittaluga, the Uruguayan actor named in one of the first Oracle predictions, whose long-awaited performance was scheduled for that very evening.

Cathy wasn't much for Shakespeare, really—she knew what the Bard's work meant to the world's cultural heritage, but parsing through the plays for meaning always made her feel stupid, and she knew that while she was many things, stupid wasn't one of them.

Cathy tapped the link to the interview and began to read. She immediately decided she liked José Pittaluga very much.

The man was completely open about the fact that the Oracle's prediction had made his career, and that it had nothing whatsoever to do with his ability as an actor. He seemed to relish that point, in fact. He knew he wasn't an Olivier, not even a Nicolas Cage, but that didn't matter. The Oracle had made him completely, one hundred percent critic proof. And rich.

You and me both, buddy, Cathy thought.

Cathy set down her tablet, smiling. She didn't just like Pittaluga—it was possible that she loved him.

The man was unrepentantly gleeful in telling the entire world to fuck off—a point of view she could respect, not so different from her own career in the software industry. She'd never had time for people who didn't recognize what she could do, or who somehow thought it was less just because she had a pair of tits. If the patriarchy didn't want her talent on her terms, then they would have to get along without it, while she sat in the shadows, making their lives miserable from time to time, getting rich off their mistakes, exploiting flaws in their security, and selling the solutions back to them.

Or, on occasion, being the IT security consultant for a man who could predict the future.

Cathy picked up her tablet again and pulled up an app. It was a search program of her own design, a spider, searching the web in all its flavors—light, dark, and deep—for mentions of a single man's name.

John Bianco. Who was obviously not actually named John Bianco. She thought back to the early days of their acquaintance, when he'd been fumbling around in the blackhat forums, trying to find someone to help him. Cathy had watched him for a while, trying to understand what he was really after—he hadn't acted like a cop, or a Deep Web tourist. He'd acted . . . like a child. Defenseless, with no real understanding of the dangers inherent in the depths he'd some-how managed to find. He seemed to really need help, but the first people he had found—a group of truly brutal Slovakians—would eat him alive.

And so, GrandDame had stepped in, and here she was today, sipping coffee on her patio, seven figures richer.

But money alone wouldn't buy off her curiosity, or her natural tendency to dig, and dig, and hack away until there were no secrets left in the world. That had always been the real reason she wanted to work with the Oracle. Secrets were Cathy Jenkins' drug, the Oracle knew them all, and the path to the Oracle ran through John Bianco.

She didn't know very much about the man. Just his name, and that he lived in New York. She'd only met him twice. Once when they finalized the deal for the Florida Ladies to work for the Ora-cle, and once when he gave them their bonuses. Bianco had been ex-tremely cautious with personal information, too. He didn't talk about himself, ever.

But a name and a city wasn't nothing, and Cathy's little digital spider was patient. There were plenty of John Biancos in New York City, but she'd been able to bring up photos of all of them, in time, and none of them looked like the man she'd met. John Bianco wasn't John Bianco. He was someone else.

She set the spider to crawl through the web, looking for new men-tions of John Bianco anywhere in the NYC area—news stories, ac-count registrations, traffic tickets, tax payments. It had been working patiently and diligently for all these months since the Site had gone up, and every time it found something, it delivered a link to Cathy's app. Her theory was that fake identities were complex to set up, and

chances were good that if a false name was used as part of one trans-
action, it would be used somewhere else.

So far, all the spider's hits were useless, unrelated to the man
she was looking for. But you never knew, and so every time the app
chimed, signaling that her software had found something new about
one John Bianco or another, Cathy looked.

The latest find: a piece of video footage, locked away in the supposedly secure Dropbox cloud storage of a woman named Leigh
Shore, who seemed to be some sort of reporter. The footage was labeled "Interview—John Bianco—Union Square—Oracle Riots,"
with a date from last December.

Cathy tapped the clip, expecting to see one of the other John
Biancos she'd encountered in her cataloging of the many New York
City residents with that name.

But no. There he was.

John Bianco—*her* John Bianco, standing next to an irritated-
looking Indian man, being interviewed by an attractive young black
woman. Cathy tapped the footage again, freezing it, then scrolling it
back until she found a decent headshot of the man, with his mouth
closed, looking directly at the camera. She took a screenshot, then
opened the headshot in her image editor, cropping it until it was just
Bianco's head.

Cathy opened another app and fed the new image into it, then
activated the program, and waited.

The problem, all along, was that she didn't have a photo of John
Bianco, and there hadn't been an easy way to get one in their limited
set of interactions. Now, though, she had what she needed, and it was
relatively simple to ask the web to kick back photos of people who
looked similar to the image she'd fed into her app. Hell, even Google
could do something along those lines.

These moments were always wonderful—when the secret was

about to be revealed, when the vault was about to be breached. When she was about to learn something she wasn't supposed to know.

A photo appeared, on a dating website, accompanied by a description that danced a fine line between wittily self-deprecating and enormously desperate.

The name attached to that photo was Will Dando.

Will Dando had John Bianco's face. Or, most likely, vice versa.

Cathy grinned in triumph, feeling a rush of victory. She enlarged the photo so it filled the screen, then set it down, staring at it, wondering if she was looking at the Oracle.

The rush was already beginning to fade. Cathy frowned.

It was obvious that the Oracle's identity was something the Oracle didn't want anyone to know. Her knowing it, or even knowing more than he wanted her to, might very well screw up the deal he'd offered her. After all, this wasn't really about money. It was about the Oracle giving her a prediction that would save her life. And Becky's life.

It wasn't necessarily a problem. All she had to do was keep her mouth shut.

But those two words—Will Dando—they felt a little like a ticking bomb.

CHAPTER 18

A s you from crimes would pardoned be," the swarthy man intoned, one arm extended in supplication toward the audience, standing alone on a mostly darkened stage, "let your indulgence set me free."

His eyes closed. His head dropped. The lights went out. The audience sat very still.

Will looked at Iris, sitting next to him. She wore a tight red dress. Short, impeccable. Will wore a tuxedo—something the concierge had helped him procure that afternoon. It was nothing like the tux he had at home, a rarely cleaned $200 number he wore for wedding gigs. This was an *item*. Custom-fit that day, while Will waited in the tailor's shop, sipping a small glass of pisco.

Iris looked back, her eyebrows raised slightly in an expression of bemusement.

José Pittaluga was possibly the worst actor Will had ever seen.

The audience was beginning to rustle. Apparently, Will was not alone in his opinion. No one was clapping. Poor José stood alone on the stage, in the darkness. Waiting for the applause the Oracle had promised him.

Will had taken a quick look at a plot summary for *The Tempest* earlier that day, and he knew the ending was bizarre. The last bit of

Act Five had Prospero literally asking the audience to play him off with applause—it was supposed to free him from eternal imprisonment on the island where the play was set. If no one clapped, presumably Prospero was trapped forever, and José Pittaluga had to stay onstage until the end of time.

Pressure seeped into the theater, mounting as the quiet extended. People were looking to either side, as if daring each other to stand.

Will's eyes returned to Pittaluga, erect on the stage, his eyes closed, alone, silent.

This isn't possible, he thought. *The predictions all come true. All of them.*

He considered that his presence might have changed something, influenced the prediction. It hadn't worked at the Lucky Corner—the opposite, really, but maybe, somehow . . .

Will's gaze didn't waver from the actor. Possibilities flooded through his mind. He felt light, open. If the predictions could actually be changed, that meant—

A sound, from the front of the theater. Loud, and sharp, like a huge firecracker going off. Pittaluga fell to the ground, just a complete collapse, as if every bit of animus within his body had vanished at once.

Gasps arose from the seats closest to the stage. A few people got out of their seats and rushed up the aisle toward the theater exits. Stagehands appeared from the wings, running toward Pittaluga.

Will watched, his heart pounding, trying to convince himself this was somehow part of the play. It was possible. It was still possible that's all this was. Most of the audience was still in its seats, even though the first several rows had emptied quickly, their former occupants still sprinting toward the theater doors.

The atmosphere in the theater was expectant, pregnant, thick—something had happened, and no one understood what it was, and no one wanted to move until they did. Perhaps five seconds had passed since Pittaluga's collapse. The tension was growing, like a downed power wire snapping and sparking across an intersection during a storm, waiting for someone to get close enough to fry.

Another sound, this time to Will's left.

Will turned and saw an older man, wearing black tie. On his feet. Applauding, rapping his palms together, his expression afraid and desperate. Around the theater, a few other people lunged to their feet, joining him, apparently those people unwilling for whatever reason to allow one of the Oracle's predictions to be false, or wanting to become part of it now that it was coming true.

And then one of the people gathered around Pittaluga onstage turned and shouted out to the audience, something in Spanish that Will didn't catch. Quick, short, anguished, and angry.

The meager standing ovation tapered off, the men and women lowering their hands and sinking back into their seats. Next to him, Iris gasped, her hand to her mouth, a sound echoed across the theater by other members of the audience, following by a growing surge of disturbed murmurs.

"What is this?" Will asked Iris. "I didn't understand what he said."

She turned to him, her face pale.

"Someone shot Pittaluga," she said. "He's . . . he is dead."

The bubble of tension exploded, the audience beginning a panicked surge into the aisles. Will stood, looking toward the stage, trying to see. Other theatergoers jostled him as they shoved past him out of the row, Iris among them.

On the stage, José Pittaluga lay on his back in a slowly spreading pool of blood, shining crimson under the stage lights.

RIPPLES

Finely dressed men and women spilled out of the Teatro Solís, clogging Plaza Independencia, slowly filling the sidewalks leading up along Soriano and Bartolomé Mitre. Approaching sirens could be heard in the distance.

Most of the patrons stayed in the area, clumping into knots, fervently arguing about what they had all just seen, and what it could mean. Sweat trickled down their backs from the unaccustomed exertion of fleeing the theater, compounded with the midsummer heat. Men removed their tuxedo jackets, and women fanned themselves with programs, but no one felt as if they could leave. Not yet.

Across Montevideo, in its parks and public spaces—the Plaza España, just blocks away from Teatro Solís; the manicured landscape of the Parque Rodó; the sandy sweep of the Playa de los Pocitos—great screens had been erected, to allow residents and tourists alike the chance to experience José Pittaluga's forty-third performance of Prospero live, alongside the privileged few wealthy enough to afford tickets to see the show in person.

Thousands of people, of all backgrounds, packed tightly together, fueled by liberally consumed portions of alcohol and street food—fried, greasy sopaipillas and empanadas and chivitos, washed down by endless bot-

tles of Pilsen and Barbot and Mastra. Stunned, confused, worried, fearful people.

The screens still showed the stage at Teatro Solís, where emergency workers—medical, police—and tearful, traumatized members of the production, milled around Pittaluga's corpse. No one had thought to end the broadcast, and while there wasn't very much to see, the images were a reminder of how wrong things had gone.

The Oracle, for whatever reason, had wanted the world's attention focused here. Had wanted millions, if not billions of men, women, and children, all around the planet, to watch a man's murder.

It began on the beach. A bottle arced up above the crowd and smashed against one of the poles of the metal scaffolding holding the large screen, with Montevideo Bay visible behind it. Fragments of green glass rained down amid a shower of foam, sparkling in the light cast by the image on the screen. Almost immediately, more bottles, crashing against the supports and the screen itself. Inevitably, the rain of glass found upturned faces below, and cries rang out. Shoves, anger, shouts as perpetrators were sought, leading to blows.

At last, the screen went dark, either via damage from the glass or because a technician realized what was happening, but too late. A critical point had been reached, and the crowd broke, spilling out from the beach into the city in a panicked, gleeful, drunken surge.

Word spread quickly, and the group from the beach was joined by others, from all across the city—windows were smashed, cars overturned, people were hurt or killed or burned or trampled.

Three days later, an overwhelmed police force was

finally relieved by army units from the Ejército Nacional, who restored order in the city through an indiscriminate application of force. An uneasy peace, and then a checkpoint close to the city center was firebombed, with responsibility claimed by a group calling themselves the Nuevo Tupamaros, after the infamous liberation movement of the '60s and '70s.

Their public statements claimed no connection to the Oracle, insisting instead that they simply wished to free Uruguay from the long-standing political oppression now finally, tangibly evidenced by armed soldiers on the streets infringing upon the freedoms of citizens. More bombings, robberies, manifestos, and at last martial law was declared within the municipal borders, until such time as the threat posed by the Tupamaros was neutralized—clearly their goal from the start.

Decisions, consequences, adaptation, and further decisions, all based on a future that was becoming impossible to predict.

CHAPTER 19

S it down, Tyler!" Miko said, in that special tone of voice all teachers could produce on demand—sharp with irresistible authority and barely restrained exercise of higher disciplinary powers, from ruler raps (once, anyway), to visits to principals' offices. Or, if the infraction was sufficiently dire, the ultimate threat—a black mark on the never viewed but monolithic set of documents governing the future of every child in every school—the permanent record.

"I'm sorry, Mrs. Sheikh," Tyler said, slinking away from the classmates he'd been distracting and returning to his own desk.

Miko shifted her gaze away and scanned across the rest of the room, where twenty-five fourth graders worked through their free-choice reading with varying degrees of engrossment.

Teachers developed any number of superpowers—the voice was one, but another, almost as important, was the read. The same batch of kids could be working quietly on two different days and appear identical to an outsider. But on one of those days, the serene pods of children scattered around their beanbags and desks and wedged into corners might be mere moments from an eruption into undisciplined chaos. Impossible to foresee, unless you had the power of the read— and any experienced teacher did. Knowing the moment to strike, to head off the tornado before it had the chance to develop into anything more than a few isolated wisps of curling wind.

Miko ran her hand across the increasingly pronounced curve of her stomach, thinking about the future. She glanced down beneath her desk, at her long, battered teacher's purse, suitable in dimension for carrying stacks of folders filled with essays and math work home to be graded. A slim manila envelope projected from the top of the purse, where it had been sitting since she picked it up a few days earlier—and would sit until she figured out what the hell to do with its contents.

She watched as Tyler turned pages in his book much too quickly to be reading them, making furtive glances over at the group of friends he had been harassing moments before, with a particular focus on Linden, a long-haired blond specimen.

Miko considered singling him out again, but too much could make things worse—Tyler could decide, whether consciously or not, that the attention he was getting from the teacher was making him cooler in the eyes of his fellow students (or more particularly, Linden), and a feedback loop of misbehavior would begin. She flicked her eyes up at the wall clock—the day was almost over. She could let this one go.

Miko touched her stomach again, feeling a little flutter that might have been the baby, might have been her. She glanced down at the envelope in her purse again, then back up to the wall clock. Just a few more minutes.

She reached out with her teacherly senses again to take the temperature of her class—they were anxious, beyond just the end-of-day readiness to get the hell out of school—and it was no surprise. The state-run standardized tests were just a few months away, and they were required by the DoE to spend a certain amount of every day preparing for them. These kids were nine and ten, and they were already losing sleep over a test that supposedly would have a significant impact on their futures.

She wished she could tell them how little it would really matter, and how lucky they were that by and large, they don't have a damn thing to worry about. Give it ten, twenty years, and life would settle into a steady drone of obligation, punctuated with the occasional peak of joy and pit of worry—things that wouldn't disappear after spending a few days penciling little dots on an answer sheet.

But even if she tried, they absolutely would not—no, *could* not believe her. Kids were so focused on the moment they were currently living that they barely understood that the future existed, beyond regularly scheduled events like Christmas, birthdays, and Halloween.

Maybe they'd believe the Oracle, but they sure as hell wouldn't believe her.

A chime sounded, ringing out from the school's PA system, and the kids all looked at her, in one synchronized motion, like a bunch of prairie dogs popping their heads from their burrows.

"Go ahead," she said. "Thank you for a lovely day, everyone."

The children began the process of assembling their things to head home.

Fifteen minutes later, everyone was properly handed off—no late buses or caregivers today, thank God—and Miko was on the subway, the weight of the envelope in her bag disproportionate to its weight on her mind.

I have to tell Hamza, she thought, gratefully accepting the seat offered to her by an older woman, who gave her a sisterly glance as she stood up. *But then . . . maybe I don't.*

Her husband was winding tighter and tighter the longer Will remained out of contact, but it wasn't just that. He'd found something to occupy himself—some puzzle or question he was trying to work out, and it was making him crazy. He was intently focused on the news, watching and reading. Pieces of scratch paper covered with notes and numbers and circles and arrows were accumulating on every flat surface in their home.

It all had to be Oracle related—everything he did these days was Oracle related—but so far he hadn't seen fit to explain. He just got more and more stressed out with every article he read.

Miko ran a fingertip over the edge of the envelope in her purse. Its contents might make things better, but they could also make things worse, and she wasn't sure which way to go with it.

Hamza was brilliant, but because he was brilliant, he assumed that no one else could see the things he saw. And maybe that was true—no one saw everything he saw—but people could see *some* of it. For instance, she was very aware of how bad it could be for her, him, and their unborn child if the Oracle was outed. The disaster in Uruguay after the murder of José Pittaluga made that point crystal clear. When it came to the Oracle, and anyone connected to him, emotions ran high.

That was why she'd held on to the envelope for a few days. Maybe it was better if the Oracle was out of their lives. But then again, maybe it was better if he wasn't, so they could at least exert some influence on his choices.

Hamza was sitting at the kitchen table when she walked into their apartment, one hand buried in his dark hair, the other holding a pencil with its tip poised above a yellow legal pad covered with the familiar circles, arrows, and angry scratch-outs. A tablet lay next to the notepad, showing some sort of article. Miko walked over to him, kissing the top of his head. She saw what looked like an offshore oil platform on the screen, surrounded by dense columns of text.

"Hi there," Miko said.

Hamza set his pencil down and looked up at her.

"Hi," he said. "Can you sit down? I want to tell you something."

Miko, instantly wary, took off her coat and slung it over the back of a chair, dropping her purse beside it as she sat.

"Did you figure it out?" she said, gesturing to the notepad. "Whatever it is you've been working on?"

Hamza glanced down, frowning. He took a few long, deep breaths, then looked at different parts of the kitchen, then down at his notes, then finally back up at her.

"I don't know. I want to see what you think."

He tapped the tablet screen, indicating the oil platform.

"You see this?" he said, swiveling it on the table so she could read it, and then, unsurprisingly, leapt in before she could get through more than a paragraph.

"TransPipe Global, GmBH. Oil company. This article's about one of their drilling platforms off the coast of Uruguay. Yesterday, it was nationalized as part of the declaration of martial law."

"Okay," Miko said. "And?"

"TransPipe is one of our clients. Like . . . ours. You know."

Miko nodded. She did. An Oracle client.

"We made like two hundred million off them, back at the beginning. Will sold them a prediction that caused them to expand their exploratory drilling on these platforms—they bet huge on it. TransPipe isn't enormous, as oil companies go. This was a big play for them. All their eggs in one basket, and now they are completely fucked. Those eggs are broken. Or, more accurately, now they belong to Uruguay."

Hamza now spun the notepad toward her and tapped his pencil on the first circled element, which Miko could now read as containing the word *ACTOR*.

"It would never have happened absent two things: Will putting up the prediction about Pittaluga on the Site and the Oracle selling a different prediction to TransPipe. We did them both."

Miko read through the notepad, seeing the path. She looked back up at Hamza.

"Don't you think it's just a coincidence?" she said. "No one knew about your deal with TransPipe—you told me all those clients paid most of their money to you to keep the predictions secret. No one could have known that the prediction about the actor would end up with martial law in Uruguay. Coincidence."

Hamza repeated his routine of looking everywhere in the room but at her, then finally took back the notepad and flipped it to the next densely covered page, tapping his pencil against the yellow paper.

"I don't know, Meeks," he said. "Even if TransPipe doesn't completely collapse, this has thrown a ton of instability into the markets. No one knows what Uruguay will do with that oil, if anything. Gas prices are starting to spike. It's getting all wibbly-wobbly out there. Globally."

"So?" Miko said. "This is like the thousandth time you've told me a story about the market falling, or rising, or hedging, or calling. Why is this different?"

"Because it kind of feels to me like maybe someone planned it."

"You mean Will did this?" Miko asked. "Why would he—?"

Hamza laughed—bleak, worrisome.

"Will couldn't have done this. Not in a million years. He doesn't know anything about the way global financial markets work, and planning something like this . . . you'd need a thorough understanding of all the pieces. Not just oil, but old political stuff in Uruguay, the way their society works . . . Will's smart, but he's . . . he's a musician, you know?"

"Okay, then. Like I said, it's a coincidence," Miko said. "No one could know all that."

"They could . . ." Hamza said, absently doodling on the notepad, his gaze distant, ". . . with hindsight."

"I thought the predictions don't mean anything, Hamza. There's no big plan . . . no purpose behind it all."

Hamza's eyes snapped back to meet hers. He looked . . . afraid.

"Miko . . . what if I'm wrong?"

Miko considered. Part of her wanted to run as far as she could from anything connected to the Oracle or Will Dando—but another part, apparently larger, wasn't sure that would do any damn good.

"You need to tell this to Will," she said. "Talk to him in person. You both need it."

"How?" Hamza said, spreading his arms in frustration. "I don't know where the fuck he is!"

Miko reached down to her purse. She pulled out the envelope and tossed it down on the table, where it landed between them with a muffled slap.

"Now you do," she said.

"What?" Hamza said, confused, looking at the envelope.

"Uruguay," Miko said. "Will's in Uruguay."

Hamza let out a long sigh.

"Yeah," he said. "Of course he is."

CHAPTER 20

A sign hung on the door to room 918: POR FAVOR, NO MOLESTAR, with the English equivalent printed below it.

"Uh-huh," Hamza said.

Hamza rapped his knuckles against the door, hard enough to hurt a little, making a sharp noise in the otherwise empty hallway.

"Can you come back later?" came Will's voice through the door, muffled.

"No, Will, I can't," Hamza said, loud. "Open the goddamn door."

A long pause, and then the sound of latches releasing, deadbolts chocking back, and a low creak as the door opened, revealing Will Dando's very surprised face.

He looked like he'd just woken up—hair sticking up in greasy clumps, an overall vibe of groggy unwashedness.

"Hamza?" he said. "How the hell did you find me?"

"I didn't," Hamza answered.

He turned and pointed back down the hallway.

"She did."

Will moved forward, looking in the direction Hamza indicated, to see a slim, lovely woman whose belly showed the faintest curve, nothing that anyone but her husband would ever notice.

"Hi, Will," Miko said.

Will's head turned, slowly, to look at Hamza. His face was almost blank.

"Does . . . does she . . ."

"Yeah," Hamza said. "Everything."

Will looked down, his fists slowly clenching, his forearms trembling with the strain.

"I can't believe you fucking told her," he said, then turned and stepped back into his room, leaving the door open.

Hamza opened his mouth to shout out a reply, then felt a hand on his arm. He looked and saw that it was Miko, her face pale but composed.

"We don't know," she said. "We don't know what he's been dealing with. It's all right. Let's just talk to him."

Hamza nodded and entered the hotel room where Will had been living. He stopped, shocked. It was a sty. Unmade bed, half-eaten trays of room service, empty beer cans and bottles, towels and papers scattered across every surface.

Behind him, he heard Miko follow him in and close the door. Will was waiting, staring at him, his face dark.

"Jesus, Will," Hamza said. "This is a hotel. They'll clean up for you. This is . . . this is just filthy."

Will glanced around the room. He shrugged.

"They won't clean while I'm in here, and I don't want to leave. I paid for a month in advance so they won't bother me."

Hamza thought about this.

"You've just . . . been in the room?"

"Mostly. Bad things happen sometimes when I go out there."

Hamza also thought about this, then looked at Miko. She shook her head slowly, helplessly.

"How did you figure out where I was?" Will asked Miko.

"It was easy, Will," Miko said. "I hired a PI, told him to look for hits on the name Will Dando in places you might go, with Oracle-related stuff high on the list. He found you here, and then Hamza bribed the desk clerk for your room number."

Hamza stepped forward.

"You are not safe, Will. You are not anonymous."

"Oh, I'm safe. Trust me on that. But . . . why? Why did you go to all that trouble?"

Hamza looked at him in disbelief.

"Will, I haven't heard from you in *six weeks*. No calls, texts, e-mails . . . why the fuck do you think I've been looking for you? I thought you were de—"

His voice cracked. He turned away, pushed a pile of dirty towels and old newspapers off a chair and sat down.

Will collapsed onto the bed. He was looking at Miko, his face tight.

"Is it really so bad that I know you're the Oracle, Will?" she said. "I mean, at least you'll have someone other than my husband to talk to about all this, right? I mean . . ."

Will's face relaxed a bit, the side of his mouth twitching upward.

"Heh," he said. "Yeah. He's no picnic."

"Don't I know it," Miko said, smiling.

Hamza watched this exchange, marveling, as always, at his wife's ability to smoothly navigate situations that he would manage with brute force, assuming he could manage them at all.

"I'm not mad that you know, Miko," Will said. "I'm afraid."

Will ran a hand through his hair, resulting in a brand-new clump pointing toward the ceiling. He flopped down on the bed, threatening to upset a tray of half-eaten food sitting on the fumbles of sheet and bedspread. He reached out and grabbed a half-eaten piece of toast from the room-service tray.

"Oh, Will, that looks like it's a week old," Miko said. "Don't eat—"

Will crunched down on the toast, chewing absently.

"I didn't mean to, you know, drop off the grid," he said. "I just needed some time. I was getting . . . overwhelmed. I went to Florida, and then I just decided I'd come down here to see José Pittaluga perform. No big plan. Just a . . . a whim. I was there in the theater when it happened. When he was killed. I took the concierge with me. And I stayed, while the country went nuts. You know people here are all freaked out about it? Uruguay's supposed to be a stable country. This is very out of character for them."

Will looked at the piece of toast in his hand, apparently considering a second bite, then tossed it back on the tray.

"I put up those warnings on the Site, and I saved people, sure, but people just keep dying, don't they? It's like a tennis game. The Site kills some people, so I save some people, and then the Site kills some more. Back and forth. Back and forth."

"So why is it still up?" Hamza asked. "We have an exit plan. We can take it down whenever we want."

"It wouldn't make any difference. I've already put so many predictions into the world—you think people would just forget them if I took down the Site? No. None of them are going away, ever. Whatever's going to happen because of those predictions is going to happen. Taking down the Site wouldn't change anything. It'll do what it wants."

Hamza looked closely at his friend.

"You just referred to the Site like it's alive, Will. Twice. Why did you do that?"

"Because I think it is, Hamza. In its own way."

Hamza considered. A week ago, he'd have taken this statement as evidence that Will had finally cracked under Oracle-related pressures. But now . . . it sounded pretty goddamn plausible.

"Things went nuts down here after Pittaluga died. I couldn't really go anywhere for a while—it was too dangerous even to get a cab to the airport. So I just stayed here, and I watched it all happen out the window, and I *thought*. And sitting there, watching things burn and hearing gunfire and knowing I was a part of it, I ended up asking myself a question. Over and over again."

He looked at Hamza and Miko, his eyes hollow.

"Whoever or whatever is the source of the Oracle dream can see the future. Or they're in the future, looking back. Whatever. So . . ."

Will gestured toward the window, in a sweeping flail of his hand that Hamza took to signify the chaos in the city beyond.

". . . couldn't they see all this coming?"

He dropped his hand.

"And if they could see it, then why would they want it? Why wouldn't they try to stop it? Hell, the Site gave me that prediction. The Site caused this. It wanted it. And everything else that's happened since I put it up."

Will stood up suddenly. A half-full glass of water on the room service tray teetered and fell, adding to the mess. Will ignored it. He stood up and walked across the room, bending to rifle through the pile of newspapers and printouts Hamza had shoved to the floor when he sat down.

"I had a system for this," he muttered.

He pulled out a sheet of paper, then discarded it.

"I've been trying to understand why the Site's doing what it's doing," Will went on. "What it wants. I don't have all the pieces yet. I'm not really built for this. It's all over the place. Economics, politics . . . all kinds of things. But I think I see some of it. None of this is random. I didn't get the predictions just so you and I could get rich. Something else is happening."

Hamza took a deep breath. He thought about men with guns, and the sandbagged checkpoint he'd had to cross to get into the hotel, and riots at the Oracle rallies, and the near-constant attacks on the Site from governments all over the world, and the Lucky Corner, and several billion dollars, and Miko, and his child.

He held his breath, not sure that Will was ready for what he was about to tell him. Not sure that he was ready to know it.

"Tell him, Hamza," Miko said.

Will looked at him, curious.

"Tell me what?"

Hamza exhaled.

"I know what it wants," he said.

Will paused his paper shuffling and looked up at him.

"Please, Hamza—don't tell me there's nothing here. Don't tell me I'm too worked up about this or some bullshit like that. I'm not. This is real."

Hamza reached out and put his hand on Will's shoulder.

"I know," he said. "Just listen."

He spoke. He described the connection he'd found between Pittaluga's death and martial law in Uruguay and the nationalization of the TransPipe offshore operation. He talked about the way these things had affected the global economy, the precision and foresight needed to engineer such a chain of events, and his strong belief that it almost had to be intentional.

Will went very still.

"Well," he said.

"It's all true," Hamza said. "I know it sounds impossible, but I think that's what the Site was doing, this whole time. I don't understand why, but—"

"Heh," Will said. "TransPipe. I missed that one."

Hamza narrowed his eyes.

"What?" he said.

"Right in front of me," Will said. "Right out the damn window. Should have seen it."

He bent back to the pile of papers and pulled out a single sheet—something that looked like a heavily annotated list. He folded it and shoved it in his pocket, then stood up. He turned and walked to the door, slipping his feet into a pair of sandals.

"Come on," he said, and left the room.

Hamza and Miko looked at each other, but there wasn't really anything to be said.

The elevator ride was silent. Miko reached out and took Hamza's hand, and they rode down all ten floors that way, with Hamza regretting involving Miko more with each floor they passed.

The doors opened, and they stepped out into the Hotel Carrasco's ornate, nearly empty lobby. Will headed for the hotel's exit, avoiding eye contact with the many security guards stationed strategically throughout the huge, open space—guards armed with automatic rifles, in uniforms that were one flag patch away from full-on military fatigues.

A few members of the staff milled around, attempting to look like they had something to do in a city that had been depleted of luxurious travelers by a declaration of martial law. A lovely young woman at the concierge desk looked up, hopeful, but dropped her eyes as soon as she saw Will. Hamza wondered fleetingly if Will had somehow taken *her* to the Pittaluga thing.

Will pushed through the revolving doors and out into the plaza beyond.

Miko tugged Hamza's hand, pulling him to a stop.

"How is he?" she asked. "Because he seems bad."

"I . . . yeah," he said, feeling entirely helpless.

Miko gestured at the revolving doors.

"Let's go."

Will stood on the wide plaza in front of the hotel near a large, sparkling fountain. The white sand of the Playa Carrasco was visible past the heavy traffic on the double-lane road between the hotel and the beach, the Rambla República de México, and the dark, sun-dappled sea beyond. The fountain provided a light, tinkling accompaniment to the breeze coming in off the beach. It was all very inviting, if you ignored the military emplacements.

"Before I say anything," Will said, "especially because of that . . ."

He pointed at Miko's belly.

". . . I want you to know that I think you both should get as far away from me, and the Site, as you can. Stay out of it. This isn't your problem. It's mine. You've already done so much for me, and if you want to go, this is the right time to do it. I won't be angry."

Will folded his arms and looked back out at the sea.

"You're better off in the dark," he said. "I mean it."

Hamza turned to look at his wife. A long moment, and then Miko gave a little nod.

"Tell us," Hamza said.

Will sighed.

"Okay. There's something happening with the Site," he began. "It's not just TransPipe and that one prediction about Pittaluga. It's all of them. The predictions are connecting. They're . . ."

Will stopped and took a breath.

"The predictions are working together. I don't know how else to say it," he said simply.

Neither Hamza nor Miko spoke for a moment.

"Can you try?" Miko said slowly.

Will looked at the fountain, its basin full of clear water shining in the sun. He reached into his pocket and pulled out a few coins, then held one up.

"Okay. I release a prediction, either by putting it on the Site, or selling it."

Will tossed the coin into the fountain. Circular rings radiated out from the spot where the coin broke the surface of the liquid.

"Make a wish," Miko said.

"Oh, I did, believe me," Will answered. He pointed at the ripples.

"Things happen in the world because the predictions are out there. People do things they wouldn't otherwise have done. I'm changing the future."

Will took more coins and dropped them into the fountain, a few inches apart, one after the other. Each created a new set of ripples, which interacted with the tiny waves generated by the others. Interference patterns—miniature geometries.

"There," he continued. "Each prediction is a coin. It ripples out into the world, changing things, and sometimes those changes meet up with ripples from another prediction. They bounce off each other, and then something else happens."

Will splashed his hand across the surface of the fountain, breaking the patterns into chaos. He pointed at the roiling surface of the water.

"It's impossible to predict what will happen next. Unless you're in the future looking back," he said. "Then you can see all of it. And then you send the information back to a person in the past who will use it how you want. He'll put some of it up on a website, sell another bit to an oil company . . . all of which you'd already know, because from your perspective, he's already done it."

Miko broke in.

"I know I'm new to all this, but just playing devil's advocate, couldn't it just have happened randomly?"

Will pulled the folded sheet of paper from his pocket and handed it to Miko.

"Read that," he said.

Miko unfolded the paper. Hamza stepped closer, reading it over her shoulder.

"The chocolate milk fad, right?" Will said. "It was the most popular nonalcoholic drink in the country for the three months after the

Oracle made a prediction about it. Everything else took a hit—soda, iced tea, all kinds of juice—including orange, grapefruit, all of that. But we told that hedge fund . . ."

"SWBG," Hamza said, not taking his eyes off the paper.

"Right. SWBG. We sold them a prediction that made them invest heavily in citrus groves, expecting that the Florida frost in May will drive prices up. But with the chocolate milk thing, it went the other way—no one wanted orange juice for a while, prices went way down, and SWBG had to pump in even more cash to keep things running. Even so, half of the groves went under. So did SWBG. They shut down last month. Between paying us almost half a billion dollars and the bad investments, I guess they didn't have enough dough to keep the lights on."

I remember that, Hamza thought. *The Dow dropped four hundred points that day. But I didn't realize . . .*

He looked up, to see Will staring at him, calm.

"This is . . . this can't be possible," Hamza said.

"I wish it weren't. That list is what I've been doing down here. Researching, figuring it out. Those fourteen connections are all I've found so far, but there have to be more that I just don't see, or that haven't happened yet. Like TransPipe. That makes fifteen, I guess."

Hamza focused on the sheet of paper his wife was still holding. It was trembling.

"I can't see the whole picture," Will said, tapping the surface of the fountain's pool with a fingertip, watching rings radiate outward, "but I think the Site's working toward three or four minor goals at the same time. Then, I think those things are supposed to come together too, to make something else happen. There's a tune to it, almost; like a song with most of its tracks stripped away. Just the backing vocals and the drums and the horn lines—you know there's more."

"So this is a puzzle?" Miko asked, her voice scaling up in pitch. "A game?"

"Not a game," Will said. "It's more like one of those Rube Goldberg machines, or, no . . . a giant engine. It feels like someone's out there, driving all this forward."

"What's it driving?" Miko asked. "If it's an engine, what's it pushing?"

Will shrugged.

"The world, I think.

"And yes," he continued, "I know I've never been the kind of guy who talks about stuff like this, even cared about it, but you'd be amazed how interesting it all becomes when you think you caused it."

He scooped his hand into the fountain, filling his palm with water, letting droplets fall back into the basin.

"Will, this is insane," Miko said. "We have to do something."

"We can just step away," Hamza said. "We have all the money in the world. The Coral Republic is almost done. I got a construction progress report for the capitol building yesterday. All the other places we set up are ready. We can go with the exit plan."

Will opened his hand, letting the remaining water fall back into the basin, then stood up, wiping his hand on his shirt.

"I think the Site might be hoping we do," Will replied. "I think that's why we got so many predictions we could sell. It's like the prize it's offering me so that I'll just disappear and let it get on with whatever it's doing. But I can't. I have to clean up my own mess."

He straightened, looking at them.

"But not you two. I can't let you get any more involved than you already are. I mean it."

Miko shook her head.

"You want to do all this alone? Will, for God's sake, you were about two days from storing your pee in jars up there!"

"I'm fine," he said, a little annoyed. "You don't have to worry about me. Nothing bad can happen to me. Not right now. Not to the Oracle."

"Will, that's ridiculous," Hamza said, his tone alarmed. "There is no Oracle. There's just you."

"Sure," Will said. "Listen. I can beat this. I know I can. I've been experimenting. Here—let me show you."

He turned and walked away from them, striding rapidly toward the busy street between the hotel and the beach.

"Where are you going?" Miko called after him.

Will didn't respond. Without slowing, he walked up to the side of the road, just a step away from the speeding flow of cars, motorcycles, and multiton trucks.

And then he took another step.

"No!" Miko shouted.

Hamza sprinted toward the street, seeing in the corner of his eye that the soldiers at the nearest checkpoint had perked up at the disturbance. Any alarm he felt at that fact was swept away by the certainty that he was about to hear a squeal of brakes and a deep, meaty thud as his best friend was embedded deep into a semi's grille.

He skidded to a stop at the edge of the street, catching a glimpse of Will striding across the Rambla Républica de México toward the beach, keeping his eyes straight ahead, as if he were walking across a lawn in Central Park instead of a four-lane road packed with traffic speeding along at what looked to be an average of about forty miles per hour.

Horns blared, cars swerved. The soldiers in the checkpoint closest to the street unslung their rifles from their shoulders, trying to see what was happening.

The light changed, the crosswalk cleared, and Hamza and Miko ran across to the beach. Hamza looked left and saw Will about fifty yards away, sitting on a bench, looking out at the sea.

"What the fuck was that, you idiot?" Hamza said, shouting as he approached.

Will looked up and smiled. It was an odd smile, empty and full at the same time.

"I told you. Nothing's going to happen to the Oracle. I'm completely safe," he said.

"That's crazy, Will," Hamza said. "That's . . . just stupid."

"No, it's not," Will answered. "I still have predictions I haven't put out in the world. The Site must want me to do something with them, and it won't let me die until I've done it. Those predictions are my insurance policy. I'm invulnerable."

Will's smile grew wider. Too wide.

"I'm Superman," he said.

He looked back out at the sea.

"I'm going to beat it," he said. "I'm not just a tool for some . . . spider-thing, burrowing behind the walls of the world, making everything weak. I'm the Oracle. I can make things better."

"Stand up, Will," Miko said.

Will stood, the smile gone, his face suddenly unsure. Miko stepped forward, her arms outstretched.

"Don't say I," she said.

Will looked at her, confused. Miko enfolded Will in her arms, wrapping him in a tight embrace. Will awkwardly patted her between the shoulder blades.

"Dammit, Will, just hug me back," Miko said, the words somewhat muffled by Will's chest.

Will surrendered to the small woman's gesture and circled his arms around her. They stood like that for thirty seconds, while Hamza watched.

Finally, Miko released Will and stepped back, sniffling a little.

"You need people," Miko said. "You might think you don't, you might wish you didn't, but no one can deal with all this alone. And since Hamza and I already know, and we love you, we're going to help you whether you want us to or not."

Will gazed at her.

"Let's go home," Miko said.

PART III

SPRING

CHAPTER 21

Will felt the pattern under his fingers, deep in the pocket, quarter notes locked in sync with the bass drum. Nothing he needed to think about, just a line to play under the solos, holding down his end of the song's foundation. He glanced at Jorge Cabrera, whose eyes were closed, his arms extended toward his keys as he entered minute five of his solo over the verse changes to the Talking Heads' "Psycho Killer."

He shifted his gaze to the audience, just indistinct silhouettes against the stage lights shining in his face, although he could see Hamza and Miko sitting at a little table to the left. He sent them an entirely sincere smile.

In the weeks since Uruguay, they'd both been pushing him—shoving, really—toward some kind of distraction from the endless effort to try to understand what the Site was doing to the world. All three of them were working on it, studying news reports, making spreadsheets . . . but it just felt futile.

The scale of the Site's plan was obviously vast, a densely coordinated global effort, constantly in motion. Evolving into . . . something. And the team trying to understand that evolution, maybe even stop it, included a failed musician, a grade-school teacher, and an ex-investment banker.

It was like trying to play chess in a pitch-dark room, where you had to determine your opponent's moves by sense of smell alone. And you had a cold. And your opponent was God.

Futile.

But still, they plugged away, dutifully studying the board, trying to win a game they didn't and most likely couldn't understand.

Hamza and Miko had each other. They could share the weight of learning that the Oracle's predictions had almost certainly resulted in the rise of the Sojo Gaba movement in Niger, and the subsequent U.S. bombing campaign that was slowly but surely pulverizing that nation in an attempt to destroy its leader while giving President Green a new hook upon which to hang his reelection campaign. Or the slow, endless downward spiral of the global economy. Or any of the other things the Site was doing to the world. They could share that weight.

Will was alone. His friends knew that, and they had concerns. Possibly justified concerns, after what they'd seen him do in Uruguay.

And so, they had gently suggested, then firmly suggested, then flat out insisted that he find an outlet for his Oracle-related tensions, which led to Will calling Jorge and asking to sit in at one of his Sunday jam nights.

They were always held at the same club—the Broken Elbow, down in the Village. A rotating cast of New York's musical elite attended, whoever wasn't on tour or booked somewhere, just to catch up with one another, trade gossip, and play a bit. Technically, anyone could ask to sit in—it was an open mic—but you got up on that stage at your peril. Jorge called a song, and the band played it, and that was it. No rehearsal, no prior discussion. If you couldn't hold up your end, no one would be a dick about it, but you were out of the cool kids' club, without much hope of ever getting back in.

Playing at that moment were, among other luminaries, two musicians from the SNL band and a guitarist who had laid down studio tracks for at least three top-ten singles in the past year. And Will Dando on the bass, holding down the line. Sitting in that pocket.

He felt light. He wasn't the Oracle. He was just a musician, on a stage with some of the best players in New York City, holding his own.

The song wrapped up, clanging through the snarl of little guitar licks and drum fills and sax squeals that tended to end jams like this, culminating in one big punctuation mark hit on the snare. The four men and one woman onstage started removing their instruments, placing them on stands, trading nods and in-jokes and subtly joyous appreciation of one another's skill.

Will turned to Jorge.

"Okay if I do one during the break? Just something I've been playing around with. Want to see how it works with the audience."

Jorge hesitated—this was a breach of etiquette. It wasn't an originals night, it was a covers jam, and moreover, no one was supposed to be featured. Even more, if someone *was* going to get a feature, Will Dando probably wasn't first on that list.

But Jorge shrugged and clapped Will on the shoulder.

"Sure, man," he said. "Have fun. I'm glad you came out tonight. You've been missed. Not the same without you. Let's talk after, too—I've got some gigs I'd like to put you up for."

He gestured at the microphone at the front of the stage.

"All yours."

Will moved to the center of the stage, pulling a few of his effects pedals over from his amp and arranging them in front of the microphone stand. He tapped a few—a loop, a thick layer of distortion and some chorus—and tested the sound as the rest of the band left the stage and headed for the bar.

A bark of snarling distortion whipped out across the club, fading into pedal-assisted echoes. Will could see the front rank of the audience lean back a bit, all at once, as if they'd all been hit by a blast of arctic wind.

"This is a new song," Will said. "It's about where things are for me, right now."

Will began to play—thick, effects-driven chords rippling out from the amp. Loud, grainy and low, with a little melodic hook kicked in from higher up the neck every few measures.

He sang, almost speaking, his voice intent and focused.

> I don't speak to my family,
> They don't know what I know.
> Twelve people gone, many more, many more.
> You don't know what I know.

The song went on, Will's voice rising to a wailing lament, the final chorus just a repetition of the words *I know* . . . over and over again. He finished, his eyes closed, the last note drifting out into the silent club.

Applause, but scattered, barely registering over the background chatter. The room had taken the band's break as an opportunity to fire up conversations. Will didn't know why he was surprised. A lone bassist they didn't know playing a song they'd never heard? It barely qualified as entertainment. He was lucky they hadn't booed.

Futile.

Will began to play again—a short, repeated pattern, just an appealing little anchor line.

"How about the world these days, huh?" he said, talking to the room. "I've been paying a lot of attention to the news lately. More than I ever used to. Shitty out there, right? What's a gallon of gas these days—like four bucks?"

He played a little flourish, then settled back into the three-note pattern.

"Here," Will said. "Let me give you what you want."

The extinction of the scarlet kingfisher
A brawl erupts in the Taiwanese Senate over the issue of
     returning certain items of antiquity to the mainland.
Twelve people die during the commission of a robbery at
     the Lucky Corner Deli in New York, New York.
A plane crashes in the Niger desert forty-three ki-
     lometers southwest of Tabelot.
Fourteen infants are born at Northside General Hospital in
     Houston, Texas. Six are male, and eight are female.

Will could see screens appearing in the audience—people check-ing the Site. To the left, he could see a silhouette, someone standing, body language communicating extreme tension. Hamza, most likely.

He didn't care. Will opened his mouth to sing the next predic-tion, the one about the Malaysia Airlines flight, and his bass amp cut out. The robust, effects-assisted pattern he'd been playing immedi-ately transformed into a thin, jangly skeleton of its former self.

Oh, he thought. He turned to look to the side of the stage, to see Jorge Cabrera standing with the sound guy at the mixing booth. Jorge's face was a little hard to read—the lights were still shining in Will's face—but he wasn't smiling.

Will unslung his bass and leaned it up against his amp—*as if Jorge will let you back up to play again after that little adventure,* he thought—and stepped down off the stage. He walked past Hamza and Miko, past Jorge and the other musicians, and found a seat at the far end of the bar.

He ordered a beer and a shot, and as they came he could hear Jorge on the microphone apologizing and promising the band would be up again soon.

Will drank the shot and signaled for another, then began work-ing to get through the beer before it showed up.

A hand touched his arm lightly, and he flinched.

"Will," Miko said.

He turned toward her.

"Hamza wanted to tackle you right there onstage," she said. "I wouldn't let him. I thought it would just draw attention to what you were doing. That second one, about the fight in Taiwan—you gave it to Hamza to convince him the predictions were real, right?"

"Yes," Will said.

"I remember that day. He came home early from Corman Brothers. Very out of character for him back then. Most days I barely saw him before midnight. He told me he was going to quit, and he didn't seem worried at all. Said he had something spectacular lined up."

She caught Will's eye.

"That was you. Turns out you were the spectacular thing, Will Dando."

"I guess so," Will answered.

Miko went silent.

Will watched her, wondering what she was thinking. In hindsight, it had been stupid to be so reluctant to let Hamza bring Miko into all this. She had dived into the work to figure out the Site's plan with both feet, and she had a flair for making connections that neither he nor Hamza saw.

More than that, though, she was kind in a way Hamza wasn't. She was thoughtful. She wanted to help.

Will picked up the second shot and downed it.

Miko was wonderful.

"What did you think of the first song?" he asked.

"Grow up, Will," Miko said, her tone mild.

He looked at her, surprised. Wounded, even.

"You aren't as special as you think you are. You aren't the only person who can see the future."

She reached out across the bar, sliding his half-empty pint glass away from his hands.

"I'm a teacher. I see the future every goddamn day with those kids, me and every other teacher out there. And then there's this."

She touched the swell of her stomach.

"The future doesn't just belong to you. We all get our piece."

Miko's eyes narrowed.

"I know how to deal with children. And so I've been nice, I've been sensitive, because no one wants you playing chicken with a truck again or jumping off a roof because you're convinced you can fly. But shit like that"—she pointed at the stage—"is absolutely not okay. You aren't allowed to implode. You'll pull me, Hamza, and who knows who else down with you when you go."

Will frowned.

"Children?" he said.

"Yup," Miko said. "You are acting like a fourth grader. No. Not even. Second grade, tops."

"You've seen what the Site is doing," Will said, hearing the defensiveness in his voice and hating it. "It's ruining the world, and I don't know what to do. I don't understand what's happening. I just know it's happening because of *me*."

"So you decided to sing the predictions at open mic night?" Miko said, pointing back at the stage.

"This isn't an open mic night," Will said, a little offended. "It's invite-only. It's actually sort of a big deal to play with these guys."

"I hope you enjoyed it. I don't think they'll have you back any time soon," Miko said, blunt.

Will sighed. He eyed his half-drunk, just-out-of-reach beer.

"You know I talked to a priest?" he said. "Went to confession, for the first time since middle school. I didn't really have anything to confess, but I wanted to talk to an expert. Someone who knew about prophets. Had to be a little careful with my questions. Didn't want him to put two and two together."

"What did he say?" Miko asked.

"He told me that prophets usually get killed. People don't like what God has to tell them, so they kill the messenger. Either that, or the prophet has to remove himself from society because he's scared he's gonna get killed, or because he just goes nuts from pressure. If you're a prophet, your choices are either to get your head served up to some king on a platter, or you can become a hermit for the rest of your life. Sometimes both."

"I didn't know you were religious," Miko said. "Do you really think the Oracle predictions were sent by God?"

Will turned back to her.

"Not really, but that's the thing. I don't know. I mean, I'm a prophet by every definition I can think of. And when I hear about the way people talk about the Oracle, out in the world, decapitation seems very damn possible, you know?"

"Right. That's why you almost outed yourself to the whole damn bar?"

"No. It's because . . . this whole thing's just too heavy. I guess I . . . just wanted to get out from under it. We've decided it's our job to figure out what the Site's doing, maybe stop it—I don't see how we can. It's not that you and Hamza aren't really smart—you are, much smarter than I am—but this is all just on another level. The picture's too big for us to see."

"You don't think that thing with the . . . what was it . . . the *Aberdeen* will help us? I think that sounds pretty promising."

Will nodded.

"Sure, it might. Maybe. But even if it helps us understand, it's hard to think that one little thing will break the whole puzzle open."

"So . . . what do you want to do? Give up?"

Will took a deep breath.

"No," he said, "I don't think we have to do this all by ourselves. I want to get help."

Miko's face turned puzzled.

"Can you . . . explain that?"

Will pulled out his phone and turned it on.

"You know all those e-mails Hamza and I got in the beginning? The ones we used to find clients to buy predictions?"

"Yeah," Miko said. "Hamza explained that whole thing. What about them?"

"I've been going through them in my spare time, answering one or two a day. Just saying something vague and reassuring. I didn't want people to think they were being ignored. I wanted to do something, you know?

"I've been giving money away, too—anonymous donations to charities. A lot of money. Don't tell Hamza. I'm sure he'd call it a waste or something."

Miko's mouth twitched up at one corner.

"You're a good man, Will Dando."

"Sometimes."

Will held up his phone to Miko. It was displaying an image—a photograph of a sheet of paper.

"I found something in one of the e-mails that gave me an idea. I took a picture of it—I've been staring at it all day, just thinking about whether I should actually do it."

Miko took the phone and zoomed in on the image. She looked up at Will, her eyes wide.

"Wow. You don't mean . . ."

"Yeah. It could be a way to sort of crowdsource the Site puzzle. We'd have to be safe about it, but we could figure that out."

Miko looked at Will's phone again, shaking her head in disbelief.

"You know, this could help with your other problem, too. It could humanize the Oracle to the world. Make it less likely your head will end up on that platter. But my God, Will . . ."

She glanced back toward the stage, where Hamza was visible, arms folded, silently watching them.

". . . Hamza will hate this."

CHAPTER 22

Dr. Jonathan Staffman, former professor of computer science at the University of Pennsylvania and self-labeled expert in illicit technological infiltration, stared intently at three glowing monitors set side by side on his desk. The middle screen displayed a Mercator projection map of the globe, the countries overlaid with an ever-shifting skein of yellow, green, and black, with pinpoints of red here and there. Most of the eastern seaboard of the United States was covered by various colors, while more sparsely populated areas like northern Africa were almost completely black. The monitor to the left of the map contained scrolling text readouts, changing rapidly as the colors on the map flickered and pulsed. The last screen, to the right, was a simple status bar, with a percentage readout. The bar read 0.008 percent complete.

"Too much in Des Moines!" Staffman shouted. "Dial it back, goddammit!"

Iowa's capital was bright red. Over a period of about ten seconds, it faded back to yellow and then to green.

"Pay attention, Hernandez, you clown," Staffman said. "You should have caught that."

"I'm sorry, Dr. Staffman," came Hernandez's reply. "Won't happen again."

Staffman scowled and dipped his left index finger into an open jar of peanut butter on the desk—Jif Chunky. He pulled out a hefty gob and plopped it into his mouth, sucking on it as he examined the map. It looked suitably green, at least for the moment.

The status bar ticked over another thousandth of a percent—0.009 percent. Staffman grunted in satisfaction around his finger. He looked up from the monitors at the control room beyond. His desk was at one end of a large room with white walls, floor, and ceilings. It was arranged in a classroom configuration, with Staffman in the teacher's spot. Twenty desks for "students," each holding a computer setup similar to Staffman's, but with only two screens, not three.

At each desk sat a technician, occupied with monitoring a different section of the world. Staffman eyed his crew suspiciously.

It was a solid group of coders, all handpicked, but that didn't mean they could do as well as twenty copies of himself would have. This was delicate work, and if one of his subordinates screwed something up, the Coach sure as hell wouldn't hold *them* responsible.

Staffman turned his attention back to his screens, flickering his eyes across them for anything out of the ordinary, until he was momentarily distracted by movement in his peripheral vision. He looked up and froze.

A large glass window took up most of the wall at the back of the room, where people could observe the goings-on in Staffman's lab, if they were so inclined. On the other side of that window, smiling, stood the Coach.

Staffman froze, his hand halfway through its journey back to the peanut butter jar.

The woman made a motion toward the door with one hand, a sort of "mind if I join you?" gesture.

Staffman gave the Coach what he hoped was a genuine-seeming smile and waved for her to come in. She gave a hearty nod and disappeared from the window, entering the room a moment later and striding to Staffman's desk. A few of the technicians glanced up as she passed, then returned to their work when they saw it was just an old woman, hardly worth their notice.

The Coach wore a simple gray dress with a navy cardigan. The expression on her face was the definition of nonthreatening. Staffman felt like he was going to throw up.

"Dr. Staffman," the Coach said. "Forgive me if I don't shake your hand. I've got a pretty good idea where it's been."

Her gaze shifted to the jar of Jif, and she chuckled. Jonathan smiled weakly.

"Tech team working out all right?" the Coach continued.

"Yes, they're all good people. No worries there."

"Good, good. Real glad to hear it. Now, Professor, tell me what it is you're doing. Looks like you've got something up and running here," the Coach said, turning the monitors on Staffman's desk slightly to get a better view.

"Ah, yes," Staffman said. "That is, I think I have a way we can access the Oracle's systems."

"Well, of course you do. Although I seem to recall you told me that was impossible when we first started discussing this project. And what did I say, Dr. Staffman? Nothing's impossible. Not one thing."

As always, whenever the Coach pulled out that little chestnut, Staffman was tempted to list any one of a hundred things that popped to mind immediately that were, in fact, scientifically impossible— surpassing the speed of light, a human mating with a crocodile, proving the existence of God—but he refrained.

"That may be true, Coach, but there are things that are so improbable that they might as well be impossible. That's the real problem with the Oracle's systems. They're brilliantly organized. I can see the whole structure, but I can't get into it. Not easily, anyway."

He reached for a pad of paper and a pencil sitting to one side of the desk and drew two circles on it, of equal size. He labeled one with the word *SITE* and tapped it with his pencil.

"This is where everyone is focusing their attention—all the hackers around the world, big and small. Everyone wants to figure out the password to access the Site, to alter the text. Put up their own predictions, maybe. It's the most visible part of the system, and anyone who breaks into it will have bragging rights like no operator ever has. It's a big target. An obvious target, and it's well protected. I've seen this type of system before. The password is generated by a code phrase, and without that code phrase . . . forget it."

The Coach made a "get on with it" gesture, her eyes focused on the second, as-yet unlabeled circle. That's how you could always tell what the Coach really was; what she wore, how she talked—none of that was her. Her eyes, though.

"But we don't care about the Site," Staffman said. "We don't want bragging rights. We just want to see behind the curtain, to figure out who the Oracle is. That's why I'm putting my efforts here."

With that final word, Staffman moved the pencil tip to the second circle.

"You see," he went on, "the Site comes from the Oracle. It leads away from him, out into the world. What we want is something that goes *to* him."

He wrote the word *E-MAIL* inside the second circle and underlined it.

"Somehow, somewhere, the Oracle is receiving all those e-mails. Must be millions by now. Hundreds of millions. That's an enormous amount of data traffic, which can be hard to hide. The e-mail address is the soft spot, and that's where I'm hitting him."

He outlined the E-MAIL circle several times, creating a thick, dark border around the word.

"His people know it, too. The security around that e-mail address is a big brick wall. Bricks made out of lead and steel, with big scary spikes on top. Much heavier than on the Site itself. Essentially unbreakable, at least in any reasonable amount of time."

The Coach finally spoke.

"But you just told me you got around all that. How?"

Staffman laid down his pencil and looked up.

"I borrowed a concept from SETI—you know, the Search for Extraterrestrial Intelligence?"

"I'm familiar with it. They aim antennas at the sky, listen for messages from little green men."

"Well, radio telescopes, but that's essentially correct. Their search produces immense amounts of information—space noise, if you will. All that needs to be processed, to look for a potential signal, but it's not simple. It requires a great deal of computer power—more processing than SETI's budget can afford, by a long shot.

"So they appealed to the public. They offered a little piece of software for free to volunteers across the world. Once someone installed the software, SETI could use their computer as a node on their distributed network. Whenever the person wasn't using their machine's processing power, SETI did. It worked very well—SETI ended up with one enormous processor, in effect, able to solve problems just as fast as one of the supercomputers they couldn't afford."

The Coach nodded, blue eyes twinkling behind her glasses.

"I think I see where you're headed with this, Doctor. You're using the SETI network to crunch the numbers on the Oracle's security that much faster."

Staffman shook his head. He was getting excited. He licked his lips.

"No, no, I did better than that," Staffman said. "The SETI network isn't strong enough to get through the Oracle's security. I had to use something else. I sent out a virus, something I designed a few years ago. I refined it a little bit to make use of flaws in Microsoft and Linux OSes—I decided not to hit Macs, although I could have, believe me. Maybe I should have. They're about due to get knocked off their high horse."

The Coach cleared her throat.

"Right," Staffman said. "Sorry. Anyway, my virus lets me access every system it infects and utilize some of its unused processing power. Most computers don't run at one hundred percent of their operating capacity. Oh, they might, for short periods of heavy activity, but most of the time it's down at twenty percent or less. That leaves me an enormous amount of computing power to access. The whole thing, tied together, is called a botnet. As of right now, the virus has gotten to about three-quarters of the world's systems in just under seventy-two hours. That's a record, in case you're wondering."

"I wasn't," the Coach said, her voice turning a bit frosty. "What do you say you cut to the chase here, Professor? I'd appreciate it."

"A botnet lets me crack the Oracle's systems much more quickly. This bar"—he indicated the third monitor—"shows how we're doing. We've only been at it for about twenty-four hours, and we're nearly at a hundredth of a percent. That's remarkable progress for the level of encryption we're trying to break. It should have taken months."

"Dr. Staffman, if I understand you right, it means we won't get this done for more than a year."

The twinkle had vanished from the Coach's eyes. Staffman swallowed. She had done some very quick math to come up with that figure, that absolutely correct figure.

"Coach, you have to understand how incredible it is that we can do this at all. We're accelerating the procedure by a thousand times! I know it's slow, but it's the only way."

"I need it faster. I need it now, Staffman."

"It can't be done. I'm already using a quarter of the world's computing power as it is. What do you expect me to do?"

The Coach raised one dark eyebrow. Staffman wondered if she dyed them—her hair was a uniform silver gray.

"Why are you only using a quarter?"

"Let me explain the situation, Coach. Look at this map," Staff-man said, gesturing to the central monitor on his desk. "I'm having my team monitor the processing power my botnet is sucking up, to make sure that it doesn't get too heavy in any one area. If we're going to be in this for the long haul, we have to stay below the radar."

"But you could use the rest, if you wanted to," the Coach said, her tone thoughtful.

"Yes, I suppose, but . . . look. I might not be explaining myself very well. If I turn up the usage, then the virus would be noticed. People would take action. We'd have to stop."

"But if you used it all, then you could get past the Oracle's security that much faster. It wouldn't matter if someone found us—we'd already be in," the Coach said.

Staffman was beginning to get frustrated. He'd paid his dues in grad school as a teaching assistant—explaining concepts to laymen was never pleasant, and the worst were those with a little knowledge, enough to think they could second-guess him. The only problem was that he couldn't exactly give the Coach a D-minus.

"The thing is, though," he said, trying valiantly to keep any trace of sarcasm out of his voice, "the computer processing power we'd be stealing is being *used* for things right now. Air traffic, the Internet, military—and not just here, but all over the world. The entire globe would go haywire, Coach."

"But you could do it."

Staffman ran a hand through his hair. He adjusted his glasses. He looked across the room, to the window at the back. He let his gaze rest there for a moment, then shifted his eyes back to the Coach.

"Yes, I could do it," he said.

"How much would it speed things up?"

"Exponentially. I could have your answer in a matter of hours."

"So do it."

"Coach, I can't. People would die."

The Coach perched on the edge of Staffman's desk. The scientist unconsciously leaned back in his desk chair, as far away from the woman as he could.

"Dr. Staffman, listen to me. You aren't a good person. You know it and I know it. You're selfish and you're cowardly. That's all right. It's not like you're unique. Most people I've met are just like you.

"And so," she continued, "I think we also both know there's no way you'll give up your life to save the lives of a bunch of people who *may* die when you fulfill your duty as a member of my team. You don't know any of those people. The truth is, the only person you give two shits about is yourself. So save your life, save me the bullshit, and do it. Now."

Staffman stared at the Coach. He thought about the money he had been promised as payment for successfully breaking through the Site's security. Almost a decade ago, he had done another job for her, and the money from that effort had funded his own research for years. Years without groveling before university tenure boards, and worse, teaching cow-eyed, dull-minded, disinterested undergraduates. That money was almost gone.

"Okay, Coach," he said.

"Good," she said, her voice cold. "Get on with it."

Staffman cleared his throat.

"Stop monitoring the nodes," he called to the rest of the technical team. "Shut down your workstations and leave. I'll contact you if I need anything else."

A chorus of questions and complaints arose in the room. People wanted to know if they were getting paid what they were promised, why the project had stopped. Staffman's mouth tightened.

"Just get out!" he shouted. "You'll get your money. Just go."

No one moved.

"Now, Doctor, that's not the way you handle a situation like this," the Coach said. She slid off Staffman's desk, getting carefully to her feet.

"People, you'll all be taken care of. You have my word. Now get on out of here and enjoy yourselves. Hell, you've just been given the rest of this beautiful spring day off. What are you still doing inside? Go throw a Frisbee, or ask someone on a date! You'll like it, I promise."

She chuckled. The technicians looked at one another uncertainly.

"Go on, now," the Coach repeated, more firmly.

A tech near the door shrugged. She hit the switch on her computer and powered it down. The rest of the team followed suit. Within a few minutes, the room was empty.

"You need to learn to handle people, Dr. Staffman," the Coach said. "You catch more bees with honey, as the saying goes."

"Right, Coach," Staffman said absently. His hands fluttered across his keyboard, preparing to increase the draw from the botnet. It didn't take long.

"It's ready," he said. "Just hit the enter key and it will start."

"No, Professor, you start it up. You made the decision to do this. You need to take responsibility."

Staffman gritted his teeth. He extended his index finger and tapped his keyboard. On the map of the globe, red plague spots began to appear in the midst of the green, expanding quickly, like bloody welts on the surface of the world. Immediately, the progress bar on the third monitor began to speed up, clicking through the 1 percent mark in just under a minute.

Staffman watched, awed.

"How long will it take?"

"I didn't think it would be so fast. The virus must have infected more computers than I realized. It's . . . amazing."

He watched, mesmerized, while his creation did its work. The botnet chewed its way through the world, behaving exactly as designed. Pride filled his chest.

The Coach stood next to Staffman's chair, hands on her hips, peering through her glasses at the monitors.

"Say," she said thoughtfully.

"Yes, Coach?"

"Something occurs to me. The way you explained it, your virus will take over damn near every computer system in the world, so they can't do what they're supposed to do. They'll be working on our little Oracle problem instead."

Yes, Coach, Staffman thought, *the sky is blue. Yes, Coach, two plus two equals four.*

"Well," she continued, turning to look directly at Staffman, "doesn't that include the power grid?"

Staffman stared at the Coach for a moment. He lunged back to his keyboard and began to type furiously.

"Your face just went like a slaughterhouse cow after it gets hit with the air hammer, so I guess that answers my question," the Coach said. "How will all those machines keep working on our project when the lights go out?"

Staffman didn't look at her, just continued to type.

"Come on," he muttered.

"Boy, you've got an answer for me?"

Staffman bit back the withering response that leapt to the front of his mind.

"I built some degree of control into the botnet, Coach," he said, not taking his eyes from his screens, his fingers flying. "I can give it commands—explain that it needs to keep the power on, but it's not easy. It's just a piece of code—it's smart, but it's stupid. It doesn't re-member what I've told it to do, so I have to keep pulling it back from power nodes over and over again. It's like . . . it's like putting out a forest fire by dumping glasses of water on it one by one."

The room fell silent, except for the rattling of the keys.

"Will that work?" the Coach asked.

"Does it sound like it will work?" Staffman snapped. "I'll keep it going for as long as I can. We'll lose parts of the grid for sure, but hopefully I can maintain enough processing power to crack the Oracle's security before we lose too many machines."

The Coach rested a hand on Staffman's shoulder, its psychological weight all out of proportion to its physical weight.

"Listen, son, if there's anyone who can do this, it's you. I wouldn't have put you on my team if you couldn't do ten impossible, sorry, ten *improbable* things before breakfast, as Lewis Carroll put it. I'll let you work, but just know I've got all the faith in the world in you."

Despite his personal distaste for the woman, despite knowing that the Coach had threatened his life not ten minutes ago, Staffman felt a blush of motivation flow through him. The lady had a gift, that's all there was to it.

"Wait and see, Coach," he said. "We'll have him."

CHAPTER 23

I t's a bad idea, Will," Hamza said. "That's all I'm saying."

"It's all you've been saying for three days," Will answered. "How about you just let it go?"

The light changed, and they crossed Lafayette. Hamza watched, frustrated, as Will stopped and peered along the street.

"Was it on Great Jones?" Will asked.

"I don't know," Hamza said. "Look it up."

"I've been to this place before. I know it's around here. Let's go this way, and if we don't see it in a block or two I'll check it on my phone."

"Or you could just look it up now."

Will shot him a glance.

"What's your problem tonight, Hamza?" he said.

"My problem is not tonight. My problem is long-standing and eternal. My problem is this: it makes no sense to give our whole god-damn game away to some stupid website. I mean, Christ, Will, if we had to do this, at least we could have gotten it on TV. Or the *New York Times* or something."

Will rounded on Hamza.

"TV? Every stupid talking head on every news show takes potshots at me. And all those televangelists preaching that I'm the devil—that fucker Branson and all his cronies, with their Detectives for Christ bullshit."

"Easy," Hamza said.

"Branson's almost mellow compared to some of the stuff coming from people overseas," Will went on, his eyes tight. "They're talking about declaring a . . . shit, what the hell is it? The Salman Rushdie thing."

"A fatwa," Hamza said. "I did notice that, actually. You've got both Sunni and Shiite leaders united on that point. That's impressive. Get a rabbi on board and the Oracle might just get peace going in the Middle East."

"Hilarious," Will said, a sharp edge to his tone.

Hamza held up a hand, palm out.

"Peace. Listen, I'm just saying—you don't have to do an interview," he said. "You could post something about the Oracle's intentions up on the Site."

"The Site's the problem!" Will answered. "The only real contact anyone has with the Oracle is a bunch of words on a computer screen. When I was down in Florida, talking to the Ladies about the Oracle, they were terrified. And they work for us!

"We kept the Site up once we figured out that the predictions were connecting so we could speak to the world if we needed to, use its influence in a positive direction. But if everyone's just getting more and more frightened, how's that going to work? We need to turn that around. I want a chance for people to see that I'm nothing to be scared of, that I'm a person, not some freak.

"That's not even the main part, either. We need to tell people about what the Site's doing. Having more brains on it just makes sense. I almost think we have to do that. This is bigger than us. It always was."

"Will, if you tell the world about all the terrible things that are happening because of the Site, hell, even if you do it anonymously . . .

they'll blame the guy who put it up. You and I know you didn't create the predictions—they aren't *yours*—but the world won't make that distinction. They'll blame the Oracle. They'll blame *you*."

"Maybe that doesn't matter," Will said. "Maybe telling people about all this is more important."

Hamza shoved his hands in his pockets and gave Will a direct look. They stared at each other, standing on the cold, East Village sidewalk.

"What?" Will shouted, finally.

"I'm just trying to protect you," Hamza said. "And I'm trying to protect myself, and Miko, and our kid. Just . . ."

He trailed off, watching Will's face, hoping to see some sign of agreement. Understanding, even. He'd take what he could get.

"Okay," Will said, finally. "I'm sorry. I mean it. You're right. I wasn't thinking straight. All of this . . . it's just so heavy. The idea of setting it down, letting someone else handle it . . . it sounded really good, for a while."

Hamza took a deep breath, then released it slowly.

"Okay. I'm not trying to be a dick, Will. I'm just . . . trying to figure all of this out. I just think that should be the priority. We can put this together, I know it."

"Yeah," Will answered, turning and walking up the street toward the corner. "That's why we're down here tonight, isn't it? And tell you what. If we learn something tonight that cracks the case, then I'll cancel the interview."

"Wait, what?" Hamza said. "You're still going to do it? But you just said—"

"I'll do it. I just won't talk about what the Site's doing. I think I need to get out there. Change some minds about the Oracle. Let them know I'm not a monster. I need this, Hamza. I know we can do it safely. You'll make sure."

Hamza kicked at a piece of trash on the sidewalk, trying to decide if it was worth pushing back, visualizing Will in front of a reporter and feeling panic rising along his spine.

No. Let it go for now. Take the half victory and see what tomorrow might bring. Or tonight, even. After all, there was a chance this whole *Aberdeen* thing could actually pan out. Maybe they'd break it wide open, figure out what the Site was doing—if they could just find the damn bar.

Will pointed up the block.

"Look. There it is. MacAvoy's."

Halfway up the block, several clusters of people in identical dark coats stood smoking outside a bar with two huge bay windows that projected slightly over the sidewalk. A sign hanging above the door swung in the wind, a wood panel carved with an overflowing pint glass and the name of the bar.

The smokers all wore small, round white caps. As Will and Hamza drew closer, they could make out a dark stripe around the crown of the hats and could see that their jackets were classic navy peacoats.

"See?" Will said. "Those sure look like sailors to me."

"Hey, I would never doubt the Oracle," Hamza said. "I just questioned your intimate familiarity with the location of the sailor bar."

They stopped across the street from MacAvoy's. The sailors were now producing a chorus of low, raucous laughter.

"You're sure they're the ones we want?" Hamza said.

"Only one way to find out," Will answered.

Hamza watched as Will crossed the street and approached the group. He said something—Hamza couldn't quite make it out—and as one, the sailors' heads swiveled to look at him.

They seemed amiable enough, but somehow still projected an undercurrent of chaos, like they were just killing time waiting for their evening to truly start, full of shouted imprecations, smashed bottles, and smashed heads.

The conversation seemed to draw to a close, and Will turned around and crossed the street to rejoin Hamza.

"Did you get the sense that you almost got your ass kicked there?" Hamza said. "Because I did."

"I'm sure it's just those guys. Smokers, you know. The ones inside will be friendlier," Will said.

"That makes zero sense," Hamza said. "Are they at least from the right ship?"

"Yeah," Will said. "HMS *Aberdeen*. They wouldn't tell me anything else, and I didn't want to push it."

"Oh man," Hamza said. "There's no way this doesn't end with us both getting punched in the face."

"We have to try. This is the first time we've seen a ripple hit New York since we started working on the Site's plan. This is a chance to get ahead of it, for once. We might never get another opportunity like this."

Hamza looked across the street at the bar, a spiked ball of nerves spinning in his stomach, counterbalanced by the fact that he knew Will was right.

MacAvoy's was a dark-paneled enclave with all but a few square inches of wall space covered with photographs and framed newspaper articles from various points in the bar's hundred-and-fifty-year history. The space was narrow up front by the bar, but widened in the back to a room with a few thickly constructed tables and chairs. Both sections were packed nearly wall to wall with men in dark blue uniforms, women to whom they were paying a great deal of attention, and pints.

Will and Hamza fought their way through the crowd and found a spot in a corner near the back.

"Okay, game plan?" Hamza said.

"Well, we know that the *Aberdeen* wasn't due to dock in New York for months," Will said. "It's supposed to be part of that big NATO war game exercise in the North Atlantic, according to the articles we read. But it's not there—it's here, and we know that's because of ripples from the Site. The connections are pretty clear."

"'Clear' is relative when it comes to this stuff," Hamza said, "but for the sake of argument, sure."

"So it has to be one of two things," Will continued. "Either the Site wants the *Aberdeen* here, or the Site doesn't want it wherever it was originally supposed to go once the war games ended. What we really need to know is the ship's mission. Until we figure that out, we don't know what the Site is trying to accomplish."

Hamza scanned the room.

"And even if we do, then what? Stop it? I hate to bring this up, but it didn't work very well with the Lucky Corner."

Will frowned.

"This isn't like that. We aren't trying to stop a prediction. We're trying to handle a ripple."

"You think that makes a difference?"

Will shrugged.

"Better idea?"

"Okay," Hamza said. "Go ahead. But I'll stay back here. I've got your back if you need it, but I sure as hell hope you don't."

"Thanks, pal," Will said, as he looked over the bar. "You know, this would have been easier if we'd brought Miko along. She could probably get these guys to tell her their Social Security numbers."

Hamza raised an eyebrow.

"Or the British equivalent," Will added.

"Maybe so," Hamza said. "But I have a policy of not sending my wife off to flirt with drunken sailors. Actually, what makes you think they'll talk to you at all? Last time I checked, you're a dude."

"I have a plan, sort of," Will said. "A good opening line, any-way."

Hamza watched as Will stepped toward a table with an empty seat whose occupants were talking quietly—relative to the rest of the room, anyway—enjoying their drinks without getting too crazy about it.

"Hey, fellas," Will said. The table fell silent. "Buy you gents a round?"

The sailors stared at Will. One finally spoke.

"Being honest, mate, you aren't exactly our type. Well, most of us, anyway," he continued, clapping one of his colleagues on his shoulder. "Maybe Freddy here'd give you a second look."

Freddy took a long, slow sip from his beer and looked Will up and down.

"Nah," he said. "I prefer redheads."

A chorus of good fellowship erupted from the table. From his corner, Hamza watched with some relief as Will sat down and summoned a waitress.

Hamza glanced around, looking for a men's room. Spying a sign at the back of the bar, he made his way through the crowd and waited in line for a urinal that, when he arrived at it, looked exactly as he expected it would after being well used by a succession of sailors.

Hamza finished and ran his hands under the tap. The only nod to hand-drying was a cloth ring towel running through a metal box that supposedly sanitized it. He wouldn't trust something like that under the best of circumstances, and sure as hell not in MacAvoy's when the *Aberdeen* was in town.

Wiping his hands on his pants, Hamza had a hand on the door back to the bar when he heard shouting—angry voices rising above the rest of the cacophony. He slowly pushed the door open, fairly certain he knew what he was about to see.

Pushing through the packed ranks outside the men's room, Hamza came upon a little circle of cleared space around the table Will had chosen. Everyone at that table, including Will, was on his feet. One of the sailors had the front of Will's shirt gathered in one hand and an empty bottle gripped by the neck in the other.

"What the fuck you playin' at?" the sailor shouted, his face red, spittle visibly striking Will's face.

"Nothing, man, listen," Will began.

"I ain't your fuckin' man, you fuckin' Yank. What in the good goddamn makes you think it's any of your bloody business asking about my ship's mission?"

"I was just curious," Will said.

"Just curious, he says," the sailor said. "You know what that did to the fuckin' cat, don't you?"

Phenomenal, Hamza thought.

He shoved through the front ranks and stepped up to the sailor holding Will.

"Hey now," Hamza said. "No need for that. Let's all just settle down. Let me buy a few more rounds. Hell, let me get one for the bar."

Sporadic cheers went up at that, but the sailor holding Will wasn't having it. He rotated his head slowly, staring at Hamza with bulging eyes.

"So here's this poof's little Paki friend, then," he said, addressing the other sailors at his table.

Hamza felt his entire body go cold.

"What did you just call me?"

"I called you a Paki. Why don't you sod off and get me a kebab, boy? I've got some business here with your friend."

Hamza took a step back.

"Listen, you racist son of a bitch. You let my friend go, right now, or I'll rip your goddamn balls off, and then I'll put you through that wall right there."

"Ooooh," the sailor said. "I'm supposed to believe some little ten-stone nothing's going to keep me from doing whatever I bloody well feel like doing?"

Hamza clenched his jaw.

"It doesn't matter if you believe it or not. I'm going to do it anyway. You've got three seconds. One."

The sailor grinned at Hamza, revealing teeth that were fairly white and straight, defying expectations.

"Two," Hamza said.

The sailor smashed his bottle on the table, leaving a jagged, ugly-looking stub clenched in his fist.

"Three," the sailor finished, his grin widening.

CHAPTER 24

omeone else get on, Leigh Shore thought. *Please.*

Four floors intervened between the cubicle farm housing the writers, art teams, and assorted other low-level employees and the floor containing the executive offices. Four chances for the elevator to pause, the doors to open, someone to get on, and the doors to close again. Five or six seconds each time. Even one stop would be something. But no. The elevator rose smoothly, bringing her closer to unemployment with each passing moment.

She wished she'd been able to go out on her own terms—quit in a blaze of glory, maybe. She'd never actually been fired before.

Five minutes before, Leigh had been in the conference room with the rest of the office, watching coverage of the ongoing American military efforts to liberate Niger from the insidious grasp of Prophet Idriss Yusuf. Actually, that had supposedly already happened—the president claimed that the Prophet had been killed in a precision drone strike a few weeks before—but no one had told the Prophet's soldiers. They had continued fighting, even ramping up their efforts, and had taken control of a place she hadn't even known existed until the news started to cover it—Niamey, the capital.

U.S. forces had expanded their bombing campaign, but there

was only so much an aerial campaign could accomplish. The Prophet's forces had entwined themselves with the local populations, forcing them to remain in the cities and villages to act as human shields. It was becoming increasingly clear that either ground troops would need to go in to clear out the capital, or the United States would have to cut its losses, declare victory, and leave the people of Niger to figure out their future for themselves.

Watching the footage, Leigh was horrified to realize that she was almost bored watching the familiar sight of U.S. warplanes pulverizing a desert country's infrastructure into sand.

Then Reimer's assistant had appeared and dragged her out of the conference room, telling her she needed to be up in Johannes' office immediately. None of her colleagues—even Eddie—would meet her eyes as she got up to leave. She was finally done—she'd pushed too hard. That's all it could be, and honestly, she'd be lying if she said she hadn't seen it coming.

Reimer was furious when she'd skipped out on her scheduled interview to film the Oracle riot. She'd gotten an extremely expensive camera damaged, the company had to cover Eddie's medical bills, and while she'd managed to retrieve the footage he'd shot, none of it was particularly newsworthy . . . all in all, a nightmare of wasted time and money for Urbanity.com.

Leigh hadn't stepped out of line since, but evidently Reimer had just been letting her twist in the wind. Time was up.

The elevator doors opened. Leigh stepped out and made her way across the executive floor to Reimer's office.

The door was open. She knocked on it anyway. Her boss looked up.

"Ms. Shore," he said. "Come in, and please close the door behind you."

Leigh closed the door and stood in front of Reimer's desk. He gestured for her to sit. As she did, she noticed that his tie was a bit loose, and the top button of his dress shirt was undone. For Johannes Reimer, that was on the same level as anyone else running through Central Park wearing a glitter-studded thong.

He was fiddling with a sheet of paper on his desk—a printed e-mail, maybe.

Leigh frantically thought back over every piece of communication that had left her computer since she'd started work at Urbanity. com, trying to remember if she'd ever written anything inappropriate, resulting in a flood of correspondence she would rather die than see on her boss' desk washing through her mind.

"Ms. Shore," Reimer began, not looking at her, then stopped. He picked up a pencil on his desk and tapped it against the paper a few times. "Will you read this and tell me what it means to you?"

With the eraser end of the pencil, he pushed the paper toward Leigh, rotating it so that it faced her. She reluctantly picked it up. It was, in fact, an e-mail, but she hadn't written it.

YOUR PROPOSAL IS ACCEPTED. THE ORACLE WILL MEET WITH AN INTERVIEWER FROM URBANITY. HOWEVER, THERE IS ONE CONDITION. THE PERSON TO CONDUCT THE INTERVIEW MUST BE LEIGH SHORE. IF THIS IS SATISFACTORY, INSTRUCTIONS FOR CONDUCTING THE INTERVIEW AND DEPOSITING THE NONREFUNDABLE FEE WILL BE SENT TO YOU. RESPOND WITHIN 24 HOURS.

Her heart began to pound. She read the e-mail three more times.

"I . . . I don't understand," she managed.

"You don't know why you are mentioned specifically?"

"No, I don't. Honestly. What's going on?"

Reimer sighed heavily.

"You know about the e-mail address on the Site? For questions to the Oracle?"

Leigh nodded.

"I think everyone does, Mr. Reimer," she said.

"I sent in a question."

In the little corner of Leigh's mind not consumed by whatever the hell the e-mail might mean, she wondered what Johannes Reimer could possibly want to know about his future, and more importantly, if he was actually about to share that with her. Poking around in other people's Oracle questions had become a sort of taboo subject in polite society, like talking money or politics. You told your closest friends, maybe, but that was about it.

"I asked him if he would do an interview for our site."

Leigh's heart, already revving pretty hard, jumped up a few gears.

Reimer frowned heavily.

"I never thought he would answer. I mean, he doesn't answer anyone, right? We'd have heard about it. So asking for an interview . . . it was a lark, I guess. Just part of feeling connected."

Leigh had never seen Reimer with an expression anywhere near the one he was currently wearing. He looked lost. Afraid, even.

"I got the Oracle's e-mail yesterday afternoon," he said. "I spent last night considering what the hell I was going to do. I didn't sleep."

"What? Why?" Leigh blurted out. "You said yes, right? I mean, this is the best thing that could ever happen for this place. And me, too, I'm not pretending it's not. Why wouldn't you just go for it?"

"Because I proposed an interview fee of ten million dollars," Reimer answered.

Leigh's eyes widened.

"That's the operating budget for this business for the next four years, Ms. Shore. I chose ten million because I thought it was probably half what other outlets had to be offering. I never thought it would happen. It was a safe bet, just something to let me feel like I was in the game."

Reimer rubbed a hand across his forehead.

"And then he called my bluff."

"So fucking what?" Leigh said. "It doesn't matter what it costs! There is no bigger thing than this. This is the . . . the biggest thing."

Shock rippled across Reimer's face, then anger.

Leigh didn't care. The Oracle wanted her, and there was no way she was letting that slip away.

"Look, I'm tempted," Reimer said, wrestling himself back under control. "The Oracle's the most famous person on the planet. An interview with him would pay for itself almost instantly. We film it, license it out, maybe do a documentary, even. It's not really the money.

"The problem," he continued, taking the e-mail printout back from Leigh, "is you."

Leigh felt her eyes narrow. She knew she was getting angrier than she probably should, but she couldn't help herself.

She opened her mouth to speak, but Reimer held up a hand for silence.

"You're a junior reporter on what's basically the gossip beat for a fourth-rate website," he said. "Why you and only you? It makes no sense."

He looked her directly in the eye.

"Do you know the Oracle?" Reimer asked. "Personally, I mean? I thought maybe it was some sort of plan between you two, but that made no sense. But if not that, then what? Why does he want you, Ms. Shore?"

Leigh smiled.

"You got me, Mr. Reimer. Maybe he wants a reporter with a little vision. Maybe he read that goddamn great story I posted about him on Urbanity last year. The one you wanted to kill."

"Do you really think right now is the time to bring all of that up?" Reimer said, real anger emerging behind his voice.

"Actually, yes. You haven't recognized my skills since I got here. I've paid my dues on shit assignment after shit assignment for absolutely no recognition. Every time I come to you with a proposal that could elevate your stupid site into something approaching, you know . . . good, you send me back down to my cubicle with a spanking.

"And now . . . and now . . . you've got the chance of a lifetime, Johannes, but you can't get it without me. Nothing at all happens without me. You probably think it's terrible. Really burns you up."

Leigh folded her arms and smiled.

"I, however, kind of dig it."

Reimer stood up from his desk and planted both fists on it.

"Leigh, I'm trying to decide if I should spend ten million bucks here. Do you really think reminding me of the fact that you tend to do whatever the hell you want helps your case?"

"You're not deciding," Leigh said. "You already decided. If you hadn't, then you never would have called me up here, and you sure as hell wouldn't have shown me that e-mail."

Reimer sat down heavily. He pulled an immaculate white handkerchief from his pocket and patted at his forehead.

"So what next," he said, "the demands?"

Leigh's face softened. Her anger dissipated slightly.

"Obviously. But it won't be that bad. First, I want a promotion to lead correspondent. You'd want to do that anyway. When we do our piece on the Oracle interview, it would look a little strange if you sent out someone junior."

Reimer nodded.

"Sure."

"Including the salary bump, benefits, the whole deal."

"I already said yes. What else?"

Leigh thought for a minute. She really only had one other demand that mattered, but this wasn't the kind of opportunity you let slip by. She considered, thinking of other things to request.

"I want my own office—no more cube—and a parking space downstairs."

Reimer nodded again, more slowly. She could almost see the calculations spinning behind his eyes.

Guess I'll have to buy myself a car, she thought.

"One more, Johannes, and you'll like it. It's free.

"This story, no matter where it goes, it's mine. I don't just want to do the interview, I want the byline. I want final edit, and I do any follow-up pieces."

"Impossible," Reimer said flatly. "You aren't ready."

"You have no idea what I'm capable of, Johannes. Besides, you don't have a choice. The Oracle asked for me. If you want this interview, those are my terms. And I'll want it in writing."

Reimer slumped visibly. He opened a drawer in his desk and pulled out a small silver flask. The smell of juniper berries wafted into the air when he opened it and took a sip. He didn't offer any to Leigh, which she didn't mind at all.

He took a long, deep, shuddering breath, then looked at Leigh, seeming more in control of himself.

"Fine. All good. Done."

Leigh endured a surge of nervous elation so intense that it left her feeling hollowed out, like a spent Roman candle. She felt her face stretch into a wide, unhinged smile.

"Look, I know you're happy, Ms. Shore," Reimer said. He seemed exhausted, like he'd suddenly realized he was completely unprepared for the life he found himself living. "You won. Congratulations. But please at least think about *what* you've won. I think most people would stay a thousand miles away from anything like this. I sure as hell would."

Reimer cast a glance at his flask, then back to Leigh.

"I almost deleted the Oracle's e-mail the second I got it. I mean, what do we actually know about him? Or her? Or it? Nothing, nothing at all, except that the Oracle can apparently do magic and doesn't want anyone to know who he is. Doesn't that . . . scare you? Because it scares me."

Reimer stood up and held out his hand.

"If I'd known he would answer, I'd never have asked," he said.

Leigh took the offered hand. They shook.

"Too late now," she said.

The lights went out.

Leigh dropped Reimer's hand, looking up at the ceiling in confusion. The darkness was . . . complete, which was unsettling. It was never dark in New York.

There was always someone else's window, a neon sign, a late-night restaurant that leaked its illumination into your sight line. But now—nothing. Leigh released Reimer's hand and walked carefully across the office to the big window behind his desk. He had already turned to look out at the city, and she took up a position beside him.

It took her a moment to understand what she was seeing.

No lights in the windows of the building across the street. Leigh craned her neck to look up and down Third Avenue. Other than the lights of cars on the streets below, no signs of electricity in any direction.

Somewhere downtown, a siren began to wail.

CHAPTER 25

MacAvoy's was dark. Sounds of confusion filled the bar, accompanied by a few alcohol-soaked, derisive boos.

"What's this then?" the sailor holding Will's shirt said. His grip slackened slightly.

Will took the opportunity and wrenched himself backward. His shirt came free, and he grabbed Hamza's coat sleeve.

"Come on!" he shouted.

They slipped toward the front of the bar. Splinters of light from car headlights came in through the big plateglass windows, supplemented by people holding lighters and cell phones over their heads. A delay as they pushed their way through the knot of people shoving their way outside.

They ran to the corner. Will glanced back, but it didn't look like anyone had decided to follow them. He slowed to a stop, panting, feeling his heart throb.

"I think we're okay," he said.

Hamza leaned against the side of the nearest building, catching his breath. He held up a hand in acknowledgment.

Will looked up the avenue. People had spilled out of every bar and restaurant and were goggling up at the city gone dark all around them, their breath steaming in the cold April air.

"What's going on?" Hamza said.

"Blackout," Will answered.

"I can see that. I wonder if it's the whole city. Did the Oracle see this coming?"

"Nope," Will said. "Surprised me as much as it did you."

Hamza tried his cell phone.

"No signal," he said. "Weird. The phones still worked down here when Sandy shut the power off below Fourteenth. The towers are on a separate grid from the rest of the city's power."

"Maybe they changed it since then. Who were you trying to call? Miko?"

"Yeah. I'm sure she's fine—we have tons of candles, batteries, all that. Just want to let her know I'm okay."

Will looked up and, for the first time he could remember, saw stars in the city's sky.

"What are the chances the trains are running?"

"No chance," Hamza answered.

"Mm," Will said. "You know, there had to be people on the subway when this happened, down in the tunnels."

Hamza shuddered.

An aproned man stepped out of a nearby bar and set down a sign with a message chalked on it, letting passersby know that the taps were still flowing, but it was cash only until the lights came back on.

Will gestured at the sign, giving Hamza a questioning look.

"No, man. I just want to get home," Hamza said.

Will nodded.

"Yeah. All right. Probably for the best," he said. He looked uptown. "I guess we're walking."

"I guess we are. Figures," Hamza said. "Stupid sailors had to pick a bar way the hell down in the Village. No way in hell we'll find a free cab. Not tonight. I've got like fifty blocks to walk, and it can't be much over thirty degrees out."

"Could be worse. You could live on Ninety-Fourth."

"Yeah," Hamza said. "That would suck."

Will shot him a look.

"I'm just playing around," Hamza said. "Come back to my place. Sleep on the foldout tonight."

"You sure? Miko won't mind?" Will said.

"Don't be an idiot," Hamza said.

"All right, good," Will said. "I'll take you up on that. Feels like a weird night to be solo. I'm sure the lights will be back on in an hour, but you know."

"I do."

They headed north, hunching their shoulders against the cold. After a few minutes, Will spoke.

"Thanks for trying to help back there. You sort of did a crap job, but thank you."

"Just pray life never puts me in that situation again," Hamza said. "I don't like being forced to hurt people."

"Uh-huh."

"Did you actually get anything from those guys before they decided to kill you? What did you say to get them so riled up?"

"I asked them if they were in New York for some kind of leave, and they said no, they were supposed to be carrying a bunch of soldiers from a base in Northern Ireland to somewhere in Asia, one of the 'Stans, I think. It was hard to understand them—they were Welsh. But then their boat got diverted, and they put in here instead."

"Huh," Hamza said, considering.

"That's about it. I tried to ask them what the soldiers were going to do over there, and that's when it fell apart. I guess I pushed too hard."

"I guess so."

"So what we get from that is this: either the Site doesn't want soldiers in that 'Stan or does want them here. But why? I have no idea."

"And so here we are, out in the cold, having learned essentially nothing. Great night out, Will."

"Mmm."

"And so I suppose you still want to do that interview."

"Suppose so. But I'll stick to what I said. No crowdsourcing."

"It's a start," Hamza said.

They trudged along Lafayette Street in silence for a few moments, both taking in how dark the streets were, even with the lights from traffic.

"You know," Hamza said. "The walk uptown will take us through Union Square. I don't think I've been back there since the riot."

"Me neither," Will said, his voice tight.

"You remember that woman who interviewed us for a minute that day? The hot one?"

Will stopped. He turned his head, meeting Hamza's eyes.

"Yeah," he said.

Will looked away.

"Thought so," Hamza said. "I looked her up. Leigh Shore. I don't even know why you told me her name. You didn't think I'd look her up? Why her, Will?"

"I've read her work. She's actually written about the Oracle before, and she's good. Maybe I thought I'd give the interview to someone who could actually use the break," Will said. "Or maybe it's because she wasn't afraid. You saw her, man—even when those riots started, she wanted to rush right in. If I'm going to do this, I want to talk to someone who isn't afraid."

"Uh-huh. Whatever you tell yourself, just remember that she's seen you before. She's talked to you. You don't think she could make the connection? I know you want to do this in disguise, but still. It just seems . . ."

"What does it seem like? What?" Will said, shouting.

"It seems like . . . you're walking into traffic again," Hamza said, his voice quiet.

Will looked out at the dark city, the streets lit only by headlights, shadows trudging along the sidewalks. Sirens from every direction.

"Maybe I am," he said.

He put his hand on Hamza's shoulder.

"Guess you'll have to make sure I don't get hit."

He turned and walked north, Hamza following a moment later.

Fifty blocks and twenty-three flights of stairs later, Will pulled open the thick steel fire door leading out to Hamza's floor. He paused to look back down the stairwell, where flashlight beams sliced through the pitch black, weaving through the shadows. Snatches of echoed conversation bounced off the concrete walls.

Out in the hall, Hamza pulled his keys from his pocket and inserted them in the lock. The handle turned before he had a chance to touch it, and the door opened, pulling the key ring out of his hand.

Miko stood framed in the doorway by candlelight spilling out from the apartment, wearing a long coat.

"Oh thank God," she said, and immediately wrapped her arms around Hamza.

"Hey, it's okay," Hamza said, stroking her hair. "It's just a blackout."

Will looked away. This seemed very much a husband-wife moment.

Miko let Hamza go, sniffling slightly and laughing at herself.

"Not really," she said. "Hey, Will."

"Hey, Miko."

"Will's going to crash here, if that's okay," Hamza said.

"Of course," Miko said. "Come in, both of you. The stove's gas—it still works. I made coffee."

They entered the apartment, pleasantly illuminated by twenty or thirty candles in all sorts of holders—candelabras, glasses, empty jam jars. Will and Hamza unbuttoned their coats but kept them on. It wasn't anywhere near as cold inside as it was on the street, but the building had a modern central heating system. It didn't work without power, and the warmth they had generated by walking up twenty-plus floors was rapidly dissipating.

"What did you mean when you said 'Not really,' Miko?" Hamza said.

"Huh?" Miko said.

"At the door. I said it was just a blackout, and you said not really."

Miko tilted her head, puzzled.

"You didn't hear?"

"Hear what? I've been walking for the last hour."

"Turn on the radio. I was listening to it until you guys showed up."

Hamza flipped the switch on a battery-powered radio on the coffee table. Immediately, a news station came on through faint static. Hamza walked into the kitchen and came out a moment later with two coffee mugs, handing one to Will.

They listened, as the radio announcer described the scope of the blackout.

Will looked at Miko.

"This is . . ."

"I know," Miko said. "It's not just here. Power's out all over the world."

Silence.

"Do you think the Site did it?" Miko asked.

Will didn't answer.

The radio announcer solemnly proclaimed that he would continue to broadcast updates as he received them, as long as he had gasoline for the generator powering the station's transmitter. He then proceeded to describe disasters occurring all around the world as power and computer systems failed.

"Look at that!" Hamza said. He had turned to look out through his apartment's large windows across the East River, toward the dark shadows of Brooklyn and Queens. Will and Miko turned to follow his gaze. A finger of flame rose up from the darkness, spreading out into a cloud as it grew.

"What is it?" Miko asked.

"Tanker truck, maybe," Will said. "Propane or something."

As the light from the initial explosion faded into a dull glow, new blossoms of flame appeared to replace it, rising up all across the darkness beyond the river.

TÖRÖKUL

The lights of the city of Uth radiated in the deep night, reflections off the stillness of the Aral Sea creating a sort of mirror city in the water, shimmering and inconstant.

Six men sat cross-legged around a fire on a hilltop overlooking the city, sharing skewers of shashlik, passing the spits of fire-blackened mutton between them. Skins of kumis circulated as well, some of the first of the spring, as the mares produced milk for the new foals.

One set of lights in the city of Uth shone from a higher perch than the rest. A Byzantine cross, projecting from the exact center of the dome atop what had once been a mosque, built five centuries before. But for more than two decades, the cross. An insult, blazing out across the plain.

One of the men, the leader of this group, turned his gaze toward the city, looking at the defiled mosque, then back at his men. He said nothing. There was nothing to be said.

Another man tossed his skewer into the dirt, scowling at his chief. The leader held the other man's gaze for a few moments, then reached over and picked up the discarded skewer from the ground. He dusted off the worst of the dirt and took a bite, washing it down with a long swig from his skin.

The chief considered. He thought about the power he held—the men he could gather to his cause on a word, and more importantly, the Sword of God hidden away in its canyon. He thought about what it would mean to pull his army together, and what it would mean if he lost. Timing. As with so many things, it was all in the timing.

Without warning, the cross atop the mosque in Uth winked out, along with all the other electric lights in the city. If not for the firelight still twinkling here and there between the buildings, it would have been easy to assume the city had been wiped off the face of the earth.

The chief and his band got to their feet. Brownouts were nothing strange in Uth, but normally only a portion of the city would go dark at a time. This suggested a larger failure. And perhaps, an opportunity.

The mirror city off the coast was gone, swallowed up into the black water.

The chief watched the dark city for a moment, then lifted his head and shouted up at the stars, crying war.

CHAPTER 26

Staffman's hands ached, a tendons-deep pain that ran halfway up his forearms. He wanted nothing more than to stop typing, to soak his hands in hot water, and pour half a bottle of ibuprofen down his throat. But each time he pulled his fingers off the keys, his botnet shut down another portion of the worldwide power grid. Each failure meant that many fewer computers available to work on breaking into the Oracle's systems, and that much longer he'd have to keep his agonized fingers moving to try to keep the virus contained.

He flicked his eyes to the right, to the screen with the progress bar. Ninety-nine percent and counting.

It had taken nearly four hours to chew through the Oracle's security. Despite Staffman's efforts, the world map on his monitor was more than half black, with the rest an angry red, dull like the coals of a fire that had almost burned itself out. The entire American East Coast was dark, as was all of South America, Australia, and parts of Africa. He'd managed to maintain a good deal of Asia, the United States, and Europe, with their heavy concentrations of computing power. Losing Africa was frustrating, but survivable—San Francisco alone held more processors than that entire continent.

The Coach sat to Staffman's left. Neither had spoken much in the last little while. For the first few hours of watching Staffman work, she had offered what assistance she could—getting him a glass of water (although the ten seconds he'd taken to drink it had put the lights out in Brazil), or reminding him of all the freedom he'd enjoy with the money he'd earn by finding the Oracle's name. But after a while, she just sat back to watch the battle.

New consequences of the virus' release kept appearing in the forefront of Staffman's mind, no matter how hard he tried to focus on his work.

Research projects in the midst of crucial calculations that would have to be restarted from scratch, costing God only knew how much money and time.

Critical surgery was almost always computer-assisted these days, and so unless the doctors were unbelievably good, people had died on the operating tables when the hospital's machines had been diverted to run Staffman's botnet.

Governments must have lost a great deal of their monitoring power, as well as their ability to communicate with their militaries. Some would assume they'd been attacked and respond in kind.

And on it went, a hundred different permutations, his brilliant but insurrectionist brain providing estimates of how many people he'd murdered with the click of a button.

"It's done," the Coach said.

The progress bar on the rightmost monitor had hit 100 percent and disappeared, replaced by a command line with a slowly blinking cursor.

"Thank God," Staffman said, his voice cracking. He typed as quickly as his nearly crippled hands would let him, telling the botnet to release control of the world's processors back to their native networks. Yellow and green blooms began to appear on the central monitor, just pinpricks at first in the sea of red, but expanding quickly as Staffman's instructions worked through the system.

Staffman gingerly lifted his hands from the keys. He flexed very gently, and the dull, insistent pain flared up into white agony. He grunted.

"Did it work?" the Coach asked.

"Please, Coach, just one second," he responded weakly.

He was so exhausted that he had to think for a moment to remember the point of the whole exercise.

Staffman looked at the monitor on the right, with its seductive blinking cursor, promising the Oracle's secrets, if only he could endure the pain in his hands for a few more moments. He took a deep breath and set his hands back on the keys.

"Yes, it worked," he said. "I'm in. Let me just see what I've found."

He typed, much more slowly than before, his fingers having stiffened up the moment he took a break.

"Hmm," he said.

"Hmm?" the Coach said, the impatience in her voice clear.

Staffman looked away from the screen.

"There's . . . ah, there's nothing here, Coach," he said, his voice quiet.

The Coach took one birdlike, liver-spotted hand and pushed her thumb and index finger up under her glasses to press on her closed eyelids. After a moment, she removed her hand and let her glasses fall back to the bridge of her nose.

"Explain," she said, her voice solid steel, all pretense that they were anything other than master and minion gone.

Staffman swallowed.

"I'm past the Oracle's security. Every e-mail he received from the Site should be stored here—and I assumed there would be other things, too. Files, maybe. Data. Some sort of clue. But . . . there's nothing. It's just an empty volume. Small, too. Only like sixteen megabytes, which is bizarre. It's almost like a . . ."

His voice trailed off.

"Staffman?" the Coach said. "Did you find something?"

"Maybe," he answered. He typed again, quickly, the pain in his hands forgotten, then sat back, satisfied.

He pointed at the screen.

"We need to go to New Jersey," he said.

CHAPTER 27

B lessed is he that readeth, and they that hear the words of this prophecy, and keep those things which are written therein: for the time is at hand," Reverend Hosiah Branson intoned, one hand clutching his Bible, the other outstretched toward the flock of worshippers assembled before him. His eyes were closed, his head upturned to heaven, cleverly placed spotlights surrounding him in a corona of white light no matter where the observer was seated, even the cheap seats.

Jonas had seen this tableau a hundred times before. He knew the precise moment when Branson would lower his head and begin to speak again—delaying just enough for his audience to sink into a state of blissful anticipation, but not so long that it became awkward or self-conscious.

Branson started most of his sermons with this trick, and it always seemed entirely natural, unforced. Just a man communing with his own spirituality, gathering himself before giving comfort and guidance to his people.

Now, though, watching it through a monitor on his desk deep inside the Branson Ministry, Jonas saw it for what it was—stagecraft. A performance. A fraud.

Branson wouldn't deny it, either. All faith was fraud, to the good reverend. He'd said as much that evening in his relic-filled sanctuary, and he expected Jonas to simply accept that and continue working as diligently as he ever had to further the Ministry's agenda in the world.

For the most part, he had. But each time he looked out at the faces of the poor people in the reverend's audiences (he found it impossible to think of them as his congregation any longer) and seen the pure belief on their faces, the pure, empty belief, he'd felt it echo within himself. They were so sure that God was real, and that Branson was their conduit to his grace.

But they were wrong. About the second part, if not the first. And if they were wrong, how many others were? All over the world, all those billions of believers . . .

Jonas wasn't naive. He knew that charlatans had been taking advantage of humankind's search for something higher than itself for thousands and thousands of years. But he'd always assumed it was an exceptional thing. Not the norm. Now, though . . . it was as if Branson's revelations had flipped the world into something like a photo negative, and he couldn't see his way back to the light.

On the monitor, Branson lowered his head, opened his eyes, and began to preach.

"Welcome to the END TIMES, my brothers and sisters!" he shouted. "The final act of the great play! Judgment Day! When the sinners are cast down to burn in the lake of fire, and the faithful travel up to join God in heaven, and all good Christians will know the pure joy of his presence.

"Our job in all of that is simple, my friends. If we avoid wickedness and help guide our fellows to righteousness, we'll get to see that Judgment Day show from the best seats in the whole darned arena. The skybox, in the truest sense! We'll get called up early, in body and spirit, when that trumpet sounds at the Rapture. And I will SEE YOU ALL THERE! That's one journey we'll make TOGETHER!"

The audience erupted into cheers and hosannas and hallelujahs. Of course they did. Branson was reminding them they were better than everyone else.

Jonas hated himself for thinking something so cynical, but ideas like that came to him constantly now.

If Branson was a fraud, then he was a fraud. Everyone was a fraud.

Almost everyone, he thought.

Jonas glanced at his phone, feeling the temptation to check his e-mail. The phone was set to chime whenever a new message came in, so he knew there hadn't been anything new since he last checked—but still.

Instead, he turned back to the stack of papers on his desk—correspondence from the Detectives for Christ initiative Branson had started up some time back as a grassroots effort to track down the Oracle's identity. The project had been wildly successful—at least from a purely participatory perspective. Every one of the Ministry's faithful from Topeka to Tallahassee was peeping in their neighbors' windows looking for the evil Oracle.

And in a surprising twist, the vast majority of the Detectives did, in fact, find their quarry.

Or they were fairly certain they had, and wanted to tell Branson about their discovery, and asked for his guidance on how to handle the situation. Every day, a mountain of correspondence poured into the offices of the Branson Ministry—e-mail, handwritten letters, packages, phone calls. Jonas had been tasked with coordinating the effort to deal with the deluge.

Initially, Jonas had assigned one intern to go through the materials the Ministry's congregation sent in—the "leads," as they had inevitably become known. Now, there were three, each pulling twelve-hour days parsing through the endless chaff, looking for even the tiniest bit of wheat.

Most of it was simple to handle—like an e-mail from a woman

convinced that the lucky win on Bingo Night by "that dirty cheater Doris Hanson" meant that poor Mrs. Hanson was quite obviously the Oracle.

But some of it was not so obviously misguided, and Jonas needed to review those communications to see if they might contain an actual clue to the Oracle's identity. The interns weren't supposed to send leads up the chain to Jonas unless something looked quite promising—but none of them wanted to be accused of missing something important, so they ended up sending much more to his desk than they should.

Hence, the stack of paperwork on Jonas' desk, and the reason he was watching the reverend's sermon through a monitor on his desk as opposed to standing backstage watching it live.

Once, being so far from Hosiah Branson's presence would have bothered Jonas immensely. Now, though, he didn't mind all that much. The farther the better, in fact.

"You all know the signs," Branson said through the monitor, lifting a solemn hand out toward his audience. "The comet Wormwood appearing in the skies, the Antichrist slouching his terrible, oozing way toward Bethlehem, the seas of blood, all the rest. But I ask you to think for one moment. The words of the Book of Revelation were set down almost two thousand years ago by the good Apostle John. He was imprisoned on the island of Patmos, waiting for the end of his life, when God sent him a vision of how it would all go down.

"It seems to me that God perhaps showed Saint John things he didn't quite understand. This was a long time ago, after all. John did his level best to explain what he saw, to give us God's message, but what if he simply didn't have the words for it?

"You know what happened five days ago. The world went dark. The power went out, and our machines failed us. Death was visited on all the lands of the earth. Tens of thousands have died in the last few days, in every country. In fact, I can feel that some of you in this very room, and those watching me from your homes, have lost people in this crisis. For that I offer you my deepest sympathy and my assurances that you will see your loved ones again—soon."

Hosiah paused and bowed his head. He removed a crystal-white handkerchief from his lapel pocket and ran it across his perfectly dry brow before continuing.

Do I hate him? Jonas thought. *I might. I really might.*

Jonas picked up the next sheet of paper from the stack. "Dear Reverund," it began. He sighed heavily and started to plow through the theories of one Donny Winston, from North Carolina. Donny seemed to favor tying the Oracle by his ankles to the back of his pickup and dragging him through the streets from town to town, making stops for him to be stoned by the good God-fearing folk along the way. "Like they done with St. Paul," Donny concluded, failing to realize that the people doing the stoning in that instance were not generally seen to be the heroes of the story.

He slashed a large red *X* across the page with a pen conveniently placed for the purpose and set it into an out-box, atop the other rejected leads.

"It is not only death that concerns us today," Branson went on. "It is also war. You've heard of the terrible fighting on the plains of Central Asia, in Qandustan. Our Christian brothers have been forced to defend themselves against the Muslims, who took the opportunity offered by the dark days to invade. And the Philippines, that good, God-fearing country, torn asunder by rioting and fear as the military pulled power from their president. And of course, our own soldiers in the armed forces of this great country, stitching together the blanket of freedom in Africa and the Middle East. I could list many others, but I'm not here to talk about that kind of news. The only news I'm going to give you is the GOOD news, straight from the Lord to you.

"And this is good news, my brothers and sisters, for when you hear talk of death, and talk of war, and when you know famine and pestilence cannot be far behind, what does that sound like to you?"

Jonas considered. Branson was a liar, but he had a point. The world did seem like it had a dark cloud covering it these days.

"Why," the Reverend said, ramping up his intensity, "it sounds to me like the FOUR HORSEMEN come a'ridin'! Not the riders of the dusty sage, not the cavalry, but the riders of the APOCALYPSE! This is the END of DAYS, my fellow children of God, and I am so pleased to be your source of guidance in this time of trial."

The crowd, hushed until this moment, boiled over, becoming a cauldron of exaggerated cries of fear, pledges to Jesus, devotions and exhortations and covenants offered.

"Oh, yes," Branson said, his amplified voice cutting through the din, "this is it. Prepare your souls for God's reckoning.

"Brothers and sisters," he shouted. "Calm yourselves. You are all bathed in God's light. These days should be days of hope, of anticipation, not fear. If there's one thing I know, it's that good people go to Heaven. And you, my friends"—he spread his arms wide—"are good people."

Branson dropped his arms. He let his face grow serious.

"But there's another thing. You know that the Bible talks of an Antichrist, an evil beast that will stalk the earth in the days before Jesus' return. I tell you he's already here. We've talked about him before, and I'm ashamed to say that I underestimated the threat to goodness that he posed. Someone out there knows whom I'm talking about. Shout it out to me, right n—"

Jonas clicked off the monitor. He lifted his phone, swiped it open, and checked his e-mail.

Nothing.

He stared at the screen for a moment, then placed it facedown on his desk and returned to work.

CHAPTER 28

Jonathan Staffman grabbed a backpack containing his toolkit— customized Raspberry Pi processors designed to inject zombifying malware into any number of common electronic lock systems, a few laptops filled with his preferred code-breaking algorithms, and even a set of analog lockpicks, just in case. He stepped out of the back of the overheated, stuffy van into the cold air of an April dawn, breathing in the comparatively refreshing scents of Bayonne, New Jersey, with some relief.

The sunrise-tinged Statue of Liberty was visible to the north, and Lower Manhattan beyond, their majesty a stark contrast to their immediate surroundings—a self-storage park on the banks of the Hudson River. Rows of modular steel bins of varying sizes, painted orange with blue shutter doors, stretched out in either direction. The complex was deserted. That was intentional—the main reason they had gotten there so early.

The Coach appeared next to him, along with two large, dark-suited men of unclear job description, whom she hadn't seen fit to introduce. Staffman had the sense that it was unusual for the Coach to attend a mission like this personally. The large gentlemen were probably her security team, a conclusion strongly supported by their air of competent menace.

"Which way?" she said.

Staffman pointed, and the group set out toward Unit 909.

"Is this what you expected to find?" the Coach asked, gesturing out at the storage units around them.

"Honestly, no," Staffman answered, as they made their way down the row, their shoes squelching in the mud. "I was thinking it would be a warehouse, maybe. But this could make sense too. Some of these units are wired. This company rents them out for all kinds of things, not just storage. Cheap office space, even some light manufacturing. 3-D printing outfits, lots of stuff. So some of them have Internet and power. It's not fancy, but it's cheap, and my guess is that whoever runs this place doesn't ask too many questions."

Two turns and a short walk deeper into the maze and they arrived at Unit 909, where the third member of the Coach's security team waited, holding the packet sniffer he'd used to zero in on the IP address from the Oracle's e-mail address.

A heavy padlock and thick chain hung from the shutter door.

"Anything?" the Coach asked her man.

"Nothing. Quiet in there. The lock doesn't look like it's been disturbed for a while, either."

She stepped back, thinking.

"All right. The Oracle isn't here. That's obvious. But maybe we'll just have a little look, see what we can see."

Staffman breathed a sigh of relief. The Coach's men were carrying guns—he'd seen them beneath their coats—and he had no interest in being anywhere near any sort of . . . firefight, or battle, or whatever the security team was thinking might happen that would require them to be armed.

He swung his shoulder bag around and started rooting around in it for his lockpicks.

"I can get through that lock," he said, as he searched.

"Can I help you?" a new voice said, from a little farther up the row.

Staffman turned, freezing as he saw a small, dark-skinned man in jeans and a light jacket. An orange-and-blue sweatshirt emblazoned with the logo of the self-storage company was visible beneath the coat.

He glanced to one side, expecting the Coach to order her security team to gun the man down. And indeed, one of them was reaching inside his coat.

Staffman opened his mouth, desperately hoping he could say something that would prevent another death being added to the considerable tally he already had on his head from the blackouts. He felt the Coach's hand, tight on his upper arm. He looked over, where he saw that her kindly old grandma persona had reappeared, anchored by a reassuring, friendly smile.

The fight—if that was what it could be called—went out of him. Staffman relaxed, resigning himself to whatever happened next. The Coach had said it, back when this all began—Dr. Jonathan Staffman was no hero.

The Coach's man removed something from inside his blazer— not a pistol, but a slim leather wallet, which he flipped open to show to the storage company's security guard.

"FBI, sir," he said. "We're here as part of an ongoing investigation."

He handed the badge to the guard, who inspected it before handing it back. Staffman wondered if the man might actually be an FBI agent. Knowing the Coach, it was entirely possible.

"All right," said the security guard. "But you should have checked in with me first. How can I help you?"

The FBI agent—false or real—turned and pointed at Unit 909.

"We need to get in there right away," he said. "Do you have a key?"

"Of course—but you can't get in without a warrant. We take that stuff seriously around here."

Staffman assumed that was probably because they had their share of illegal businesses operating in the complex, which was neither here nor there to him. In a way, he respected the man's integrity.

"Sure, of course!" the Coach said, speaking for the first time. She had her cell phone in her hand and was tapping its face. "Do you have a fax number here?"

The guard rattled off ten digits, which the Coach apparently memorized on hearing once. She stepped away, spoke a few quiet words into her phone, then returned to the group.

"You should have your warrant in about five minutes," she said.

It took three. The guard reviewed the papers, nodded, produced the padlock key and handed it over, asking only that they return it when they were done.

The lock fell open, and one of the Coach's men lifted the storage unit's door, sliding it up on its track. All four men and one woman crowded around the door, eager to see what had been hidden so securely, what had cost so many lives to find.

Paper. Drifts of white copy paper covered the entire floor of the unit in a chaotic pile, several inches deep, sloping up to cover a back corner of the unit to a height of several feet—thousands of pages. Tens of thousands.

Staffman bent and picked up a sheet. One side was covered with finely printed text. He recognized the familiar formatting of a printed e-mail—sender header with the outgoing e-mail address, date and time it was sent, and the subject line. In this case, just one word: *Please*.

He continued reading, aware in his peripheral vision that the Coach and her team had each picked up their own sheets of paper.

IF YOU COULD JUST TELL ME THE NEXT FEW SUPER BOWL WINNERS, OR ANY BIG SPORTING EVENT, REALLY. I WOULDN'T BE GREEDY—I'D JUST BET ENOUGH

TO GET MY FAMILY BACK ON ITS FEET. IT'S BEEN RE-
ALLY TOUGH THE PAST FEW YEARS, AND . . .

Staffman skimmed the rest, a tale of bad luck and illness and
woe, a desperate bid for sympathy that had ended up ignored in a
New Jersey storage unit.

He lifted his eyes from the paper, realizing what the unit actually
held.

"These are the questions," he said. "From the Site."

The Coach looked up from her own sheet and nodded.

"Must be," she said. "But it can't be all of them. There's a lot
here, sure, but he must have received millions of questions. Billions."

Staffman waded into the storage unit, slipping and sliding on
other people's dreams as he made his way to the back corner. Before
he'd even made it halfway, he set off a cascade that caused the higher
stack of printouts in the corner to slide away, revealing what he knew
he'd see—a heavy-duty industrial printer, the kind used at office service companies and print centers, designed to run nonstop, all day
long, doing high-volume jobs.

As Staffman drew closer, he could see lights blinking on the machine's display, indicating both a low ink supply and an empty paper
bin—a secondary unit that had apparently held many thousands of
pages, designed to continue working independently for days, even
weeks without a resupply.

"What are we looking at?" the Coach asked from behind him.

Staffman's mouth twisted. All this way, everything he'd done,
everything he'd have to live with for the rest of his life—for a
dead end.

"This is where the questions went when people sent them to the
Site. They came to this printer—it must have an Internet connection—
and then they were printed. The machine just went ahead and did that
until it ran out of paper."

"I understand that, Dr. Staffman. I would like to know why the Oracle did this."

Staffman squatted down, inspecting the printer.

"I . . . don't know, Coach. Maybe the e-mail address was a ruse of some kind. Or . . . I don't know. It doesn't make any sense."

The Coach grunted, her disapproval clear. Staffman heard her speak quietly to one of her men.

Staffman focused, trying to think through the system, trying to understand why the Oracle would have set it up.

He moved laboriously to the back of the machine, shoving away drifts of Oracle questions in order to access the printer's ports—and then he saw it.

Staffman reached down and plucked a thumb drive from a USB port on the back of the printer and held it up. He smiled.

The Coach's man returned with the security guard. Staffman walked out of the unit, holding the flash drive carefully, cradling it like a robin's egg, only dimly aware of what the guard was telling the Coach.

"I'm sorry," he heard him say. "This tenant paid in cash for a year, up front. We take names and contact information, but I'll be honest with you . . . we don't verify any of that for cash transactions. We only do it if they're paying with credit. You can have what I've got, but I wouldn't expect it to pan out."

"Security footage?" the Coach asked.

"We only keep it for two weeks," the guard answered. "And I can tell you, no one's been in this unit for a lot longer than that."

"Well, that is not very helpful," the Coach said, her tone dark. "Not very helpful at all."

Staffman tuned out the rest of the conversation. He was sitting on the cold ground outside the storage unit, one of his notebook computers open on his lap, poking around inside the flash drive. It wasn't even encrypted.

They probably couldn't, he thought. *The printer's too dumb to deal with encryption.*

The drive held just a few very simple lines of code—macros, operating instructions telling the machine how to manage its print buffer—its short-term memory.

The printer was set up to receive jobs via e-mail. Ordinarily, those tasks were stored in an onboard hard drive, which allowed for a great many options for the printer's operators. Many jobs could be queued, or they could be retrieved and reprinted if an error occurred. The code on the flash drive told the printer to bypass that system entirely. All incoming e-mails were sent directly to the printer's buffer where they were held only long enough for the job to be printed, then erased.

He had assumed something like this would be the case when he first cracked the Oracle's e-mail address. He'd expected a massive storage system holding terabytes of data—all those e-mails, stored in a huge database. Instead, he'd seen something tiny—well under a hundred megabytes. That meant, probably, that the e-mails were being offloaded somewhere else, but the network trail had stopped dead. So the e-mails were either being deleted, which didn't make sense, or they were being transitioned to hard copy . . . they were being printed.

Staffman didn't know why the Oracle had chosen to set things up this way—he presumed that the Oracle, or his people, had intended to clear away the printed e-mails on a regular basis, but obviously that plan had faltered in some way.

Not that any of this was useful, nor would it help him locate the Oracle.

He looked up at the Coach, who was giving instructions to her men. The woman paused and looked at Staffman. Her gaze was cold, sharklike. She held Staffman's eyes for a moment, freezing him down to his spine, then turned back and continued talking to her team.

He knew how the Coach worked. Do what she asked, and you would be rewarded, comfortable for the rest of your days. Fail her, and even if she let you live, she would use her apparently endless levels of influence to ruin your life, so that the next time she came calling, you'd be so desperate that you would do whatever she wanted, without question.

Staffman turned his eyes back to his laptop, scanning through the code on the flash drive for anything that could help him—any clue at all—but there was nothing. It was just two lines of incredibly simple programming.

But . . . no. There was more—a few lines of header text, the sort of thing many programmers inserted into their code as a sort of signature, the same way e-mails might have a generic sign-off at the end of the relevant text. Staffman hadn't even registered it at first—it was so common that he skimmed over it without thinking, looking for the meat of the program, the lines that actually did something.

But he looked now, and he saw that the signature consisted of a single phrase. A very particular phrase:

WOMEN, BY THEIR NATURE, ARE NOT EXCEPTIONAL CHESS PLAYERS: THEY ARE NOT GREAT FIGHTERS.

His eyes widened.

He knew that quote—Garry Kasparov had said it. He also remembered the woman who'd placed these words up on a little sign over her desk, from twenty-five years earlier when they'd both been working at PARC. She'd put up the sign, and she always inserted the phrase into her code, too.

She had apparently thought she was making some kind of point. Well, good fighter or not, she'd just lost.

"Coach," he said, looking up, relief flooding through him. "I know the woman you want. I can tell you all about her. Either she's the Oracle, or she knows him."

"Well, good," the Coach said, smiling, her eyes suddenly warm again. "I'm sure we'll be able to track her down without any trouble. Good job, Dr. Staffman."

She turned back to her men and gave them a significant look.

"Looks like the tech team's done. Time for the field team."

CHAPTER 29

Cathy Jenkins rinsed tiny, chamomile-smelling bubbles of soap off her hands. She shook the excess droplets of water into the sink and turned off the brass faucets.

She looked at her reflection in the mirror and frowned, placing her index finger on her cheek. She pulled down the skin under her eye, smoothing out the wrinkles. Tired. Or maybe just old.

Cathy fussed with her hair, thinking about lunch. Becky was down in the kitchen getting it ready. They would eat on the back deck while watching the seagulls dive. She smiled at herself in the mirror, looking old but feeling young.

Nothing from her twenty-plus years of contented marriage to Bill Jenkins, nothing from the quarter century before that, had ever shown a glimmer that she'd end up in love with a fiftysomething fellow widow. But then again, she'd never expected to be in love again at all after Bill died, so all things considered, Mrs. Shubman had turned out to be quite the wonderful little surprise.

Cathy opened the bathroom door and stepped into the upstairs hall. She looked critically at the slight patch of wear running down the center of the beige carpet as she walked toward the stairs leading down to the living room.

She was starting to think she might redo the rest of the house. Just do the whole damn thing. Why not? She had five million bucks. She could afford it, thank you, John Bianco. Or Will Dando. Whichever.

She started down the stairs.

"Becky," she called from halfway down the stairs, "is lunch ready? I'll set the table out back, if you don't need any help in the kitch—"

Cathy stopped with one foot halfway to the next step, hovering in the air. Her hand tightened around the banister.

Six men, all in khaki pants and short-sleeved pastel dress shirts, stood looking up at her, waiting. Four of them carried long, black guns—shotguns, she guessed, and the remainder held pistols with elongated cylinders attached to the barrels that she recognized from movies as silencers. The shotguns were pointed directly at her, and the eyes of the men holding them were hard.

Turn. Run back upstairs. Lock a door. Find a phone.

Turn. Run back upstairs. Lock a door. Find a phone.

Cathy didn't move. Slowly, she processed another piece of information that her eyes had been trying to feed her since she got her first view of her violated living room.

Becky was on the couch. Sitting next to her, in a pose that would almost have been companionable but for the gunmen in the room, was a woman. She was older, probably in her sixties, maybe well-kept seventies, and elegant. She wore a black suit with a blue scarf tied around her neck. She looked utterly ordinary, like a PR executive, perhaps.

Everything was ordinary. Except for the guns.

"Mrs. Jenkins," the woman said pleasantly. "I'm the Coach. Will you come join us, please?"

Cathy's foot landed heavily on the step below her, and she almost stumbled. She caught herself with a hand on the wall and felt a fingernail bend back.

Ignoring the pain, Cathy walked unsteadily down the remaining steps and into the living room. She passed two of the pastel and khaki gunmen, who moved to stand between her and the stairs. She could see Becky's face much more clearly now—terror, nothing else. Her eyes flicked back and forth wildly between her captor, Cathy, and the gunmen.

I write code, for God's sake! Cathy thought, desperate. *What is this?*

But she knew, of course.

"Sit down, just there," the Coach said. She gestured to the other couch. "You, too, Mrs. Shubman."

Becky looked at her, her face confused. The Coach smiled gently at her and gave her a slight push on the shoulder. Becky stood and stumbled around the glass-topped coffee table to the other couch. Cathy sat down next to her. Through the picture windows that looked out onto the beach, she could see sunbathers and people walking hand in hand, off in the distance.

As soon as Cathy sat down, she reached for Becky's hand and met it as it grasped across the cushions for her own.

"Are you all right?" she whispered.

Becky nodded—but she didn't talk, and Becky Shubman *never* stopped talking.

"I apologize for the intrusion, ladies," the Coach said. "We'll be out of here just as soon as possible. Before anything else, let me say the thing people in these situations always say. In this case, though, it's the truth. I promise. We don't want to hurt you."

She interlaced her fingers, nails painted a shade of blue that nicely complemented her scarf. She raised her eyebrows and tapped her thumbs a few times, as if considering how to begin. Cathy watched her, and to her surprise, felt impatient.

"Please," she said, "what do you want? Money?"

The Coach's mouth quirked. Her eyes looked almost amused.

"Do we look like we're here for money?"

"I don't know!" Cathy said. Becky squeezed her hand.

"Relax, Mrs. Jenkins," the Coach said. "We just want information. We know that at least you, and probably both of you, set up data security for the Oracle. We need to know who engaged you to do this."

Becky's grip tightened another notch. The Coach leaned forward.

"This doesn't have to go the intimidation route, either. You can just think of it as a job. We're happy to pay you for your help, in fact."

"I don't know what you're talking about," Cathy said. "Who the hell are you?"

The Coach sighed. She held out her hand, and one of the gunmen placed his pistol in her palm. The Coach held the weapon up, displaying it to the women. To Cathy, it looked singularly ugly; it gleamed dully like some sort of malevolent metal insect.

"Personally," the Coach said, "weapons like this scare the hell out of me. The idea of killing someone is horrible. You never get tough about it. I remember everyone I've ever had to kill, or even hurt. Whatever lives they had left, whatever moments of happiness they had left, disappeared because of me."

She handed the pistol back to the gunman.

"In my heart, I don't believe I'm a killer. However," she said, gesturing at the stony crew standing around them, "these men certainly are, and every one of them is completely fine with that label. I want you both to understand that, and be frightened, because the last thing I want to do today is walk out of here with another face or two to keep me up at night.

"I'm going to ask you a few questions, and I'd like you to answer me honestly. That doesn't seem like too much to ask, does it?"

A sickening suspicion began to dawn in Cathy's mind, related to a certain turn of phrase she might have inserted into her program code for the Oracle's e-mail system—just a reflex, something she included in almost everything she created.

The Coach pointed her index finger, with the nail painted that incongruous shade of royal blue, directly at Cathy's face.

"Here's why you want to answer honestly," she said.

She shifted her finger to point at Becky.

"Because of what I'll do to Mrs. Shubman if you don't."

The Coach's eyes were sincere, open, without guile.

"Imagine, Mrs. Jenkins, feeling her hands on you, feeling the missing fingers, and know that they're missing because of a choice you made . . . assuming you get to feel them at all. Hands come after fingers."

Becky's hand clenched on Cathy's.

Cathy bowed her head. She looked at Becky.

"I told her we don't know anything, but she didn't believe me," Becky whispered. Her voice was tiny, like a child's. "What are we going to do?"

The Coach waited patiently.

Cathy smiled sadly at Becky.

"His name is Will Dando. He lives in New York," she said, not looking anywhere but Becky's face. "I don't know if he's the Oracle or just works for him, but I think he's probably who you want. He's listed. I can get you the number, if you want it."

Becky sucked in a little breath. Cathy had never told her that she'd figured out John Bianco's real name. She felt Becky's hand loosen on hers.

"Thank you," the Coach said. "We'll want to verify what you've told us, but it shouldn't take long, and then you'll never have to see us again. And isn't it better this way?"

Cathy saw Becky's eyes narrow. She cocked her head at the Coach, who was dialing a cell phone she had produced from within her suit. Very deliberately, Becky extended her hand toward the other woman. She slowly, elegantly curled down all but her middle finger, leaving it standing straight up.

CHAPTER 30

L eigh Shore left room 1952 of the Waldorf-Astoria and turned
right. She walked down the broad, silent hallway, feeling the
slightly imperfect fit of her entirely new set of clothes—a light
gray skirt suit, well cut—with every step. It needed a touch of tai-
loring, but really, it wasn't bad—and it was certainly more expensive
than any other clothing she owned.

There had been three differently sized versions of the suit in
room 1952, along with underwear and shoes. Leigh had picked the
best fits from the available options, disrobing completely in front of
the obviously embarrassed, pregnant Asian woman she'd met there.
The woman had explained the rules and taken her purse, jewelry (not
that she was wearing much), cell, laptop bag, and clothes. Leigh was
given a brand-new laptop, a notepad, and a few sharpened pencils
and directed to head to room 1964.

And now that door stood before her, waiting. Her legs were tin-
gling. Why was that? That made no sense.

Leigh stared at the door, trying to calm herself. Trying to focus.
It wasn't working, and so, what? Leave?

No. Absolutely not.

She reached up and knocked.

A shadow moved behind the peephole in the door, blocking the light momentarily. The impulse to run gripped Leigh, so strongly that she half turned before she gathered herself. A click from the door handle, and then the door opened.

A man, white, on the youngish side by complexion, although these days that could mean anything from twenties to forties. Jeans—nice ones—a button-down shirt, tucked in, good shoes, all of which broadcast a picture of casual wealth. Sunglasses, and a mop of light, blond hair.

That's a wig, she thought. *He's wearing a disguise.*

"Ms. Shore," the man said.

"The . . . Oracle?" Leigh said, hesitating a bit.

"That's right," the man said.

"Very pleased to meet you," Leigh said. She extended her hand and received a brief, firm shake in return.

"Come in," the Oracle said. "Have a seat over there—couch or chair, doesn't matter."

Leigh moved inside, seeing a large, well-appointed room with a separate sitting area—a suite. A tray with snacks and drinks sat on a wooden coffee table between a couch and two armchairs. Leigh sat on the couch, placing the laptop and notepad on the cushion beside her.

"Can I offer you anything?" the Oracle said. "There's soda, water . . . uh, anything you want from the minibar."

She realized that he was nervous, too, and felt herself starting to relax. The Oracle, whatever else he might be, was clearly a human being.

Leigh smiled at him, a big, fifty-thousand-kilowatt smile, one of the most potent weapons in her arsenal.

"Just water, thanks."

The Oracle clinked a few cubes of ice into a glass from the silver bucket on the tray, then filled the glass with water. He handed it to Leigh and sat in one of the armchairs.

"Thank you for seeing me," Leigh said. "I'm glad we were able to put this together."

"It's my pleasure," the Oracle said.

Leigh smiled again and took a sip of water. An awkward silence descended.

"Well, good," the Oracle said. "Would you like to, uh, get started?"

"Absolutely," Leigh answered, putting her glass on the table and picking up the laptop. She flipped it open. "How much time do we have?"

"As much as we need," the Oracle said.

Leigh's eyebrows raised, but she nodded. A short burst of typing on the laptop, and then she gave the man sitting opposite her a look she hoped was direct and businesslike.

"First question," she said, "what do I call you? Are you comfortable with Oracle?"

The man gave an embarrassed shrug.

He's such a . . . person, she marveled. *Almost ordinary.*

"That's probably easiest for now, I guess. It's a little goofy, I know."

"But it's accurate, right? It's like calling a man who puts out fires a fireman. You are an oracle, after all. You see the future, and you tell us about it."

The Oracle nodded.

"Fair enough."

"Next—and this is off the record, just something I'd like to know. That business in the other room. Everything I brought with me is back there, and—"

"Oh, of course," the Oracle said. He pulled a plastic card from his pocket and held it out. "This is the key to 1952. You can get your things when we're done here. And I am sorry about the security stuff, too, but . . . you understand."

Leigh took the keycard and slipped it into the breast pocket of her suit.

"I do. I get it. Not even an audio recorder, though? That's pretty standard equipment for an interview like this."

The Oracle reached out and grabbed a pretzel from the tray. He chewed slowly, swallowed.

"I don't want my voice on tape. That's why we gave you the laptop, Ms. Shore. You can take all the notes you want. We'll review them once we're done here to make sure the quotes are accurate, then you get them back on a thumb drive."

Leigh nodded. She extended her hands over the keyboard, then pulled them back.

"Last question before we start. What makes you think people will believe me about any of this?" she said. "I won't have any evidence that we met, other than my word. For a lot of people, that won't be enough. After all," Leigh continued, "I'm not exactly Barbara Walters. I'm not even TMZ."

The Oracle leaned forward.

"I've read your work. You're selling yourself short," he said. "But I'll do two things. I'll put something up on the Site about this interview so that people know it's legitimate. And, second, I'll give you a prediction tonight that you can put in your story to prove that you met me."

Leigh felt her face go slack. The Oracle just watched from behind his sunglasses, and, no, he was definitely not ordinary.

"That . . . that would work, I think," Leigh said.

The Oracle smiled and leaned back in his chair.

"I think so. But you must have a lot of questions for me. Go ahead."

"All right, Oracle," Leigh began.

He winced, his forehead wrinkling.

"That's terrible," he interrupted. "I didn't realize how awful that would sound. Just call me J— Just call me Jim, all right? That will work as well as anything."

"Jim it is," Leigh said.

"So. The first question, the first real question," she continued, "is pretty simple. How do you predict the future?"

The Oracle hesitated. To Leigh, it seemed as if he was thinking about how to respond, which seemed strange. He had to have known this would be something she would ask.

He looked off to one side, smiling a little, as if sharing a private joke with himself. He sighed, then looked back to Leigh.

"I don't know," the Oracle answered. "I dreamed all of this."

Leigh looked up from the laptop.

"You . . . dreamed it?" she said, very focused.

"Yes. About eight months ago. Voices spoke to me in my head while I was asleep. A little later, I noticed that the things I dreamed were starting to come true." His mouth twitched. "And here we are."

Leigh almost felt drunk. These were the answers. What everyone—everyone—wanted to know. But . . . a dream? A *dream*?

For the first time, she wondered whether the answers she would get might not be the answers she—or anyone else—would want.

"Have there been any other dreams since then?"

"No, just that one set of predictions, but they go out for a long while from now—hundreds of them."

"Why not release all of them at once? Why parcel them out like you have?"

"The predictions came to me. I'm using my best judgment about what to do with them."

"So you came up with the Site on your own?"

"I have had some help from some people close to me. I couldn't do what I'm doing without them."

"I don't suppose you want to tell me who any of them are?"

The Oracle nodded.

"Sure, want their cell numbers? Hold on, I'll read them off slowly."

A pause. Leigh looked up from her keys.

"Nah," he said, his tone light.

"Right," Leigh said. She smiled as she said it, but she could hear a snappish tone in her voice. She flexed her fingers.

"Do you want to stop for a little while?" The Oracle asked.

"No, that's all right. Just a bunch of quick typing. I'm fine, Jim," she said.

Leigh leaned forward.

"Three things," Leigh said.

The Oracle nodded.

"First, why do you think you were sent this information? Second, do you know who sent it, and if so, who is it?" Leigh said. "And finally, what are you actually doing with the predictions? You mentioned a moment ago that you're relying on your judgment—what exactly does that mean? For months, rumors have persisted that you're selling information about the future to wealthy individuals. That doesn't seem particularly altruistic."

The Oracle crossed his legs, resting his ankle on his knee. He looked out the window, and Leigh followed his gaze, out across the roofs of the west side of Midtown.

The Oracle looked back at Leigh. His face was solemn, and he contorted it into what looked a little bit like a smile.

"I'll answer your second question first," he said. "I have no idea who sent me the predictions. Maybe there's some code or pattern in them that would give me the answer, but if there is, I'm too stupid to see it.

"There are only a few possibilities," he continued. "Number one, someone out there in the future sent all this information back to me. Or maybe someone in the present sent me a list of things they were planning to do, and they're making all the predictions come true, one after the other. Or no one's behind it at all, and it's all just some accident of physics."

"Surely you have some guess, though?" Leigh said. "You've been living with these predictions for more than half a year. If you had to gamble on one of your three theories, which would it be?"

He smiled.

"I'm the Oracle. There's no such thing as gambling when you know the future. Anyway, it doesn't matter. How I got the information, and even why I got it, isn't important. It's about what I do with it.

"Let's say I read a book that, oh, teaches me how to weave a rug. Does it matter if I bought that book, or checked it out from the library, or, hell, stole it? No. What makes a difference is whether I go out and weave a rug, or if I just let the information sit in my brain. Taken to the next level, it's how I use the rug once I've woven it. Do I sell it, do I keep it, do I give it away?"

Leigh took that down and read over her last few paragraphs.

"Okay. So what are you actually doing with the predictions? Why did you create the Site?"

Again, the Oracle paused before responding.

It felt to Leigh like he was going off script, moving away from whatever answer he'd originally planned to give. Which raised the question: Had he shifted toward the truth, or lies?

"The Site was part of a bigger plan to attract buyers for the predictions. It was a way to ease the world into the idea that someone out there could see the future."

"Did that work?" she said, typing.

"Yes," he answered. "The Oracle has made over fourteen billion dollars."

Leigh's hands froze.

"So that's really all this is about? Just . . . money?" she said, not looking up from her screen.

She could hear disappointment in her voice—no, something more profound. Disillusionment.

"That's where it started."

"And now?"

"It's more than that," the Oracle said. "I've used the money to do things that haven't been made public. I've given away over a third of that cash. To charities, anonymous donations, things like that."

Leigh raised an eyebrow.

"That has to make you the largest charitable donor in history. Why?"

The Oracle smiled.

"What the fuck am I going to do with fourteen billion dollars that I can't do with nine? It didn't seem right to take all that good fortune and not do something for other people."

The Oracle reached up under his sunglasses, careful not to knock them off, and rubbed at his eyes.

"Also," he said, "I'm trying to make up for killing twelve people when this whole thing started."

Leigh's reporter's instincts lit up, even as her disappointment in what the Oracle was turning out to be deepened.

". . . what?" she managed.

"You remember the Lucky Corner Massacre?"

"Of course," Leigh said cautiously. "It was huge news. Last year. Like eight months ago."

"I did that."

Leigh thought for a moment, trying to remember the details.

"But wasn't it just a bodega robbery that went bad over on Ninth? A couple of patrol cops walked into the store while it was happening. I don't remember exactly how it played out, but . . ."

"The bad guys saw the cops and started shooting," the Oracle said, his voice dull.

"First, the owner of the deli—his name was Han-Woo Park," the

Oracle went on. "Then one of the patrolmen. Officer Leonard Es-posito. His partner made it out of the store and called for backup, and it turned into a hostage situation. SWAT had to go in, eventually. The kids who were robbing the store weren't interested in negotiat-ing. They'd already made their minds up to go out as street legends, have songs written about them."

"How can you know that? Did you know them?"

"I bought transcripts of the negotiator's conversations with them."

"Is that legal?"

The Oracle shrugged.

"Anyway," he continued, "the cops went in after a few hours, and it all went to shit. Twelve people. The thieves—they were just kids, only sixteen. Robert Washington and Adewale Deluta. Customers—Andy Singer, Maria Lucia Sanchez, Barry Anderson, Chantal L'Green, Amanda Sumner, Jim Roundsman, and Peter Roundsman. He was eight. And another officer, Jerry Shaugnessy."

Leigh thought this over.

"You weren't there," she said, finally. "Were you?"

"I was standing outside the Lucky Corner with the rest of the crowd, behind the police cordon, waiting."

"Then how . . . ?"

"Why do you think those cops went into that store in the first place, Leigh? I told them to. One of the first predictions I dreamed was about the Lucky Corner. Back then, I didn't understand the rules. I was trying to figure out whether the predictions had to hap-pen, or if they could be changed."

"Can they?" Leigh broke in.

"No," the Oracle said, one short word, like a vault door closing.

They were both silent for a moment.

"I wanted to stop it," he went on. "I thought, you know, why would I have been given these predictions if I couldn't do something about them? It just . . . made sense. I called 911 and said I'd overheard the two thieves planning to rob the deli. That's why the cops went in the store, and that's how the whole thing started."

"You can't hold yourself responsible," Leigh said.

"You sure? If I hadn't called the cops, those kids would just have taken their money and left. Because of my action, what I did, trying to be a goddamn superhero, all those people are dead."

Leigh hadn't typed anything for a few minutes. She watched the Oracle. He was emotional, upset. He wasn't lying—and honestly, about causing the death of twelve people—why would he?

The Oracle stood up and walked over to the window. He stared out in silence. She was getting such a sense of weight from him, of a burden he could never set down. It radiated out from behind the sunglasses and the stupid wig, a haze of sad dignity.

He turned away from the window, returning to his seat.

"Look. I didn't just ask you here to tell you about myself," the Oracle said. "I wasn't originally planning to talk about this, but there's something else—something I think the world needs to know. Get ready to take this down. It's important to get the details right."

Leigh put her hands on the keyboard. She leaned forward on the couch, watching the Oracle's face, feeling the gigantic change her life was about to undergo looming over her like a tsunami.

"Go ahead. I'm listening."

The door to the room burst open with a gigantic crash, the locks shattering as the screws pulled out of the doorframe. A large circular dent could be seen in the center of the outside of the door as it smashed open and bounced off the inner wall of the room. A man dressed in black coveralls, holding a metal tube with handles attached to either side of it, stepped back from the destroyed door.

The Oracle bounded up from his chair. His knees jolted the coffee table, and the pitcher of water spilled, along with the ice bucket and the pot of coffee. Liquid soaked the tray and dripped over the sides of the table.

Leigh inadvertently slapped the laptop closed, clutching it to her chest like some sort of wholly inadequate combination of shield and prized possession.

Someone appeared in the doorway—an older woman, something like a sharp suburban grandmother.

"Will Dando?" she asked, eyes cast in the Oracle's direction.

"Yes?" he said, and then he cringed with his whole body, as if realizing that he had just made some sort of a gigantic, unfixable mistake.

Will Dando? Leigh thought, trying to process.

"Pleased to meet you," the woman said.

The woman lifted her hand. She held a little black object, a bit larger than a deck of cards. Her hand clenched, and two darts shot out into the Oracle's chest, attached to the object by long, curling wires.

The Oracle—Will Dando—fell to the ground, his limbs convulsing. Leigh leapt to her feet, looking desperately to either side for somewhere to run.

A moment of sharp, invasive pain in her stomach, dwarfed a moment later by agony in an entirely different category, juddering through her muscles.

She fell to the floor and landed facedown in the thick carpet, narrowly missing cracking her head open on the coffee table. She felt water dripping down from the table onto the center of her back. Her vision dimmed.

"Bring them both," she heard the woman say.

CHAPTER 31

Will opened his eyes. He was lying on his back on something soft. Fading in above him was a rapidly moving hallway; dark-green-on-gray-striped wallpaper and a beige ceiling rushing past on either side, illuminated by brass light fixtures on the walls.

He tried to sit up and found that he couldn't. He could lift his head, although something was pressing down on his forehead, keeping it from moving more than an inch or so. He peered down his body, seeing straps across his chest, his waist, and over his wrists and ankles.

Men in light blue, short-sleeved shirts hovered above him. He decided to ask them about the straps, but found something in his mouth. A little exploration by a very dry tongue suggested that it was a thick piece of cloth.

Pain. It felt like every muscle in his body had been occupied with holding up something very heavy for six or seven hours without a break. The pain was localized somewhat around two small spots on his chest. An image came to Will's fogged mind: he was standing on an olive carpet, looking down at two long wires extending out from his chest, curling like overstretched Slinkys. And with that came the rest.

Will cried out against the gag in his mouth, but the resulting noise was muffled, barely audible even to himself. The men on either side of him were dressed like paramedics, might even be paramedics, and they were rolling his gurney down the hallway of the Waldorf. An IV bag dangled from a hook on a pole above him, but as far as Will could tell it wasn't connected to his body. Will caught a glimpse of a room number as they passed—1904. They hadn't yet left the floor where he'd been taken.

I must only have been out for a few minutes, he thought. *What was that thing? A Taser, I guess? And that woman.*

He tried to fight through his rising panic. Someone had figured out that Will Dando was the Oracle, and they'd known where to find him. But the only people who had known Will was at the hotel were . . . Hamza and Miko.

Will could see it in his head. Somehow, the name Will Dando had been connected to the Oracle, and whoever had done that had simply . . . well, they'd probably just googled his address and headed on over. If his arm hadn't been strapped down, Will would have punched himself in the face.

Hamza had been after him for months to move into a new apartment, someplace with more security, more room, an address they could hide behind one of the shell companies Hamza had set up— somewhere with a doorman, at the very least, but he hadn't wanted to take the time.

Will envisioned the older woman and her cronies breaking through the door to his apartment in much the same way she'd broken into the hotel room. Hamza would have been there, and probably Miko by then as well.

Will began, involuntarily, to think about the methods the woman might have used to get his location out of Hamza—or Miko and her unborn baby, for that matter.

And then, another idea, just as unpleasant.

Hamza and Miko weren't the only ones who had known where he was. Leigh Shore had known too. She'd set him up.

The paramedics rotated Will's gurney and pushed it into a waiting elevator. A second gurney rolled into the elevator, directly to Will's right. He turned his head as far as his strap would allow and rolled his eyeballs to the point where they began to hurt with the strain. On the other gurney, her eyes wide and locked on Will's, restrained and gagged, lay Leigh Shore.

I guess she didn't set me up, was his first thought. His second: *I'm so sorry.*

The elevator doors opened and the paramedics pushed both gurneys out. Will's view changed to a low ceiling of smooth concrete and long fluorescent lights. The parking garage.

A quick glimpse of the rear doors of an ambulance—white, with orange and blue stripes and a logo for New York Presbyterian Hospital. The doors opened, and Will felt himself being loaded headfirst into the back of the vehicle. Alone.

A nasty thought—Leigh wasn't the Oracle. They didn't need her.

He wondered if he'd gotten her killed. Selfishly, foolishly . . . gotten her killed, all because his ego was getting a little bruised by bad press.

Will heard the front doors of the ambulance open and close and felt the shift as the two paramedics got in. The vehicle started up, began to move. A second later, he felt the gag being removed from his mouth. It was replaced by a straw, which Will sucked at involuntarily, before the thought to wonder what he was about to drink made it from mind to mouth.

Cool water spilled down his throat, pure joy across his chalk-dry tongue, and he drank three huge gulps before the straw was pulled away.

"Easy now," a light, pleasant voice said from behind his head.

"Who's there?" Will said, attempting to muster some authority in his tone, but finding it hard to rise above a whisper.

The woman from the hotel room came around to the side of Will's gurney and sat down on a bench running the length of the rear compartment. She reached over and loosened the strap holding Will's forehead.

"You can call me the Coach, son," the woman said.

"Coach of what?" Will croaked.

"Why, of the team that figured out you're the Oracle."

With the strap loosened, Will was able to turn and take better stock of the woman than he'd had time to do back in the hotel—she was slim, with gray-white hair, dark eyebrows, and a sharp nose. She wore a pair of pressed khaki trousers, a blue blouse, and elegant glasses framing bright blue eyes, and she was smiling in a way that conveyed both good humor and concern for Will's well-being. The Coach looked like she belonged in a library, expertly handling misshelved volumes and interbranch loan requests and late fees and rowdy children.

"How are you feeling, Will?" she said.

The lady seemed so sincere, so genuine, that Will found himself considering the possibility that this was all a mistake. That things had spiraled out of the Coach's control, and now she just wanted to set everything right.

"Better, a little," Will said.

The Coach patted him on the shoulder.

"I'm sorry about the Taser," she said. "But we didn't know what you were capable of, and it seemed much easier to get you out of the hotel if you were down for the count."

Will's jaw clenched, all warmth he'd felt toward her evaporating.

"You probably feel like a grilled cheese sandwich right about now, but it will pass," the Coach continued. "Your body just needs to work through all that hurt. No lasting damage, I promise."

"Leigh," Will said.

The Coach looked puzzled for a moment, then her face cleared.

"Oh, the young lady. She's in the other ambulance. She'll come along with us, for the time being."

She moved an object into Will's field of vision—the laptop Leigh had been using to take notes.

"Some very interesting material here, Will," the Coach said. "If I'd known all this before I met you, we wouldn't have had to toast your bacon at all."

She chuckled.

"See, what I was worried about, my concern, was that if you could see the future, who knew what else you could do? Maybe you could set people on fire, or stop their hearts, or who knows what? I've seen those movies."

She set the laptop down.

"You seem pretty safe, though. That's why I decided to take this little ride with you. I have to hand you over to my client in a little while, but I didn't want to miss a chance to meet you in person. I've met some movers and shakers in my time, Will, but you're right up there. Right up there."

"Who's your . . . client?" Will managed.

"You'll find out," she said and gave him a hearty, surreal wink.

"How did you find me?" Will said.

His voice was almost quaking with need. He hated it, hated saying anything at all to this woman, but he had to know.

The Coach gave a slow nod, acknowledging the question.

"There's always a way, Will. I've been in this business for forty years. I've taken a lot of tricky jobs, and I'll tell you—I never take a job if I don't see a way I can get it done. That doesn't mean the clients always have the gumption to see it through. They might not want to expend the resources, or they don't have the will. But there's always a path to the finish line.

"You were tough, though," she said, pointing a delicate, bony finger at Will. "I did some jobs for Mossad, finding Nazis, and those were hard—those Krauts knew how to cover their tracks. You were in their league, for sure."

Did she just call me a Nazi? Will thought. And then: *How did she find me?*

The answer to this question had become the one thing Will wanted to know most in all the world.

"Computers, son," the Coach said, her tone apologetic. "These days, you want to find someone, it's almost always computers. It's no fun anymore, you ask me. Used to be you'd break into someone's office and dig through their files at four in the morning, or send a girl in to loosen a man's lips after a little romance. Sometimes, I even was that girl, hard as it might be to believe."

At this, the Coach tilted her head at Will, waggling her eyebrows lewdly.

"Those were good times," she went on. "Adventures. It seemed fairer, somehow. But now, you hire some pencil-neck to sit in an office and type for a few days, and you've got your answer. It's not the same."

Will closed his eyes. He thought of the Florida Ladies and wondered if the Coach had paid them a visit as well.

"But like I said," the woman went on, "you weren't easy. The head of my technical team—now there's a strange duck, believe me! He had to jump through some hoops to find you. But it's like Archimedes said: give me a lever long enough and I'll move the world.

"My guy had his lever, he just didn't want to use it. He was scared of his own creation. And maybe he was right to be—it blacked out half the world, didn't it?"

The Coach kept talking, rambling, but Will had stopped listening. Headlines ran through his head—WITH LIGHTS OUT, DETROIT RAVAGED BY LOOTING; ALITALIA FLIGHT 579 CRASHES ON APPROACH TO DARKENED MILAN RUNWAY; UKRAINIAN NUCLEAR PLANT VENTS CLOUD OF RADIOACTIVE STEAM WHEN SAFEGUARDS FAIL . . .

He screwed his eyes shut. Little flashes of white light flared on the inside of his eyelids.

All those people . . . all of them . . . they were on him too. His fault.

He felt himself recede, until he was drifting in an interior space, floating on a black sea of guilt and uncertainty and helplessness. Floating—no, he was drowning.

". . . from my perspective," the Coach was saying, "I have to say that I admire what you've been able to accomplish. I don't know if I would have used those predictions the way you did, but I can't argue . . ."

"Enough," Will said and opened his eyes.

The woman stopped in midsentence. She looked a little surprised at the interruption, and irritated, and not much like a librarian anymore—more like a pissed-off old Viking queen.

The ambulance was slowing.

"Why?" he said. "Why didn't you just leave me alone?"

"Well, maybe I would have, Will, if you hadn't made yourself so damned interesting," the Coach said.

The ambulance came to a stop.

"In fact," she went on, a smile returning to her face, "I'd say you're probably the most interesting man in the world."

The rear doors of the ambulance opened. The paramedics reappeared, pulling Will's gurney from the back of the ambulance and extending the wheeled legs beneath it. They undid the straps and helped Will sit up. His head swam, and he almost fell back off the gurney. One of the paramedics caught him by the arm.

"Just relax. You should be completely fine in an hour or so," the man said. "Don't exert yourself too much before that."

"Thanks for the concern," Will said. He swung his legs over the side of the gurney and stood, feeling unsteady and slow.

He was outside, in the middle of a large, fenced-in area, standing on concrete in the center of a circle of cold-eyed men holding assault rifles and wearing sparse military uniforms, blank except for U.S. flag patches.

Past the cordon of soldiers stood an enormous corrugated steel building—an airplane hangar. Similar buildings stretched off to either side of it. In front of the open doors of the hangar, perched on three delicate wheels that seemed too small to hold its bulk, was a large, two-tone helicopter—white on top, navy-blue on its lower two-thirds. Painted on the white section, just below the rotors, was an American flag.

The helicopter's ID tag was visible on the tail section—five numbers: 42132. Will stared at them, trying to understand why they seemed familiar to him.

A trim, middle-aged man, graying around the temples and wearing a dark suit, appeared from behind the helicopter and came toward Will. He cut through the circle of marines and, unbelievably, put out his hand for Will to shake. Will ignored it. After a moment, the man dropped his hand. He reached inside his suit jacket and pulled out a slim black wallet, which he flipped open to reveal an FBI identification card and badge.

"I'm James Franklin, director of the Federal Bureau of Investigation. You can call me Jim," the man said, snapping his ID closed and replacing it in his jacket. "You're Will Dando."

Will nodded.

The FBI director looked past Will. He turned to follow Franklin's gaze and saw the Coach, standing near the back of the ambulance.

"Coach, thank you. For everything," Jim Franklin said. "We'll take him now."

The Coach raised a hand, her eyes sharp and focused behind her glasses.

"Anytime, Jim," she said and shifted her eyes to Will.

"It was a true pleasure, Mr. Dando. As you make your way through this next bit, just remember what I told you. You're interesting, and they need you more than you need them."

Franklin frowned.

"Uh, Coach, why . . ."

"Oh, you know me," the Coach said. "I'm a confirmed pot stirrer. Besides, I see a lot of myself in this kid. I'm actually pretty excited to see what he does next."

The Coach turned and ambled away across the tarmac, ignoring the marines, expecting them to move out of her way—which they did.

Will watched the woman vanish into the darkness of one of the hangars, like she'd never been there at all.

"Please come with me, Mr. Dando," Franklin said. "We're going for a ride."

Will walked with the FBI agent to the helicopter, the marines pacing them. The door was open; a set of steps had unfolded from the side of the aircraft for easy access to the interior.

Will's eyes returned to the five digits painted on the vehicle's tail.

42132. 23–12–4 in reverse, he thought.

The Site suddenly became very present—almost a physical pressure, as if Will were caught in the gears of a great machine, turning him to some new configuration.

He reminded himself that it had almost certainly wanted this.

Several of the marines entered the helicopter first and turned, their faces blank, to cover Will while he climbed the steps.

The helicopter's interior was huge, nothing like he'd expected, almost like a small airplane's cabin. The seats were upholstered in white leather, each with the seal of the United States of America on a piece of navy blue fabric on the headrest. Five were empty, three were occupied.

"Will!" Miko said. "Thank God."

Hamza sat next to her, staring fixedly at the bulkhead in front of him. Leigh Shore sat alone in the row behind them.

"Have a seat," Jim Franklin said, climbing into the helicopter behind him. Will immediately took the open seat next to Leigh.

"Are you all right, Leigh?" he said.

Leigh nodded, her eyes wide, staring at him.

He put a hand to his head, realizing what she was seeing. The wig and the sunglasses were long gone, presumably still sitting on the floor of room 1964 at the Waldorf. A marine entered the cabin through a small door in the front of the aircraft.

"Seat belts, ladies and gentlemen. We'll be lifting off in about five minutes," he said, then turned around and returned through the little door.

Will leaned forward and reached through the seats in front of him. He clasped Hamza by the shoulder.

"It's going to be all right," he said.

"No. It's not," Hamza said.

CHAPTER 32

Anthony Leuchten sat and stared at the Oracle. He looked so young. Like one of the White House interns.

This man—Will Dando—had thus far refused to sit down at the long, undistinguished faux-wood table that took up most of the government-standard windowless conference room. He stood with his arms folded, his friends behind him, a dark expression on his face. His eyes moved across the room without pause, scanning back and forth across its few features of note—a pitcher of water and some glasses on the table. A contingent of Secret Service and U.S. Marine guards, Leuchten himself, and a few of his aides. A small camcorder was placed on a tripod at the head of the table, oriented to capture both sides at once, which seemed to occupy a good deal of the Oracle's attention—his eyes kept returning to it, several times for each pass around the room.

He wasn't reacting the way Leuchten would have expected. He was, in fact, cool as a cuke—acting like he was annoyed some cop had pulled him over for speeding.

At least his friends were terrified.

Hamza Sheikh had both arms around his wife, as if he were trying to protect her from an oncoming tidal wave. Leigh Shore stood near them, still with the deer-in-headlights look she'd had ever since she'd been offloaded from the helicopter.

They obviously understood their situation.

But not the Oracle. He'd been abducted by agents of questionable provenance and flown to Quantico Marine Base in Virginia. He'd been bundled into this little room and introduced to the chief of staff to the goddamn president of the United States of America. And then . . . nothing. Barely a word so far.

Leuchten considered the many tactics at his disposal—anything from women to waterboarding was just a phone call away. The choice of direction was important, of course—manipulation that worked on one target could be a complete failure on another. And failure, here . . . it could not be allowed.

He took another look at Will Dando, taking in everything he could understand from the man's body language, adding to it the things the Coach had learned about him, and the dossier the FBI had hastily prepared once they'd learned the Oracle's real name.

When Leuchten added all that together, the truth was that he knew quite a bit about Will Dando.

Apparently not enough, however.

The Oracle wasn't acting like a man in his position should act. The jig was up. They had him. He was powerless, but he was acting like he held all the cards. Like he knew something they didn't— which, frankly, was almost certainly true. He was the Oracle, after all.

Leuchten turned and addressed his aides, a self-absorbed batch of position jostlers who'd sell their mothers into slavery in exchange for face time with the right influencer.

"I'm going to need you out of here, folks," he said.

For a moment, Leuchten thought he'd get some pushback. Frustration was apparent on each smooth, well-groomed face, despite the fact that these were career politicians, better than poker champions at hiding their emotions. There was no influencer more influential than the Oracle. This was nothing they wanted to miss.

"Today!" Leuchten shouted.

The men and women grudgingly left the room, most taking the chance for a last, lingering look at the Oracle and his companions.

"Folks," Leuchten said, once the room was empty other than the Oracle and his companions, "I'm going to interview you one at a time, and we'll need to keep you separated while I do that."

Hamza shook his head and closed his arms more tightly around Miko.

"No. No, that will not happen," he said. "I'm not leaving my wife. Not after what you bastards did."

One of the marines, a captain, caught Leuchten's eye with a questioning look. He considered.

"All right. We're not trying to be inhumane. This is Quantico— one of the safest places on the East Coast. Huge marine base. I know it's difficult to accept, but you should think of yourselves as our guests while you're here."

The Oracle hmmphed skeptically at this, which Leuchten found hugely irritating.

Leigh Shore apparently agreed; she was staring at Will like he was completely out of his mind.

"Son," Leuchten said, turning to address Hamza directly, "I was told about what that woman did to you and your wife. You have my sincerest apologies. She's an independent agent. We had no control over her methods."

"I—" Hamza began.

"But you did send her, right?" Dando interrupted. "Let's be clear here. Whatever that woman did, she did it because you wanted her to."

Leuchten frowned. He waited several long seconds before responding.

"The three of you can go together to a waiting room," he said, indicating Hamza, Miko, and Leigh. "Anything you need, just ask one of the marines, and they'll get it for you." He pointed at Will. "You. Stay. Have a seat."

A small group of soldiers stepped away from their posts against the wall to escort everyone but the Oracle out of the room. Dando took a few steps after them, but stopped when rifle barrels rose from resting positions to track his head. He held up his hands in surrender and called after his departing friends.

"Guys, it's going to be all right. Really. We'll be back together soon."

Once the door had closed behind them, the Oracle sat down across the table from Leuchten and folded his hands.

"Why did you kidnap us?" Dando said.

Now it was Leuchten's turn to snort skeptically.

"Mr. Dando—you have not been kidnapped. We are the United States government. We do not kidnap. You and your friends have simply been detained."

The Oracle spread his hands, palms up.

"Is there a difference?"

"Absolutely," Leuchten said. "When we do it, it's legal."

"Fine," Dando said, frowning. "Why did you detain us?"

"Really, son, that's not a game you want to play. You know who you are, I know who you are. You're here because Will Dando is the Oracle."

Dando shrugged.

"Am I under arrest?"

"Not exactly," Leuchten answered. "We just want to talk to you, to tell you something you need to know. We've been looking for you for a long time, so we could tell you this thing. But you made it so goddamn hard to track you down that we had to go through, well, quite a bit of effort."

"Effort? You killed people, you caused those blackouts, you threatened me and my friends, you—"

"Shut up," Leuchten cut him off. The kid was working up a head of steam, and maybe with good reason, but the Oracle needed to understand that he was not in control of this discussion.

"I talk, you listen. There are things you need to hear."

Dando opened his mouth, clearly ready to start blatting again.

"Will," Leuchten said quickly, before the Oracle could speak, "I can tell you where the predictions came from. I can explain everything that's happened to you, if you *shut the fuck up* for two minutes."

The Oracle's mouth snapped closed, which Leuchten noted with no small satisfaction.

"Before I begin, do you want anything? Water? I know how getting hit with one of those Tasers can dry out your mouth."

Dando hesitated, then nodded. A pitcher and a stack of paper cups sat on a tray in the middle of the table. One of the marines filled a cup and handed it to the Oracle, who drank half at a gulp.

Leuchten didn't care at all about the relative parchedness of the Oracle. Not even a tiny bit. But he did want to take a moment to consider his next play.

This was the moment. Being in this room, on this day—every bit of power and access he'd amassed in his life had been about making sure it would happen. He hadn't seen it coming, hadn't known the opportunity would fall into this particular configuration, but in the end, that hadn't mattered. When the moment came, he'd been ready.

This was what he'd been searching for his entire life. He knew what the world of tomorrow should look like—he knew better than anyone else—and now he was sitting across a table from the man who could make it happen.

The future was within his grasp.

He just had to close his fist and squeeze.

"I'm listening," the Oracle said and put the cup down.

"Here's the situation, Will," Leuchten said. "For more than ten years, the U.S. government has been working on a way to transmit information directly into the minds of people on the ground—by that I mean soldiers, agents, whoever, using signals sent from satellites. Whatever they send just appears in the brain of the receiver, like it's a thought they generated themselves."

Across the table, Leuchten saw the Oracle's eyes narrow.

"The technology isn't perfect. The biggest problem they've had, from what I understand, is the targeting—making sure the transmission ends up in the right skull. If you had ten people standing in a thirty-foot circle, you could be sure one of them would get the data. Unfortunately, you wouldn't know which one."

"What are you telling me?" Dando said. His voice had risen half an octave, which Leuchten thought was a promising sign.

He held up a hand for patience.

"During the tests, long strings of data were sent to test subjects," Leuchten went on. "The receivers wrote down the information. If they got it all, fantastic. If there were gaps, well, then they knew where the problems were. You get the idea."

He paused.

"Will, your predictions were one of those tests. The agency working on this technology had a run-through about a year ago. Something went haywire in the satellite, and the transmission beam landed way, way off course. Where, exactly, the techs didn't know, except that it was probably in New York City. Which, of course, it was."

"But they all happened," the Oracle said. He sounded bewildered. "The predictions all came true. It's impossible."

Leuchten nodded, molding his face into a sincere, earnest expression.

This was his masterstroke. The moment where he brought it all home.

He took a deep breath.

This was his destiny.

"Not impossible, Will," Leuchten said. "We've been making them all happen. We needed to know how successful the test really was. Imagine someone hearing voices in their head, seeming completely real, with no idea where they came from—well, it opened up a new realm of applications for the device that we hadn't considered."

"Mind control, I guess?" Will said. "Pretend you're the voice of God, put an idea in someone's head to do something."

Leuchten chuckled.

"The psych guys said you'd probably be smart. We kept expecting someone to start shouting from the rooftops that they could see the future. Then, we'd find that person for a chat. But you didn't do that. We never expected you would keep your identity a secret. Or if you did, that you'd be this hard to find."

"Why did you keep it going so long?"

"Because of you, Will. What you did. You've got the entire world believing everything you put on that website of yours. No one questions it, no one second-guesses, they just believe. That's incredible power. Useful power."

The Oracle leaned back in his chair, wincing a little—he was probably still hurting from the Taser.

"It sounds like you want me to lie for you—make up new predictions. And you need me to do it because you still haven't figured out how to hack into the Site," Dando said.

Leuchten leaned back, shaking his head—just a touch.

"You aren't too far off. By carefully considering the effect a pronouncement from the Oracle might have, we—and by we I mean your country's government—can influence world affairs in a positive way."

The Oracle frowned.

"The only reason people trust me is that I've never lied to them. The first time something I predict doesn't come true, they'll never believe again."

"Well, that's sort of in our hands, isn't it?" Leuchten said. "We can stop fulfilling the predictions any time we want. And then you're just an ordinary guy again. One with a lot of enemies, I'd like to add."

"I just . . . I just can't believe this," Dando said. "All this time, I thought . . ."

"I know, Will," Leuchten said kindly. "But you've got nothing to worry about. All we're asking is that you help your country. And we'll compensate you for your services, of course. Maybe not as much as you were making by selling your Oracle predictions, but no one's asking you to do this for free. If nothing else, you and your friends will be completely free from prosecution."

Dando cast his eyes down to the table. He toyed with his glass of water, tipping it back and forth from one edge to the other, almost spilling it, but stopping so the water just barely lapped the rim of the glass. Finally, he looked up. He was smiling. His whole demeanor had changed, in fact. He was back to the cocky twentysomething asshole he'd been when he'd first walked into the room.

"Good try," the Oracle said. "But I won't be doing any of that."

"Excuse me?" Leuchten said. "You don't seem to understand, Will. We don't have to let you or your friends walk out of here. In fact, most of the people I work with are firmly against that idea.

"The Oracle has disrupted the world in countless ways big and small. People are afraid of you, and you use that fear to achieve your goals. You know what that makes the Oracle? What that makes you in the eyes of the law, Will Dando? A terrorist."

He waited, letting the impact of the word sink in.

"You've heard about those black sites the whistle-blowers say we have, right? Detention centers in the middle of nowhere, no one knows what the hell happens inside?

"Well, it's true. All of that. We've got plenty of 'em, and the rules say we can hold you indefinitely. Guy like you, I think it's pretty doubtful that you'd ever see the light of day again."

The Oracle just kept smiling at him. It was unnerving.

Dando had just been told that all his predictions were trumped-up bullshit, and he clearly didn't know any better, based on the interview notes he'd given the pretty black reporter. His friends were being held prisoner down the hall, and the idea that they might be used as hostages to secure his cooperation would surely have occurred to him. He was in the middle of a United States Marine base. He could be disappeared in less time than it took to sneeze.

But he was smiling.

"Is he listening?" the Oracle said.

"Listening?" Leuchten said. "What do you—"

"No, I bet he's watching, through that. The red light's been on this whole time."

He pointed at the camcorder.

"I've got something to say to him," Dando said. "To him. Not to you. And it's something he wants to hear. Believe me. The Oracle doesn't lie."

Leuchten didn't move. Across the table, the Oracle seemed completely relaxed.

Cool as a cuke, Leuchten thought, feeling sweat run down his back.

"You've got ten seconds," Dando said, "or I'll say this thing out loud, right here in this room. He'll hear it, but so will everyone in here."

He gestured at the marines and Secret Service agents in the room and began to count backward from ten.

"Son," Leuchten said, "I don't know what you think you're doing, but you're in no position to make threats. It's just you and me. No one is watching."

The Oracle paused in his count and gave Leuchten a sour look.

"If you call me son one more fucking time," he said. "Five."

What is he going to say? Leuchten thought.

"Four."

What the fuck is he going to say? I . . . I can have the marines knock him out, or gag him, or . . . shoot him, for God's sake. I can keep him from talking. I can still stop him.

"Three."

Leuchten recognized, far too late, that this was indeed a moment of destiny, here in this dingy conference room deep inside a Virginia military base. The future would emerge from this moment, shaped into some new configuration.

"Two."

He was present. He would witness it. All his choices, all his sacrifices . . . they'd bought him that much. But ultimately . . . the future belonged to the Oracle.

Leuchten reached forward and pressed a button on the speakerphone in the center of the table.

"Sir, there's someone out here who wants to speak with you."

A pause. A long, thick pause.

"Send him in," the president said through the speaker, his voice icy. "By himself."

The Oracle stood up from the table, a satisfied look on his face. Two of the Secret Service men walked to stand on either side of him. Leuchten watched as the agents escorted Will Dando from the room.

Leuchten stayed where he was. The marines were still in the room—they probably didn't know what to do either—but he had no interest in talking to them. Five long, silent minutes passed.

The door opened, and the Oracle returned to the conference

room, followed by Daniel Green, the president of the United States. Leuchten rose to his feet.

"Sir, are you all right?" he said.

Green did not look good, not good at all. He usually glowed with ruddy good health. Now, though, his skin showed a waxy under-pallor, and the wrinkles on his face stood out as deep canyons etched into his forehead and cheeks. His eyes stared, unfocused.

"Let them go," the president said, his voice distant. "Take them home and leave them alone."

"Sir . . . are you sure?" Leuchten said. "We can't do that. This isn't the plan, Mr. President. You know that . . ."

"Let them go, goddammit!" Green roared. The dead look had left his face, replaced by an expression of rage and despair. Leuchten had never seen him so uncontrolled before, not even in private moments, behind closed doors. He glanced at the Oracle, who was standing to one side, his arms crossed, looking very self-satisfied.

"Well," Will Dando said. "I guess that's that."

CHAPTER 33

Jonas Block watched from a seat in the corner of the dressing room as Reverend Branson dismissed the fourth centerpiece option presented to him by the preternaturally patient set designers working to help create the visual presentation for the big dinner broadcast planned for the twenty-third of August.

A number of ideas had been considered—run it as a banquet, with Branson surrounded by family and friends. Or perhaps a more intimate affair, with only a few guests—theologians and politicians and significant men of business, to underscore the importance of the great man on this day that he would demonstrate his power over the false prophet.

Ultimately, Branson had decided that he would be the only person onstage, eating his meal while delivering a sermon on the power of personal choice and every individual's capacity to resist the pernicious influence of evil—demonstrated viscerally, once and for all, when he declined to allow pepper anywhere near his steak.

A huge PR campaign was in full swing for the big event—donations were up, for the first time in months. Of course, the cost of promoting the dinner was in danger of outstripping any gains they'd seen, but from what Jonas could tell, Branson didn't care at all. This was his moment—his line in the sand. He would spend any amount to win. Beating the Oracle was everything, and it had to be done in public, with the world watching, or there would still be room for doubt.

Never mind that every other prediction had come true. Never mind that Branson was trying to convince the world that the Oracle was a liar, when from all appearances the Oracle had only ever told the truth.

A fifth centerpiece was set aside, the professionally plastic smiles on the designers' faces beginning to waver.

Jonas' cell phone rang. He pulled it from his pocket and glanced at the screen.

Matthew Wyatt? he thought. *That is unexpected.*

Wyatt worked in DC—in the White House, in fact. Jonas knew that political types, especially of the less senior variety, liked to exaggerate their access. Wyatt was the real deal, though, an aide to the chief of staff. He worked directly with the hundreds of lobbyists who constantly attempted to push their agendas into the Oval Office, determining which, if any, might merit the attention of Anthony Leuchten, and then, possibly, be placed on the desk of the president.

Matt Wyatt was an old friend—they had both attended the same small Christian college in South Carolina and had kept in touch as they found themselves working in the orbit of powerful men. An old friend, certainly, but it was unusual for him to call unprompted. An occasional text, or an e-mail update once or twice a year, but a call out of the blue? Odd.

Jonas tapped the screen to answer the call and lifted the phone to his ear.

"Hey, Matt," he said. "What's up?"

"Hey, man," came Wyatt's voice, sounding excited. "Just listen. I can't talk long. I know who the Oracle is. The FBI found him, and the president just met with him, down at Quantico. It wasn't on his itinerary—we were on our way to a campaign speech in South

Carolina when we diverted to Virginia. Jim Franklin—he's the FBI director—called, and after Green hung up, he had us turn around. A briefing sheet came through before the meeting, and I snuck a look at it once he got off the plane."

"That's . . . that's incredible," Jonas said. "Who is he?"

"His name is Will Dando. He lives in New York."

Jonas closed his eyes.

Will Dando, he thought, realizing the depth of the choice that had just been laid before him.

"Matt, why are you telling me this? Isn't it . . . I mean, I'm sure this isn't the sort of thing the president wants getting out."

"It's not," Wyatt said, "but I've been listening to Branson's sermons. I know the danger the Oracle represents, and how hard you've been working to find him. That whole Detectives for Christ initiative you guys set up—it resonated with me, I guess. I think that if anyone should know who he is, it's the reverend."

Jonas marveled. Branson's idiotic idea had, somehow, worked.

"I need to go," he said. "I need to get this to Branson right away."

"That's smart," Wyatt said. "I'm not the only person who knows the Oracle's name, and I'm sure word will get out soon. I think Branson should be the one to tell the world, though. He should be first. He deserves it, after everything he's done."

Jonas lifted his eyes, to see Branson across the dressing room, powder being applied to his face as he angrily berated the set designers for some small failure.

"Yes," he said. "He does. I need to go, Matt. Thank you. I owe you."

Jonas disconnected the call. He watched Branson for a few moments, thinking.

He thought about faith, and whether it was ever anything other than a Hollywood back lot, a beautiful façade with absolutely nothing behind it.

The Oracle was a man named Will Dando.

He lifted his phone again and swiped it on. He checked his e-mail, giving the Oracle one last chance. Jonas noted with absolutely no surprise that there was nothing—no response from the man, Will Dando, who knew the future.

At that moment, for the first time in his long life as a believer, faith suddenly seemed ridiculous—a game for children and idiots. Useless, except as a tool to manipulate other people. A lie.

Branson had told him that, back in his saint-filled study. He had used almost those exact words.

Faith was gone. Faith wouldn't—couldn't—help him. Jonas cast around in his soul for something that might replace it and settled on the face of the man who had told him the truth from the very start.

Branson was a liar—but he had never lied to him.

Faith had failed. All he had left was loyalty. Loyalty made sense. Loyalty might actually get you somewhere.

Jonas addressed the makeup artists and set designers and assorted hangers-on clustered around Branson.

"I need you to leave now," Jonas said.

Branson looked up, surprised.

"What? We're not finished here, Brother Jonas."

"Trust me," he said to Branson, and then "Go," to the attendants, gesturing at the door.

After an uncertain look at the reverend, looking for some sort of contravention of Jonas' directive and finding none, they left.

"What is this?" Branson said, sounding annoyed.

"The Oracle's name is Will Dando," Jonas said, and then he explained how he knew.

Branson's face went pale under the stage makeup, then returned to his normal, hearty color as he smiled at his own reflection in the mirror.

"Well," he said, "thank God for small favors."

CHAPTER 34

W hy is she here, Will?" Hamza said, not looking away from the monitor, his fingers flying across the keyboard.

"I promised her an interview," Will said. "She just went through hell because of me. It's the least I can do."

"That's not my point. I thought we were scrubbing this place before we run. We need to be gone in ten minutes, twenty at most."

"I still have to finish packing," Will answered. "I'll talk to her while I do that."

Will walked toward his bedroom, glancing into the bathroom as he passed, where Miko was standing over the bathtub, busily stirring a paper-dissolving slurry of water, vinegar, and salt with a broom-stick handle. Next to her on the floor stood a large shredder, with a pile of papers—notes on the Site's plan, printouts of e-mails—sitting on the sink, ready to be consumed.

"Almost done," she said, not looking up. "Hurry up, Will."

The bedroom was tiny and cluttered, occupied mainly by instruments, recording gear, and an unmade bed. Will reached under the bed and pulled out a duffel bag. He looked around the room, trying to decide if he actually needed to bring any of this with him.

"I can't believe you called me," Leigh Shore said. "We got off that helicopter yesterday and I thought I'd never see you again."

She was leaning against the wall in jeans, a black MISFITS T-shirt, and an unzipped hoodie.

"I felt like I owed you one," Will said, throwing a few changes of clothes into the bag. "And I wanted to tell you that you're safe. They won't come after you. At least until November, and this should all be over by then."

"November?" Leigh asked, making no move toward any sort of recording or note-taking technology. "I'm safe until . . . November?"

"Yes. From the president, anyway. From the rest of the world, I don't know, but the U.S. government is off our backs for the next six months."

"How did you do it?" Leigh said. Her tone was flat, odd. "I thought we were dead. How did you make them let us go?"

"I knew we were all right as soon as I saw U.S. flags," Will said. "I was always afraid it'd be Libya, or someplace like that."

"Libya?" Leigh said.

"Libya, North Korea, whatever. France. You know what I mean. Some country we wouldn't want to be kidnapped by. It doesn't matter."

"Will, please," Leigh said, a note of frustration creeping into her voice. "How did you do it?"

"The president was there. Just in the other room," Will answered, speaking quickly. "After they took you guys out, that Leuchten guy fed me a line of bullshit about the government sending me the predictions in the first place."

"What?" Leigh said, her voice sharpening.

"It's bullshit, Leigh. And I'll tell you why."

Will tossed a few framed photos into his bag.

"One of the predictions was . . . well, if the U.S. government was behind the Oracle, they would never have sent it. There's no way. You know I didn't put all the predictions I got up on the Site, right? I held some back?"

"If you tell me that's what you did, then all right, that's what you did," Leigh answered.

"Well, I did. Not even Hamza knows them all, and some of them I held back because it seemed like they could come in handy if certain things . . .

"Look. I'm getting off track," he said. "Back in Virginia, I insisted that I needed to talk to President Green directly. After a while, they let me, and then I told him two things, and all of us were out of there ten minutes later."

Leigh looked at him.

"Are you going to tell me what you told the president, Will?"

Will hesitated. He knew better. But then he thought about this woman, who had been sucked up into the Site's tornado through no fault of her own. Worse than that—it wasn't like it was an accident. He had picked her, and now she would spend the rest of her life wondering what had actually happened down in Virginia, and if it would ever happen again.

He asked himself whether that was something he should be particularly concerned about, considering the big picture of everything else the Site was doing. And then he decided that, yes, it absolutely was, because this—unlike every other terrible thing he'd caused in the world—was something he could fix.

"Off the record," he said. "It has to be, and you'll understand why as soon as I tell you."

Leigh nodded, making a zipping gesture across her lips.

"I told the president that he was going to be diagnosed with Stage IV lymphatic cancer in January of next year. And then I said that I had set up all my predictions to be released on the Site, including that one, unless I tell the system once per day to hold them back."

Leigh whistled.

"Jesus. Is that true? Is he going to die?"

"I don't know if he'll die, just that he'll get diagnosed."

"What did he say?"

"Nothing, at first. I mean, what do you say to that? His face went really still. You could see him thinking it through. If the country finds out about the cancer thing, then no second term. No one will vote for a terminal president."

Will shrugged.

"I told Green to let us go and gave him my word that I wouldn't let that particular prediction leak before voting day. But if he comes anywhere near us, out it will go."

"That's why you said we're safe for the next six months," Leigh said.

"Until the first Tuesday in November," Will said. "Election day. Hopefully longer, though. We knew something like this might happen eventually—we made plans."

Will took a small hard drive that held demos of most of his original songs and stuffed it into the bulging duffel. He looked at the basses and other instruments leaning against the walls, some in cases, some not. Some of them he'd had for ten years or more. There was just no way.

Will zipped his bag closed. He stepped over to Leigh and looked her in the eye.

"For all I know, you're taping this. Maybe you've got me on video. I don't know. I don't really know you. Hamza's pissed at me for bringing you here."

"I noticed," Leigh said. "Why did you?"

"I'm guilty about a lot of things. I didn't want stiffing you on your interview to be one more."

Leigh raised an eyebrow.

"Will, honestly . . . that's stupid."

"Guilty of that too," he said.

Leigh was blocking the way out of the bedroom, standing with her arms at her sides, looking at him.

"Can I . . . get past?" Will said.

"I'm still going to write a story," she said. "I'll do my best to make your quotes from the hotel interview accurate—it'll be from memory, but I think I've got it. Hell, I've got material from three Oracle interviews, including today. If I can't put a story together by this point, I should quit."

Three? Will thought. He gazed at Leigh for a long moment. She met his eyes without blinking.

"I didn't think you remembered," Will said.

"Union Square," Leigh answered. "I recognized you right away when I saw you on the helicopter without the wig. Is that why you chose me? I've got to say, Will, I still don't get it."

Will felt his face flush.

"I, uh, used to read all the articles that came out about the Oracle," he said. "Everyone speculating about who I was, if the whole thing was real. I stopped after everything started to get so dark. But back then, you wrote an article about me. It was different from the others—it talked about me like I was a person. Tried to get into what I was thinking and feeling, maybe how hard it would be to have to deal with all this."

He shrugged.

"I never forgot it. It's why I talked to you in Union Square. I recognized your name."

They stared at each other for a long moment.

"I knew that piece was good," Leigh said. "It almost got me fired, but I *knew* it was good."

"Yeah," Will said.

He turned and yelled into the living room.

"Hamza, how we doing?"

"Getting there," Hamza called back. "You could have organized your files a little better, you know. You've got stuff all over the place here. I just want to make sure I get everything we need."

Will looked back at Leigh, who was just watching him, waiting.

"Before I forget," he said. "You'll need that prediction, so that people believe you interviewed me. I'll put something up on the Site about you, too, like I said I would."

"Thank you, Will. That will make my life a lot easier."

"Okay. Can you write this down?"

Leigh reached into the pocket of her hoodie and produced a small notepad and a pen. Will thought through the ever-shrinking set of predictions he hadn't yet put out into the world in one way or another. It didn't take long. He only had three left, and two—the ever-confounding 23–12–4 and a vague phrase about a Laundromat—weren't anything Leigh would be able to use.

The third, though . . . it was perfect. Will found that he wasn't even all that surprised. The Site had given him exactly what he'd need for every step along the way—no, not what he would need. What *it* would need.

The devil's toolbox, almost all of which had been used. But not all—at this moment, when he needed a prediction, he had exactly one left that would suit the purpose. Of course.

"In about two weeks, on the fifth of July, a guy named Manuel Escobar will hook a two-hundred-and-twelve-pound tarpon while fishing off Santa Monica. It will happen at about half past three in the afternoon."

He watched Leigh write that down, imagining the Site grinning fiendishly as he let another chunk of it loose. Leigh gave him a doubtful look. "Presidents getting cancer, and Manny Escobar catching a fish. Whoever sent you this stuff, they've got a weird sense of what's important."

"It's all important, Leigh," Will said. "If I didn't get the Escobar prediction, which didn't seem important enough to put up on the Site, I might not have had anything left for you to prove you met me."

Leigh shivered involuntarily.

"What does that mean, Will?" she asked.

"If you figure it out, let me know. I stopped thinking about it a long time ago," he lied.

"There was something else," Leigh said. "Back at the Waldorf. You were about to tell me something important that you thought the world needed to know."

Will looked at her for a long moment.

"I'm not sure what you mean," he said.

Will hoisted his bag over his shoulder and stepped past Leigh into the living room.

"Miko, can you come in here for a second? I want to talk to you and Hamza."

Miko stepped out of the bathroom, wiping her hands on her pants. Hamza looked up from the computer, his face frustrated.

"Come on, Will. We need to get this done and get the hell out of here. This is the one place people can connect to you. If we didn't have so much Oracle-related stuff here, I'd never have let you come back to your apartment. We need to get it cleaned and get gone."

"The safe house will be nice," Miko said. "Almost a vacation. New York sucks in the summer, anyway."

"No," Will said.

Hamza gave Will a questioning look.

"Are you thinking the Republic?" he asked.

"No," Will repeated. "I'll go to the safe house, but you two need to take your stuff and go someplace else, someplace I don't know about. Set up a new life for yourselves, have your baby, forget you ever knew me."

Hamza and Miko turned to look at each other. They were silent for a moment, then looked back at Will.

"Are you sure?" Hamza said.

"Yes. Go. It's all right. I'll figure the rest of this out on my own."

"Oh, Will," Miko said.

"It's all right," Will repeated. "I'll be fine."

Miko reached out and took Will's hand. After a pause, Hamza did the same. Will held his friends' hands for a long moment. Leigh watched, quiet.

"Thank you," Miko said.

"We'll all be back together before you know it," Hamza said. "My kid needs a godfather. Once this is all over."

Will released their hands.

Once this was over. He couldn't even picture it.

Will's cell phone rang. He reached for it without thinking and checked the caller ID.

"It's my mom," he said.

"You aren't home," Hamza said. "No time."

Miko snatched the phone from Will's hand. She gave him a disapproving look.

"You're about to vanish for God knows how long," she said. "Don't be a dick." She answered the phone.

"Mrs. Dando, hello!" she said. "It's Miko Sheikh. We haven't spoken in ages. How are you?"

Mom, Will thought. He hadn't spoken to her in . . . what? He'd called once or twice since the Oracle dream, but the conversations had always been short. *Two months ago?* he thought. *Three?*

Miko wasn't talking. Whatever Will's mother was saying, she didn't like it. A deep frown cut across her face. Will raised an eyebrow. *What?* he mouthed at Miko.

"Yes, he's right here," Miko said. She held out the phone.

Will didn't want to talk to his mother anymore. This felt like a bad-news call—a someone-just-died call. But he took the phone.

Miko turned to Hamza and pointed at the computer.

"Finish. Now," she said, her voice ice cold.

"Hi, Mom," Will said, hearing Hamza begin a burst of intense typing.

"Is it true?" his mother asked him. "Are you the Oracle?"

Will's veins turned to glass.

"It's on CNN, Will. Is it true?"

Will could hear fear in his mother's voice.

For me, or of me? he thought.

He held the phone away from his mouth.

"Miko, turn on CNN, quick."

Miko nodded. She picked up the remote from Will's coffee table and turned on Will's fifty-five-inch television, far too big for his apartment, one of the things he'd bought for himself in the early days of the Oracle windfall.

An anchor was speaking, over a news ticker running across the bottom of the screen: "BREAKING NEWS—Presidential spiritual adviser Rev. Hosiah Branson identifies the Oracle . . ." Footage appeared in a window over the anchor's shoulder, of Hosiah Branson standing in some sort of television studio, in front of an easel that held a blown-up photograph that Will recognized.

The glass in Will's veins shattered.

He used one picture for everything—Facebook, Twitter, dating sites—always the same image, the one time he thought he'd been photographed decently well, at a gig a few years back. His hair was a bit long, and he was smiling, and it looked like he thought he should look. And there it was, on CNN.

"According to Branson, the Oracle is a New York City resident named Will Dando," the newscaster was saying. Will's mother spoke in his ear, but he couldn't hear her.

"Reverend Branson issued his announcement, which included descriptions of an Indian or Arab man, an Asian woman, and a dark-skinned woman with dark hair and eyes that he claims are associates of the Oracle. Beyond that, we're waiting for developments. I have one of CNN's legal advisers here with us this morning, Sarah De-Koort. After the break, we'll get her opinion on whether Reverend

Branson is opening himself up to liability by essentially having outed the Oracle."

"That MOTHERFUCKER!" Will screamed at the television.

"Will!" his mother said in his ear, shocked.

"Listen, Mom, I'll be fine. Don't worry about me. You need to take care of yourself—you and Dad. It won't take them long to track you down. I'm going to send you money, to you and everyone else in the family. A lot of money. Take it and disappear for a while, and tell Emily to do it, too. Go overseas, if you can.

"I'll get back in touch soon, I promise."

"Oh, Will. Oh my God," his mother said, almost sighing into the phone. "Why didn't you tell me?"

She sounded stunned. Hurt.

"I didn't want you to worry, and I didn't want to have to deal with questions that I don't know the answers to. I'm . . . I'm sorry, Mom."

"Oh, Will," she said. Her voice seemed stronger. "I don't understand how this all happened, but I'm so proud of you. The people you saved with your predictions—you're doing something good, Will, something amazing."

Will closed his eyes.

"Thank you, Mom," he said. "But I have to go now. I love you, and I'll see you as soon as I can."

His mother was crying.

"I love you, too, Will. Please be safe."

Will screwed his eyes even more tightly shut. He ended the call. His phone immediately started to ring again. Hamza's phone lit up, and a second later, Miko's.

Hamza stood up quickly, pulling his phone from his pocket and holding out his hand.

"Phones, quick. They can track us through them even if we turn them off."

Hamza took all three phones and disappeared into the bathroom. A small sound a moment later—a splash.

"God," Will said. He felt an arm around his shoulders. He opened his eyes. It was Leigh.

"I'm sorry, Will," she said.

"It's okay," he said, pulling himself together. "It's time to go."

Hamza emerged from the bathroom, empty-handed. He looked at the monitor on Will's desk. He hesitated, then stepped quickly over to it and started typing.

"Leave it!" Will shouted.

"Will, I have to finish this. If I don't do it right, information can still be pulled off it. They'll figure out how to find us, find the cabin, the Republic. The *money*."

"Hamza!" Will cried in frustration. "They're probably downstairs right now. We've got to go! You guys can come on the plane with me—we'll separate once we're away."

"Listen, you take Miko and go," Hamza said. "I'll be right behind you. It's a charter. It's not like we'll miss the plane. But this has to be done, or there's no point in going at all."

"I'll wait with Hamza," Miko said immediately.

"Don't be silly, Meeks, just go," Hamza said, frantically trying to finish wiping Will's computer clean.

"I'll stay," she said in a quiet but very firm voice.

"Dammit," Will said. "Let *me* do it, at least!"

Hamza spared Will a half-second glance.

"You're terrible with computers. It'd take you fifteen minutes. It'll take me three. There's no question. I'm not the Oracle. You are. Go, Will."

Will hesitated for another moment.

"All right. Get out as quickly as you can." He looked at Leigh. "Come on," he said. "Let's go. I've got a car waiting downstairs. I'll drop you on the way."

Will picked up his duffel that held his clothes and ran toward the door. He grabbed a baseball cap and a pair of sunglasses from the small table to the left of the door and put them on. Poor excuse for a disguise, but it was all he had.

He looked back at Hamza, Miko standing next to him with her arms crossed across her chest. Hamza was intent on the screen, his hands moving quickly. Miko's face was heartbreaking—beautiful and pale.

"Hurry," Will said.

"Sure, man," Hamza said, not looking up. "Five minutes behind you, tops. Get going."

Leigh was already in the hall. She'd picked up Will's shoulder bag and stood at the top of the stairs. She looked scared, but exhilarated.

"Every time I see you is chaos," she said.

"Try living it," Will said. He took his duffel and followed Leigh down the six flights of stairs.

Two Lincoln Town Cars sat idling at the curb just outside his building. Will ran to the closer one and knocked on the driver's window. "Trunk!" he said.

The driver, a dark-skinned man with the look of central Africa, nodded amiably. Will ran to the back of the car and threw in his bag. Leigh pulled open the passenger door and tossed the shoulder bag into the backseat. She looked up the street. Her whole body tensed.

"Will," she said. "Look."

Will looked. Advancing in their direction along the sidewalk, still a block and a half away, was a group of about twenty people, men and women of different ages and races, unified only by a similar look of purpose. The one in the lead, a tough-looking man with graying hair and a long coat, held his phone in his hand, and kept looking from it to the address of each building they passed.

"Get in the car, Leigh," Will said, slamming the trunk closed. "We have to go."

She got into the Town Car and scooted across the seat to the far side. Will piled into the car after her, hoping that the driver hadn't been listening to the news while he was waiting.

"Macallan Airfield?" the driver asked, consulting a clipboard on the seat next to him.

"That's right, but we'll make a stop on the way. Just drive, okay? Just get us rolling."

"Of course, sir," the driver said. The car pulled away and drove to the corner, where it stopped for a red light.

Will and Leigh rotated in their seats to look back at the entrance to Will's building. The group had reached it and stood in a loose cluster around the door, in the midst of a heated discussion. Will imagined they were trying to decide whether to buzz up or just smash through the doors.

And then Hamza's head appeared from the alley next to the building, peering out cautiously at the people waiting on Will's stoop. He'd left the building through the side door from the basement laundry room. Brilliant.

Hamza turned to speak to someone behind him—Miko, had to be. The two of them emerged from the alley, each holding their own duffel bag, ignoring the second Town Car idling at the curb, trying to make it to the corner without being seen.

Leigh reached out and took Will's hand in an iron grip. Will barely noticed—he couldn't take his eyes off his friends.

"Please," he said out loud.

Will heard shouting. He shifted his gaze back to the crowd around the building's front door. They had noticed the two figures trying to slip away and were running down the sidewalk toward Hamza and Miko.

"No!" Leigh said.

The traffic light turned green. Will's Town Car pulled through the intersection and continued up the street.

Will watched, helpless, as Hamza and Miko ran. They held on to their bags for a few crucial seconds longer than they should have, and Miko fell behind. They dropped their luggage to the sidewalk and sprinted, but the crowd caught Miko. Someone shoved her to the ground from behind, and she went sprawling.

Leigh gasped.

Will saw Miko's face bounce against the pavement. Hamza turned and ran back to help her, and in moments the mob had surrounded them both. Will heard himself repeat "no, no, no" over and over again as he watched someone's shoe plant itself in Hamza's midsection, someone twisting Miko's tiny, thin arm. It was like a slide show—single frames of violence as the thicket of the mob's individual parts shifted every few seconds to allow another glimpse.

"Stop the car!" Will shouted.

He reached over and yanked on the door handle, but the driver had locked the doors when they started to move.

Leigh wrapped both arms around Will and held him as tightly as she could. Will fought her.

"Let me go, they're dying," he cried.

"Will, no, there are too many of them. You can't go back. They'll just get you, too. We have to go."

"No, you don't understand. Nothing will happen to me. The Site wants me alive!"

"Sir?" the driver asked from the front seat. "Is everything all right?"

The car had slowed. Will fought free of Leigh's arms and gave the door handle a savage yank. He spilled out to the street, sprawling on his hands and knees. He pushed himself to his feet. Now that he was out of the car, he could hear the roars of the crowd—shouts about the Oracle, and God, and the devil. Will's mind went white with fury.

"Will!" Leigh yelled behind him, from inside the car.

Will ran back down the sidewalk, toward the group surrounding Hamza and Miko. The second Town Car was still idling on the curb. Through the windshield, Will could see the driver talking excitedly on his cell phone while watching the crowd.

With two great steps, Will leapt onto the hood of the Town Car. The driver stared at him in shock.

"Call the police!" Will yelled at the driver. "Now!"

Without waiting for an answer, Will took another step onto the car's roof. He looked down into the crowd. He could see his friends. Miko was curled into a tight ball, and Hamza's arms were around his wife, trying to shield her.

"Stop!" Will shouted. "I'm here!"

The men at the edge of the crowd heard him and looked. Eyes widened, and a moment later, almost as one, the rest of them turned to see him. He could hear Miko sobbing.

"You know who I am," Will said. "What I can do. Get the fuck out of my way."

Will jumped down from the roof of the car. He stared into the face of the first person he saw, an older man, grizzled with stubble. The man stumbled back, and Will stepped forward. And so it continued through to the center of the mob, people parting to let him through, Will staring through anyone who met his eyes until they looked away.

He bent down over Hamza and Miko. Hamza's eyes were closed, his face bruised and swollen. Blood leaked from his nose and mouth, giving a thin, dark shine to the lower half of his face. Miko looked up, saw him. She looked better than Hamza, but only just.

"Will . . ." she managed, barely.

"Come on," Will said. "We have to go now. Can you get up?"

"I don't know. I'll try. Hamza . . ."

"I'll help him."

He slowly helped Miko to her feet. She cradled her belly protectively with one arm, and with the other she held out an arm to help Will pull Hamza up. Hamza stirred briefly as he was lifted, but didn't open his eyes. Will put Hamza's arm across his shoulder and looked up, half expecting the crowd to have surrounded them again. They hadn't. The path was clear, and the people who had, just moments ago, been screaming with exultation as they beat two people to death now just watched in eerie silence.

Will hobbled with Hamza and Miko to the street, grabbing their dropped bags on the way. The second Town Car was still at the curb. Miko opened the back door, and Will pushed Hamza into the car. Hamza had come around enough to help—he dragged himself to the other side of the car to make room for Miko.

Miko suddenly let out a cry of pain and clutched her stomach. She wobbled, almost going to her knees.

"Oh no," she gasped. "No, please."

"Here," Will said.

He got Miko into the backseat as carefully as he could. Her breathing was rapid, and tears coursed down her face.

"Get them to the goddamn hospital!" Will shouted at the driver, who nodded, his eyes wide.

"Will!" Hamza managed. "Get out of here."

"I can't leave you two."

"Yes, you can. You have to. It's . . . safer. Just go."

Will looked into his friend's face, realizing that "safe" in this context meant as far away from the Oracle as possible, and understanding, and agreeing.

He stepped back and closed the car door. The Town Car peeled out from the curb. Will turned back to face the crowd. In the distance, he could hear sirens approaching, and apparently so could they. People were glancing at one another, awakening to what they'd just done, drifting away down the sidewalk in small, shamed groups.

"How dare you?" Will said. He looked from face to face. Not one of them would look him in the eye. "What are you people?"

"God is with us," a man with long, gray hair said. "That's all you need to know, monster."

If Will had been holding a gun, he would have shot the man dead. As it was, he used the weapon he had.

"I am," he said. "I am a monster. You're all going to die. Horribly, and in pain. Every single one of you. You're dead. Trust the monster. The Oracle never lies."

The crowd recoiled, shock on every face. Will turned and walked away, toward the first car. He could see Leigh waiting for him.

Behind him, shouts of confusion and apology spiraled up from the crowd. Will didn't look back.

CHAPTER 35

The Town Car moved north along Ninth Avenue, inching its way through heavy traffic on its way to the George Washington Bridge.

The Oracle was hunched down in his seat, his arms clenched around his torso, sunglasses on and a baseball cap pulled down low over his face. He presented like a pill bug curled up into an armored ball after being poked.

Leigh wanted to talk to him, but the man in the front seat was a problem. Every driver in New York City understood the beautiful illusion of privacy offered by the backseat of their ride, be it a cab, limo, or Uber—that sacred trick of solitude. But this particular driver currently had the Oracle as his passenger, and the minute he learned that, all chaufferly codes of honor were likely to fly out the window.

So Leigh sat quietly, thinking about how much danger they might be in—attempting to calculate her personal threat level versus the Oracle's. She wondered where they were headed at that moment, and whether Hamza and Miko were all right, and what could possibly happen next, taking thorough mental notes toward the moment when she might be able to write it all down.

Will unclenched, sitting upright in a quick, convulsive movement. He looked around the backseat, his hands casting across the leather until they found his shoulder bag, forgotten since they had first entered the car. He ripped it open, fumbling inside until he pulled out a cell phone. He swiped it on, cursed, then flipped it over.

"What is it?" Leigh asked. "What's the matter?"

Will didn't answer. He popped open a small compartment on the back of the phone and levered out a small chip of plastic—the SIM card, Leigh realized. He pressed the control to pull down the car's window and tossed the SIM card out onto Ninth. Then, he removed the phone's battery and, a block or two farther north, threw that out too. The last item to go was the phone itself.

Leigh noticed the driver was watching the Oracle through the rearview mirror—but he didn't say anything. The holy veil was holding, at least for the moment.

She understood what Will had done. Hamza had done the same thing, back in the apartment. Phones could be tracked, easily, and the device Will had gotten rid of probably had some connection back to his actual name. She thought about news offices all over the world, and trending topics, and hacker collectives, all, finally, with something to work with. Two words: Will Dando.

Leigh tried to imagine it, tried to put herself into Will's shoes. She couldn't. Privacy, even the illusion of privacy, was too central to how she viewed herself. The ability to decide what parts of you were shared with the world seemed like it should be a basic human right—no longer an option for Will Dando. Everything he'd ever done, or thought, or bought; everyone he'd ever slept with; every choice he'd ever made . . . within a day, all that would be public knowledge.

Will reached back into his bag and pulled out a second cell phone. It looked cheaper than the one he had destroyed, less sleek, maybe a prepaid burner. He powered it on and thumb-typed for a moment, then showed the screen to Leigh.

Will: Let's talk this way?

She reached into her own pocket and removed her cell, opening a similar program and typing for a moment.

Leigh: I get it. Where are we going?

Will: Private airport just outside city. Chartered jet was supposed to take me, H, M to a safe house. Can't go now.

Leigh: Why?

Will: Paid for plane with Oracle accounts. Don't know if bad guys made connection—can't take chance.

Leigh thought about this for a little while before responding.

Leigh: Chance of what? Everyone already knows you're the Oracle. Why worried now?

Will read her screen, then looked at her, frowning. He typed for a moment, then held up his phone for her to read.

Will: Best friends just almost got killed. Maybe just beginning. You forget?

Leigh recoiled from herself. Of course she hadn't forgotten—the sight of Miko's face hitting the sidewalk would be embedded in her soul forever like a tick—but she had just meant . . . it didn't matter.

Leigh: No. Didn't forget. I'm sorry. What now?

Will: Still need to go to safe house. H set it up so it wasn't

connected—off grid, bought with cash. Private. Can finish this there.

Leigh: Finish what?

Will hesitated.

Will: Long story. Have to stay hidden until it's done. If
world knows where I am, no peace. Too many questions.

Leigh nodded.

Leigh: Okay. But if you can't fly, how?

Will looked at the driver, who was ignoring them, concentrating
on navigating the slow-moving traffic approaching the bridge across
the Hudson. He bent to his phone and went through a long burst of
typing.

Will: Need to buy this car. Twenty thousand in bag in
trunk. Emergency cash. Can offer to driver.

Leigh responded:

Leigh: He might not own the car. Sometimes they're just
hired by the company.

Will: We'll figure it out. Will you help me?

Leigh stared at the phone, focused on the last four words, seeing
all the opportunity and hazard they offered, trying to understand the
magnitude of the situation she had fallen into. She looked up at the

Oracle—no, at Will Dando—trying to see him as a person. Trying to decide whether she should leap from the car and sprint down the side of the road.

An hour later, a strange negotiation with their wary, confused driver was concluded, the Oracle was almost nineteen thousand dollars poorer, and Leigh sat behind the wheel of their new car, driving at a decent clip over the George Washington Bridge.

A sign welcoming them to New Jersey flashed by overhead, momentarily illuminated in their headlights.

"We're almost over the bridge," Leigh said. "Then what?"

"West," the Oracle answered, his eyes on the road ahead. "Then up."

PART IV

SUMMER

CHAPTER 36

This is almost over, Will thought.

He had started with one hundred and eight predictions. All but two had been released into the world in one way or another—posted on the Site, sold, used to prove his bona fides, used to escape from the goddamn president of the United States . . . and now just two.

One was the numbers, the final prediction, still incomprehensible. The other was just nonsense, a short phrase including so few details that it was impossible to understand or use. It was set to occur later that day, though, so Will assumed he'd find out what it meant eventually. The Site would probably use it to do something dire—make Hoover Dam collapse, maybe.

Will glanced out the window, watching as northern Ohio streamed steadily past, a nondescript set of flatlands interspersed with toll plazas and interchangeable towns. I-80 was a hell of a road—it would get them halfway to their destination—but not much for scenery. Everything seemed calm, ordinary. Relaxed.

That was not, in fact, the case. It wasn't just that almost all the predictions had been used. Things were accelerating. In just the past few days, he'd been abducted by agents of the president, the world had learned the Oracle's identity, he and his best friends had been attacked, and he'd run from his city like a rat scuttling down subway tracks ahead of an oncoming train.

It felt like a moment from his childhood, when he was eight or nine. He'd been riding his bike in the neighborhood and had found himself at the top of a hill. He was new to bikes at that point—his father had only taught him how to ride a month or so before. He pushed off, his speed almost instantly increasing beyond the point where his legs could keep up with the pedals, seeing traffic in the cross-street at the bottom of the hill and realizing that there was absolutely nothing he could do to avoid it other than ditching the bike, but being more afraid of the pavement than the cars, breathlessly waiting to see which catastrophe would end him.

That was this. The Site was the bicycle, and Will was riding it right into traffic. But not just Will. Everyone. The entire world.

He looked down at the newspaper in his lap, frowning.

The front page—every front page—was using the same photograph CNN had run in its original broadcast outing the Oracle's identity. Will Dando, sitting on the edge of a bandstand at a club, bass on his lap, tuning up before a show. He remembered the gig—a quick one-off in support of a hedge fund guy who could afford to hire a great support band to play under his crappy Dave Matthews-y originals. He'd had a photographer at the show, like it was some epic showcase for the ages instead of a 9 P.M. Thursday slot at the Mercury Lounge.

The pics went up on the singer's website a few days later. One shot had caught Will's eye, so he'd copied it and used it as his profile picture on a dating website or three a few years back, not unsuccessfully, either.

Now it was in the corner of every screen, on every landing page, above the fold of every paper, and Will hated it with everything he had.

He skipped past the first three articles—all Oracle related, delving deep into his past, already featuring quotes from people his life had touched in one way or another. He skipped it all. He needed to function, and sinking into the ongoing dissection of his existence would paralyze him, if he let it.

Every story not about the Oracle described a planet in revolt. Economic turmoil; significant military actions on four continents: cleanup of U.S. operations in Niger, saber rattling by a warlord in a tiny nation in Central Asia who had gathered an army and besieged a city, unrest in France, many other battles large and small; coups, plunging markets, fear.

Behind it all, the Site.

Will's mouth twisted in frustration. He folded the paper and tossed it behind him, where a small but growing pile of other publications covered the backseat and spilled onto the floor.

He opened a notebook on his lap and reached for a set of colored pencils in the passenger door's storage bay—purchased the night before, along with the papers and magazines now avalanching across the backseat, at a travel plaza off the New Jersey Turnpike. He flipped through the book and started to jot down notes from the morning's reading. Page after page was already covered by scribbled notations in various colors—Will's attempt to analyze the Site's plan, to understand what it had done, and what it was attempting to do.

The original Oracle predictions, all one hundred and eight, were written on the first several pages in black, and the fact that he had done this twice, in two separate notebooks, did not escape his notice. He'd burned the predictions. They still came true.

Events listed in green represented confirmed aftereffects of an Oracle prediction being put into the world, either by selling it or putting it on the Site. Ripples.

Anything in blue was unconfirmed, but likely—a maybe. Red events were dead ends—things that had originally looked connected but had ceased interacting with the rest of the Site's web. Will included them because it was always possible that he just hadn't seen the full set of connections yet, or that the Site would loop back and reconnect with them down the road.

Finally, purple for the big stuff. When green events meshed together to do something else, to move toward a larger purpose. As far as Will could tell, that larger purpose was represented largely by the litany of woes he had just read in the paper.

They'd only been on the road for two days, but dear God, Will missed the Internet. Staying updated on the Site's activities using only hard copy was maddening. He had a few prepaid phones he could use to get online if he had to, but he was saving them for emergencies, and checking cnn.com didn't count.

Will had tried listening to radio news as he and Leigh drove west, to stay updated in something closer to real time, but even a few hours of that had been too much. Too many breathless DJs and talk shows and morning zoos enjoying their deep dive into the life of Will Dando.

Will finished making notes on the morning's reading and closed the notebook, setting it and the pencils on the dashboard.

He looked at Leigh, sitting behind the steering wheel with her hands sensibly at ten and two. He wanted to talk through his theories, explain what the Site was doing, but the truth was that he didn't know this woman at all. They'd managed some small talk in the early hours of the drive, but eventually it became clear that Leigh wanted answers Will wasn't willing to give, and a stilted silence had descended.

The whole situation was almost breathtaking. He'd known Leigh Shore for something like three days, and now he was relying on her completely. Everyone in the world knew the Oracle's face, which meant he couldn't pump his own gas, couldn't eat in public, couldn't do anything at all without risking . . . what?

The sound of Miko's head knocking against the concrete.

Leigh was a risk, but he needed to get west, soon—because things were accelerating—and she could get him there. As long as the illusion of the Oracle held up, with all the leverage it brought him, all the things she thought he knew, they should be fine.

That was partly why he had kept the radio off, and why he'd kept conversation to a minimum. If Leigh learned too much about Will Dando, the man sitting next to her might stop being the all-powerful Oracle and become just a kid on his bike, rushing down a hill, wondering how he was going to die.

All that, and underneath and above and around it all, sick worry for Hamza and Miko. He didn't know their condition and couldn't call—didn't even know where they were. For all he knew, they were back at Quantico, being questioned by that asshole Leuchten.

Will eyed the radio, that saucy temptress, holding out its promise of world news that wasn't a day out of date.

"Just for a few minutes," he said out loud, earning him a raised eyebrow from Leigh.

He pressed the power button.

"—don't know the Oracle," Hamza said, his voice tainted with a slight overlay of static, "but if I did, I'd tell him to just keep doing what he's doing. My wife and I were hurt in the attack by Hosiah Branson's people, but that's not his fault. He's saved a lot of lives, helped a lot of people. I don't want what happened to us to stop him from what he's doing. I think he's a hero."

"Holy shit," Leigh said, "is that Hamza?"

"Yes," Will said, listening, understanding the gift that Hamza was giving him.

A second voice—a woman, assured and confident.

"You claim not to know the Oracle, but as we know, he's been revealed to be a man named Will Dando, whom you definitely *do* know. You went to high school with him, and we've spoken to people who say you two are extremely close friends. And yet—"

"He hasn't been revealed as the Oracle. Reverend Hosiah Branson just claimed he's the Oracle. I didn't hear any proof—but then again, I didn't have much time to listen before my pregnant wife and I were attacked by an angry mob Branson sent our way."

"That's how you see it?" the interviewer asked.

"Not just me," Hamza said. "I spent the morning speaking with extremely skilled and expensive attorneys, and they all agree. Branson spent months convincing his millions of followers that the Oracle's the devil. Then, he claimed Will is the Oracle and released his name and address on live TV. Branson knew exactly what would happen. That's attempted murder. He is a criminal, and I intend to do everything I can to make sure he pays for the injuries to me, my wife, and our unborn child."

"And Will Dando?" the interviewer asked. "No one has seen him since the attacks outside his apartment."

"I have no idea," Hamza said. "But if I were him, I would be far away, under the radar, getting ready to sue the shit out of Hosiah Branson."

"There we have it," the interviewer said. "Strong words from Hamza Sheikh, victim of an attack by a mob seeking the Oracle. After the break, we'll have our legal experts on to discuss the merits of the sort of claims Mr. Sheikh described."

A commercial began, and Will reached forward to turn off the radio.

"He was setting me free," he said, looking at Leigh.

"Wait," she said. "Did you know he was going to be on the radio?"

"No," he said.

"Then how did you . . ."

"Because I'm the Oracle," Will answered, lying and telling the truth at the same time.

Leigh took her eyes off the road for a minute, evaluating him.

"You said he set you free," she said. "Set you free to do what? What does that mean?"

"Right now, it means driving," Will said.

"Seriously?" she said, her voice tense. "You are aware that all this is . . . a little terrifying?"

"I know," Will said. "I'm sorry. I'll explain more when I can. Right now, it's probably safer if we just keep going."

"Yeah, well, I'm sorry to tell you this, but this is over. We have to stop."

Will whipped his head to the left to stare at Leigh.

"What? Why?"

She turned and stared back at him for a moment, then her mouth turned upward into a smile.

"Because we're almost out of gas," she said.

"Jesus," Will said, exhaling.

Leigh laughed.

"I'm sorry, man, I just wanted to fuck with you a little bit. Send a little of that terror back your way."

"Yeah," Will said. "I probably deserved it."

"Wig time," she answered.

Will looked up to see that they were pulling off the expressway. He popped open the glove compartment, revealing a blond wig, a baseball cap, and a pair of sunglasses—replacements for the disguise he'd lost back at the Waldorf when the coach had found them.

Leigh tsked in disapproval as they pulled into the gas station.

"Over eight bucks a gallon," she said.

"Yeah," Will answered, adjusting the baseball cap over the wig. "Hard to believe."

But it wasn't. The Site had been pushing up gas prices for months. All part of its devotion to making the entire world a poisoned, awful mess.

Will reached for his wallet and pulled out three twenties, handing them to Leigh, not without a twinge. They had at least a four-day drive ahead of them. ATMs weren't an option—they were just as trackable as cell phones, and his accounts were all linked to his name or Oracle-related businesses, all of which he had to assume were blown by now. They'd started the drive with about a thousand dollars, but between food and gas and cheap hotels and the daily newspaper budget, it would vanish quickly.

Will heard Leigh pop open the gas tank cover and start to fill the tank. He reached for the notebook again, flipping through it, trying to make sense of all the lists and diagrams and seeing nothing more than a tangled web of patternless colors.

Out of the corner of his eye—something. He looked and saw a man—older, dark skinned—across the gas station's parking lot, standing next to a beat-up green Celica . . . and staring right at him with a puzzled, intent look on his face. The man pulled his phone out of his pocket, fiddled with it, stared at the screen, then looked back up, his expression sharpening.

There was no question as to what his phone was displaying—a photo of Will Dando on the bandstand, with his bass, smiling a little.

"Oh shit," Will said.

He opened the passenger-side door and leaned out, catching Leigh's attention.

"We need to leave, right now," he said.

"I've only got twenty bucks in," she answered.

"Leave it," he said. "I think someone recognized me."

Leigh's eyes narrowed. She pulled the nozzle out of the tank, slammed the cover closed, and slipped behind the wheel.

"Who was it?"

"Guy in a green Celica. Go slow, don't make him sure he saw what he saw. Just get back on the highway."

"All right. Dammit."

The car coasted up the ramp back to I-80, gaining speed as it merged into traffic.

"Is he there?" Leigh asked, accelerating. "Did he follow us?"

"I don't see him," Will answered, trying to glance behind them without seeming obvious about it. "Maybe we . . . shit."

The Celica changed lanes about six cars back, emerging from behind a semi like a striking snake. It was going fast, speeding, obviously trying to catch up to them.

"Go!" Will said.

"Where?" Leigh said, her voice admirably even toned, under the circumstances.

"Next exit. We won't be able to shake them on the highway, it's a straight line. Maybe if we can get ahead of them, though, we can turn off somewhere. Hide."

"Like in the movies," Leigh said, the suggestion clear that this was not, in fact, a movie.

"Yeah," Will answered, looking back through the rear window, not trying to hide it anymore, feeling the push of acceleration as Leigh hit the gas.

The next exit, another small town. Leigh hit the ramp too fast, skidded a little, and corrected. The Celica had been caught in a little snarl of traffic and they'd gotten some distance, but not enough. Not miles.

Leigh turned off the bottom of the ramp, the tires squealing. Will wondered how the hell she'd ever learned to drive like this, then decided to stop wondering, because what if she hadn't ever learned to drive like this?

The notebook slid off the dashboard into Will's lap, flopping open. He glanced down, steadying it with his hand, and saw that it had opened to the list of Oracle predictions. One in particular caught his eye, and his eyes flicked to the dashboard clock—11:03 A.M.— then back to the notebook.

Will ripped his eyes up to the road, examining the tiny, depressed, depressing town they were zooming through. He knew they were inviting the attention of whatever police department Starling, Ohio, had to offer, and didn't care.

"Look for a Laundromat!" he said.

"What?" Leigh said, not understanding. "What will that do for us?"

Will looked back behind them and saw the Celica rocket off the ramp.

He didn't know what their pursuer wanted, didn't know if there was a reward out for him or if it was about bragging rights. Or if he wanted him dead. Most likely, he had a question, and Will didn't have any answers left.

"There," he heard Leigh say. "Up on the right. Now what?"

"Turn in," Will said, taking a deep breath.

Leigh pulled into the parking lot, screeching to a stop next to a white panel van with a logo on it—Will didn't take time to read it. He scrambled out of the car and ran to the Laundromat's front door, aware of the Celica pulling into the lot behind him. He yanked open the door and dashed inside, Leigh a few steps behind him.

The Laundromat was . . . a Laundromat. Washers and dryers and folding tables. Vending machines for soap and fabric softener and snacks. A few beat-up arcade cabinets—treasures in any Williamsburg bar, here dusty and ignored. Patrons, not many, but more than a few, most wearing matching T-shirts, all staring at Will and Leigh, eyes wide.

Will reached up, grasping his wig, hat, and sunglasses.

Leigh looked at him, dismayed.

"What the fuck are you doing?"

Will removed his paltry, stupid disguise.

The reaction was instant. Everyone, every single person in the place knew who he was. The Oracle had come to Starling.

"You," said the man closest to him, a silver-haired, slim fellow wearing one of the matching T-shirts. "You're him."

"I am," Will said.

The door swung open behind him, and the man from the gas station stepped inside. Will spun to look.

"I knew it," he said, pointing. "The goddamned Oracle!"

He took a step forward, his expression intent, manic, one hand in his pocket, pulling an object out. Probably his phone, to snap a picture. Maybe something else—a knife, or a gun.

Will stepped backward, grasping Leigh by the arm and pulling her with him.

"Stop," Will said. "Stop now."

But the man didn't stop. A smile appeared on his face.

"No," he said. "You know what this means?"

And then the other man was there, the older man in the T-shirt, stepping between the Oracle and his . . . attacker? Supplicant? Fan? He held up a hand.

"You heard the Oracle," he said. "Please stay back."

Other customers stepped up, surrounding the man from the gas station, all wearing the same T-shirt. Will finally read it: CINCINNATI MEN'S CHORUS in elegant navy letters against white.

"Fuck's this?" the Celica man said, his face uncertain, even a bit afraid.

"Nothing," the first man said, apparently the leader of the Cincinnati Men's Chorus. "Unless you make it something."

He turned to Will.

"What do you need? How can we help you?"

Will considered.

"I just want to go. I need to get some distance on this guy. That's all."

The older man nodded and turned back to Celica man.

"All right. You're going to stay here with us while the Oracle leaves, and you're going to let him go wherever he wants, and you aren't going to follow him. Right?"

Celica man glanced at the ring of silent men surrounding him, the Oracle's defenders, taking their measure. He slipped his hand from his pocket and held it and its mate up, palms out.

"Right."

The chorus leader turned back to Will. He reached into his pocket and pulled out a set of car keys, tossing them through the air. Will caught them and gave the man a questioning look.

"This gentleman knows what you're driving. So you'll want to take my car. It's next to the van outside, a rental, in my name. Take it wherever you need to go. I'll cover the cost."

Will looked at Leigh. She looked completely lost, like she had no idea what was happening. To be fair, neither did Will, not really.

"Thank you," Will said, looking back at the chorus director. "We'll leave you the keys for ours, on the driver's seat. Sell it, do whatever you want with it. We appreciate the help, more than you know."

He looked at the silent chorus members, and the Celica man, and then down at the wig, hat, and sunglasses still clutched in his hand.

"Why?" he asked.

The director blinked, surprised.

"Don't you know? I mean, if you don't know, then why did you come here, right now . . ."

"Just tell me," Will said. "It was one of the warnings, right?"

"Yes. We were on tour, in Wisconsin. We tour a lot. The route we were taking would have had us on the Hoan Bridge in Milwaukee right at the minute it collapsed. I mean, give or take, sure, but the odds were damn good. Only reason we weren't is because you told us it would fall. Way we see it"—here he gestured at the rest of the chorus—"you saved all our lives. Helping you out here seems like the least we can do."

"Yeah," Will said. "Guess so."

He turned and went to the exit, Leigh at his side.

"Please," Celica man said as they passed, from within the ring of singers, "just one thing. Let me ask you just one thing."

Outside, Will and Leigh gathered their belongings from the Town Car and transferred them to their new vehicle, a late-model light blue Nissan sedan. Will left the Lincoln's keys on its driver's seat, then they got in the sedan and drove away, back to I-80 West.

That lasted for about two miles, until Leigh abruptly pulled over to the side of the expressway, slamming on the brakes and sliding to a stop. She looked at Will, her eyes wide, her face ashen.

"How?" she said. *"How?"*

Will nodded. He reached for the Oracle notebook and opened it, flipping to the front, to the fourth page. He ran his finger down the list of predictions, stopping about two-thirds of the way through. He held the notebook up for Leigh to read.

JULY 21, 11:07 A.M.—A MAN REVEALS HIMSELF IN A LAUNDROMAT.

CHAPTER 37

So the Oracle's in Ohio?" the president asked.

Daniel Green tapped the end of a pen against his desk, a dark, elaborately carved thing built from the timbers of the HMS *Resolute*. Queen Victoria had presented the desk to the United States in 1880, and every president since Hayes had used it in the Oval Office, with the notable exceptions of Johnson, Nixon, and Ford.

Anthony Leuchten, sitting in an armchair on the other side of the desk, knew the president hated the thing, but he was superstitious enough not to want to be lumped in with the guys who hadn't used it.

"Yes," Leuchten said. "Or he was. The Coach is on it, though. We'll know where he is, wherever he goes."

"The Coach," the president said, his tone sour. "Okay. What's Mr. Dando doing?"

"Nothing, as far as we can tell. Just driving. No new predictions, nothing. He's with the reporter."

"Huh. Okay. Let's keep our distance. We have a deal with the man, after all. What about the other two? The Sheikhs?"

"They've left the United States. Chartered a jet with an onboard medical suite, hired doctors, and flew on out."

The president narrowed his eyes.

"We let them go?"

"We can't hold them. They're covered under the, ah, arrangement with the Oracle. They don't seem to want to cause any trouble. Hamza Sheikh is focusing his energy on making sure Reverend Branson spends the rest of his life in prison. As for that, sir . . . it looks like the New York D.A.'s office is seriously considering issuing an indictment."

Leuchten hesitated. Ever since the fiasco in Quantico, he'd felt wrong, like his instincts were on the fritz somehow. He could still see the strings, but he no longer felt like he could touch them, much less pull them.

For the first time in his life, he felt the allure of letting someone else make the important decisions.

"Should we intervene?" Leuchten said. "I know you and Branson are close. We could exert influence on his case. Behind the scenes, of course."

The president frowned, his pen tapping out an irregular rhythm against his desk.

"No," he said, the pen going still. "I warned that asshole to stay away from the Oracle. He deserves what he gets."

"Anything else?" Green said. "This has been a long day. The doctor will be here in about fifteen minutes, and I need a little recharge time."

The president had asked for a daily cancer screening ever since the meeting with the Oracle, and it was taking its toll. Not the physical invasion of the blood tests, but the wait for the results. So far, all negative, but one day they wouldn't be, and the weight of that knowledge was pulling Green down, a little more each day. The price of the future.

"One last thing," Leuchten said. "The situation in Central Asia. I have an update."

"Qandustan?" the president asked. "I saw something about it in the security briefing this morning. It's still developing, right?"

Leuchten nodded.

"Yes. I'll briefly summarize for you, sir. We have a warlord—Törökul," he said, stumbling slightly over the unfamiliar pronunciation. "He's the leader of a tribe, an ethnic minority that has a history of squabbling with anyone and everyone in the area over the past several hundred years. He's apparently managed to organize his people, and he's come out from the hills with a small army and invaded the capital—a place called Uth.

"It's street-fighting. Ugly, bloody stuff. Törökul says he just wants control over a mosque with some historical significance to his tribe, but based on what the CIA pulled together on this guy, he's probably planning to slaughter everyone he can."

The pen started tapping again.

"But as I said, I have an update," Leuchten said. "Good news, potentially."

"I'll be damned," Green answered. "I think I've forgotten what good news sounds like. Do tell."

"Representatives from the two sides have brokered a temporary peace—apparently there is a cultural system in place in the region for resolving disputes. It's called a council of *biys*. Elders from both sides convene in some hidden spot in the mountains and try to work it out. This particular council has thirty-five people in total—seventeen from each side plus a neutral party acceptable to both who can vote to break a deadlock. If things go well with the process, then that's that. The fighting stops and they all get on with their lives."

"Huh," the president said. "Wouldn't that be nice? Nice enough that I can't imagine it will ever happen. I'll give you two-to-one odds the old guys all kill one another and things get even worse."

Leuchten nodded.

"Certainly possible, sir."

"Should we step in before it gets out of hand? Maybe send some troops to make sure this truce sticks no matter what the *biys* decide?" Green said.

Leuchten shrugged.

"I don't see how. I've spoken to the joint chiefs. Before Niger, maybe we could have done something, but now . . . We're stretched damn thin." Leuchten began ticking off items on his fingers. "Beyond Africa, there's the Iran occupation, plus the peacekeeping forces in Iraq and Afghanistan. General Blackman says we're on the edge of not being able to properly defend the country from an attack, and the rest of the Joint Chiefs agree."

Leuchten lowered his hand.

"We just don't have anyone to send."

The president frowned, thinking. The pen started moving again, then froze before it reached the desk.

"That's not true," Green said. He looked at Leuchten and smiled. "I can send you."

CHAPTER 38

L eigh was a desert.

Any movement would split her, broad cracks opening in her skin. Her eyes were full of grit—she wouldn't, couldn't open them, but she could feel the particles moving behind her eyelids, scratching against the lens. Her mouth was a gulch, parched and dead.

She was baked dry, and hyperaware: the weight of the sheet and the heavy hotel-bed blanket, pushed down to around her knees; her clothes from the night before still on her body; the air conditioner's hiss; the sound of running water from the bathroom, tantalizing, soothing . . . but out of reach, as getting to it would require leaving the bed.

So, she lay there, eyes closed, still, waiting for her body to give her a signal that she could move without shattering, pain cradling her skull like a mother's hands around her newborn.

Flashes from the previous night ran through her mind. Staring at the prediction in Will's notebook, trying to understand what it meant. Pulling back onto the highway, driving in silence until they reached the outskirts of Toledo, exiting, pulling up at a Hampton Inn.

"I feel like this is my last stop," she'd said. "Convince me I'm wrong."

"How?" Will answered.

She'd seen the fear in his face and knew she wasn't being fair, or kind. Will needed her desperately, and she was about to use that need to force him to tell her the things he'd been holding back. She wanted the story, and up to this point she'd been willing to be patient. No longer, apparently.

Leigh didn't mind being involved in something huge—in many ways, that's all she'd ever wanted—but she needed the narrative, so she could place herself within it. Helping the Oracle escape angry mobs out for his blood—that was one story, sure. But that prediction— *A Man Reveals Himself* . . . just those few words had made it clear that the story she'd been telling herself was tiny, just the smallest part of what was actually happening.

"Tell me the rest. The pieces you've left out. Otherwise you're on your own."

This was a bluff. But Will didn't know that, and so he started to talk.

He showed her the notebook, the lists, the color-coded calamities, the scribbled, scratched-out efforts to make sense of the Site's slowly tightening grip on world events.

Will told her about the billions of dollars, money that he had come to feel was essentially a bribe from the Site, a prize for being its agent in the world. He told her about fifteen thousand people dead in Uruguay, about the blackouts, about Niger, and how those things and everything else were locking together bit by bit, more each day. He told her about his last prediction—the numbers 23–12–4.

He told her about the walk into traffic in Montevideo, and other attempts like it, things he had kept to himself. He called them tests of the Site's control. That wasn't what they were.

He gave her, at last, details about the Oracle safe house waiting in the west—a cabin hidden in the mountains, bought, prepared, and stocked by Hamza and Miko in anticipation of a day when

Will's identity might be blown. It wasn't connected to any of their other accounts or identities, which meant that if he could just get there, he could put the pieces together—come to understand the Site's plan from a place of blessed anonymity. Figure out his part in all the terrible things the Site had done and decide what the Oracle could do about them. Will's vaunted plan—the driving force for their trip west—at the end, it wasn't some huge, complex machination that would magically turn everything around. He just wanted to feel safe.

The Oracle spoke for more than an hour, there in the parking lot of the Hampton Inn in Toledo, Ohio, as the sun set and the sky turned dark. Leigh just listened. When he stopped, she put her hand on his, letting it stay there for a moment.

Leigh started the car and left the parking lot, driving until she found a liquor store, where she purchased too much alcohol. Then back to the Hampton Inn, where a room was obtained for cash, and too much alcohol was consumed by both of them, and they kept talking.

She came to understand that Will hated that the Site had saved them at the Laundromat. It wasn't benevolent—it was a sign of the Site's casual power over him, a message that all his struggle, all his pain—it had been anticipated, it was part of the plan. The Site put Will in danger, and then it saved him from it, each time the message getting stronger that Will should just lie down, surrender, let it all happen.

The Oracle lived in constant anticipation of the next horrible thing the Site would do, mixed with the knowledge that if he had just kept his mouth shut in the beginning, if he hadn't become the Oracle, then it would never have happened. It was a contradiction he could not reconcile. The Site was in control, but yet, somehow, the choices all belonged to Will, from the start. No one had forced him to do anything—but he'd done it all.

The causality of it escaped him. The why of his own existence completely incomprehensible and impossible to ignore.

She remembered Will drunkenly suggesting an idea to her, a way to subvert the Site's plan, or at least do something good for the world with the Oracle's influence. She remembered her drunken, enthusiastic agreement. Him pulling out one of his burner phones and fiddling with it for a while, laughing.

Her enthusiastic, clumsy pass, which Will, to his credit, deflected. More drinking, and finally not sleep but a span of darkness, unawareness, each in their own bed.

Now, morning, and Leigh was a desert.

She heard Will sit on the bed opposite her.

"Awake?" he said, his voice soft.

Leigh raised a hand off the sheets, not wanting to risk opening her eyes.

"I have a glass of water here, and a cup of room coffee," Will said. "It's terrible, tastes like chemicals and poison, but I can't go out to get anything better. I had two Advils, too—I had to take one, I'm sorry, but the other's next to the water, if you need it."

"I do," Leigh said.

She rolled onto her side, taking the water and ibuprofen first, drinking the whole glass. Then the coffee, and her first sip confirmed Will's description—chemicals and poison. But better than nothing.

"I need to get back on the road," the Oracle said. "Are you coming with me?"

Leigh looked at him, just a man, and not just a man at all, trying to save the world.

"Yes," she said. "You deserve my help. You deserve everyone's help, but I want to be clear about something. There's a . . . mercenary angle to this for me. I'm sorry that you've had to endure so much, but that's not the only reason I want to stay. I want the rest of the story. For me."

"Obviously," Will said. "I'm not an idiot."

Leigh braced herself and sat up, her head pulsing in time with her heartbeat.

"How do you keep going?" she asked. "If it were me, I might just . . . hide, I guess."

Will closed his hands around his coffee cup, staring down into it.

"I could do that, but then I'd just be surrendering. At least this way I'm still making choices. I'm still trying. I'm still me. The minute I stop, that ends. I'm just a tool for the Site. Maybe it's an illusion, but it's what I have."

He glanced at the small table between the two beds, noticing a cell phone, facedown. He frowned.

"Do you remember me using that last night?" he said. "It's one of my last phones."

"Yeah," Leigh said, "but I don't remember what for."

He picked it up, turning it over.

"Me neither. I need to get rid of it, but let me just see what I—"

Will swiped the phone's screen. He stared at it, his frown deepening.

"Oh yeah," he said. "That's right."

"What?" Leigh said. "What did you do?"

He turned the screen so Leigh could see it.

On it, a prediction, in the same format as all the others on the Site:

ON SEPTEMBER 4, 2022, THE GOVERNMENT OF CHINA WILL BE TOPPLED BY A REVOLUTION THAT STEMS FROM MORE THAN FIFTY YEARS OF PERSISTENT HUMAN RIGHTS VIOLATIONS.

"Whoa," Leigh said. Her voice was hushed. "Is this real?"

"No," the Oracle answered. "I made it up."

CHAPTER 39

ON AUGUST 15, 2024, A BREAKTHROUGH IN STEM-CELL THERAPY WILL ALLOW COMPLETE REPAIR OF SPINAL-CORD-RELATED PARALYSIS.

Will tapped the screen, and the prediction went live to the Site. They were just crossing the border between Nebraska and Colorado, finally off I-80. I-76 would take them to Denver, and then it would be I-70 for all but the very last leg of their journey.

He thumbed the phone off and performed the now-familiar ritual of removing the SIM card and battery, tossing the pieces out the window as the car sped along the interstate.

Will adjusted his headphones slightly and tapped the volume control on the little MP3 player he'd bought at an Iowan travel plaza, a compromise that allowed Leigh to listen to the radio while she drove. He'd stocked it with songs ripped from the small set of CDs also available for purchase, mostly greatest hits collections. Right now, it was Prince, a bunch of the '80s classics. Will liked the tunes, but the real star for him was always the production. No one built an arrangement like Prince.

The Oracle notebook lay open on his lap, every page covered with his cramped handwriting in various colors.

The pattern had evolved past just the blue, red, yellow, and green he'd started with. He'd added a whole new run of shades to deal with the effects of the false predictions he'd been putting up—purple, orange, turquoise. The prediction about China was just the first. He'd been kicking around the idea ever since meeting Anthony Leuchten and realizing that the government had planned to use the Oracle's influence to affect world affairs.

Leigh's reaction to this plan had started skeptical and shifted to hugely alarmed once she'd had a little time to think over the implications. For one thing, she thought that trying to essentially trick China into improving human rights inside its borders could backfire in any number of ways. She'd taken some Asian poli-sci courses in college and knew the country's history much better than Will did. But it was done.

He'd put up several more false predictions since, although he'd discussed them with Leigh first. The idea was to run interference patterns across the Site's plan, possibly disrupt it in some way. Barring that, just to help. To improve things.

Will knew he was slowly but surely burning the Oracle's credibility—but he wasn't sure that was such a bad thing. The Site was using that same credibility to sow chaos. Maybe it was better to try to do something good with it. If the real predictions were destroying the world, maybe a few false ones could fix it.

The spinal cord thing was designed to spur research in that area—he'd been reading about it in *Wired*, and it seemed like something that should be getting more money. Likewise, a prediction about large, easily accessible mineral deposits in near-Earth asteroids, and a few others.

So far, it had been a lot of effort, some extra colors for the notebook, and not much else. His new predictions generated their own streams of aftereffects but never really connected with the Site's existing web; just dead flies on a windowsill.

He only had one untraceable phone left, and he was saving it for one last Site update—a Hail Mary pass he'd only use if he absolutely had to.

Will leaned back, looking out at the mountains through the windshield, letting his mind drift, listening to the radio edit of "Alphabet Street," which lacked the five-minute instrumental coda. He thought about the Site, free-associating. It was strange. The web wasn't growing the way it originally had. The nexus points that had combined early on to create what Will thought of as the "big" effects—the problems with the global economy, the Niger invasion, and so on—had stopped interacting.

The first, second, and third rounds of connection had all been relatively quick. Quick, that was, for events happening on a worldwide scale. Like dominoes falling. Now, though, it was as if everything was in slow motion, as if the gears of the Site's great machine had pulled apart and were no longer churning the world along to some unknown destination. It felt like the Site was holding its breath, waiting.

Will sighed. He closed the notebook and reached down between his legs to the floor, where a small stack of unread newspapers and magazines awaited. The top item was that week's copy of *The Economist,* on stands that morning. The cover story was about Qandustan.

He opened the magazine, looked at the article, and frowned. He was exhausted, it looked long, and *The Economist* used tiny type. Most importantly, he still wasn't sure the Site had anything to do with Qandustan at all.

Virtually every event he was certain was part of the Site's web had several Oracle-related triggers—more than one string connecting it to other sections of the web. But Qandustan only had one—the warlord Törökul's decision to attack the city of Uth because the United

States was too busy stepping on the forces of the Prophet in Niger to intervene. And even that was speculation—no one knew for sure if it had played a factor.

Will forced himself to dig into *The Economist* article. Not much new, really. The elder *biys* in the council were still sequestered up in the mountains above Uth, as they had been for the past several weeks. Anthony Leuchten was on the ground, talking to both sides, trying to find a diplomatic solution to an increasingly tense situation, which conjured up a nice image of Leuchten sweating in some desert hellhole surrounded by men who might kill him at any moment.

The magazine had sent a reporter to the other side of the world to obtain an interview with Törökul. He had proven elusive, but the reporter had managed to track down one of his subordinates, a Colonel Bishtuk.

He repeated most of the facts Will knew from his own research: his ancestors had built the mosque; his people still had every right to the mosque; their heritage had been stolen; his leader, the great Törökul, would lead them to victory . . . but then there was something else. Something new. Will's eyes widened.

"Holy shit," he said.

Will grabbed a green pencil from the passenger-side door. He flipped through the notebook on his lap until he found the pages related to Qandustan. All the entries were written in blue. Will drew big, green, dramatic circles around the edges of the page, designating it as firmly Site related.

"I knew it," he said to himself.

According to Colonel Bishtuk, Törökul had decided to attack Uth when he saw the city's lights go out during the worldwide blackouts that spring. He called it a sign from Allah, and at that very moment Törökul had vaulted onto his horse and ridden to gather the tribes.

The invasion in Niger had given Törökul the opportunity, the blackouts had given him the inspiration—and the Site had caused them both.

Will reached up, pulling off his headphones.

"Leigh!" he said. "Check this out. Qandustan's definitely a big part of the picture."

He looked up to see Leigh staring straight ahead, her face slack.

"Qandustan," she said in a dazed voice. "Yeah? Qandustan. How about that?"

"What's the matter?" Will asked.

"Listen to the radio, Will," Leigh said.

He hadn't even realized it was on. He focused his attention on the words, a deep voice speaking in a language Will didn't understand, emphatic and angular.

"What is this?" Will asked. "I can't understand it."

"It's audio from a clip that a local TV station in Qandustan broadcast last night our time—that's their morning. The translation will come through in a minute. They've already run it a few times," Leigh answered.

"Can you just summarize?" Will said.

"Yup," she said. "Törökul's got a nuke."

"What?" Will said. Leigh glanced at him. She looked ill.

"The anchor said it's an old missile from the USSR, an SS-24. They used to mount them on trains and trucks, I guess, and drive them around. They were completely self-contained, and they kept them moving all the time so a U.S. strike couldn't take them out."

Leigh reached down and turned off the radio.

"They aren't even sure if it works, and he's not saying how he got it, or where it is. But Törökul's calling it the Sword of God, and he's saying that the council in the mountains is taking too long to come back with their vote. He thinks they're screwing with him—stalling until his enemies can regroup."

Will hunched forward, gripping the notebook in both hands, his mind deep in the Site's web, trying to understand.

"What does Törökul want?" he asked.

"The elders need to come down from the mountains within forty-eight hours, or he'll launch the Sword of God against Uth. If his people can't have the mosque, he doesn't want anyone to have it."

Will leaned back.

"Jesus," he said. "They better get word to the old guys to hurry up their vote."

"They can't," Leigh said. "They're hidden, in a cave or something. That's the whole point, remember? No one knows where they are. They'll come back when they come back."

"To a big, smoking hole in the ground," Will said. "I don't understand why the Site would do this. What the fuck would be gained from some city in Central Asia getting vaporized?"

"Will, you don't understand. It's not just Uth. All night long . . . while we were asleep . . . the world . . . it's all falling apart."

Leigh's knuckles were white on the steering wheel.

"Qandustan has a defense treaty with China. So China said that if Uth gets nuked, they'll send attack bombers into the mountains where they think Törökul is hiding. Half the Muslim countries in the world said they'd fight to stop that, and that includes Pakistan and Saudi Arabia."

"Pakistan and China both have nukes, too," Will said.

"And the Saudis," Leigh said. "Apparently for a while. They thought now would be a good time to announce it. The U.S. has a defense treaty with them, just like China with Qandustan. So if China starts fighting the Saudis . . ."

"So that'd be it. Everyone would jump in. Boom."

Will closed his eyes, his gut churning, thinking about the Site laughing at him for putting up his idiotic fake predictions, trying to change a world that wouldn't even exist in a few days.

"In one fucking night?" he said.

He felt Leigh's hand on his back, a tentative touch.

"What's going to happen, Will? Tell me you know what's going to happen."

Will thought, and wondered, and had nothing to say.

CHAPTER 40

L eigh pushed her cart down the aisle, looking at the nearly empty shelves, attempting to ignore the news broadcast running on the store's speaker system, giving an update on the global crisis— nothing she didn't already know, and nothing she wanted to hear.

Panner's Market was the only grocery store in Feldspar Creek—a market, really. A small store for a small town, never with all that much in stock.

Still. This was apocalyptic. Gaping holes where the staples should have been. No flour or sugar, no toilet paper, no coffee.

They had almost reached the cabin. According to Will, it was a fifteen-minute drive up the mountain from the town. The place had taken on a talismanic quality in Leigh's mind—a refuge where they could finally settle in and think, figure out a next step.

Until, of course, the world ended in a huge nuclear fireball.

The feast had been her idea. A celebration of their arrival at the cabin, and a sort of screw-you to the Site—a dance to the graveyard.

Hamza had supposedly stocked the safe house—and "safe" was relative, under the circumstances—with canned goods, bottled water, and other nonperishables. Enough to last for a while, if they needed it, but fresh was fresh, and so Leigh had pulled into Panner's Market in search of milk, eggs, fruits, and vegetables. A few good steaks, if they could be found. They had talked about grilling that night, maybe splitting a bottle or three of wine.

Apparently, though, she wasn't the only one in Feldspar Creek thinking that way. The tiny butcher's case held only a few graying packages of ground chuck. Leigh grabbed them and made her way to the register, where she waited her turn behind a line of still, silent shoppers.

The checkout clerk—a well-padded older woman with brilliant, bottle-red hair and a name tag labeling her as a Claire—worked the line with quiet efficiency.

Claire looked a little off her game. Her makeup was unevenly applied, and her hair was messy.

"Hi there," she said, as Leigh stepped up.

"Hello," Leigh said. She began unloading her cart and placing the groceries on the conveyor belt. Claire swiped Leigh's items across the scanner. She rushed it and hissed with impatience when the laser didn't ring up the price on the first try.

Leigh opened her purse and pulled out her wallet. She unsnapped it and thumbed through the sheaf of bills inside, literally the last of their cash.

She considered the fact that her trip west with the Oracle had used almost exactly, to the penny, the amount of money Will had brought with him from New York, and let her mind skitter away. She'd only known Will Dando for about a week, and she was already largely postcoincidence.

"You're lucky you made it," Claire the clerk told her. "We're closing early today."

"I get it," Leigh said.

"I just want to be home, you know?"

"I do," Leigh agreed. "I really do."

Claire stopped scanning Leigh's items and settled back, holding a thin plastic bag containing the one anemic-looking head of lettuce the market's cold case had left to offer. She looked bleakly at her empty market.

"You know, I've made more money this week than I do in the whole down season up here. I should go spend it, you know? Buy something nice, while I still can."

She pressed a button on her cash register.

"Forty-eight ninety-seven," she said.

Leigh nodded, and looked down at her wallet, then dimly realized that words from the news broadcast were penetrating her consciousness despite her best efforts to screen them out.

"President Daniel Green." "Cancer." "New prediction." "The Site." "The Oracle." "Three to four months."

"The Oracle."

The Oracle.

Leigh's head swam. Nausea churned in her gut. Hazily, she fumbled a few bills from her wallet and dropped them on the checkout scanner. She grabbed the grocery bags and walked toward the exit, ignoring Claire, dimly aware that the woman was holding up the money and calling after her. She had paid too much or too little. It didn't matter.

Leigh walked quickly to the Nissan, parked at the edge of the market's small lot. Will was visible through the windshield, in a cap and wig and glasses—he was always in disguise now, unless he was behind a locked door. His head was down. The pose felt to Leigh like he was looking at his phone. The phone he had just used to fuck them both.

She ripped open the car's rear door and tossed the grocery bags into the backseat, then slammed it shut. She took a deep breath, held it, released it, then opened the driver's-side door and slid inside.

"Everything all right?" the Oracle asked.

She was wrong—it wasn't his phone. He had the notebook on his lap, the Notebook in which the Oracle attempted to figure out the plan of the Site. The green pencil was in his hand, and an entire page was covered with lime-colored text. She knew what that meant—he had explained his color-coding system to her during a particularly dull stretch of road in Indiana. And so, she knew it was unusual, unprecedented, probably represented some significant breakthrough— and she couldn't manage to give even a single shit.

"Fuck you, Will," Leigh said. She pulled the door closed and sat with her hands on the wheel, almost shaking with tension.

The Oracle considered this, then closed the Notebook, marking his place with the green pencil.

"You heard," Will said.

"Yeah," Leigh said. "I heard. Of all the things you could have done, all the predictions you could put up on the Site, you gave up the one thing that's keeping the president of the United States from coming after us—not to mention poor Hamza and Miko—and, at best, throwing us into prison for the rest of our lives. I heard."

Will sighed heavily.

"Well?" Leigh asked.

"I figured it out," he said. "I know what the Site's doing. I know what the numbers mean."

Through the windshield, she could see a helicopter making its way through the sky. Will had told her that Feldspar Creek was a wealthy town, a little mountain paradise for rich Californians who flew to Denver or Grand Junction and choppered in. The Oracle's cabin was probably just one of many secluded, helipad-equipped getaways currently being used to ride out the end of the world. She wondered who was in it. A studio head, a movie star, a politician . . . did it matter? No. Not at all. Very little did, at this point.

"You figured something out. So what?" Leigh said. "Too little too late, you know?"

"But it's not," Will said, his voice calm. "That's the whole thing. That's why I put up the prediction about the president. Can I just explain this?"

Leigh looked out the window, breathing hard. She could call her dad, could call Reimer, and get some money wired to her. She could get back to the city, could write all this up, could . . .

Leigh turned the key in the car's ignition, and the engine came to life.

She pulled up to the exit from the lot, the front of the car nosing onto the main drag through Feldspar Creek. A turn to the right would head out of town, back east and eventually, home. The Oracle could get out, or not. His choice.

To the left, she saw a waterfall, a silver ribbon winding its way down the face of the mountain that waited at the end of the road. The cascade split into two streams as it hit some ledge or promontory, dividing into two paths.

Left or right. She thought about good decisions, and bad decisions, and how hard it could be to tell them apart.

Leigh chose the mountain. She turned left.

Will exhaled.

"I thought about Hamza and Miko," he said. "They're safe. They're out of the country, and we know from the radio and stuff that he's hired guards—twenty-four-hour protection. Plus, really, this isn't about them. It's about *me*. I had to do something, Leigh. I just couldn't sit here and let the Site . . . end everything."

"But why did you have to do *this*?" Leigh said. "How could giving up the cancer prediction possibly affect things in Qandustan?"

"You've read the same op-eds I have. The U.S. is staying out of Qandustan because Green doesn't want another military action in an election year on top of Niger and the others.

"But if he knows he's going to lose the election, and stops worrying about how he'll be perceived by the voters, he's freed up to do something beyond just sending that idiot Leuchten."

Leigh opened her mouth to respond, but Will cut her off.

"And you know what? It sucked that he was going to win again. He put the Coach on to us, he's the reason for those blackouts, *he's the reason Branson outed me.* Fuck him."

Will glared out through the windshield. Leigh saw the sign for Laird Lane, the long dirt road that led up the final stretch of road to the cabin, and turned. She hadn't seen another house for at least a few miles—it seemed that the safe house was as isolated as promised. Small consolation.

"Why couldn't you just let us be here, together?" Leigh said, her voice rising in pitch. "Even if there is a war, we could have ridden it out here. We would have been safe. Doesn't that matter to you? Do I even factor into this decision?"

She realized she was yelling. She realized she had said "together" and "we." She realized how frightened she was, for herself, for everyone.

"Don't you think it's a little fucking selfish to do something like this without discussing it with me?"

"Selfish? Leigh, that's the whole point. This is something I'm doing for everyone *but* myself."

"While ignoring the one person who's been standing by you through all this bullshit."

"Leigh, listen, of course I thought about us. I told you, I know what the numbers mean. I have a plan, and . . ."

"Come on, man! Getting the predictions doesn't make you Batman or whatever. The Oracle is a fiction, Will. You're just a guy."

Laird Lane ended in a large clearing, and there, at last, was the cabin. Small but perfect, wood and shingles, a front porch complete with rocking chairs, everything Will had claimed it would be.

And next to it, perched on the dirt, was a black, insectile helicopter—the same aircraft Leigh had noticed back at Panner's Market.

"What the hell?" Will said, and then noise, incredibly loud.

Four distinct reports, echoed a moment later by the sound of all four of the car's tires blowing out. Leigh fought the wheel.

Black-clad men holding rifles rushed out of the tree line on all sides, sprinting up to the car as it slewed to a stop.

They lifted their weapons, pointing them directly at Leigh and Will. One man—imposing, granite-faced—stepped close to the car on Leigh's side. He tapped the driver's-side window with the barrel of his rifle, making a small metal-on-glass tink that was possibly the worst sound Leigh had ever heard.

"Out," he said.

CHAPTER 41

A slow, cautious exit from the car, then an escorted walk to the cabin. Up the porch steps, through the front door, and into the living room, the first time Will had seen it in person.

He saw evidence of Hamza and Miko's careful planning everywhere—the CB radio, the metal crate pushed against one wall that Will knew contained over a hundred burner cell phones ready for use, the encrypted laptops and satphone, the safe holding cash, gold and gems, instrument cases, rustic but tasteful furniture, the stocked kitchen. Everything the Oracle would need to survive in a world that knew his name.

And sitting on the couch, holding a steaming mug in one delicate hand, nails painted a bright, pretty shade of blue, was the reason he would never use any of it—the Coach.

"Hello, Will," she said. "So nice to see you again."

"Fuck you," Will said.

"It sounds interesting, but I think my men are in a hurry to finish our work before the local law enforcement comes looking to figure out what's going on."

"How did you know we were coming here?"

"Oh, please. I found you once, what makes you think I'd ever let you go again? I've been tracking you two kids ever since you left

New York. Swapping out the Town Car for that rental made it a snap, really. They all have transponders, so the companies can find them if they're stolen or something. Did you not know that?"

Will glanced at Leigh. She looked terrified, of course, but also angry. He felt incredibly stupid. Will Dando was emphatically, now and forever, not Batman.

"What do you want from me?" he said.

"Nothing," the Coach said. "Nothing at all."

A sound, behind them, the unmistakable *ka-chik* of a pistol's slide being racked.

"Oh, Jesus," Leigh said.

He turned to see one of the Coach's men—the same man who had ordered them out of the car—was now pointing a dark, gray hammer of a gun at Will's head.

"No," Will said, his thoughts fuzzed, adrenaline streaking through his system. He knew there was a pistol in a small plastic case in a closet upstairs, and a few rifles in a cabinet in the kitchen, but they might as well have been back in New York for all the good they could do.

"You don't want to do this," he said, trying hard to project a note of authority into his voice. "I have to do something. If I don't, it's going to be bad, really bad."

"What do you need to do?" the Coach said, a note of curiosity in her voice.

"Let me go and I'll tell you. I can tell you all kinds of things. I'm the Oracle."

The Coach shook her head.

"I'm sorry, Mr. Dando, but my employer gave explicit instructions. You see, you appear to be more dangerous alive than dead. You've been a busy boy up here. That business with China, and the bit about stem-cell research?"

The Coach made a small, chiding noise, clicking her tongue against her teeth.

"I've been getting calls for days to end your rampage across the geopolitical landscape. The only reason I said no was because you had the president protecting you. But then you sold him out."

She made a small gesture, and her mercenary placed the pistol at Will's temple. The circle of metal felt red-hot against his skin, a tiny stove burner making it impossible to think about anything else.

"Forgive me, Will, but that was stupid. President Green was absolutely furious. He personally gave the kill order for you. No plausible deniability this time, I guess."

She scratched the side of her nose with her free hand—a gesture too casual to seem remotely real, considering the circumstances.

"I'm almost disappointed," the Coach continued. "I guess I expected something more . . . interesting from you. Considering, you know, all this buildup."

She shrugged.

"Should have known better. Expectations. They'll get you every time."

"I've got money," Will said, desperate. "I can get you anything you want. Goddammit, what do you think all of this has been about? Can't you understand that there's a point to everything that's happened, and if I die it will all fall apart?"

The Coach held a finger to her lips.

"Shh," she said. "It's time to go."

And then, for the first time since the dream, Will could breathe. There was nothing left for him to do.

No decisions to make.

No globe-spanning drama with the Oracle in its starring role.

No future.

Just Will Dando, at the end of his life.

He closed his eyes, entirely focused on that little circle of metal against the side of his head.

"In the car," he heard Leigh say. "There's a notebook. Go get it.

Read it. You'll understand. If you kill him, you kill yourself. You kill everyone."

A long silence.

"Open your eyes, Will," the Coach said.

Will did. She had stood and was considering him carefully.

"Okay. I'm interested. Go get it, Grunfeld," she said, and the circle of metal disappeared from the side of Will's head.

A moment or two later, and the leader of the Coach's team—Grunfeld, apparently—returned with the notebook. He handed it to her without a word, and she paged through it, one eyebrow raised, making an occasional noise of interest.

"Huh," she said, snapping the notebook closed. "When I take a job, I tend to get a bit . . . focused. I can be extremely goal oriented. Big picture bores me. I'd even go so far as to say it's my tragic flaw."

She tapped the cover of the notebook with one fingernail.

"But this . . . this is all big picture, isn't it? This is The Big Picture, you might say."

"Yeah," Will said. "It is."

"Mm," the Coach said. "It pushes plausibility to suggest that you prepared this on the off chance you might run into me. I just skimmed, but it seems to strongly suggest that something very bad will happen unless you, personally, stop it."

"That is exactly what I have been trying to say."

"Fine, fine," the Coach said, her tone irritated. "But you have to understand—it is a very big deal for me not to follow through on an assignment. Getting things done is my entire brand. So, if I am going to consider not killing you, then I will need a very good reason."

She held up the notebook.

"This—" she said, "how bad are we talking?"

"End of the world," Will said. "And we have no time."

"About what I thought," the Coach said. "So saving you means

I'm saving myself, and my husband, and my children and grandchildren, just as the lovely Ms. Shore suggested."

She looked out the window, toward the waterfall visible through the slightly warped, imperfect panes, and tapped her fingers against her lips.

"Okay," she said, turning back to Will and holding out the notebook. "Do what you have to do."

Feeling a bit dazed, Will took the notebook.

"But please, don't forget that I came here to kill you," she went on. "I am not your friend. Bluffs, trickery, or chicanery of any kind will result in . . ."

The Coach gestured at Grunfeld, who lifted his gun in a mildly threatening way.

"I'm sure it won't come to that, though," she said, smiling. "Now, where are we going?"

Will stared at the Coach, trying to think of any ruse, any bluff that could get them away. He looked at Leigh, the woman who had, without any doubt, just saved his life. Her eyes were wide, clearly hoping he would return the favor.

"Denver," he said.

CHAPTER 42

We believe the Chinese incursion into Pakistan's airspace was entirely intentional, Mr. President."

The chairman of the Joint Chiefs, General Ira Blackman, pointed with his pen to the large screen taking up most of the far wall of the Situation Room. It was currently showing a satellite image of the Pakistan/China border, with various air- and land-based military units from both sides overlaid on the map as graphic chits—China in red, Pakistan in yellow.

The scans are all clean, Daniel Green thought, *but the doctors made it clear that doesn't mean anything. Lymphatic cancer comes on quickly. I could be clean one week and have one foot in the grave the next.*

"A display of power in the wake of the Oracle's prediction about the revolution in a few years. They want to show they're as strong as ever," the national security adviser added.

Green reached for a cup of coffee in front of him—full, black—and took a sip. It was hot, and perfect. The world was ending, but God forbid they let the president's coffee get cold.

"But they turned around, right?" Green asked, sending the question out to the twenty or so uniformed military advisers crowded into the room. "It wasn't an actual attack?"

"Correct, Mr. President. The Pakistanis scrambled fighters to intercept, and the Chinese returned across their own border," the chairman said.

"Do we think they *will* attack?" Green said.

A long, not entirely reassuring glance between the national security adviser and the chairman.

"Not without provocation, sir."

"Define provocation," Green said, almost—almost—wishing he hadn't sent Tony Leuchten away. He was better at dealing with the military.

"Almost anything. A misunderstood order from home, an itchy trigger finger . . . but the most likely cause would be Török̈ul launching his nuclear weapon at the city of Uth," the national security adviser replied.

"The Sword of God," Green said.

"Correct."

"And we still can't find the goddamned thing?"

"Not yet, sir. We have drones scanning the region looking for radiation signatures, but the terrain makes it extremely challenging. If he's got it stashed in a cave, or a deep valley, we might never—"

The door to the Situation Room opened—in itself an unusual enough situation that every head in the room turned to look. Green's secretary, a formidable woman named Meredith, entered and walked over to him. She leaned down and spoke quietly into his ear.

"Telephone call, Mr. President."

"I presume it's extraordinarily important, or you wouldn't be telling me about it," Green said.

Meredith nodded.

"It's a Major Carter Grunfeld, Mr. President. He used an authorization code I wasn't familiar with: Sundown. Do you want to speak to him?"

Green's mouth quirked upward.

"Sundown," he said. "Yes. Put him through."

"Very good, sir," Meredith said.

She lifted the handset for his secure phone, tapped a few buttons on its face, and handed it to him.

"Major. What's the status? If you're using Sundown, I'm expecting good news," Green said.

"Mr. President, this is the Oracle," an all-too-familiar voice said. "I need a favor."

The president's grip tightened on his phone. He could feel its edges digging into his palm and fingers and wished he could squeeze the damn thing until it shattered.

"What makes you think I'd be interested in doing you any favors at all?"

"Because then I'd owe you one. And because it would make me much more willing to forget about the whole kidnapping thing in New York, and the fact that you tried to have me killed today."

"Son, I have no idea what you're talking about," Green said. "What I do know is that you're not very good at keeping your promises. Why the hell you chose to release that prediction, to make a private matter so drastically public, I'll never—"

"This is bigger than you," the Oracle snapped. "You know what I'm capable of, as much as anyone can. Will you help me?"

The president looked back into the Situation Room. The chairman of the Joint Chiefs was pointing his index finger at the national security adviser, red-faced, indignant. The screens along walls displayed fifteen different versions of the next twenty-four hours— twelve of which resulted in the end of the world.

"What are you looking for?" Green said. "No promises. Just tell me what you want, and we'll see."

"I need to speak to Törökul," the Oracle said.

The president spasmed out a sound—something between a chuckle and a groan.

"How the hell do you suppose that'll work? Maybe you haven't heard of the Sword of God. Catchy name, right? I should have him manage my campaign. Man has a gift for marketing."

"I can stop that, Mr. President. I can keep him from launching that missile. You just need to get me in front of him," the Oracle said.

"What makes you think I have that power?" Green asked.

"You're the president of the United States," the Oracle answered.

Green waited, but that appeared to be all Dando had to say on the matter.

Ordinarily, he enjoyed the average citizen's belief that the president could do more or less anything he wanted, like some sort of wizard in a fantastic suit. The reality was significantly less impressive. But you couldn't tell the Oracle that.

He looked at the screens mounted all around the room—twelve apocalypses, and the other options weren't much prettier. He shifted his gaze across the faces of his advisers, all brilliant men and women, all with enormous power and experience, none of which was doing him a good goddamn. The only person offering him any sort of lifeline was, of course, the fucking Oracle.

"I can try to get word to his people," Green said.

"Good," the Oracle said. "Look, do this, play your role, and you can spin it so that it looks like you saved the world. I don't care—I really don't. But do it right, and it should help you get that second term, cancer or no cancer."

"Will it?" Green said.

"What?" came the Oracle's voice, sounding genuinely puzzled.

"Will I win?" the president asked.

A lengthy pause from the other end of the line.

"You will," came the answer. "If you help me. How long will it take you to make contact with Törökul?"

The president exhaled loudly.

"No time at all," Green said. "We know exactly where he is.

We've got a Special Forces team out in the mountains keeping him under surveillance."

"Wait, why?" the Oracle said. "If you know where he is, why don't you just—"

"Because we can't find the damn missile," the president broke in. "The goddamn Sword. He's got it hidden somewhere in the mountains, and his people have orders to launch it if Törökul is killed or captured."

Another pause from the Oracle's end of the phone.

"All right—the Special Forces team can get to him?" the Oracle said. "It's important that someone conveys to Törökul that I just want to speak to him. He needs to know he'll be released once we're done."

"Of course," the president answered. "We don't want any misunderstandings, believe me. I have Tony Leuchten on the ground there. You remember him?"

"Rings a bell," the Oracle said, his tone bone-dry.

"I bet. He'll get it done. What will you say to Törökul?"

"Wait and see," the Oracle answered.

"Listen, you arrogant little . . ." the president began.

He took a breath.

"Ah, fuck it. When will you be ready?"

"Not long."

"All right, I'll give the orders. I'll call this number when it's all set up. You know what you're doing?" the president said.

"Absolutely," the Oracle answered.

The phone went dead.

CHAPTER 43

The Coach took back her phone without a word, her expression impressed, and full of questions she had apparently decided not to ask. For the moment.

Will looked out the window. The helicopter had just completed a steep climb up a mountain range, and as they crested the peak, a city came into view. It sprawled next to a deep blue lake, with a cluster of skyscrapers near the center and endless suburbs scattered across a broad plateau.

Will was doing his best to ignore Grunfeld. The man had his pistol resting lightly on one leg, pointed roughly in Will's direction. His finger wasn't on the trigger, but Will had absolutely no illusions that he had any chance of getting his hands on that gun.

"Is that it?" Will asked, nodding toward the window.

"That's it. Denver," the Coach answered. She made a show of pulling up her sleeve to look at her watch, a slim-banded, elegant thing. "This will all be very public. I hope you know what you're doing."

"I do," Will said.

Across the cabin, Leigh was in the far seat against the window, surrounded by three of the Coach's men. She had her arms crossed, staring straight ahead, boring a hole through the chest of the mercenary seated opposite. She looked tiny in comparison to her guards, but all attitude, all defiance.

Will's confidence faltered a few degrees. If he was wrong . . . But no. It was too right.

And if it wasn't, then he and Leigh would both be dead, and there was never anything he could have done about it. Not at any single point since the day he was born.

"All right, Denver. Time to get a bit more specific about your plan, Mr. Oracle," the Coach said.

"Hold on," Will said. "Just give me a minute."

"Sure thing. How about this. You've got twenty minutes to show me something before I call this whole thing a bad investment and shove you both out the door over the Rockies. Take your time."

Will swallowed.

"Leigh," he said. "I need your help."

Leigh blinked. She turned. She'd been all but comatose for the ride thus far, but seemed to dial herself back to life at the sound of Will's voice. She flashed him a quick, faint smile.

"Shoot," she said.

"I need the biggest TV station in Denver," Will said.

Leigh raised an eyebrow.

"Okay . . ." she said. "You want KUSA. They're the NBC affiliate."

"Do you know where they're located in the city?"

"They have a headquarters building just outside downtown. It's this weird round-looking thing."

"Could you recognize it from the air?"

"I think so," Leigh said. "It's just up the road from the Denver Country Club. Find that and I'm sure I could spot it."

"They'll have some sort of satellite linkup, right? A way to get footage out beyond Denver?"

"Of course. Even the smallest local stations can do that. But why do you need a TV station, Will?"

Will gave Leigh a placating gesture and turned back to the Coach.

"Tell your pilot to look for the country club. A golf course. Leigh will direct him from there. And I need you to make a call for me."

The Coach tossed her phone to Grunfeld.

"Eighteen minutes," she said. "Use them well."

Will turned to Grunfeld.

"Dial information," Will told the man. "Get . . . what was the station, Leigh?"

"KUSA," she said.

"Right. Ask for their direct line, then call them and tell them that you've got the Oracle, he wants to make a statement, and he'll be landing on their roof in ten minutes."

The Coach reached out and put her hand on Grunfeld's forearm, keeping him from lifting the phone.

"I don't think so," she said.

"Do it," Will said.

The Coach leaned forward.

"Will, you've clearly decided I'm an idiot, which surprises me. If there's anything you should have learned from our time together, it is that I am exactly the opposite of an idiot. I said I'll help you, but I'm not letting you out of my hands, and I'm sure as hell not letting you near any television cameras."

"Listen," Will said, keeping his tone level, "it has to be this way. I have to get in front of a camera. There's no other way to do it."

"Nope," the Coach said. "I won't be able to keep you under control if you've got an audience. Find another way."

Will closed his eyes and took a deep breath. He opened them and gave the Coach what he hoped was a look of the utmost sincerity.

"Here's how we do it," he said. "You guys stay in the helicopter. Let me outside just for five minutes to say what I have to say, and then I'll get back in here and go with you. You can do what you want with me. You have my word, as long as you let Leigh go. You don't need her."

"Will!" Leigh said, horrified.

"It's okay, Leigh," Will said, although he kept his eyes on the Coach's face.

She leaned back in her seat, thinking.

"Your word," she said. "What's that worth? I don't know you, and I've been threatening to kill you for the last few hours. Why would you keep your promise to me?"

"Because of her," Will said, pointing across the cabin at Leigh.

The Coach's head turned slowly, following Will's gesture. She looked at Leigh for a long moment, then turned back.

"This is the only way to do it?" the Coach said.

"That I can think of."

She gestured to Grunfeld, spinning her fingers in a go-ahead movement.

"It'll go like this," she said. "You can have your little TV show, but the girl stays in the chopper while you do. We'll tie a line around your waist, so that if we need to lift off in a hurry, you're coming with us. When you're done, get back in here, and we'll let your girlfriend go at the same time."

"No," Leigh said. "I'm not going anywhere without him."

"Leigh," Will said, "it'll be fine. Don't worry."

"It's not going to be fine, Will! What the hell are you doing? There has to be another way!"

Will dug deep and gave her the most reassuring smile he could muster. He closed his eyes and leaned back against his seat's headrest, listening to Grunfeld making the call.

"They're connecting me," Grunfeld said. "How do I convince them I really have the Oracle?"

"You're the badass son-of-a-bitch soldier of fortune," Will said, without opening his eyes. "I sure as hell hope you're tougher than a TV station receptionist."

CHAPTER 44

A helipad was clearly marked on the widest section of KUSA's roof: a large black *H* in a white circle. A crowd had gathered around that *H*, at least a hundred people.

The Coach turned from the helicopter cabin's window and spoke to the pilot.

"Keep them spinning," the Coach said. "We'll need to get out of here in a hurry."

Grunfeld tested the knots on the length of black nylon cord tied around Will's waist. The other end was lashed securely to one of the seat supports in the cabin. Without a knife, it would take half an hour to get free. At least.

"So," the Coach said, almost apologetic. "I feel like this has to be said. Try anything, and you'll get a bullet in the back of the head."

"Won't that happen anyway?" Will said.

"Probably. But act up and"—she pointed a thumb over her shoulder at Leigh—"she'll be next. We'll toss her out after you and fly away."

The eyes of everyone in the cabin were on Will. From the corner of his eye, he saw Leigh move—slowly reaching for the pistol in the belt of one of the guards next to her.

Oh no, no, he thought. *Leigh, don't—*

She managed to get it halfway out of the holster before her hand was slapped away and the guard's fist closed around her throat. Leigh made a strangled noise. The guard looked to the Coach for instructions.

"Jesus," she said. "Doesn't know when she's got a good deal."

She leaned in, putting her face close to Leigh's.

"Just relax," the Coach said. "You'll be out of here in five minutes, if Mr. Dando sticks to the plan."

The guard holding Leigh relaxed his grip but didn't let go. She shoved at his arms, but she might as well have tried to topple an oak.

"Keep her quiet," the Coach instructed. The guard's other hand went over Leigh's mouth.

"Take it easy, for God's sake," Will said.

"You want her out of here? Get on with it," the Coach said.

Will glared at her, then put his hand on the cabin door and shoved the handle down. A meaty click as the latch released. He pushed open the door, which split at the midway point, the upper half sectioning up and the bottom expanding into a short flight of steps descending to the roof.

Will stepped out of the helicopter into an eruption of rotor wash, trailing the black nylon tether. The blades were still spinning, as the Coach had instructed, but even over the noise they generated Will could hear the shouted questions from the assembled crowd.

"Is it the end?"

"Will my husband stay with me?"

"Should I play fifteen or twenty-six in the match game?"

"Who's going to win the next Super Bowl?"

"Is the Sword going to launch?"

"Will we ever land on Mars?"

"Where's my daughter?"

The faces surrounding the helicopter were manic, frightened, awed.

Will hadn't been exposed to this much raw need since he'd sifted through the e-mails people sent to the Site—forever ago. It was disorienting, like a hot spotlight shining right in his face.

Will took a deep, focusing breath. He turned back to the helicopter. "Shut it down!" he shouted.

Grunfeld, waiting back in the open door to the helicopter's cabin with the ropes in his hand, apparently couldn't hear him—his face was stone blank, as ever. Will made a spinning motion with his hand, trying to evoke the rotors, then made a throat-cutting gesture, signaling for him to stop.

Finally, a reaction—Grunfeld's eyebrows lifted almost to his hairline. He shook his head. Will covered his ears with his hands and shrugged. Grunfeld frowned deeply, but shouted something back into the cabin. A long moment, and then the deep thrumming of the helicopter's engine ceased. The rotors slowed to a stop.

Ignoring the pleas from the crowd for information about loved ones' futures, stock tips, answers, answers, answers, Will pointed at the nearest camera crew and motioned them forward. A trim, middle-aged man with salt-and-pepper hair seemed to be the man in charge—he was wearing a suit and had a microphone in his hand and had the polished vibe of a news anchor.

Once he was close enough, Will leaned over and shouted over the crowd noise, right into the man's ear.

"You're going to have to do an uplink with this signal," Will said.

The anchor gave him a puzzled look. Will pointed at the camera.

"I need this to go someplace specific," he said, in an attempt to clarify. "What's your name?"

"Crandall Fontaine," the anchor said, who didn't seem like he had completely processed the situation.

"Okay, Crandall, do you have a tech guy I can talk to?" Will said.

The anchor nodded. He waved to a heavyset man standing nearby.

"Jerry! Get up here," Crandall Fontaine called.

The tech approached warily, his eyes never leaving Will's face.

"Jerry," Will said, keeping his voice calm and patient. "Hold on just one sec. I'll need your help."

He turned back to the helicopter.

"I need the phone again," he shouted at Grunfeld, still lurking in the open cabin door.

Will was expecting to have to spend another few minutes convincing the Coach to give him the phone, but it sailed out of the helicopter door without a word. Evidently she had decided she was in for a penny, might as well be in for a pound. Will caught the phone neatly. He turned back to Jerry the tech and held it up.

"Now, Jerry, in a little while, someone will call this number. You're going to talk to them and get the signal where it's supposed to go. The footage from here will need to be sent someplace else, I think via satellite, and you'll be receiving another feed the same way. The person over there needs to see and hear me, and I need to be able to see and hear them. Can you do that?"

"Yes, sir," Jerry answered. "Should be simple, if they have the right gear."

"Good."

Will handed Jerry the phone.

He stepped back and looked around the roof, making eye contact with different faces in the crowd, seeing the surge of eagerness whenever someone thought they'd made a connection. They wanted him to help. They wanted him to save the day.

Will turned around and climbed back up into the helicopter. He pulled the door shut behind him. The aircraft had good soundproofing—it had to, because of the rotors' din. The sudden silence once the door latched shut was a balm to Will's noise-lacerated ears.

Will stepped toward the seats containing Leigh and the mercenary guarding her.

"Move," Will said to the man.

They locked eyes.

A beat.

The soldier stood. Will sat down next to Leigh.

"What's happening?" she said.

"It's all getting set up. It'll take a few minutes."

Leigh considered this.

"Can I ask you something?" she said.

"Of course," he answered.

"What do I do, Will?"

"For a living?"

"Yes," Leigh said. "For a living."

"You're a journalist," Will said.

"What kind?"

Will thought this over.

"For a website," he said.

"Correct," Leigh said. "So why in the world would I know anything about TV stations in Denver?"

Will frowned.

"I . . . guess I didn't think about it. Just seemed like something you would know. But you did, right?"

Leigh looked at him, very intent.

"I used to date a guy in college. After graduation, he moved out here and took a job with KUSA. I visited him a few times, saw where he worked. That's the only reason I knew. I shouldn't have, but I did. We had zero time—the Coach was two seconds from ordering her guy to shoot us, and I had exactly the information you needed, at exactly the right moment. What *is* that, Will?"

Will exhaled, a long, slow breath that communicated an utter lack of surprise at what he'd just heard.

"What can I say, Leigh?" he said. "The Site provides."

Leigh reached out and gripped his forearm.

"Please, Will," Leigh said. "Tell me you've really got a plan."

"Answer the lady," the Coach said. "What are you doing, Mr. Oracle?"

"Waiting," Will said.

He leaned back in the seat and closed his eyes.

CHAPTER 45

The streets swarmed. An immense crowd, thousands strong, had gathered around KUSA headquarters, filling every open spot around the building, flowing across the grounds of the golf course up the street. People screamed, their hands in the air, tears running down their faces.

The Oracle had descended from the mountain—he was, in fact, standing on the steps of a helicopter on the roof of the television station with a thick black cord tied around his waist—and, oh, the things he could tell them.

"Jerry!" Will shouted over the crowd noise, calling over to the KUSA technician, who was standing not far away next to a nervous-seeming cameraman, each holding portable video equipment with cords trailing back across the roof and into the building through an open access door. "How we doing?"

"Hello, sir," Jerry said. "It's all set up. Good to go."

Will looked at the crowd.

"This won't work. I can't hear anything. Can we do it in the helicopter?"

Jerry thought for a moment.

"I don't see why not."

"Good. Bring the camera guy inside."

"What about Mr. Fontaine?"

Will had forgotten about the station's anchor. He looked now and saw him standing slightly off to one side, anxiously awaiting what he thought was his golden ticket—mediating some sort of conversation between the Oracle and Törökul. Crandall Fontaine flashed Will a broad smile.

"We don't need him, I'm sorry. There's not much room in there, anyway."

"I'll let him know, sir."

Will thought he detected a little satisfaction in Jerry's tone.

Moments later, Will was back in the helicopter, sitting opposite a cameraman with a monitor next to him displaying a grainy, poorly lit image of the rock-strewn floor of a dry desert canyon. It was night in Qandustan, and outside the circle of light shown in the monitor, the canyon faded quickly into inky blackness. Members of the U.S. Special Forces team who had presumably captured Törökul patrolled the canyon, looking in every direction at once.

Leigh sat with Grunfeld on the other side of the helicopter, along with Jerry and the Coach. The rest of the Coach's men had been forced to leave the aircraft—no room.

The scene on the monitor shifted as the camera panned quickly to one side. It stabilized, bringing into focus a dark-skinned man wearing desert camouflage gear and a head wrap. The man's arms were extended before him, tied at the wrists by plastic quick-tie restraints. Two huge Special Forces soldiers covered him, rifles held at the ready. Will studied the prisoner, who could only be Törökul. He stood straight, unbowed, unafraid, almost curious. Will wondered what Leuchten had told him about what was happening.

As if responding to Will's thought, Anthony Leuchten stepped into the frame. He looked thoroughly miserable—hot, filthy, with some sort of rash covering most of the diminished pouch of fat on his neck.

"Is the Oracle online?" Will heard him say. "We're too exposed out here. This is taking too long."

Will took a deep breath and motioned to the cameraman.

"Turn it on," he said.

The cameraman flipped a switch on the side of his camera, and a red light blinked on.

"Mr. Leuchten," Will said. "Nice to see you again."

"Mr. Dando," Leuchten responded, his tone clipped and short. "Are you ready?"

"Yeah. What about Törökul? What did you tell him?"

"I told him that the Oracle wanted to speak to him, that he was not under arrest, that he would be released as soon as the conversation was complete, and that whatever you tell him has nothing to do with the U.S. government in any way."

"Of course you did," Will said. "That's all I need from you, then. Tell your men to cut him loose and step back. I want him free when he speaks to me."

"Impossible," Leuchten said flatly. "We can let him go once we're done."

Will raised an eyebrow.

"Tony, doesn't the fact that your boss set this whole thing up, *just because I asked him to,* suggest that I'm the one calling the goddamn shots? Get the restraints off him. Now."

Leuchten's mouth clenched, but he turned and gave the order. Without a word, one of the Special Forces soldiers sliced through the plastic cuffs and stepped back. Törökul immediately began to massage his wrists, but his eyes stayed focused on the camera.

"All right," Will said. "Does he speak English?"

"No," Leuchten said. "But one of our men can translate."

"Good. The rest of you, get back."

Leuchten and all the soldiers but the translator stepped out of the circle of light, fading back into the darkness.

Will watched Törökul for a moment, who seemed content to wait and see what happened next.

"Do you know who I am?" Will asked.

He realized how much of what was about to happen hinged on Törökul's answer to that question.

"Yes," came the translation. "The Oracle is known to me."

Will released the breath he'd been holding, a big, relieved sigh.

"How?" Will asked.

"The leaders of my faith have spoken about you for some time."

"All good things, I hope?" Will said, and instantly asked himself what the hell he was thinking.

Upon hearing the translation, Törökul gave Will a blank look.

"No. No good things."

Will considered this and decided it didn't matter.

"Will you listen to what I have to say?" he asked.

"Everywhere I look, guns are pointed at me. What choice do I have? But I will tell you what I told your companion—even now the Sword of God is being prepared to fly. Say what you like. Every moment brings me closer to victory."

"But you were told you would be released."

Törökul gestured at the translator and spoke, his face cold.

"These soldiers storm my camp in the dark of night, kill three of my men," he said.

Will winced.

"They tell me," Törökul continued, "that the famous infidel prophet wishes a word with me, after which I will be set free."

Törökul stared fiercely at Will.

"The imams teach that you are no true prophet. It is one of the few points upon which all sects of Islam agree. They say that you lie with every word, that you are the devil's child, casting evil words into the hearts and minds of men.

"So," he said. "Lie to me."

Törökul spat, the impact on the ground clearly audible.

"I will listen, and when I refuse you, these soldiers will kill me. That is apparently the will of God, and what choice do I have but to accept it?"

"The will of God," Will repeated. "I know more than I want to about the will of God."

Will stopped thinking. Nothing he could say would make things worse. He just spoke.

"I have nothing to do with the devil, Törökul," Will said. "I'm just a man. But I am a man who can see the future, and the things I see happen.

"The *biys* will be twenty-three to twelve in favor of returning your mosque to you and your people. I don't know when the council will come back. I don't know if they will meet your deadline. I only know the results. Twenty-three to twelve in your favor."

Will leaned forward, doing his best to look directly into the other man's eyes.

"I am asking you to wait. If you launch your missile, the entire world will burn. You have to know this. But wait until the *biys* return, and you will get what you want. You have my word."

Will waited while the translation filtered through to Törökul and watched the man's expression harden.

"So. You want a favor," Törökul said. "Interesting."

He looked away, out of frame. A long, long pause.

Will gripped the armrest of his seat.

Törökul looked back at the screen, back at the Oracle.

"You do not understand the reason I fight. You do not know any-thing about me. You just want me to do something for you. To keep you safe, in your soft homes in your soft land across the sea."

Törökul took a step forward, toward the screen. His face was twisted in a snarl.

"Fuck you, Oracle. I do not care if you are safe. I do not care if your children are safe. They mean nothing to me. Everything that matters to me and my people is here, and here is where I must act.

"And, so, as I promised, I refuse your request. You have only two choices, false prophet. Kill me now, and the Sword of God flies within the hour. Your world will burn, and I will laugh at you from hell.

"Or, release me, and gamble that I will not launch my weapon just because you have offended me. It is your choice, but I am done with waiting. I have power, and I must use it to help my people."

Törökul crossed his arms and, unbelievably, smiled.

Will stared at him in silence and tried to figure out what the fuck he had been thinking when he assumed a twentysomething white American guy would be able to convince a Central Asian warlord with a nuclear missile pointed at a city to do anything at all. Törökul was never going to listen to him, would never believe a word he said. It had been so goddamn arrogant to think that the Oracle could say a few words and boom, happy ending. The Site had been taking care of him for so long—keeping him alive, protecting him from presidents and lunatics in Laundromats and assassin grandmothers—that he just hadn't really even considered that this might not work.

But it hadn't—of course it hadn't. Arrogant.

Why had the Site spent so much time and effort, burned through so many lives, just to bring the world to the brink?

Either the Site wanted chaos, or it didn't. If it didn't, then there had to be an answer. There had to be a way to balance the scales.

And with that thought, Will understood. At last, the pattern became clear.

Yes, the Site had done everything it possibly could to bring fear and misery into the world. It killed people, it made them afraid, it took away things they loved, it made them wonder if the future would even arrive at all.

But that was not all it had done.

The Site had created balance. It had created a roiling, spinning engine of chaos and doom, but it had also created a person with the power to stop it.

Love him, hate him, fear him. It didn't matter. Will Dando, the Oracle, was the most powerful person in the world, and it was time to stop fighting the future.

"Leuchten," Will said.

Tony Leuchten stepped into the circle of light. He didn't say anything, but his body language communicated immense fury—he was almost quivering.

"Look at Törökul," Will told Leuchten.

Tony inclined his head and narrowed his eyes, but he did what he was told.

"Törökul," Will said. "You know who this man is?"

Törökul nodded.

"He is your president's"—the translator hesitated for a moment—"special friend," the soldier finished, obviously choosing a diplomatic way to express the term Törökul had actually used.

Will saw Leuchten's hands clench.

"He is the chief adviser to the leader of America," Will said. "He speaks for the president. He is an extraordinarily powerful man."

Törökul nodded.

"Yes, I know this. So he told me. This is why he was sent to treat with me."

"Here, Törökul," Will said, "a gift."

Will took a breath, held it, let it go.

"Captain, stop translating," Will said.

The soldier nodded.

"Leuchten," Will said.

Tony half turned to look at the monitor.

"Get on your knees in front of him."

"Fuck you," Leuchten said.

"Do it, or this whole thing's done," Will said. "You want that election, you want to save the world? Get down in the sand."

"I represent the United States of America," Leuchten said. "I can't do it."

"Do you really want that goddamn missile to launch, Tony? You can't be that stupid. You can stop it right now. I'm telling you, I know what's going to happen. I'm the Oracle, for fuck's sake."

Will smiled at him.

"Sometimes we all have to surrender to a higher power, Tony. Today, that higher power is me."

Even through the monitor, Will could see Leuchten's face flush. He slowly turned back to face Török.

Laboriously, Anthony Leuchten lowered himself to his knees, his eyes far away. Down in the sand, facing Török, the chief of staff to the president of the United States of America bowed his head.

Török watched this happen, and then looked back at Will. His attitude had changed; for the first time since their conversation had begun, Will saw a touch of respect in the other man's face.

"Captain, start translating again," Will said.

The soldier nodded, waiting.

"So here we are, Török," Will said, "you and me. The men with all the power. You say you need to use yours to help your people. I'm using mine for the same thing. I'm giving you my word, right now. When the *biys* come down from the mountains, the vote will be in your favor, twenty-three to twelve."

Will waited for the soldier to translate his words, then continued.

"If you wait, you win. If you don't, everyone dies. I can't tell you what to do. But think about everything I could have done with all this power I have, and then think about what I actually did here tonight. From one powerful man to another, just consider that I am telling you the truth."

Törökul watched Will's face. Will felt calm, calmer than he had been in a long time, possibly since the dream.

The warlord glanced at Leuchten, still kneeling silently in the dirt, and then back up at Will. He looked off into the distance, his face blank, unreadable, and remained that way for perhaps thirty seconds.

Törökul spoke briefly.

"I will wait," came the translation.

Will was dimly aware of sounds of relief erupting around him in the helicopter.

"Thank you," Will said.

Tony Leuchten looked toward the screen, a question on his face. Will kept him waiting for a long moment, then nodded. The other man slowly pulled himself to his feet. Once he was standing, Leuchten brushed sand from his clothes and gave Will a look of pure, burning hatred. Will was severely unimpressed.

"Thank you, Tony," he said. "I'm sure that wasn't easy."

"You're a son of a bitch," Leuchten spat.

"Hey, pal, you were the one who wanted to work with me so badly. You get what you get, asshole," Will said. "Let Törökul and his men go. You heard him. He's going to wait."

"How do we know?" Leuchten said.

"Because he made a deal with someone he thinks he can trust," Will said. "Good-bye, Leuchten. I hope I never see you again."

Will looked at the cameraman in the helicopter.

"Shut it off," he said.

The cameraman flipped off the monitor and lowered his camera. His face was pale, and his eyes wouldn't leave Will's face.

Leigh squirmed past Grunfeld into the helicopter's aisle, her eyes wide.

"Holy shit, Will!" she said.

"I told you I knew what I was doing."

"Time to go," the Coach said. "Step lively."

She nodded at Grunfeld, who spoke briefly into a radio wired into his collar. A moment later, the door to the helicopter opened, and the Coach's men appeared, motioning to Jerry and the cameraman to exit. As soon as the door opened, Will heard cheers and screams from outside, and more questions.

The Coach looked at Leigh.

"As I understood the deal, Ms. Shore," she said, "it's about time you were headed on out of here too."

Leigh shook her head and looked at Will. He nodded.

"It's okay, Leigh," he said. "I'll be all right. Just go, be safe."

"She's going to kill you, Will!"

"It's all right," Will repeated. "Go. We don't have time."

"He's right, you know," the Coach said. "Get down those stairs in the next ten seconds, or you're coming with us."

Leigh abruptly sat down in one of the seats and buckled her seat belt.

"Oh, Leigh, no, come on," Will said.

"Lady wants to stay, her call," the Coach said.

"Get us up," she shouted to the pilot.

The helicopter's rotors cycled up, their pitch running higher, as the pilot made preparations to return to the sky.

Will collapsed into the seat next to Leigh.

"Why?" he said.

"Come on, Will, shouldn't you know by now?" she replied. "The story's not done."

Her face turned sober. She looked at the Coach, who was giving them both a speculative look.

"Can I ask him a few questions, or are you planning to throw us out over Mile High Stadium?"

"Knock yourself out," the woman said. "I've got some questions of my own."

Leigh returned her focus to Will.

"Will, how did you know that, about the numbers? Are you sure that's what they mean?" she asked.

"There are thirty-five elders in the council of *biys*, Leigh. It was in the news stories from the beginning, but I didn't make the connection until I saw it in the paper again this morning and everything clicked. I can't believe I didn't see it earlier."

She looked at him askance.

"And the four? How does that fit in?"

Will shrugged.

"You remember how I told you that the predictions came to me in a dream? They were all *spoken*. I heard two numbers and assumed the third was a number, too. But it's not. It's *for*, like 'in favor of'— not the number. I just couldn't see it until today."

Leigh shook her head, silent for the moment.

"My turn," the Coach interrupted. "I have one question."

Will looked up at her.

"Did you just stop the Qandustan situation from going hot?" she asked.

Will didn't hesitate.

"Yes," he said. "I did."

"A thank-you would be nice," Leigh added. "Preferably before you shoot us in the head."

The Coach crossed her arms and looked out the window for a long, long moment.

"Where to, ma'am?" the pilot asked. No answer.

"Well, huh," the Coach said, finally. "I guess I've got my limits. I can't do this. Looks like you two get to see tomorrow after all."

"Uh, boss," one of the guards spoke up, "I have to ask . . . doesn't that screw us? I mean, the president gave us a job . . ."

"True," the Coach said. "But as we've heard, he's going to get cancer and probably die. I'm not worried about the president. We're not going to kill the guy who headed off a nuclear war by making Tony Leuchten kneel in the dirt. *That* is an interesting person. You want a guy like that owing you a favor."

The Coach, this small, elderly, unarmed woman, looked at her team.

"Any of you try to take him down, you will be stopped. By me. We clear?"

"Clear," the guards said in unison.

"Now," the Coach said, looking back at Will. "Can I drop you two anywhere?"

Will felt Leigh's hand curl around his. And with that small gesture, the future opened to him.

AUGUST 23

"And in another example of what is being called the Oracle Effect, a historic peace accord was signed last night in the Gaza Strip between representatives of Israel and Palestine. The terms of the accord were negotiated by U.S. President Daniel Green, seen here at the signing in—"

Of the many, many things Reverend Hosiah Branson wished he currently had access to, perhaps highest on the list at the moment was a remote control, so as to mute the goddamn TV.

But the television was inside a wire cage mounted high on the wall, and the remote control was in the hands of the guards who oversaw the cafeteria as their own personal fiefdom, and Branson wasn't getting anywhere near either of them.

He glanced around the cafeteria, a quick, furtive look designed specifically to avoid eye contact with any of the other prisoners. Light blue jumpsuits as far as the eye could see, a rumble of conversation. The sights and sounds of about a hundred men shoveling the garbage this facility called food into their mouths.

No one was looking directly at him, but he somehow had the sense that they were all very aware of his pres-

ence. Aware of the tray sitting on the table. Aware of its contents.

Aware of the date.

How did this happen? he thought, *just the latest cycle of a question that ran on an endless loop in his head.*

But of course, he knew. He had made himself the Oracle's most public enemy. And the world loved the Oracle now, because the Oracle had saved the world. And so the Oracle's most public enemy was the enemy of the world.

That included the prosecutor who had made the argument that Branson was a flight risk, and so should be held in jail until the criminal trial related to the attempted murder charges levied against him by the New York City District Attorney's Office. It included the D.A. himself, who was once part of Branson's circle of influence. It included the judge. It included his wife, whom he hadn't seen since his imprisonment.

He looked back at the TV, where an oh-so-dignified Daniel Green was watching the Jew and the Arab shake hands.

It included the president of the United States, who had most assuredly cut ties with Reverend Hosiah Branson.

It included the entire world.

Everyone but Brother Jonas, at any rate. He visited fairly often. The man had proven to be loyal, when all was said and done.

Not that his loyalty would gain him all that much. Poor man had backed the wrong horse.

Branson looked down at his tray. On it was a yellowish puddle of instant mashed potatoes, a fleshy pile of limp, overcooked green beans, and a gray slab of protein covered by a splat of thick, sewagey sauce.

It was inedible. All of it. You just had to season the hell out of it and hope for the best.

Branson reached for his government-issued spork, made of a bendable nylon/plastic mix that could under no circumstances ever be used as a weapon.

It was August 23. It was Sunday. And so, it was Salisbury Steak Day.

He looked up again at the other prisoners. Now, many of them were looking at him, nudging each other.

They knew what day it was, too. They were Oracle tourists, in their way.

All around, men started to stand from their seats. The guards moved in from the edges of the room, unlimbering weapons from their belts, but they didn't stop the prisoners as they moved into a loose circle around Branson, sitting alone at his table.

The guards glanced at each other, then stepped forward, joining the prisoners.

Branson stared at them all, watching silently, their faces still and expectant.

Well, look at this, *he thought.* The Oracle gave me back my audience.

He looked back up at the television, which was continuing to discuss the Oracle Effect in all its many world-altering forms. Goddamn Will Dando, still running the world, even though he hadn't appeared in public since that stunt in Denver and hadn't communicated at all beyond his last, one-word update to the Site. One word, and it changed everything.

Everything.

The Oracle Effect. Goddamn Will Dando, still running the world.

Branson moved his eyes back to the lump of meat on his tray.

I still have a choice, *he thought.* No one's making me do this. I have free will.

He reached for the pepper shaker placed conveniently close to his plate and heard a rustle of movement among the assembled watchers.

What if I just . . . don't? *he asked himself.* Word would get out. I could still do exactly what I was planning all along. The Oracle's just a man. I know it.

He looked up at the men standing around him, not meeting anyone's eyes, just taking their emotional temperature. Excitement. The beginnings of impatience. Certainty.

They know what I'm going to do. The Oracle said it, and they believe it, and that's that.

But I can show them they're wrong. I still have free will, *he thought again.* I have a choice.

He stared at the pepper shaker in his hand. He did have a choice. But he knew what would happen to him if he disobeyed the Oracle in front of these men who were so deeply invested in their prophet's infallibility. He would be made to season his steak as specified, and there would be pain then and pain to follow. Punishment for his defiance.

These people <u>believed</u>, certainly more strongly than anyone Branson had ever touched with his ministry. They wanted to see the Oracle's enemy brought low with their own eyes. The prediction would come true, one way or the other. They would see to it.

The easy way, or the hard, cripplingly painful way. That was his actual choice, his only choice. It didn't matter what he believed, and it didn't matter what the Oracle was, god or man.

The things he said came true.

Reverend Hosiah Branson put pepper on his steak. He replaced the shaker on the table, lifted his spork, and carved himself a bite.

EPILOGUE: TOMORROW

Leigh shaded her eyes and peered out across the water, looking for three curved palm trees, partially uprooted by some long-past storm so that they hung low over the beach, nearly horizontal, like permanent, natural limbo sticks. The few channels into the shore weren't visible above the waterline—the sovereign nation of the Coral Republic was, in fact, ringed by a large coral reef, and the only safe way through was marked by the limbo palms.

A concrete pier jutted roughly a hundred yards into the sea from the beach, with mooring slips jutting out from the main pier at right angles. Once she was through the gate in the coral, Leigh spun her boat's wheel to angle toward the nearest slip. She could see a figure walking along the beach to the pier to meet her. She smiled, but turned her attention back to bringing the boat in safely.

Several vessels were already docked at the pier—a motorboat that was too small for Leigh to feel comfortable using alone in the open ocean, and a palatial, screw-you-I'm-rich yacht that was too large for her to pilot by herself. Leigh thought Hamza had acquired the yacht just for the sheer satisfaction of owning a boat that big.

She was driving the *Florida Lady,* a thirty-foot fishing boat. Leigh thought of it as hers, although technically she supposed it belonged to the Oracle organization. Will rarely took it out to any of the nearby islands. Too many people would recognize him, even down here.

Hamza had arranged the Republic as its own country—she wasn't clear on the details—but the upshot was that it had its own set of laws, and it very pointedly had no extradition treaties. As long as the Oracle remained on the sandy ground of the Coral Republic, he was—in theory—legally untouchable.

As Leigh pulled the throttle back to idling speed and inched the *Lady* forward into the mooring slip, she glanced to her right, where a short way back into the jungle off the beach, the orange tile roofs of what she and Will had both come to call the Capitol Building poked through the treetops.

It was really just a large, comfortable house built on stilts in a cleared area of the jungle, although it did house the entire population of the Republic. A flag flew out front—a stylized branch of yellow coral against a turquoise background.

The boat bumped gently against the rubber tires placed at regular intervals along the side of the mooring slip. Leigh turned off the motor and slipped quickly down from the cabin. Will had made it to the end of the pier and stood waiting, his hands in his pockets. He was wearing shorts, sandals, and sunglasses, looking very appealingly sun-touched.

"Hey," Will said. "Any trouble?"

"Nope. Had to haggle a little bit to get a good price on dinner, but otherwise smooth sailing."

Leigh picked up one end of a coil of rope on the deck and tossed it across to Will.

"What'd they have?" Will asked, catching the line neatly and bending to secure it to a metal mooring cleat anchored into the pier. "Did you get that blue one, tastes like salmon?"

They repeated the procedure with a second line at the stern.

The whole operation was smooth, rehearsed, a far cry from their fumbling attempts when they first arrived at the island four months earlier.

"The Kalu Palu market didn't have any today," Leigh said. "But I got a couple of the big silver ones with the red tails."

Kalu Palu was the nearest inhabited island—home to a fishing community of about two hundred people.

"Okay?" she asked. Will tugged on the line he had just tied down. He gave her a thumbs-up, then looked at the boat's bow for a moment.

"We should rechristen this, call it the *Italian Lady,*" he said.

"What do you mean?" Leigh asked.

"I finally heard from Cathy and Becky. They went to Italy, to Portofino, after the Coach thing. They've been lying low, but I guess they thought it was safe to get in touch."

"Are they okay?"

"Half the e-mail was about obscure Italian wines they've discovered. They're fine."

Leigh returned to the bridge briefly to gather her purchases. She pushed a button on the control console. A section of the *Florida Lady*'s railing flattened and extended out with a subtle whirring noise into a gangplank across to the slip. She shouldered her bags, climbed down to the deck, and left her boat.

Will took most of the bags, and they walked down the pier together. As they headed in toward the beach, Leigh looked down at the sea. It was an impossibly clear shade of turquoise—like looking through an old Coke bottle at the seafloor. A school of red-and-gold tropical fish darted across the white sands, like a fleet of autumn leaves zipping through gently waving tendrils of seaweed.

The one satchel Leigh had kept was cold against her back, welcome in the equatorial heat. It was filled with ice, and inside that was a selection of fish caught earlier that morning by Kalu Palu fishermen. Like the Feldspar Creek cabin, the Capitol Building's kitchens were stocked with every type of freezable or nonperishable food imaginable, but there was no substitute for freshness.

They crossed the beach and walked into the shade of the trees, along a gravel path cut into the jungle. A clearing opened up, revealing the Coral Republic Capitol Building in all its splendor. It was basically a wide, square box built atop pillars, with double windows circling the entirety of the upstairs living space to ensure that the interior was always filled with air and light. The house was bright white with black accents, including shutters on the windows that could be closed against storms. Parquet floors, verandas everywhere—it was like something out of a Somerset Maugham novel.

Will had told her the plan was based on something called a "black and white" house, which were used as quarters for British officers in Singapore during World War II. Whatever the provenance of the design, Leigh loved it. She liked to sit upstairs, in front of the windows facing the sea, and remember her tiny box of an apartment back in Manhattan.

They entered the house and climbed the stairs. Will took the last bag from Leigh.

"I'll put this stuff away. I found a recipe for a sweet fish curry with mangos I want to try. It'll probably be better with the redtail anyway. Does that sound good?"

Leigh smiled.

"Sure, give it a shot."

Will's first tries at new recipes didn't always work out particularly well. They usually improved over time, but he was definitely sort of a trial-and-error cook. It made him happy, though, and she didn't mind the experiments. He was always quick to admit if something was inedible, and they'd scrounge up something else.

"Okay—it has to simmer for three or four hours. I'll take this stuff to the kitchen and put it together in a little bit, after my call. What are you going to do?"

"I think I'm going to finish the story."

Will smiled.

"Really? You got your ending?"

"Maybe."

"Well, good luck," he said. "I'm sure it's great."

Will kissed her on the cheek and turned to lug the bags into the kitchen, whistling as he went. Leigh watched him go, struck for the hundredth time at the change that had come over him since the day in Denver. It had taken her a little while to understand, but the truth was that she'd never really seen Will happy before they got to the Republic.

Leigh crossed the house to the room she had turned into her office, a small space with an ocean view. She sat down at her desk, flipped open the laptop, and pulled up her current work in progress: the story she had been planning since Reimer had first told her she would be interviewing the Oracle. It had evolved into a fairly long piece of work; really a narrative describing everything she knew about Will and what he'd done. It could be the foundation for a book, if she thought it was something she'd ever want to publish.

She scrolled through the document to the end and reread the last section she'd written. It was an account of the first few days after the Denver broadcast; the details of their journey to the Coral Republic: a five-day ordeal that left commercial airports behind on the second day and ended with a ferry over from Kalu Palu in a leaky motorboat piloted by a wrinkled old walnut of a man.

Leigh was thinking about cutting it—it wasn't that interesting, although she supposed it was important from a historical perspective. There were a few good bits, though. For one, after the Coach had dropped them off back at the cabin in Feldspar Creek so they could make good their escape from the United States, she'd asked

Will if he was really sure that the 23–12–4 numbers would be the result of the Qandustan vote.

"Eighty percent sure," Will had answered. "We'll know soon enough."

Leigh had laughed, but she was pretty sure what Will had said wasn't funny at all.

He ended up being right, of course. The Oracle's predictions always came true.

Törökul got his mosque back, although he didn't keep it for very long. President Green spearheaded a multinational military effort that captured the warlord—an action which, incidentally, looked to have won him a second term, cancer or no cancer.

Most of that had happened while she and Will were on their way to the Coral Republic—Will knew by the time their boat hit the beach that he was right about the numbers. And from that moment, it was like he'd shed a two-hundred-pound suit of armor he'd been wearing as long as she'd known him.

He'd done one last thing before, as far as she knew, retiring the Oracle forever. One last update to the Site. He'd removed all the predictions, and the e-mail address, leaving only the phrase:

THIS IS NOT ALL I KNOW.

And then he'd added one word:

BEHAVE.

Leigh reached the blank section of the page where she was planning to write her conclusions. It was a good story—strong, almost beautiful—but it wouldn't be finished until she tried to put down in black and white what she thought it all meant.

Music wafted into the room—just idle noodling on a guitar, but good. Very good. A lot of that, recently. She had begun to wonder if that's why the Site had chosen Will in the first place—a musician, used to improvisation, able to hear the tune in what it was doing, even if just on a subconscious level.

Leigh leaned back in her chair, turning her head. She could just see Will sitting in an armchair, with an open laptop on an ottoman in front of him and a guitar on his lap. A smiling, captivated infant was visible on the screen, being held up by two hands around her midsection, the hands somewhat darker than the baby's light caramel skin. Hamza and Miko had named her Wilhelmina.

Leigh smiled. She put her hands to the keys and began to type.

It has been four months since the Oracle averted a nuclear catastrophe that would at the very least have destroyed the city and people of Uth and could quite possibly have consumed the world.

The Oracle Effect has ushered in a new era of compromise: people of all nations seem to feel that we came closer to the brink of destruction than ever before, and a global statement of purpose has been issued: Never again. Mankind has stepped away from hostility in favor of understanding.

Or, more likely, humanity's leaders are terrified that the Oracle will make good on the implied threat in his final update to the Site and issue new predictions that will drastically rearrange the world in whatever direction he sees fit. And so, they behave.

Either way.

But in the end . . . who, and why? Who sent the predictions to the Oracle, and why did they try to achieve their goals in this particular way?

We know the predictions were sent by someone with a unique viewpoint, someone able to see problems humankind would suffer in the years to come, with a desire to help us avoid them. That's the who.

That person, that entity, chose Will Dando as its instrument of change. It plucked him from an ordinary life and thrust him into an extraordinary one. He suffered through pain and uncertainty the likes of which the rest of us can barely comprehend.

Beyond that, we know nothing at all, which leaves us with the why.

The Site could have given Will its entire scheme, step by step, right from the start. It didn't. Its plan depended completely on the fact that the Oracle, paradoxically, *didn't know what was going to happen*.

He had to navigate the same way any of us do in our lives—with free will. He wasn't a puppet. He was never under anyone's control. Every decision he made along the way was his, made using whatever skill and knowledge he had amassed in his life, in the hope that he was doing the right thing.

Each of those decisions was, at its heart, a gamble—but he kept making them. He could have surrendered, let the Site do whatever it was going to do. He didn't. He fought, every step of the way, trying to move his own life—and, in the end, all our lives, in a better direction. In the end, he succeeded.

I believe that may be the why.

Fate, destiny—they're myths.

We are the sum of our choices.
Choose well.

Leigh stopped typing. She read over the text, and for the first time in many attempts at ending the Oracle's story, she didn't hit the delete key.

Notes from Will's guitar drifted through the air.

She stood, turned from her desk, and walked toward the music. If it turned out that she did have more to say, well, there was always tomorrow.

ACKNOWLEDGMENTS

This book has had many hands on it, and it wouldn't exist without every last one of them. There are people out there who have read endless drafts over (what seems like) endless years, and their smart observations and general support were what made this book what it is. Let's start with them, since they read *The Oracle Year* in its earlier incarnations for no other reason than they wanted to help me realize a dream I've had since I was very young. So, THANK YOU to those brave first readers: Amy Soule (who is not just a reader, but also my wonderful wife, and has been there every step of the way on all of this), Shawn DePasquale, Shoumitro Goswami, Sam Soule, Michael Pereira, Carl Marcellino, and Roger Yoo, all of whom read a not-ready-for-prime-time book just because I asked them to (often more than once). And to the more recent readers: Ray Fawkes, Ben McCool, and especially Matt Idelson, all of whom helped me with some of the last, crucial tweaks that brought it all together. To Andy Deemer, Shawn Hynes, Scott Snyder, Jake Laufer, Jorge Pertuz, and all the other friends who support and encourage me in countless ways. To Brad Meltzer, who is nicer than he has any reason to be, and whose presentation to a Columbia School of Law IP class in my second year set me on the road to writing not just *The Oracle Year*, but everything else I've written, too. To Jeff Boison—a strong argument could be made that this book would not be in your hands if he hadn't done a very kind thing some years back. To my incredibly sharp, perceptive agent Seth Fishman at the Gernert Company, whose patient guidance through this process was everything a writer could ask for. And Seth's colleagues, especially Will Roberts. To Angela Cheng Caplan, who rolled the dice with her time and insight perhaps earlier than she had any reason to—I'll never forget it. To Sara Nelson, my editor at HarperCollins, who has championed the novel since the first moment she read it, and all her colleagues, from publishing to PR, who have done a wonderful job designing, copyediting, promoting, and selling this book.

To my family—Amy, Rosemary, Sam, Hannah, and Chris. And to my extended family who are my family. And especially to Mary and Jim, whom I miss very much. I think they would have been proud.

To everyone who had a hand in this who I have egregiously failed to include here—and I'm sure you're out there—you're the best, never doubt it.

And thanks to you, for reading.

ABOUT THE AUTHOR

CHARLES SOULE is a *New York Times* bestselling, Brooklyn-based comic book writer, musician, and attorney. He is best known for writing *Daredevil, She-Hulk, Death of Wolverine* and various Star Wars comics for Marvel Comics, as well as his creator-owned series Curse Words from Image Comics and the award-winning political sci-fi epic *Letter 44* from Oni Press.